FAMINE

J.R. ANDREWS

Hardback ISBN: 978-1-7343958-0-8
Paperback ISBN: 978-1-7343958-1-5
eBook ISBN: 978-1-7343958-2-2

E-mail: jr@jrandrewsbooks.com
Website: http://jrandrewsbooks.com

For Querida,
Te amo mas que tengo las palabras. Siempre.

CHAPTER 1

THE DULL ACHE OF ANA'S hunger gnawed at her.

She cursed herself in silence for not having eaten anything before she broke into the hospital. Oddly, she rarely thought of anything but food these days yet often neglected to eat until it was absolutely necessary. Today, though, she should have known better. The last thing she needed was to lose focus in a place where any tiny lapse in concentration might ruin everything.

She took a breath. She would *not* be responsible for the starvation of what remained of her people because she'd forgotten to feed.

Ana squeezed back against the wall beside the open double doors of the ER's medical supply room. Sneaking peeks around the corner into the room every few seconds, she watched a Feral examine items from a cabinet at random.

The humanoid monster with leathery, ash-gray skin picked up a roll of gauze, its razor-sharp talons leaving incidental gashes. It sniffed at the roll but, finding it uninteresting and inedible, dropped it and turned its attention back to the supply cabinet.

Holding her breath, Ana waited for it to turn away

from the doorway. She was lucky as it was apparently one of the dumber ones. A more clever or observant plaguer might have sensed her in the hallway. Of course, the overwhelming stench of death lingering in the hospital and the lack of air movement favored her too. Under these conditions, smelling anything or anyone other than the decaying corpses littering the hallways on rolling beds would be a challenge.

That cut both ways, though. Her own usually sharp senses were just as dull.

At last, the somewhat human-like beast turned its back to the doorway to investigate the chrome handle of a restroom door.

Ana flung herself from one side of the doorway to the other, pressing against the wall on the far side.

Still holding her breath—she didn't need to breathe anyway—she listened for signs that she'd attracted its attention. But the thing continued to huff and sniff in a steady rhythm, keeping its distance from the door.

Turning away, she crept along the hallway, avoiding the rotting bodies, and exhaled only when she reached the stairwell at the end. With a glance back the way she'd come, she climbed up the stairs, mindful to make no sounds.

The first time she'd done this had been much easier. She strolled right in, snatched the patient, and walked right out. The second had been a little more difficult but not much. One of Alexander's sadistic thugs would march a few Feral through the building twice a day like bomb-sniffing dogs, as regular as clockwork. Avoiding them had been as simple as making the grab between rounds.

But Alexander had learned his lesson. At least two plaguers were in the building at all times now, and one or two members of his Family would also make daily visits to check on things. He was taking his last three patients very seriously. And who could blame him—they were, after all, human.

Whether or not she got away with another one tonight, this was almost certainly her last attempt. Alexander would likely station an entire group of his most reliable Family in here afterward.

Not making a sound, Ana reached the intensive-care unit and exhaled in relief. Then she frowned, realizing she hadn't crossed paths with the second Feral she knew was somewhere in the hospital. Not knowing where it was would make her exit much more difficult.

She pushed one of the unit's gray double doors open a few inches, not enough to make it creak, and slipped inside. She left one foot over the threshold, and the door came to rest against it, preventing a loud clank as it swung back into place.

Squatting, she squeezed her eyes shut and listened. Nothing was moving but soft ripples of air in three rooms around the corner and up the hall—the patients' rooms.

Still half crouching, she lurched down the corridor and around the bend, peering into each room on the ward before crossing in front of its door. The rooms weren't empty, of course. Each contained several beds holding the long dead. But those weren't of any interest to her.

She checked all three to be sure no one was waiting inside, still as death, for her to blunder into them. Only when she was absolutely certain she was alone did she stand up and lean against the counter of the nurses' station opposite the rooms.

Three rooms, three patients, and this might be her last chance without Colin sending more help. She needed some luck.

The first two attempts had both been women. She'd hoped that since studies had shown that infant girls tended to fight for life harder than their male counterparts, the same might prove true of adult coma patients. Ultimately, that hadn't proved to be the case. Both women died before regaining consciousness.

She looked at the three names on the doors in front of her: Thomas Woodford, Melanie Schmidt, and Earl Benson. Poor Melanie was out of luck—this time, the subject would be male.

Ana peeked into the first and third rooms, with Thomas in the first and Earl in the last. The latter patient appeared to have ten or fifteen years on the former, and based on the graying hair and sallow, lined skin, they looked to have been hard ones.

Moving close to Thomas, she studied his face as he slept. His slightly sunken cheeks were a hallmark of such a long coma under these conditions. A mane of dark-brown wavy hair surrounded his head, and a full, dark beard peppered with the first touches of gray reached his chest.

As with all the other patients, circular scabs and scars dotted his arms, legs, and neck. She had little doubt she'd find more once she got him out of the hospital.

She lifted both eyelids but got no response from his dull chocolate-brown eyes. Still comatose.

He wasn't the picture of health, to be sure, but by

being male and only just middle-aged, he was the best overall candidate as far as she was concerned.

A metallic clang echoed from the hallway, and she stiffened. Her heart would have been beating out of her chest if it still beat at all. As it was, she stood frozen beside the bed, straining to catch any hint of the other Feral, or anything worse, moving down the corridor toward her.

Sensing nothing, though, she counted silently to fifty. The noise must have been the ICU door sliding back into place.

Satisfied, she whispered, "Time to go, Thomas."

With practiced experience, she disconnected his IV lines but left the injection sites untouched so she could reuse them. Then she leaned forward, grabbed him by the chest, and slung him over one shoulder.

As easily as picking up a doll, she lifted the six-foot-tall man who, according to his chart, weighed just under two hundred pounds. Three years after her... change... some of the things she could do still amazed her.

Setting out from his room at a jogging pace, Ana paused only to tiptoe through the ICU doors and make sure she and Thomas were alone in the outer hallway. She resumed the brisk trot through the building when she was satisfied nothing was waiting for them.

Moving with stealth and caution had been the obvious choice when she entered the hospital, but Ana would have sprinted out if she thought she could manage it without dropping her patient, especially considering he was breathing and human. The pair of Feral inside with them would be much quicker to notice those factors than they would her alone, and the smell of him—and his blood—outside the ICU they'd been guarding would likely incense them. Getting out as quickly as possible was by far the best course.

She took a different path from the one she'd taken into the hospital, making a direct line to the parking garage—down a hall then two flights of stairs, followed by another length of corridor and a few more steps, constantly dodging hospital beds littering her path. She paused for only a second or two before each new leg, to be certain to avoid running blindly into trouble. So far, so good.

She stopped at the exit to the subterranean garage. Through a grimy pane of glass in the door, Ana studied the expanse of concrete beyond. Between rows of abandoned cars left by long-dead owners, the ambulance she'd backed up to the door sat waiting. The rolling gurney she'd set up was still exactly where she left it.

Satisfied, she pushed through the door, moving with care to keep the man from knocking against the frame. After clearing it, she laid him on the gurney and belted him in.

Ready to roll the bed into the ambulance, she yanked the latch on its back gate and sprang back at the sound of a startled, angry hiss. The second Feral, the one she hadn't found, glared back at her, its dead, coal-black eyes blinking through a few limp strands of ash-colored hair hanging from a mottled scalp.

It opened its mouth, flashing a full set of wicked, pointed teeth complemented by a pair of curved fangs.

The thing lunged, growling. She stepped to the right and turned sideways, her back to the gurney, and its sharp claws passed through the space where her head had just been.

The Feral lunged again, this time diving completely out of the truck. Ana stepped back and pivoted, smacking it as it flew by. The Feral fell away and rolled to the ground but managed to swipe her across the stomach in the process.

Blood gushed from a set of jagged slashes beneath her shirt.

As the Feral lumbered to its feet, she grabbed it by the neck and spun it back toward the ambulance. Shoving with all her strength, Ana drove the monster's head into the corner of the truck's frame and was rewarded with a deep crackling sound. The body in her hands went limp.

Holding it in place, she reached for the truck gate and swung it closed, hard against its skull, which popped like an engorged tick, spreading brains and blood throughout the ambulance interior.

Ana stepped back and touched her belly. The wound wasn't deep. It would heal quickly enough.

Opening the ambulance gate again, she pulled the lifeless Feral away. It fell to the ground with a dull thud. She then dragged it clear, leaving a messy path.

After pushing the patient into the vehicle, she locked the wheels in place, closed the gate, and jumped into the driver's seat. Company—the unwelcome variety—would arrive at any moment.

Tires squealing, they rocketed away from the door. The bloody corpse with the rotten-pumpkin head grew smaller in Ana's side-view mirror. Nothing else followed.

Hitting the street in the dark hours just before dawn,

she breathed a sigh of relief. Then she glanced back at her patient in another mirror hanging beside her.

"You had better live, Thomas Woodford. You had better be worth all this trouble."

CHAPTER 2

TOM WOKE UP SLOWLY, UNABLE to remember having fallen asleep, and drew a raspy breath. Another labored exchange of air brought starbursts to his eyes, still shut against the light. Breathing had never seemed such a struggle.

Grimacing at the raw dryness of his throat, he tried to swallow, hoping some saliva would ease the pain. Unable to coax out more than a few drops of spittle, though, he earned nothing from the effort but a hard, painful gulp and a hoarse cough.

He opened his eyes, and light seared his vision. With a groan, he squeezed them shut again.

Steeling himself, he tried again, blinking repeatedly. Flashes of light stung him with each blink, a stabbing pain contrasting the dull ache already thrumming through his head. With each flutter of his eyelids, he adjusted to the light as the pain eased.

When he could finally see, he found himself in an unfamiliar bed, looking through a strange window at the pale sun, floating in a cloudless sky. Turning away from the window, he lolled his head to the right. Fire lanced across his shoulders and down both arms, making him yelp.

Forcing himself to exhale while trying to ignore all his various pains, the man consciously relaxed each part of his body, from shoulders to toes. It was a familiar trick, one he'd used often during long cross-country flights or on nights when his mind was too busy to fall asleep.

Releasing the tension from his muscles soothed the pain in his head to some manageable degree, and for the first time, he took a good look at his surroundings. He was lying on a rolling hospital bed, positioned at the side of a room reminiscent of the eleventh-grade chemistry lab at St. Philip's. Four pedestal tables with smooth octagonal black-finished tops stood to his right. A large vacuum hood at the front of the room partially blocked his view of the only door.

Otherwise, the room was unfamiliar. He could be anywhere on earth—or heaven or hell, for that matter.

His face crinkled in frustration. Odd to recall restless nights and being jammed shoulder-to-shoulder with strangers on an airplane but nothing about how he'd ended up in this room, on this bed.

He drew another rasping gasp of breath just as a glint of chrome caught his eye. Inset in the top of each table was a sink with a shiny goose-neck faucet. He sighed with longing, imagining water flowing from it.

The man wiggled the toes peeking out from the dingy, too-short blanket covering him only from waist to ankles. Dozens of fresh circular scabs covered his feet, bringing cigarette burns to mind. Matching scars dotted his legs, too, as well as his arms. He frowned at them, but they would have to wait.

An IV, taped to his right hand and running from an empty fluid bag beside the bed, was a much more pressing issue if he was going to reach that faucet. He could remove the line, but that might cause other problems. It probably wasn't worth the risk. Besides, the bag was hanging from the kind of wheeled, hooked pole designed to roll along with a patient.

The four feet of space between the bed and the faucet might as well have been the Grand Canyon. While considering the empty span of tiled floor, he took two deep breaths: inhale, exhale, inhale, and exhale. Nothing to do but go for it. He swung his legs over the side of the bed with a grunt of effort.

He wiggled his toes again, and they brushed the cool floor below.

As before, he took two measured breaths in preparation for sliding off the bed: deep breath in, slow breath out, deep, slow. Tensing, he dropped his bare feet onto the tiles. Each foot flattened against the solid floor but for barely more than a second. His legs buckled, and the world spun out of control as the rest of his body followed his feet to the floor. As his vision faded, he thought how pleasant the coolness of the tiles was against his cheek.

The man came to sometime later, groggy and with no way to guess how long he'd been crumpled on the floor in a heap. Gingerly, he touched his head. A stinging knot stood where it'd hit the hard tile. In a way, he was lucky he'd had such a throbbing headache to begin with—at least cracking his skull hadn't made it worse.

He pushed himself up to a sitting position, ignoring the flare of pain that accompanied the movement.

Darkness had covered the room. In the clear sky through the window, though, a breathtaking number of stars twinkled, providing the only light. Moonlight would have been a welcome addition but was missing from his small view of the world outside.

Instead of trying to move again right away, the man listened for any hint that someone else might be nearby. A rustling of cloth, a shuffling of feet, or even a tremble of vibration would have been welcome. But the air was as quiet and still as death.

"Hello? Hello?" he tried to shout. "I need help!" It was a weak croak at best.

The closest lab table was still an agonizing distance away, and its prized faucet loomed above him. He grunted in an effort to climb to his knees, but his weak legs refused to cooperate. With a sigh, he sank back down, chest to the floor. Shifting elbows and shoulders alternately, he scooted forward a few inches with each motion, like an infant army crawling for the first time.

After what had to have been an hour of snaking across the floor, the gaunt man reached the base of the table, arms and lungs burning, breath rattling in his chest. He stopped to rest, wheezing. Reaching the faucet several feet above was going to be quite a trick.

Almost panting but with no alternative, Tom pulled himself up into a seated position, mustering every ounce of strength possible. He reached over his head and grabbed the edge of the shiny black tabletop. Then, with a grimace, he heaved himself up onto his knees, pushing from below with what little strength his legs had to offer.

He was one step closer, with the top of the table at eye level, and the silver gooseneck teased, just out of reach.

Next came the hardest part. He spread his elbows to gain some leverage on the table, forearms flat against the surface, and closed his eyes. A few careful breaths, as before: inhale, exhale, inhale, exhale, inhale. Power coiled in his elbows, forearms, and shoulders. He released it with his next breath, visualizing a mechanical spring.

He rose from the floor, his feet sliding into place beneath him for support. Coming to rest, he leaned precariously over the table, propped up on a base made from his arms and chest.

Relief washed over him.

His fingers touched the flat metal lever engraved with a *C*, and he pushed down. Panic flared as it refused to yield at first. Begrudgingly, it gave way.

First, nothing. Then came a hollow rattle in the pipes below. Finally, a few desperate sputters of warm water splashed on his arm before resolving into a steady stream of clear liquid.

He leaned forward and drank deeply, selfishly. The water was stale and tasted of minerals, but his body ached for every drop. After several long drinks, having conquered his tremendous thirst, he turned the lever the opposite way until the flow became a trickle then drops.

He held himself over the sink, catching his breath again, the cool weight of the water sloshing in his belly. Instead of the contentment he'd expected, a quiver roiled his stomach. Drinking so much so quickly had been a mistake. A series of burps was followed by a painful, gagging heave. Then he retched most of the water back into the sink.

"Among the living, are we?" An icy voice came from the doorway.

Startled, he nearly collapsed at the sound but caught the edge of the sink to prevent himself sliding from the table.

The shadow of a woman was standing at the door.

"Who—" he started.

"My name is Ana," the shadow replied, "and you should be in bed." She crossed the space between them quickly, faster than he expected.

He shrank back but had little chance to move away. As she moved out of the shadows and into the starlight, he got a better look. She was not quite tall—maybe five feet eight or nine—and seemed trim. The jeans and baggy knit sweater she wore made it impossible to be sure, though, especially in the dark room.

Her face confirmed she didn't carry even one extra pound of weight, with a slender neck and prominent cheekbones. Smooth, white skin gleamed in the pale light, and dark eyes stood in sharp contrast—hard to say what color, exactly, and not focusing on them was even harder. They were stunning and piercing and sparkling, somehow all at once.

He had married the last person he'd seen with eyes like that. How long ago was that?

"Do you remember your name?" she asked.

"Um, Tom," he replied, still shaky from throwing up. "Thomas Woodford."

"I'm going to help you, Tom. You need to get well. Let's get you back in bed." Her strong yet oddly delicate hands took him by the shoulders. She helped him away from the table and ducked beneath his left arm. He hesitated but then leaned into her tentatively, afraid she couldn't hold him. She did, though, easily, and moved him back to the empty hospital bed.

"Ana, you said?" he asked as they shuffled across the room.

"Yes."

"Do I know you?"

"No. But I've been taking care of you. You have been asleep for a very long time. I wasn't sure if you would ever wake up. Now that you have, you need some time to recover fully."

"How did I...?" he started, nearly whispering.

"How you came to be here is a long story and part of an even longer one. My guess is that you were in a coma for more than ten years. What year do you last remember?"

His brow furrowed. "I can't remember. I think the Cubs had won the Series? Wait, that can't be right."

When they reached the bed, she helped him lie down. "More than ten years, then. Do you need anything else? More water?"

Tom shook his head a fraction of an inch to each side as he settled back into the bed, letting that nugget of information sink in. "Not now—I'm tired now. But ten years? Are you serious? What year is it now?"

She hooked a full bag of clear fluid to his IV post and took a syringe from her pocket. After removing the cap with her teeth, she pushed the needle into a port on the plastic tubing. She squeezed the plunger steadily, and the contents of the syringe flowed down the line. "The year has little meaning anymore."

He'd been tired a moment before but the kind of tired you could fight for a while. After the syringe, though, his eyelids drooped against his will. He fought to keep them open.

"The world you know is gone, Tom" was the last thing he heard her say.

CHAPTER 3

TOM SAT IN AN UNCOMFORTABLE *chair by the elevators, pretending to read a newspaper. Was this the day, finally? He'd had no reason not to do it already except that he hated confrontation and knew that there would be no going back afterward.*

The elevator chimed, and the doors opened. A teenager in an ugly eggplant vest with the hotel's crest stepped out, carrying a basket of fruit, a pair of wineglasses, and a bottle of wine. He looked barely old enough to have passed his driver's test. Hopefully the kid could use some gas money.

The boy strode past him, focused on the hallway beyond. Tom frowned to himself. Now or never. How many weeks of Wednesdays and Fridays had he spent putting off the inevitable, waiting in hard-backed chairs in hotel hallways that were never meant to be sat in? Time to be done with it—get it over with, like ripping off a Band-Aid. Before he could change his mind, he coughed and stood up.

The room-service boy stopped and turned back with a sigh, rolling his eyes. "Can I help you, sir?"

He glanced at the kid's name badge. "Tell me, Brendon, is that for room 1517?"

"Um…"

"Yeah, okay. Why don't you let me take that for you?"

"Look, mister, I shouldn't—"

"Fifty bucks," Tom interrupted, pulling a folded fifty-dollar bill from the front pocket of his faded jeans. "A little gas money, maybe a movie and some popcorn for your sweetheart, just to let me do your job for you."

The kid gnawed his bottom lip. Finally, he surrendered to material sense. "Um… okay."

A minute later, Tom's fist hung over the door of room 1517. Blood pounded in his ears.

Last chance, no going back after this.

He hesitated for a split second then rapped on the door three times in quick succession.

"Who is it?" a woman called from within.

"Room service," he said, trying to channel a pubescent teenager. He succeeded, somewhat, as nervousness made his voice crack.

The bolt withdrew, and the chain slid back on the other side of the door. It cracked inward, then she was in the doorway. She wore a fuzzy white hotel robe that exposed the delicate curves of her chest, exactly the same as on the morning after their wedding.

Her shoulder-length hair, the color of milk chocolate streaked with amber highlights, was disheveled, out of place. Her eyes, a deeper, darker brown, grew wide in recognition.

She let out an almost inaudible gasp. "Oh my God. Tom." She stepped into the hallway, pulling the door behind her.

It didn't matter now. The hiding was over.

"Oh my God. I—"

"Who is it?" a man asked inside the room. "Where's the damned wine?"

"Shut up!" she yelled back.

Tom's blood pressure had to be off the charts. His face flushed, his hands shook, and his jaw clenched tightly enough that he could feel the muscles standing out at his temples.

"Calm down, Tom. You're going to pop a blood vessel."

"So fucking what?" he screamed, spittle landing on her face.

She recoiled as if slapped. It was a good start, but he wasn't finished, not by a long shot. He wanted to unload all the hurt and suspicion he'd been carrying around quietly for weeks. Opening his mouth to lay into her, though, he was suddenly mute, as if the rage had rendered him speechless.

Words. He needed words. They whirled in his head, just out of reach, like bills flying around some lucky retiree in one of those lottery booths, which left him nothing to work with but the anger itself. Giving up, he spat, "You fucking whore."

"Tom, please," she started, clutching the openness of the robe at her chest, "please, I'm… I'm sorry. This was a mistake. It doesn't mean anything. Please."

He dropped the basket and the wine, vaguely noting that something cracked at his feet. His fists curled into balls at his sides, the knuckles going white. Hitting her or putting a hole in the wall wouldn't help, but he needed to pour the anguish, the rage, the hurt—so much hurt—into something else before it overcame him.

"Did it mean nothing last week? What about last month? You've been at this for six months, Heather, just that I know about! Things that mean nothing don't last half a year or more, you conniving bitch!"

"Please. Tom." Tears now, real ones, slid down her cheeks, leaving shiny, wet trails in her makeup. "I just… ever since… I couldn't get over it… and we were… different together. I needed to not think about it."

He hung his head and exhaled. Deep down, he'd known the why of it already, which had made him wait, hoping she would get over it, hoping they could move on together. That hope was gone.

He knew it would be before he knocked on the door.

"I can't tell you how much this hurts me, Heather," he whispered, "but honestly, no matter how much that is, you'll always be more broken and alone than me."

He turned his back to her and walked down the hall.

"Tom, wait," she called, sobbing. "Tom! Tom! Tom."

A hand shook his shoulder. "Tom. Tom?"

He opened his eyes, but the woman he saw wasn't Heather. She was too thin, too pale in the moonlight. Her name… He knew her name.

"Ana?" He coughed.

"Good. You remember. You seemed to be having a bad dream. How do you feel?"

He cleared his throat. "Thirsty. And maybe hungry."

"Good. I have soup, chicken noodle or vegetable. Would you like to try one?"

"Water first. Then the chicken."

She nodded, filled a cup from the same sink he had crawled to before, and held it to his mouth. "A few sips. Slowly. Then I will get you soup. We have much to discuss."

Tom drank two full cups of water and slurped every

last drop of the soup, which she brought back to him on a brown plastic lunchroom tray. His stomach gurgled. He had no idea when he'd last eaten anything, even something as simple as soup. More than a decade could've passed, based on what Ana had said. Hopefully his body would remember how it worked.

"Okay," he said, wiping his mouth with a raggedly torn paper towel from a washroom. "How did I lose more than ten years of my life? And where the hell am I?"

She was sitting on a tall metal stool beside the chemistry worktable. She held her hands in her lap, picking at the skin around her left thumbnail.

Seeing him watching her, she frowned, folded her hands, and took a deep breath. "We'll get to that soon, but there's something else I need to tell you first."

"I'm… all ears," he replied, sensing her apprehension.

She cleared her throat and looked at her lap. "We know that it started in Los Angeles but not exactly why or how. Maybe if there'd been more time, we would have found the source. What we do know is that one day, the world was normal. The next, people were getting sick. The first case was reported on October twenty-ninth—"

"First case of what?"

"Please don't interrupt," she snapped. "This is difficult enough. Let me get to the end."

Tom started to say something sarcastic, but the hard set of her eyes warned against it. He swallowed the comment and motioned for her to go on.

"They ended up calling it Charon, named for the ferryman of Greek mythology that carried souls to the world of the dead. The first case was reported on the twenty-ninth. The first death was the next day. On average, once identified, a patient had about seventy-two hours to live, three very unpleasant days.

"It began with congestion, followed by a fever and welts, then vomiting and diarrhea. Eventually came profuse bleeding, both internally and externally. The old, young, and those already weak were generally lucky enough to develop pneumonia in the early stages and died before it got to the painful end."

"What are you talking about?" he asked. "This isn't funny. And what's it got to do with—" She cut him off with a cold, flat stare.

"Two days after Halloween, LA was quarantined. On November fifth, with cases being reported among the soldiers maintaining the quarantine and fear of an epidemic mounting, the president authorized use of a nuclear warhead on Los Angeles.

"Someone told me later that it was launched from the Nevada desert and basically went up and came right back down. I don't know if that's true, but I know that every living soul in the area evaporated in a blinding flash of light."

"Okay, lady, look," Tom said, "let's stop this right here. I don't know who you are or what your game is, but this is about the worst joke I've ever heard. Why don't you just get me a phone so I can call my wife before this gets unpleasant?"

"Are you not listening to me?" Ana exclaimed. "Your wife is dead. *Everyone* is dead. Believe me, I wish I could just give her a call and send you home, for more reasons than you'll likely ever understand. But I can't. And I can't explain how you ended up here unless you let me tell you the whole story."

Her intensity caught him off guard. Jesus, she wasn't joking. "Heather is…?"

She sighed. "Yes, I'm sorry. Forgive me for putting it so bluntly. I promise, I'll get to it in a minute. But you need to hear everything."

He shook his head, numb. How could Heather be dead?

"One day after LA's destruction, with the nation in mourning and the inevitable finger-pointing just getting started, the first case of Charon was reported in New York. The next day, Washington. And then Baltimore, Philadelphia, and Boston followed. After that, we lost track. Charon was everywhere, and there was no stopping it. The president died exactly six days after ordering the missile launch, his successor eighteen days later.

"Charon spread worldwide like a summer wildfire, and almost no one survived. It took only eight weeks, give or take, for humanity's dominance on Earth to come to an end. There are only a handful of us left now, and no one escaped being… changed… by the plague one way or another. I'm sorry, Tom, but the world you remember, your loved ones, friends… It's… Everything is gone." The last few words were nearly a whisper, as if she'd run down like the ballerina in a music box. She sat motionless, watching him.

Tom idly wiped at a discolored spot on the food tray with his ragged paper towel while staring at the floor. "I don't… know what to say. I don't believe you. Can't believe you. It's too much. I want to make a phone call."

She sagged visibly and sighed. "I looked into your wife, Heather. She died two years ago, on November thirteenth. I am very sorry." She stood, reached behind herself, and produced a stack of old newspapers. "I know it's a lot to process. This is a collection of material for you to read"—she placed it next to him on the bed—"starting with the *LA Times* from October thirty-first."

"Look, Ana—" he began.

She cut in. "I've got a number of other errands to deal with at the moment, and you need time to absorb all this. Read these while I'm gone. Hopefully, they will help you see that I'm telling you the truth. I'll be back in several hours, and then we'll talk more. You are still weak. Stay in bed."

She handed him a flashlight, turned, and left the room without another word, leaving Tom with the stack of newsprint and a look of shock.

She'd promised to return in a few hours, but he didn't see her again for days.

He ignored the papers at first, defiantly refusing to accept whatever they were meant to prove to him. But with nothing else to do, he eventually worked his way into the stack. He found few related stories at first but did read an article buried deep in the first *Los Angeles Times* that warned of a strange outbreak of some deadly infection at Cedars-Sinai. She apparently wasn't feeding him a complete line of bullshit. One story, though, wasn't going to convince him.

He read late into the night until exhaustion from slurping a bowl of soup and reading about the deaths of everyone he loved caught up with him. He fell asleep while desperately looking for something to contradict Ana, trying to catch her in a lie. But the yellowing papers supported her every claim.

He woke up the next day with the sun filtering through his nearly closed blinds. They had been twisted all the way open when he drifted off the night before, so she must have come back while he slept.

He found a note from Ana and a thermos on a wheeled table beside the bed. The thermos contained tomato soup somewhere between warm and hot. He was disappointed, though, when he tasted it and found it had been made with water. He preferred it with milk but allowed that probably not too many milkmen were making runs if civilization had come to an end.

Her note was direct: "Tom, get as much as rest as possible. You must regain your strength as quickly as possible as we will need to move soon. I hope you have been reading what I left for you. Parts of the building have power, but do not turn on any lights. If you find you can walk, there is a restroom across the hall. I will return tonight. I am sorry I cannot be there, but I have much to do. There is dried food in the cabinets. Ana."

Tom frowned at the note. Those cabinets seemed awfully far away for him to reach on his own.

For the next two days, he read and dozed in the dusty sunlight that drifted in through the blinds. At dusk on the second day, he folded the last newspaper from her stack and set it on his "finished" pile. In all the stuff she'd left, he found not a single story to contradict her. It was an overwhelming pile of corroboration.

He'd wanted to vomit when he read about the destruction of Los Angeles and couldn't have said what made him sicker in the following day's *New York Times*: the story about the first cases of Charon on the east coast or the political piece about the president's re-election chances as he'd just nuked the state with the largest number of electors in the union.

Tom spent the third day trying to escape the mounting boredom by filling out whatever puzzles and games he could find in the papers. In the afternoon, he wheeled his IV hook and bag into the hall, just to prove he could. From the middle of the hallway between his room and a restroom, sets of matching double doors mocked him from both ends of the corridor. He considered picking a direction and setting off on a short adventure. His legs, though, still felt a lot like jelly from simply standing there in the doorway.

Promising himself to venture farther in the next few days, he climbed back into bed and fell asleep in the early evening. He dreamed of riding his motorcycle along the ocean; of playing with his childhood Lab, Chester; and of having a spring picnic with his beautiful Heather—that is, the wife she had been in the days before their problems.

He also saw disturbing things: a white-hot fire that burned out millions of lives; a mob of moaning plague-ridden friends clamoring for his help; and his wife, blood leaking from her nose and mouth, reaching for him while calling his name from an open grave.

He woke, shouting into the darkness.

Ana, her dark eyes wider than usual, set a thermos on his side table. "You startled me."

"Sorry, bad dream" was all he could think to say.

"Do you want to talk about it?" she asked.

"No. Not… not now."

She nodded in understanding. "I have about an hour before I need to go. Would you like to talk about the news I left?"

"Yes but not now. Not first. First, you're going to explain to me where the hell I am and how the hell I got here."

CHAPTER 4

ANA RESUMED HER PERCH ON the same metal stool, untouched since their last meeting. "What is the last thing you remember before waking up here?"

Tom opened his mouth to answer and paused. He had given that exact question a good deal of thought in the handful of days since he first woke up, but he'd yet to come up with a good answer. He remembered walking away from Heather in that hotel and wandering through an underground parking garage in a daze, looking for his car. He remembered his hands shaking as he drove and thinking that he needed to stop before he killed someone. But most of his memories after that were a hazy collection of bars, smoke, and alcohol.

He remembered being served those papers, for sure. Try as he might, though, he could not recall anything after opening the manila envelope holding Heather's divorce filing. Did he even talk to an attorney?

"My wife filed for divorce. That's the last thing I remember."

Ana frowned. "A pity—I was hoping for more. It is common, though, in cases of head trauma, to not recall events leading up to the responsible incident. I suppose we'll never know how you ended up in the coma."

"Once I became aware of your... situation," she went on, "I began looking for background information. Eventually, I managed to locate your original hospital chart, but it was partially damaged, and large sections were missing. From what I can tell, at some point you suffered a massive head injury and became comatose."

"What happened?" Tom asked.

"I never found out, and my search was fairly extensive. If the computer system at the hospital had been working, I might have gotten some additional information, but many places no longer have electricity."

"Well," he mumbled, "it was February, I think, when I got the papers. Maybe I drove myself into a tree or over a cliff."

"Perhaps," she said. "Regardless, you ended up with a significant head wound and a grave prognosis. No one expected you to ever be conscious again. You were lucky, though. The hospital was participating in a medical study for coma victims. As a result, rather than being shipped off to whatever establishment your family could afford, you stayed for nearly ten years. You apparently received a variety of experimental drugs intended to boost your brain activity. You were closely monitored and well cared for—at least, until Charon."

"So everyone got super-flu and died, but I didn't get it? How'd that happen? And even if I didn't get it, how'd I manage not to starve to death? Don't people in comas need feeding tubes or something?"

Ana smiled wryly. "Yes, feeding is necessary. I don't

know exactly what happened when everyone else died. As I told you, though, some people did survive, but they are largely… different… not truly human anymore."

"What do you mean, different?"

"We'll get to that. The important thing is that they found you somehow, and they had to have found you relatively soon. You could not have survived long, help-lessly comatose and without food."

"Okay, fine. Someone else—some people like, what, the post-apocalyptic Red Cross—took care of me for three years and kept me warm, dry, and fed? Great. I don't much care that they're not exactly human beings anymore. I don't care if they're a bunch of psychos or elves or whatever. They kept me alive. They can't be all bad. I'd at least like to meet them and maybe find a way to thank them."

Ana jumped up from her stool. "You will make *no* attempt to find them!"

"Whoa, Ana," Tom began.

Her eyes narrowed, and she stabbed a finger at him. "Whoa nothing. Listen to me carefully. If you ever try to return to those who kept you, you will surely be killed. You were held captive by a very twisted man for three years, kept alive solely because, well, you weren't dead already. You cannot go back. It isn't safe. You have to trust me."

"Okay, okay. I get it. Calm down. But, I mean, why? Why would anyone want to kill me, especially now? What the hell were they doing with me all that time?"

She sighed and dropped back onto the stool. "Experiments, Tom," she mumbled. "Hundreds, maybe thousands of them. What do you think made those marks all over you?"

Tom looked down at the circular wounds dotting his arms. Some were completely healed, slightly raised and shiny pink. Others seemed more recent, having thick, dark, scabbed caps that itched enough to need idle scratching. Still more were between fully healed and freshly made. He had those mostly on his arms and legs but also a few along his neck and shoulders.

"Well, I suppose it's good to know I wasn't being used to put out cigarettes," Tom remarked. "What kind of experiments? Am I going to get cancer? It'd be pretty disappointing to live through the end of civilization and then die because someone shot me up with transmission fluid just to see what would happen. And what left the marks?"

"Unfortunately, I don't know. The man I believe was responsible for seeing to you either does not keep much in the way of scientific notes, or he keeps them with him. In any event, I was unable to determine exactly what they were doing. I don't even know for sure that they had a plan or goal."

"Great," Tom muttered in frustration. "We know I was in a coma, we know I got some experimental brain drugs, and we know some bad guy used me as a pincushion for three years but have no idea why. That about sum it up?"

"I'm sorry, Tom." Ana shifted uncomfortably and looked down at her feet. "I had hoped to find out more, maybe after getting you out, but my attempts to return to the hospital have failed. For now, we just don't know anything more than that you're awake, you seem normal, and you're getting stronger."

"Stronger, right." He scoffed. "I'm so weak I can barely make it across the hallway without needing to nap for a couple of hours. Sure, I'm not army crawling across the floor to get a drink of water anymore, but I'm an awfully long way from feeling like a normal person."

Still, her suggestion struck at something else he'd been wondering.

His brow furrowed. "If I was in a coma for thirteen years and just woke up a handful of day ago, shouldn't I pretty much be an invalid? Obviously, I'm not running any marathons anytime soon, but I can actually already walk a little ways at a time. Shouldn't my muscles be complete pudding?"

"According to your original chart, part of the coma study included regular electrical muscular stimulation. I don't know if it was continued later, but that would explain why you aren't in worse shape than you are. You are certainly gaunt, but you're not all skin and bones. Also, I'm giving you a pretty regular regimen of steroids and other growth hormones to help you recover."

"Steroids?" he snapped. "How about you check with me first before pumping stuff into me. Or at least explain what you're doing."

She gave him that glare again. "Since I'm the only one between us with medical experience, I'm quite content to make those decisions without consultation."

He frowned and grunted in resignation. "Look, I haven't been in control of my own life for thirteen years, and now the world's turned all upside down. I'm having enough trouble with that without feeling powerless as well."

Nodding, she said, "I understand that, but you need to understand that every day we stay here, we get one step closer to being found. Both of us are in grave danger, and we need to be away from here as soon as possible. I need you strong enough that you can travel cross-country, alone if necessary, and I'll do whatever it takes to accomplish that.

"And if it's the side effects you're concerned with," she added with a wry smile, "I wouldn't worry too much. The most likely ones are baldness and infertility." She leaned forward and tugged on a lock of his shaggy hair. "You could do with a haircut at the moment, so I think we can agree you have little to fear from baldness. And since I doubt you'll be having much luck on the dating scene these days, reproduction is probably not going to be a significant issue."

Tom scowled and started to reply, but she cut him off.

"Don't worry. It's only for the short term, until we get you strong enough to travel. There should be no lasting side effects. But if we don't move away from here soon, we'll be found. If that happens, side effects will be the least of your concerns."

"Boy, that makes me feel a whole lot better," Tom replied, rolling his eyes. "You know, maybe you should go," he snapped. "I'm tired. I haven't really been sleeping well. I keep having terrible dreams about Heather, LA getting fried, or packs of zombies." He didn't add that every time she explained something to him, it was generally bad news that led to more new questions than answers.

She seemed to know what he was thinking. "Tom, I know that—"

He put a hand out. "No, it's all right," he said, barely whispering. "I'm fine. Just a bit tired."

Ana cocked her head to the left and gave him a concerned look.

He regretted suggesting she leave. "Wait. I'm sorry. Please stay. I know you're not sure if I can handle all of this at once. But it's okay. I can take it."

That was complete bullshit. He wasn't at all sure he could take more bad news, but he wasn't going to admit that openly. The last thing he needed was a candy-coated version of his situation because she figured he wasn't up to hearing the facts. No, if what she said was true and they were in legitimate danger, he wanted the unvarnished truth.

"I don't know."

"Honestly, I'm fine. Let's keep going for a little while longer."

"Are you sure? Nothing is as important as your rest right now."

"Yes, I'm sure. I'll just sleep in a bit tomorrow. It looks like my schedule is pretty flexible all this week." He winked at her, hoping to allay any lingering doubts.

"Okay, then, I'll continue for a bit. Perhaps a drink of water first?"

"Sure, yeah, I am a little thirsty. That's a good idea. Thank you."

She nodded and turned to pour him a cup of water.

"Tell me why we're in so much danger here. We're being looked for? Who's doing the looking, and why?"

She handed him the water and leaned back against the stool. "I suspect we are the targets of a search, although I haven't seen any direct evidence of it, luckily. As I said, the man I snuck you away from will make every effort to get you back."

"What does 'every effort' mean, and who is this guy?"

"It means he likely has several groups of hunters out trying to track you down as we speak. And the hunters are both skilled and dedicated, which makes our situation so dangerous. They will find us eventually. It's simply a matter of time."

He sipped the water and let that sink in. Thirteen years ago he was a regular guy working his way through a boring, fairly unhappy life while trying to hold the pieces of his marriage together. Then, in the blink of an eye, he lost a decade and somehow became the focus of people intent on finding him and using him for some twisted experimentation.

The whole idea was kind of ridiculous—surreal, to say the least.

"What about 'the guy'?" he asked.

"His name is Alexander. He's in charge of this part of the United States, although there is no longer any such thing."

"What, so he's like a governor?"

"No," she replied, "more like a tribal chief. The days after Charon were chaotic, at best, and those that survived basically all tried to live independently. Before long, there wasn't enough food. No one knew anything about producing it. Worse, in places where the survivors lived relatively close together, there was invariably fighting. And that fighting almost always led to death.

"With so few of us already, some form of order and authority was necessary. In this part of the country, Alexander was able to convince survivors to follow him, to accept his rules and live by his law. In return, he brought the worst of the fighting to an end and made some progress on providing food."

"That doesn't seem so bad."

"Stories say he used threats and coercion to solidify his power and simply killed anyone who wouldn't follow along."

"Oh. That does seem kind of bad. Is it that way everywhere?" Tom asked.

"No. The continental US became six separate regions, and each has a kind of leader like Alexander. Each one came to the position in a different way. Some were well known before Charon and lived in areas still well populated enough for their influence to spread. Others were largely unknown but managed to gain support somehow, whether by force or by some other method of proving their leadership."

"Does that mean you're not from this part of the country, then? Where are you from? Who do you work for?"

"I'm from the West," she replied.

"Oh, I'm so sorry," he interjected, thinking of the remains of Los Angeles as a huge black crater.

"No, no, not LA. Seattle, specifically. Just before Charon, I lived in Atlanta. I did happen to be in California when the worst of it came, so I went north and started over there. The ruler of the West is a man named Colin. Everything I do, even here, I do on his orders. He is equally responsible for getting you away from Alexander."

"Then I'd like to meet him."

"And you will when you are well enough to travel. We'll be going out that way, where things should be safer for both of us."

"I see."

"That's enough for tonight. I should be going. There are a number of things I need to check into, and I need to start making preparations for us to leave. I will return soon."

"One more thing."

Ana turned in the doorway, and for a moment, her eyes shone like onyx. "Yes?"

"Are there hard borders to these regions? Where is the closest one?"

"In some places, where geography helps, yes. But in most places, no. It is a problem that still leads to fighting. We are currently just north of Cincinnati. To the south of the city is the Ohio River. It marks the edge of Alexander's territory. Across the river, in Kentucky, is the southern region."

Tom nodded and yawned, adding a muffled "Got it" behind his hand.

"Now, I have one last thing for you, Tom," Ana said. "You need to start taking several walks every day. Do not overdo it. The last thing I need is for you to be slumped over in a corner someplace, alone, too exhausted to stand up. Try to go as far as you can, though. It will help you regain your strength."

He nodded again and mumbled an agreement. Satisfied, she turned and left. The woman hardly made a sound as she walked away, but a few moments later, the door at one end of the hallway clanged open then fell back into place with a click.

He frowned, disappointed she hadn't stayed longer. Her visits helped to break the monotony threatening his rather tenuous sanity. Each time she left, though, he found himself more uneasy than the last. He was beginning to wonder whether she would drive him to a panic-induced heart attack before the loneliness and boredom made him crazy.

CHAPTER 5

HE DID AS SHE SUGGESTED and took a walk the next day. Whatever she was giving him was doing its job, and he managed to shuffle all the way up the hallway after making a left turn at the door to his room. At the end of the hall stood a set of large gunmetal-gray double doors, each with an inset window roughly one foot square.

Already leaning on his IV pole for support, he didn't dare try to push either open. He would probably end up sprawled on the floor, wedged between the doors. And even if he did manage to somehow stagger across the threshold, the thought of maneuvering his IV through while trying to hold a steel fire door open made him cringe.

Instead, he settled for cupping his hands to his face and peering through the window—not much to see but another hallway running perpendicular to this one. Opposite the door was a wall of windows overlooking some kind of courtyard.

He turned around and trudged back toward his room, passing more closed doors along the way. Each door frame was built with a sidelight, though, and inside he found classroom after classroom, all dedicated to some form of science.

"Why a school?" he asked a cutout face of Albert Einstein hanging over the chalkboard in room 217.

If hunter people were really looking for them, an old high school seemed an unusual choice, considering all the places you could hide in an empty world. Why not a huge high-rise, with hundreds of floors in which to disappear, protected by limited points of entry? Or some random suburban house, nestled in a cookie-cutter neighborhood. Here, with the open halls and so many windows, he was constantly getting a prickling sensation on the back of his neck.

Didn't help that the place was huge, empty, and creepy as hell.

At the doorway to his room, he paused then continued right past. His legs would no doubt pay the price for so much walking around, but he wasn't ready to climb back into bed just yet, not while the other end of the hallway beckoned.

He chuckled. *Adventurous* apparently now meant walking to *both* ends of the same hall in one day.

"Yep, you're a regular action hero, Tommy boy."

Passing another group of closed doors, Tom found more abandoned classrooms. At the end of the hall, though, the windows in those fire doors hinted at something more interesting. As on the far side, a hallway ran perpendicular to this one, but instead of windows looking out onto the world, a large set of open stairs led downward to his right. Even better, directly across from the doors was an enormous open room lined with dozens and dozens of bookshelves.

"Thank God. Finally, something to do," he said, breath fogging the glass. Other than finding himself alive and apparently not plague-ridden after waking up from a decade-long coma, finding the school's library was the only good news he'd gotten all week. Having a working computer or an actual companion would have felt like winning the lottery, but reading would do for the time being. It had always been a hobby for him. And it was certainly better than waiting to hear voices in his head.

Panting as he finally returned to the room, Tom was forced to lean against one of the worktables for several minutes before building up the energy to climb into bed. It was a not-too-subtle reminder that he wasn't even in the same zip code as "feeling normal."

Finally gathering his strength, he slipped into bed then wrote a note for Ana, in case he was asleep when she checked on him next: "Would like to do without the IV, if possible." Wandering the empty hallways would be much easier without a tether in his arm.

Tom expected to be asleep quickly after the day's efforts, but his mind raced with plans to spend the coming weeks rereading favorite novels and researching the events of the decade before. For the first time since he woke up, sleep came only with effort.

The following day, Tom struggled through the fire doors leading to the library with equal measures of stubbornness and boredom. He managed to make it to the other side without feeling too much like he'd been in a televised wrestling match, but the effort was enough that he sighed in relief after kicking down the prop leg to hold the massive door open.

Nearly the entire day was spent rummaging through the remains of the school's library. Luckily for him, the building was a high school. A library intended for teenagers meant stacks of books containing pages full of words rather than colorful pictures and talking animals. An elementary school would have had him clawing at his own eyes.

He perused the card catalog, noting new works by his favorite authors. Several series he'd followed before the coma had also progressed with the addition of new books. They were new to him, anyway—a minor benefit of a decade-long coma.

He selected a few to start with and settled into a comfortable reading chair.

The hours slipped past, and he looked up at one point to find the light outside had become a pale gray as the sun drooped. He considered trudging up the long hallway to watch it slip below the horizon from the courtyard but decided against it. He'd been out of his room for long enough, and the few strips of jerky and one bag of trail mix he'd barely remembered to pack into the pockets of the tattered robe were long gone.

He shuffled back down the hall with a couple of books, thankful to have something to do that night besides considering the possibility that he was actually insane and just living out an elaborate hallucination—or worse, the possibility that he *wasn't*. Either way, the characters in the murder mystery in his hands were a welcome diversion.

The IV line disappeared a few days later, although he

couldn't figure out how she'd removed it without waking him. Either way, losing it gave him a new sense of freedom, especially since he was making daily trips out of the room. He dared to hope that he'd soon take a more extended tour of the building.

Beside the library entrance, the extra wide set of steps leading to the floor below beckoned like a siren at sea. Every day, he would walk over to the steps and peer into the darkness, contemplating a journey *down*, to wherever they led. But visions of being stranded down there without the strength to climb back up or, worse, of losing control and taking a tumble, got the better of him. He wasn't quite *that* adventurous yet.

Over the course of the next several weeks, he developed a daily pattern to stave off the creeping insanity. In the morning, he'd have a light breakfast, often consisting of something his mysterious caretaker had left for him the previous night. If she hadn't left anything, it would be dry oatmeal packets made with water heated from an electric burner plate she'd gotten at his request. Then he'd freshen up as much as possible before strolling—no longer shuffling now but *strolling*—to the library.

After a few hours, his legs stiff from sitting for too long while reading, came a small lunch of dried meat and stale granola then a good stretch before an increasingly longer exploratory walk. By now, he'd made his way through every door and hallway on what he assumed was the second floor.

The school was laid out in a simple grid, with six parallel halls of classrooms, each ending in two long hallways running perpendicular. The "end" halls, as Tom thought of them, ran north to south. The western one also served as a viewing area overlooking the courtyard. It also offered a ghastly view of an empty, overgrown parking lot beyond. The main hall on the eastern side of the building ran adjacent to the library and had large matching staircases at both ends.

Four of the halls of classrooms were dedicated largely to one subject each, specifically English and other languages, mathematics, social studies, and the sciences. The remaining two were composed of a kind of hodge-podge of other topics, including everything from home economics to what must have been health, judging by the posters of reproductive organs all over that room's walls.

Without spending more than a few minutes in any one classroom, he made a point to investigate each, at least once, over the course of several weeks. Each day, he pushed a different door open and stepped in to survey the room. Occasionally, doing so would trigger a foggy memory of his own high-school days, and he expected an emotional wave of nostalgia to blanket him, but instead, the sensation was like watching an old movie of someone else's life from long ago.

Finally, seven weeks to the day after he'd awoken in an unfamiliar room with the kind of thirst that meant death was dogging his steps, Tom stood, again, at the top of the large stairway near the library. Most of his strength had returned. The previous few days, he'd walked this entire floor without needing to stop for rest.

He'd seen everything there was to see there.

Staring into the darkness again, he nodded. The time

had come to find out what secrets, if any, hid in the darkness below.

He checked the large police-style flashlight Ana had given him, flicking the switch on and off a few times to make sure it was in working order. Satisfied, he exhaled and concentrated, listening to the silence below.

Nothing.

He cackled at his own graveness. "It's a simple flight of stairs, Tommy boy, not the path to hell. There's likely nothing to find down there but a few rats and some dusty textbooks."

Grinning at his foolishness, he took the first step and descended.

CHAPTER 6

TOM NEARLY TIPTOED DOWN THE steps until he came to a large landing halfway between the floors, where they turned the opposite direction. Stronger or not, he knew the possibility of toppling over and rolling to the bottom was still all too real. He hadn't walked down stairs with his own legs in a long time, so he clung to the railing with his left hand just in case.

His slippers slapped against the hard steps as he moved, echoes bouncing in the dark space below. Going barefoot might have been less grating, easier on his blossoming paranoia, but he didn't want to catch a cold—or something worse—from a chilly floor that hadn't seen a mop in at least three years, especially over a little noise that no one but the rats could possibly hear, no matter how nerve-wracking.

That assumed that Charon hadn't gotten the rats too. But the damned rats always seemed to come out on top.

He reached the bottom and stopped. A few windows here and there let in a measure of pale afternoon light but not much. It was late enough in the day, too, that the sun would be sinking toward the horizon before long.

Shadows dominated the space, giving it a creepy, gloomy atmosphere.

He thumbed the flashlight on.

A long hallway ran from where he stood to a set of double doors roughly fifty yards away. He could just make out the word "Gymnasium" on a plaque above them. Immediately to his right were two sets of glass doors leading outside, and just beyond them, farther down the hall, was the school's main office. The external doors, then, were likely the main entrance.

After taking a few steps forward, he turned right just outside the office. Behind the wooden counter intended to separate the administration from the students were three standard-sized desks, two along the wall to the left and the third facing him from the center of the room. They still held a few dusty stacks of file folders and paperwork, which suggested they'd once belonged to the administrative staff. The center desk even held a picture frame, face-down on a dusty, oversized desk calendar. Hanging from the back wall was a large grid of staff mailboxes, a few still holding unclaimed mail. To the left of that stood a narrow, open doorway, no doubt leading to the infamous principal's office.

Turning his back to the office, Tom faced the school's cafeteria. It was an open area, taking up the whole side of the hall from the stairway to the gym. Twenty or twenty-five circular lunch tables were spaced throughout, reaching all the way to the back of the room, where archways opened to the food-service area that would have served institutional pizza and mystery-meat patties when students were still around to feed.

Tom's mouth watered at the thought of the food once served here. High-school lunch had never been the apex of modern cuisine, and the students no doubt mocked it endlessly, but he'd been eating reconstituted soup, beef jerky, and instant oatmeal for weeks. A tray of questionable nuggets sounded pretty good.

"I bet there's still something in there worth eating," he mumbled. "Maybe some decent canned goods." Unable to help himself, he made a path straight for the door in the back labeled Staff Only.

The gray door squeaked as he pushed past the service area into the kitchen. Inside were a pair of stainless-steel worktables, several industrial-sized appliances, and a dingy floor of orange tiles. The tables stood in the center of the room, to his immediate right. Behind them, along the back wall, was a large, flat metal griddle next to several gas-powered burners, all under a sizeable ventilation hood. A single pot sat on the cooktop, which he assumed Ana used to make his soup. Several other pieces of equipment whose purpose he couldn't guess hunkered beside the flat top.

In front of him were two large metal doors with clasp handles and a third one with a normal knob, reminiscent of a closet. He approached that one first and twisted it easily. The door swung open, and Tom barely kept himself from hooting.

A shelf full of cans meant he'd found the pantry. His moment of joy was short-lived, though—nothing but chicken soup, bean soup, tomato soup, two cans of dark-red kidney beans, and one can of creamed corn that looked at least four decades old. On the lowest shelf, he found some tomato paste and a huge can labeled "Beets" that was bigger than a gallon of paint.

After picking up the creamed corn, he chucked it at the nearest wall in frustration.

"This place is like a fifties bomb shelter. Looks like it's soup for dinner… forever. Watery glitch."

He left the pantry, closed the door, and went for the larger doors. When he pulled the handle of the first, frigid air blasted him.

The freezer was a sizeable walk-in or just seemed larger because of the general emptiness inside. It held one rather oddly shaped hunk of pale pinkish meat. Pork, maybe, but not a familiar cut. Still, the image of a big, juicy roasted hunk of meat made him raise a hand to his mouth just to make sure he wasn't drooling.

He rapped a knuckle against the solid roast several times. "It's too late today, frozen roast, but I'm coming back for you tomorrow morning. I'm going to thaw you out, cook you all day, and have a bit of a feast."

Turning around, he left the freezer, letting the door swing shut. It hit its frame with a dull thud and then a louder click as the handle's clasp settled into position.

Tom reached for the next door, the refrigerator. Its contents were even worse: two shelves of labeled bags that appeared to contain human blood, a stand-up rack of vials, and several small bottles of various types of medication—medical supplies.

The blood seemed a little strange until he realized the bags were designed to hang from an IV pole like the one tethered to him weeks before. Athletes would often use blood transfusions to increase strength and stamina.

Maybe Ana had used the blood for the same purpose early on, when he was weaker.

He took a closer look at the rack of vials. To his eye, they looked like samples, the kind a doctor would draw for an insurance physical or some type of obscure-sounding cell count. Each was labeled with just a number and a date. Two vials were labeled with the number one, and both were dated well over a year before. Six or seven carried the number two and were least six months old, while more than a dozen had the number three and seemed to be from the last couple of months.

Picking up one of the "3" vials, Tom frowned at the thick, crimson fluid. It simply couldn't be a coincidence that the dates matched when he'd been there. That blood had to be his.

He couldn't remember giving Ana any blood during the entire past two months. How had she managed to take it without him knowing? After putting the sample back on the rack, he inspected his arms, looking for needle marks to explain the mystery or any obvious sores among the puckered scars, now healed.

Certainly, taking the first few samples when he was still in a coma would have been easy. But the most recent one was dated just two weeks ago, long after even the IV line had been removed. Somehow Ana had to have been sticking a needle in his arm and taking blood without waking him. If she could do that, a circus running through the room probably wouldn't wake him.

He shuddered. Getting any decent rest was going to be a lot more difficult if he had to worry about sleeping too soundly while people hunted for them. The thought gave him a chill. Or, worse, could Ana have been slip-ping him tranquilizers at night, ensuring he'd be out of it? Probably not, since he never saw her most days. Still, the next time he saw her, they were going to have a good heart-to-heart about what medicines she was giving him.

Tom looked at the other vials in the rack and cocked his head to the side. "If the number threes are me, where did the number ones and twos come from?"

That sort of question would have him staring at the ceiling until he knew, one way or the other, and she might not show up again when he was awake for a week. A re-search journal or notebook of hers might shed some light on it, but he'd never seen her with anything like that.

"Odd," he whispered, rubbing his chin.

Ana reminded him somewhat of the girl from Psych 101 that wrote down every single word the professor spoke in class, including the time he talked about his aging Mustang. The girl never had a button undone, a shoelace loose, or a hair out of place, much like his enig-matic caretaker. If someone like that was taking samples for analysis, she had to have some kind of research journal somewhere.

If such a journal existed, odds were good she left it at the school when she went out.

"The office," he muttered.

He left the kitchen and crossed the cafeteria and hall-way, his search for better food momentarily forgotten.

He checked all three desks in the admin area but found only dusty personnel folders, aging memos, and an attendance sheet with a long list of absent names.

A doorway in the back of the room to the left caught

his eye, and he stopped in the opening. The short corridor beyond was dark. The sun had gone down while he was in the kitchen, and what little light had been coming in earlier was gone. His flashlight was all the light he had.

Three doors stood out on the right side of the hallway, each leading to an individual office and labeled Principal, Vice Principal, and Security, respectively. He spent at least half an hour in each of the first two, hunting anything not school related. The search proved fruitless. Everything he found was covered in three years of dust and was about curriculum, disciplinary action, or most commonly, the school's budget.

He looked until his stomach was rumbling enough to echo through the office. Throwing a dusty folder down in frustration, he sank into the vice principal's chair and rubbed his eyes. "Helluva way to waste a few hours," he grumbled. "I give up."

Rising, he grabbed the flashlight and left the vice principal's office. He turned to leave but stopped and reversed course. "Screw it. I've wasted this much time. I might as well be thorough." With a sigh, he trudged toward the security office.

He stepped inside, and his eyes lit up. It was the smallest room of the three, likely having been a supply closet or something similar once upon a time. Right in front of him, facing the doorway, a wall of video monitors glowed in the darkness, displaying security-camera feeds from all over the school.

Monitor one was labeled Main Entrance and had a wide view of the main doors just outside the office. Monitor two was watching the Rear Entrance. The third had the word "Subject" written on a piece of tape below the screen.

In grainy black-and-white was the empty hospital bed where Tom had spent most of the past seven weeks.

"Fuck!" He slammed a fist on the desk. She'd been watching him without his knowledge the entire time.

A fuzzy latticework on the display suggested the camera was hidden in a vent near the ceiling. Blocking it would be the first thing he did when he got back to his room. Never mind that he'd probably needed that watchful eye early on—he couldn't wait for her to appear again so that he could give her a good piece of his mind. Or whatever mind he had left.

Eight monitors in total made up the wall of video. The cafeteria, the windowed hallway upstairs that looked out over the courtyard and parking lot, the gym, the library, and even the stairway he'd come down were on camera. Was the footage recorded someplace, or only available in real time? Had Ana been going back to watch what he did when she wasn't here? He was damned well going to find out.

He turned from the screens and did a quick sweep of the room. To his left stood a bookcase filled with VCR tapes. One of the shelves, though, held no tapes. It was empty save for three two-inch binders labeled Subject 1, Subject 2, and Subject 3, respectively.

He grabbed the last one and opened it. The first page was a cover sheet: a picture of him in that same bed upstairs, with an IV and tubes everywhere. He was either still comatose or asleep. She must have taken it in the very beginning.

The Tom sleeping in that picture looked much different from how he thought of himself. In his mind, his face was ruddy and colorful, and his cheeks were full, a complement to the rectangular shape of his head. In the photo, though, his face was gaunt, skin stretched tight against the skull. His hair too, was different: shaggy, dark brown waves instead of the closely cropped style he'd always favored.

More than just the coma had changed him. He didn't recognize the age in his own face—lines around his eyes and across the forehead. His nose looked the same, at least, not too wide and just pointed enough to temper his family's typically bulbous sniffer. His eyes, of course, were closed in the image, but they likely hadn't changed much from the clear, football-leather brown they'd always been.

He flipped through the rest of the binder quickly, finding pages and pages of hand-written notes. Forcing himself to close it, he set it aside. He could take it back to his room and read it in detail.

Tom then grabbed the Subject 1 binder. The first page had a similar photo of a younger-looking woman, but unlike him, she had been connected to a respirator. The bed and the room in the picture were not like anything he'd seen in the school, though, so it must have been taken somewhere else. He scanned through it quickly, as he had the previous journal, pausing only when he came to the word "Deceased" scrawled in large letters on the last page. Beneath that he read, "Expired following removal from life support."

He flipped back to the beginning to give it a deep read, but a flicker of motion on the video displays caught his eye. Something the size of a piano leapt up into his throat. A dark figure stood just outside the back entrance on monitor two. It seemed shorter than average for a person, although it was hard to be sure. Who- or whatever was out there seemed to be half crouching and bobbing erratically. Also, the poor quality of the video feed left a great deal to be desired, which didn't help. If pressed, though, he would have guessed it was probably male and likely older. Despite that, even with the fuzzy image, he would not have said that who- or whatever was out there looked... human.

Tom stood petrified as the figure leaned toward the door and pressed its face to the glass. One hand, the left, came up to touch the door, just beside its head. The face bobbed three or four times slightly, like an animal testing for a scent. The other hand grasped the door's handle.

"Oh, Jesus, no."

The figure tugged.

The door didn't move, apparently locked.

Tom forced himself to exhale while counting to ten.

The short figure pulled the handle several times, its entire body jerking backward as it yanked.

"Holy shit. Give up, dammit. Go away." It was barely a whisper.

The figure stepped back from the door and looked up toward the sky. It opened its mouth and expressed the horrible screech of a furious, wounded animal. Tom's shoulders locked up as revulsion clawed up his back. The sound was worse than metal scraping on blacktop.

His revulsion turned to ice with the realization that

the security monitors had no audio. He was hearing the thing screaming, clear as a bell, from inside the building.

Tom's mouth fell open as the thing on the monitor raised a hand, formed a fist, and swung it against the glass door. A spider web of cracks radiated outward from the impact. Then it leaned forward, inspecting the damage.

Tom stood helpless in the security closet, his heart hammering in his chest. He held his breath again.

The thing made another fist and swung a second time, hitting the center of the existing cracks. Glass exploded into the building.

Tom's hands went numb. Horror swept up his spine and lanced across the back of his neck.

The figure stepped through the broken door, either not feeling or not caring about the jagged shards of glass jutting out around the frame.

Deep inside, Tom's mind screamed at him to do something, anything—run, hide, grab a weapon. But he couldn't think, didn't know how to react.

Nothing was left of him but panic.

Something was in the building, and he suspected it was one of those hunters.

CHAPTER 7

O N THE MONITOR, THE MAN-LOOKING thing took a half step forward, slightly crouched, as if evaluating the school with every step. Its head moved in a kind of pendulous motion, bobbing and sweeping from side to side while it looked around the hallway near the rear entrance.

Slowly, the thing crept past the camera's view and off-screen.

There had to be a back exit, right? Tom hadn't come across it while wandering the building, but it had to be on this level somewhere. It wasn't upstairs with all the classrooms, and while there could be another, lower floor, every window he'd seen on this one looked out onto ground level.

In other words, the thing was almost certainly on the same floor as he was, and he had no idea where.

Not quite hyperventilating—not yet—he took one deep breath then another, hoping to quiet the panicky buzz threatening to overwhelm him. It didn't help. Somehow, he had to get control of himself. Just standing dumbfounded in the security office was likely to get him killed soon.

That monster, even as fuzzy at it had been on the low-resolution black-and-white security display, was unlike any horror he'd ever dreamt of on Halloween. The claw-like fingers seemed like an animal's, and its eyes were dull, black marbles. Its clothing was tattered, and it had either no hair at all or hair so fine he couldn't see it. He was pretty sure he'd seen a mouthful of pointed teeth as well but told himself that was just his panic-fueled imagination.

Each passing moment, his heart, already pounding wildly, beat faster, threatening to rip a hole right through his chest. It was bound to either explode or seize up at any second, wasting all of Ana's rehabilitation efforts in a sudden, massive heart attack. He willed his feet to turn, his legs to move. Instead, he stared at the monitors impotently, frozen in place.

At last, a quiet voice, somewhere deep within whispered, whispered through the fog of horror. After all his years asleep and the work of the past two months to get himself stronger, was he going to throw it away now? Why give up just like he gave up on her?

The panic burned away just enough for him to form a clear thought. He had to act. He ticked off three options: close the door and hide in the security office, find a way to sneak back upstairs, or try to trap the thing someplace.

The kitchen had several possibilities for trapping and locking it in, but the risk was enormous. With only himself to use as bait, he was likely to be caught out in the open with it. Sure, having it locked in the freezer for Ana to deal with would be great, but trying to pull that off in his current condition wasn't a great plan. He wasn't going to try unless he had no other options.

Staying put was tempting. Being able to watch the thing move around the building on the security feeds had advantages, for sure. But if it came down the hall, he'd have nowhere to go. Being trapped in a room the size of a supply closet with it wouldn't end well.

That left only one option: getting back upstairs somehow. On the second floor, with all the classrooms and interconnected corridors, he'd have a much better chance at avoiding… whatever that thing was. *If* he could get up there, that is. It wasn't visible on any of the monitors. It could be right in the hallway outside the office.

A muted bang from somewhere nearby rattled off the walls, startling him. Scanning the displays, Tom found the thing on the screen labeled Gym, doing its tentative bob-step toward the center of the basketball court. The sound must have been the gym door closing.

He exhaled. At the moment, he was just down the hall from the thing, which made it much too close, by at least a zip code, but on the other hand, he did know its location. And with it inside the gym, this was probably his best chance to make it upstairs unnoticed.

He slid his feet out of his plastic-soled slippers and stole out of the security office. His heart continued to hammer away, but at least he had a goal and some kind of plan. He just had to move quickly and quietly. And pray he was strong enough to get through whatever happened next.

Tom tiptoed past the two other offices and back into the main area, where he clicked off his flashlight. He waited for a few seconds, letting his eyes adjust to the inky blackness. Holding his breath, he listened for noises from the hallway beyond the counter.

He could have heard a feather hit the ground. Nothing was there.

Pooling his courage, he dashed through the office space and ducked beside the counter at the opening to the corridor. Peeking beyond, he squinted out into the hall—empty. Standing up, Tom turned left and jogged to the stairway.

At the bottom, he looked at the gym doors over his shoulder and listened again. Again, he heard nothing but the blood rushing in his ears. He started climbing the stairs as quickly as he dared.

He reached the landing and turned toward the second half of his climb, but instead of starting right away, he leaned over, hands on knees, to catch his breath. He was panting from the combination of a lack of conditioning and a wallop of adrenalin.

As he regained some measure of control, his heart finally slowed to a reasonable rate. He might make it through this yet.

Tom set a cold, bare foot on the next step as a familiar metallic thud pierced the emptiness below. It was the same sound—albeit louder—he'd heard minutes ago. One of the gym doors had been opened.

The thing was in the hallway.

"Get upstairs and stay ahead of it," he whispered.

But hearing the thing's sluggish shuffle made him hesitate, partially out of stupid curiosity. He'd always been the kid that had to spend a few precious summer afternoons inside, swollen with bee stings, because he'd gotten too close while trying for a better look at the hive. Deep down, something within him cried out to watch the thing that looked so much like a man yet seem to act like an animal.

Part of him, too, wanted to know how far down the hall the thing was and whether it was headed toward the stairs or maybe, he hoped, the kitchen.

A heavy wheeze filled his ears, and his heart picked up the pace again. The thing's breath seemed labored for some reason as it huffed and grunted with each exchange of air. The sound made the hair stand up on the back of Tom's neck, and goose bumps prickled among the scars on his arms.

"Get upstairs and stay ahead of it," he repeated.

He crept up two steps. Two down, six more to go.

Another door opened with that same metallic thud but much closer than the last—right at the bottom of the stairs. He froze and ducked below the handrail.

As the door clanged shut, the thing in the hallway screeched, a twisted combination of surprise and delight. Immediately following that came a grunt and a deep, low growl, along with the slap of feet hitting the tiles in quick succession. The thing wasn't taking bobbing, hesitant half steps any longer. It was running… toward him.

"Bloody hell," a woman said in a clipped voice.

Ana.

Tom stood up on the steps and leaned over the railing. "Ana, watch out!" he screamed, just as the brightest light he'd ever seen cut through the darkness, out of the palm of her hand.

The bright beam formed a tight cone focused directly into the face of the monster charging her. Only a few feet away from her, it buried its face in its clawlike hands, squealed in pain, and turned away.

Ana spared a quick look back at him. "Upstairs! Now!" she barked before returning her attention to the thing whimpering in front of her. She raised the hand holding the light, revealing the long, narrow shape of a flashlight.

He turned away and started climbing again just as a sickening crunch and a cry of pain filled the room, followed by the heavy thud of something dropping to the tiles.

He could still hear the thing's wheezing grunts of breath, even more labored.

"Ana?" he called down the stairs.

"I'm fine, Tom," she replied, her voice huskier than usual. "We need to get out of here right now. There are clothes and a pair of boots in the closet in your room. Get up there and change. Grab some of the food, but don't bother with much. We'll find more. We're leaving and not coming back. I'd guess we have maybe ten minutes to get out of here before more guests like your friend here arrive."

Tom ran.

Minutes later, Tom was at the bottom of the dark stairs again but wearing dingy jeans, an old Harley-Davidson T-shirt, and a pair of boots new enough that they still bore their tags.

Ana was waiting with her flashlight and nothing else. "Are you ready?" she asked, heading toward the door.

"I... I guess." Tom replied, following. "What was that?"

"Not now." She shoved the door open and led him out.

Outside, in the cool night air, he stopped after a few steps. Eyes closed, he reveled in the breeze blowing against his face. He'd forgotten what a cool autumn wind felt like.

"We have to go," Ana urged. She swung her head in each direction, looking into the distance.

Tom opened his eyes and jogged to her car, an average-looking gray Honda. She was already behind the wheel, so he opened the passenger door and dropped into the seat beside her.

"What the hell was that thing? Did you kill it?" he asked.

"They're called Feral, or plaguers," she replied, buckling her seat belt. "The rest I'll explain later. I need to focus."

She whipped out of the parking space and pounded the accelerator. A few seconds later, the school disappeared behind a hill as they sped away at breakneck speed, chasing shadows in the road with no headlights.

Tom clenched his back teeth and braced himself against the dashboard. "Slow down! If I'd wanted to get killed, I would have just stayed back there with that... thing. The Feral or whatever."

"Buckle up," she replied in a chill voice, not taking her eyes from their road. He frowned, irritated. He'd just found out the Bogeyman was real, and Ana wasn't showing even the slightest tinge of discomfort.

They drove for long enough that Tom's hands cramped

from clinging for dear life. He had to force them open when she at last slowed down. They turned at a crossroad and rumbled down a narrow gravel lane toward a dark, looming warehouse. Ana pulled up to a garage door, grabbed her flashlight, and stepped out. After approaching the door, she stopped, listening. Satisfied, she raised the sectioned panel door over her head and disappeared into the emptiness.

Time stretched as he waited for her return. Thirty seconds seemed an hour, and a full minute was a lifetime. At last, Ana emerged from the building, got back in the car, and pulled it through the door without a word.

After killing the engine, she got out again and pulled a chain hanging near the wall. The garage door slid back to the ground, closing them in the warehouse. Then she leaned against the Honda, closed her eyes, and sighed.

Tom joined her. "Are you okay? Are we okay?" His voice was nearly a whisper.

After a deep breath, Ana's shining eyes gleamed back in the dark. "For now, I believe we're safe. We'll stay here for the night. Tomorrow, we're heading for Seattle."

CHAPTER 8

"**T**HANK GOD," TOM REPLIED. "I was about to lose my mind in that school." A crackling twinge in his voice betrayed him. He wasn't sure about traveling west with her, but he was sure he wasn't going to talk to *her* about that.

The darkness and silence of the warehouse pressed on him. He had to say something to fill the emptiness. "Did you, uh, know about this place already?"

She nodded. "I've been keeping my eye on it for some time, just in case."

Tom looked around, taking stock. The car sat at the head of a long aisle separating row after row of huge shelving racks running away from them on both the left and right. The racks were two or three stories tall and looked as if they were sectioned off at regular intervals into bays holding skids full of cardboard boxes. It seemed a lot like the center aisle of one of those bulk chain stores that sold five-gallon tubs of mayonnaise or fifty-pound bags of rice.

He walked away from the car but found nothing more than endless rows of shelving running off into the cavernous distance. The pale light of the moon filtered through dingy windows three stories up, where the walls met the roof, making it much too dark to see very far away.

His imagination filled the vastness in front of him with dozens of those shuffling Feral. He shivered, pretending he didn't notice the new flash of goose bumps on his skin.

Ana, still leaning against the driver's-side door, said nothing as he walked back to the car.

She pushed away and pressed a button on the key fob, making the trunk spring open. "I've got some camping supplies. There's a gas stove and some cooking pans, utensils, that kind of thing. A few canned goods as well. Are you hungry?"

Although he hadn't eaten in hours, he shook his head. "No, thanks. I'll just eat something I grabbed before we left."

She nodded, reached into the trunk, and pulled out a stack of blankets. "I set some pallets together the next row up, and I think I have enough blankets to soften them a little. It won't be comfortable, but it should be better than sleeping on the ground."

"Ana, I…" he started but wasn't sure exactly what to say. "Um, thanks. For everything. Especially for showing up when you did."

She turned to him with an armload of blankets. "I promised I was going to take care of you."

"I appreciate it."

"I'm glad I got there in time."

"So that… Feral… That's what you called it, right?" Tom asked.

"Yes."

"Feral," he repeated, feeling the word in his mouth. "What did you do? Did you kill it?"

"Yes," she replied without hesitation. "Plaguers are dangerous but, luckily, also extremely sensitive to light. With all the shadows in there, my flashlight blinded it completely. While it was trying to recover, I applied as much force as I could muster to its temple."

He nodded, remembering that sickening crunch. "It was still breathing after that, though. What did you do?"

"If you really want to know," she said, "I broke its neck and severed its spinal cord. The things are incredibly resilient. In order to completely stop one, you have to do significant damage to the nervous system. When I was sure it was dead, I dragged it into the freezer."

Tom couldn't imagine keeping a level head during the few seconds when that thing was charging down the school's main hall. Yet she'd managed to snap the light on at just the right moment and then beat it senseless with a flashlight. She must have been moving damned fast, too, to accomplish all that and stow it in the freezer in the few minutes he was upstairs changing.

"Speaking of Feral, Tom, we need to go over a few things. You'll be traveling during the day, and plaguers are almost completely nocturnal, so you shouldn't have any trouble with them. Still, I want you to take a few precautions to avoid drawing attention to yourself."

He creased his brow. "Now, hold on just a minute. '*You'll*'? I thought we were going together."

"We are," she replied. "But for a day or maybe more, you'll have to go alone. I have a number of loose ends to tie up here, and I'm not keeping you close to Alexander a moment longer than absolutely necessary. You can drive a car, right?"

"It's obviously been a while, but I'm sure it's like riding a bike. Not sure I trust the other drivers, though." He smirked.

"Take this," she continued, ignoring the jab and offering him the flashlight. "It's a high-powered light, so be careful not to do anything stupid like look right at it or flash it around windows or anywhere someone might see it."

He nodded.

"Tomorrow morning at dawn, take the car and travel as far west as you can. The fastest way is to go northwest from here through Indiana, Iowa, and South Dakota. Alexander's territory reaches west to Illinois, and you need to get through it as soon as possible. Make sure you don't stop for the night until you reach Iowa, at least. I laid out the best route for you here." Ana handed him a folded United States road map.

He scowled at it and then back at her. She was steamrolling him.

"Look," he said. "I'm not sure…"

"I'll catch up as soon as I can. Stay on the roads marked on the map, and I shouldn't have any problem finding you. The precautions are simple: don't stop unless you must, stay out of buildings during the day, and make sure you're off the road and locked inside somewhere by nightfall. Also, wherever you choose to stop for the night has to have more than one exit. Do not get cornered inside a building. And whatever else, if I'm not there by the time you stop, find a place with a working lock, make sure there are no lights visible from the outside, and try not to make much noise."

"What the hell? Make no noise, leave no trace, have no fun," Tom said with a sneer. "This is kind of ridiculous. If I have to spend the rest of my life skulking around, I might as well be dead."

Ana slammed the trunk and turned to him with fire in her eyes. "I am sorry this isn't going to be some college road trip full of pranks and co-eds, but your life is in considerable danger, and you've seen evidence that I'm not just making that up. You know next to nothing about the world outside that door, and I have limited time to teach you the basics of survival. Until we reach Seattle, nothing is more important than being cautious."

She had managed to yell at him somehow without even raising her voice. Still, she got the point across.

Tom looked down. "I'm sorry. I know you're trying to help, and I guess this isn't easy for you either. It's just that it's all so much to take. And I thought you'd be with me. I'm tired of being, well, alone all the time."

She sagged. "I know, and I wish things could be different. I know how difficult this must be. Honestly, I'm a little surprised you're not more frayed around the edges." She touched him on one shoulder.

Surprising himself, he covered her hand with his own. Her gesture had been awkward but welcome. It was the first time she'd been anything more than cold and clinical toward him.

"I keep thinking this is someone else's life or just a bad dream that I'm going to wake up from, any minute."

Ana gave him half a smile. "Before long, we'll be someplace safer. Then maybe we'll be able to relax. A little." She slipped her hand away. Gathering the blankets again, she added, "I think we should both try to get some sleep. Dawn comes early, and you need as much rest as you can get. I don't want you falling asleep at the wheel. There isn't going to be much out there to provide a diversion."

Tom followed her up the aisle and into the next row. "Oh, I don't know about that," he said. "It isn't every day I get a cross-country view of the aftermath of an apocalypse. Surely there's something interesting to see out there."

She shook her head, chuckling lightly as they approached a couple of skids together on the ground. "I hope you're not too disappointed, then, Tom."

Ana spread the blankets out across the pallets. He lay down and nestled into them, surprised at how comfortable the makeshift bed felt. "I'll be just across the aisle in the opposite row," she said, pointing, "but I'm going to look around a bit before I settle in. I want to make sure there haven't been any visitors recently."

"Okay. Good night."

After she retreated into the darkness, Tom stared at the ceiling for what could have been hours. Exhaustion overtook him at some point, but even then, it was a fitful, restless sleep, scattered with bad dreams.

Ana woke him with a gentle nudge just as the windows high above showed a sky turning pale blue. "It's time," she said.

He got up, grabbed the mound of blankets, and stumbled to the car, groggy, wishing for the first time that he had some coffee—a very big, very strong cup of coffee.

He stopped in front of the Honda and rubbed his

eyes. After blinking the sleep away, he raised an eyebrow at the car. "With all the cars in the world left to pick from, you went for the most ordinary compact sedan you could find?"

"The best thing for you is a dependable car that gets excellent fuel economy," she replied. "You don't need to be stopping any more than necessary for gas, and I'd hate to give you something that broke down a hundred miles from the nearest available replacement. There's no auto-service club anymore, and you can't very well be walking along the interstate after dark because your car died."

Tom grunted and slid into the driver's seat while Ana tugged on the chain beside the garage door. Light flooded into the warehouse.

She retreated several steps into the shadows, not quite far enough to be obscured by them.

"Wow," he whispered, seeing her for the first time that wasn't the middle of the night.

As the soft morning glow brightened the sharp features of her oblong face and highlighted the almost bluish tint of her jet-black hair—not a wisp of which was out of place even after spending the night on a palette in a warehouse—she almost took his breath away.

With all that, though, it was, again, her eyes that struck him. Their exact color remained a mystery, even reflecting the sunlight a few paces away. He decided they were simply "dark." Slightly almond shaped and perfectly spaced and aligned, they blazed in the light in a way he'd never seen before.

Blinking out of his reverie, he started the car, slid the gearshift to reverse, and backed out of the warehouse, turning the car toward the road. He put his hand up and waved. "Godspeed," he whispered. "See you soon."

He wished he felt more certain of that. Would he even make it through the day? How would she find him?

She returned his wave and gave him a half smile back.

Optimism surged through him, burning away the fear. Whatever happened, the time had come to get on with his life. "Right after I do something about this car." He chuckled.

Lifting his foot from the brake pedal, he put the car into drive and hit the gas.

CHAPTER 9

AFTER LEAVING ANA AT THE warehouse, Tom found the on-ramp to I-75. Mile after mile of deserted gray concrete and overgrown median slipped past as he drove, the only moving thing in the center of three lanes of empty highway. Despite the sense of oddness, being alone had its advantages. With a smile, he pressed the accelerator to the floor.

The little Honda accelerated well, but Ana hadn't even gotten him a V-6. At ninety miles an hour, it started making the high-pitched whine he considered a hallmark of economy cars. This was definitely not the way to travel as one of humanity's last survivors. That would have to be fixed right away.

Out of habit, Tom clicked on the radio but found nothing but static and the harsh buzz of the Emergency Broadcast System. He needed a new car and some tunes as soon as possible, or he'd end up driving into a tree just to break up the monotony.

Ana had made it as clear as day that he needed to get out of Alexander's territory quickly. She also said he shouldn't make any more stops than were absolutely necessary. And after the previous night and the incident with the Feral, he tended to agree. But this morning was a brand-new day.

Tom grinned at the thought of a little mischief. "What could it hurt to make a few quick stops close to home?" he said. "Switch cars, pick up a stack of CDs, and maybe even see what the old apartment looks like." He'd be back on the road in an hour, tops. And with a real car with a real engine, he'd make that time up before noon.

As he made his way south toward the Ohio River, he saw no signs of human life. Flocks of birds flew in loose formation overhead, migrating south with him, but that was pretty much it. Otherwise, the whole world seemed empty.

With the exception of having to dodge potholes at ninety miles an hour, his short drive was uneventful. A few winters seemed to have done a lot of damage without road crews to patch things up every spring.

Tom tightened his grip on the wheel as he approached the bridge across the Ohio River. Crossing it into Kentucky meant leaving Alexander's territory, and he checked his mirrors and windows again and again as the metal thrummed underneath the sedan. He half expected to find a barricade of Feral in the middle of the bridge. Regardless, he breathed easier when the tires hit the pavement on the far side.

The exit toward the apartment he'd shared with Heather was just a few miles south of the river, the kind of nonthreatening corporate suburban area that people used to love to make fun of. But picking up a different car and some music there would be easy—assuming things hadn't changed *too* much.

Leaving the expressway, his first stop was a Ford dealership. Tom got out of the Honda and walked the lot slowly, watchful for both the perfect car and any sign of someone or something moving. Halfway between the sensible sedans and gleaming oversized trucks, he stopped and whistled.

"There she is," he said, eyeing a ruby-red Mustang GT convertible, everything the American teenage boy dreams about. "Been looking for you since I was handed my learner's permit," he whispered.

Both car doors were locked, though. He had to find the right key. Cursing for having nothing to write with or on, he memorized the last six digits of the car's stock number, hoping that would be enough. Then he headed for the sales office.

The doors to the main entrance were locked, but several large glass display windows had been knocked out. He eased his way through the breakage and stopped to listen.

The air was stubborn inside the building, and he heard nothing like the labored cycle of wheezes and growls that Feral thing had made. He hoped that meant he was alone. Of course, he'd only heard that one. Did they all breathe the same way?

On the far side of the showroom was a large board covered with hooks and keys that had to be for the lot cars. Head swiveling, he darted across the open space and skimmed the tags hanging with the keys.

After clenching his jaws long enough for beads of sweat to form on his forehead as he checked the hooks, he found the stock number matching his Mustang. Tom grabbed the key and dashed out of the building. Back out in the sun, he was met with both a sense of relief and a refreshing blast of cool autumn air.

Returning to the Mustang, Tom pressed the unlock button on the car's key fob, and the locks rewarded him with a satisfying click. He opened the driver's door, slipped behind the wheel, then frowned, realizing there was no ignition slot to slide a key into. Eyeing a large circular button labeled Engine Start with suspicion, he gave it a soft tap as if it might shock him. Instead, the engine roared to life. Tom pushed the accelerator a few times and was rewarded with a throaty purr. The surge of power was exactly what he expected, and he couldn't help but smile.

This was how you went about being the last man on earth.

He exchanged all the supplies from the Honda and raced out of the lot, heading toward his old apartment. In all likelihood, he'd find nothing interesting. Heather had probably dropped the lease during his extended hospital stay and moved on with her life. But he had to look. He was about to drive twenty-five hundred miles west and probably wouldn't ever come back. This was his only shot at a little closure.

Pulling into the apartment complex, he found the parking lot almost completely full, which seemed odd in comparison to all the deserted roads.

A cold chill washed over him when he realized why that was the case. After getting sick, most people had likely stayed home to die. The hospitals would have been packed, and nobody would want to hang out in an ER full of plague victims.

All the parked cars were a sign of everyday life, though, which wasn't helping him adjust to the world. As he looked around, things seemed kind of normal.

But all those everyday lives had ended years ago.

The front door to Tom's old building opened easily, which didn't surprise him. It was supposed to be locked around the clock, but that hadn't ever been the case when he lived there.

He entered the building and wrinkled his nose. The air was heavy, fetid, to put it lightly. The place was probably full of bodies. A few steps leading up to the first floor confirmed that suspicion: a pair of legs stuck out into the hallway, cross-trainers pointing, motionless, toward the ceiling. His view down the hall was obscured enough that he couldn't see the rest of the corpse, though, and that was just fine.

Ignoring both the body and the odor, he checked the bank of mailboxes to his right. To his surprise, the number-five slot still bore the name Woodford.

Brow furrowed, Tom walked down the four steps to the ground-floor hallway. He stopped at the last door on the left, marked simply with the number five, and tried the doorknob. This one was locked. He flipped over the mat and pulled a piece of duct tape off the bottom. Attached to the tape was a key that fit snugly into the lock.

An image of his dead wife's body rotting on the couch inside flashed through his head. No matter what she'd done to him, he couldn't handle that. Offering a silent prayer that he wouldn't find either her or a Feral, he pushed the door open.

Everything was just as he remembered. The TV was

newer and wider, but the rest hadn't changed except a thick coat of dust. His lips compressed into a thin line, and he rubbed his chin.

This was the last thing he'd expected. Heather had never been the type to get attached to things, and much of what was there had been his before they were married. The room should have been filled with new, unfamiliar stuff—things that were hers that he'd never seen. Instead, she'd apparently gone on living in the place just as they'd had it.

"I hated this apartment after you went and..." he whispered to himself.

In the days following their confrontation at the hotel, he'd sense her touch on everything. Microwaving a bowl of soup would lead to remembering all the times she left twelve infuriating seconds on the timer because she had the patience of a toddler. On the empty couch, he would see past visions of her napping, contentedly, beautifully, in front of some rom-com movie on a lazy Sunday afternoon. Those memories and the thousand others like them were special to him now, cherished. He hated that among those was also the one in that hotel-room doorway when she was wearing nothing but a half-open bathrobe and a guilty expression.

The only thing out of place, other than the television, was a box of stationery on the coffee table in front of the couch. Inside, he found a collection of envelopes lined up in a neat row.

He grabbed the one closest to the front of the box and inspected it. Across it, "Tom" was written perfectly in Heather's unmistakable script. A single rose was embossed in the lower right-hand corner, and a vine trailed away around the back. It was her stationery, the special stationery that she used only to write personal notes to the people most important to her.

He looked back at the box and ran his fingers through the rest of the envelopes. They were all the same and all addressed to him, easily a hundred or more.

The one in his hand was unsealed, as were all the others. He lifted the flap from where it was tucked in and slid the folded note halfway out. Hands trembling, he let out a slow breath.

"I don't really have time for this," he said, more to Heather than himself. "I need to get going." But that was only an excuse, and he knew it. Deep down, he was afraid to read whatever she'd left for him.

She'd hated him at the time of the accident, and before then, she'd avoided meeting with him. The few times they had spoken, she'd told him off. If forced to guess, he'd bet that box of stationery held a decade's worth of bitterness and anger.

He frowned. Whatever was inside, he wasn't ready to cope with all that yet. No way. Especially not in the face of everything else.

Tom slid the letter back into its envelope and set it down on the table beside the box. Turning away, he put the notes out of his mind. "Clothes," he said and walked down a short hallway into the rear of the apartment.

In their old bedroom, Tom threw open the closet door and blinked at the contents. Every shirt and pair of pants he'd owned at the time of his injury hung exactly where he'd left it.

A grin split his face but then evaporated when he picked up one of his hoodies. It was much too big for him. Thirteen years in a coma would do that.

After returning to the living room, he opened the coat closet in search of his black leather jacket. He'd worn it on their first date, on the night he proposed, and on that horrifying day they went to the hospital before their marriage—never mind civilization—came apart. He'd had it for all the most important events of his life.

It was hanging just where he'd left it, pushed all the way to one side, carefully wrapped in plastic. She must have had it cleaned.

After sliding the jacket off the hanger and out of the wrapping, he shrugged it on. It was also too big for his new slim frame, but he wasn't leaving it. Maybe he would grow back into it.

Tom picked up the note from the table and stuffed it into his left-hand pocket. Then he grabbed the box of letters to read later—much later.

A quick scan of the apartment revealed nothing else he really wanted. Strange that his old life had become little more than an old leather jacket and a box of letters. Even stranger, that felt about right at the moment. All this stuff was just junk he'd filled his previous life with. He didn't have room for it anymore.

He left the apartment, pulling the door behind him until it clicked. Then for some reason he couldn't explain, he put the door key back under the mat, using the same piece of duct tape.

The car was exactly where he'd left it, untouched. He set the box of letters in the backseat, got in, and clicked the button to put the top down. As the motor whirred to retract it, Tom raised his face to the sky. He smiled, basking in the warmth of the sun, glad to know that no matter what else, at least some things stayed the same.

CHAPTER 10

Tom took one last look at the apartment complex and pulled away, leaving his former life in the rearview mirror.

The drive to the nearest music store was short, thankfully, giving him little opportunity to dwell on Heather. Picking out a stack of CDs was exactly the kind of diversion he needed.

The store sat in the center of a strip mall, with a coffee shop on one side and a dry cleaner on the other. He parked in the handicapped space closest to the door after half a minute of consideration. It still felt wrong, even with no one around to care anymore. In the end, though, Tom shrugged. "You're about to steal a few hundred dollars' worth of CDs, and you want to beat yourself up over parking, Tommy boy?"

Adjusting his ideas of acceptable behavior would take some time.

The door to RecordNow was still in one piece and, unfortunately, locked. Determined, Tom returned to the car and grabbed Ana's flashlight from the passenger seat. He gripped it like a baseball bat and, holding it by the bell, swung it butt-end at the door. Cracks blossomed in the glass.

He struck again and again, making a circle of zigzagging fissures. Still, the glass held. He frowned at his handiwork, face darkening. Summoning all his strength, he swung once more, pouring himself into it. The glass finally gave way, and the end of the flashlight popped just through the surface.

Tom pumped his fist in the air and hooted like a kid.

He widened the hole with the flashlight until it could accommodate his hand and arm. Reaching in, he flipped the lock and chuckled to himself. "Didn't think I'd need to actually break into the place."

With the door unlocked, Tom opened it slowly, expecting an alarm or some kind of bell or chime to sound. It would be just his luck to finally crack his way into the place, only to have one of those monsters appear out of nowhere. He said a quiet word of thanks that nothing rang out. Taking a breath, he walked through the door and let it close behind him. Inside, he counted to ten silently.

Nothing moved. He exhaled, shaking out his arms and shoulders. He'd been holding his upper body so tense that someone could have played him like a guitar.

The walls of the store were covered with posters of singers and musicians, but they could have just as easily been the names of families in Tucson. He recognized hardly any of them. One or two were familiar, but the rest were new and very young looking. Music seemed to have changed a lot in just ten years.

Tom made his way up the first of four aisles, looking

for a few specific favorites and anything else that caught his eye. Half an hour later, he reached the end of the rock section while struggling to hold the dozen or so CDs he'd already picked out. The country category would have several things he wanted too. A few plastic cases slipped out of his arms and hit the floor in a tiny avalanche. He grimaced at the rattle of plastic falling.

"This is stupid. I need a bag or something."

He set his CDs down in a stack behind the checkout counter at the rear of the store and glanced around. The counter and shelves beneath the cash register held only a credit-card machine, a half-empty bottle of Mountain Dew, a tape dispenser, and a couple of disposable pens—no bags anywhere. In the far back corner of the store was a door labeled Employees Only. Figuring it for the office, a storage room, or both, it seemed a promising alternative.

The door stood slightly open, barely an inch or two, and the narrow gap set off alarms in his head.

He peered inside with the slow care of someone carrying explosives and found much of what he'd expected: a desk, a metal rack of shelves, and the back door of the building, open to the outside. Nothing moved or made any discernible noise. He inched the door open farther, ready to bolt in the other direction if necessary.

Halfway, the door's hinges squeaked loudly. Tom shouted a curse and half jumped out of his shoes.

After a few calming breaths, he pushed it farther. As it swung open, a low animal growl threatened from the shadows beyond.

Tom dashed away and was halfway to the front door, CDs be damned, before he looked over his shoulder. He expected one of those Feral to be staggering after him. Instead, he found only open space.

He stopped, turned around, and cocked his head in confusion.

The Feral back at the school had shot after Ana the second she made a sound. But here… nothing. Had the growl been just a figment of his imagination? Getting paranoid already?

He shook his head. "Doesn't matter."

A very rational, very loud voice somewhere within was shouting at him to forget the CDs, forget the office, and get the hell out. But some part of him desperately needed to know what was back there—had to know whether it was a monster or his mind playing tricks on him.

Besides, that growl had seemed sort of familiar.

"You're a damned fool," he muttered, creeping back toward the office.

Reaching the door again, he focused on the space beyond it. Everything was still except for the light fall breeze blowing lightly from outside—no other noise, no movement.

Tom touched the doorknob to push it open a little wider.

Another growl, unmistakably a warning—it was louder this time, too, more urgent… and certainly familiar.

"God, could it be…" Tom whispered, poking his head past the doorway.

In the far back right corner of the room, beyond the desk and open exit door, a furry head popped up with a jingle of tags. It was a dog, growling at him again.

Tom took a step into the room and was met with two short barks and a show of wicked, gleaming canine teeth.

"Hey there, boy," he said, making his voice soft. "It's okay. I'm not going to hurt you. You don't want to hurt me either."

The dog appeared to be a good deal German shepherd and was clearly underfed. It was black in the face and body, with a tan spot just above each eye and more tan covering the legs, neck, and chest.

When Tom spoke, the dog sat up and cocked its head to the side.

He extended his hand slowly, palm up, the way he'd been taught when he was eight years old, and dropped to his knees. He shuffled forward, inching closer to the animal.

"It's okay, buddy," he continued in that same mild tone. "I don't know about you, but I could sure use a friend. I bet you'd like one too, huh? I bet you're a damned good dog."

As Tom reached the corner, the dog stretched its nose forward and sniffed at his hand. It cocked its head again then stood and took a small step forward.

"That's a good boy."

The dog emitted two quick yips, short and sharp.

He yanked his hand away and fell backward, over his heels and onto his butt, scampering away in reverse.

The dog watched him with what could be called a touch of amusement.

After getting to his feet again, Tom stooped back toward the animal. "What's wrong, fella?" He put his hand out again and, with a careful, delicate touch, stroked the animal along its neck and shoulders.

The dog barked again twice in quick succession, sharp but not deep.

"How about some beef diplomacy?" Tom reached into his pocket for one of the bags of jerky he'd taken from the school.

The shepherd shook its fur out with a resounding jingle of tags and sat down, polite and at attention. Tom gave his new friend a piece of dried beef and scratched its chest as the animal chewed.

His hand brushed the metal tags hanging from a red collar. "Any chance one of those has your name on it?"

He got a short bark in reply.

Tom lifted the tags for a closer look. The first was the city license, expired years before. The second was a record of a rabies vaccination even earlier, and the last was bone shaped and carried the former owner's address, which was a few miles away.

On the reverse side of the metal bone was one word: *Lady*.

"Lady, huh?"

She replied again with one short bark.

"Well then, Lady, I'm Tom. I'm heading for Seattle, where it's supposed to be safer. I think I could use a sidekick, or else I'm going to end up referring to myself in the third person soon. Want to come along?"

Lady barked again and stood up. She padded to the open back door and looked out the rear of the building. Satisfied, she reversed course and walked to the door of the office. She stopped there and looked back with a puzzled expression, as if to say, "Why are you still hanging around back there?"

Tom chuckled to himself. "All right, I'm coming."

Leaving the office and passing the checkout counter, he grabbed his stack of CDs. Country would have to wait for another day.

The pair left the store, with Lady leading the way. She stopped from time to time to sniff at the air but always moved on without reacting. When they reached the car, she jumped completely over the passenger door and into the seat.

Tom started the engine, unwrapped one of his new discs, and fed it to the dashboard. As the music started to play, he scratched Lady between her ears then backed the Mustang out of the parking space. Squinting in the sunlight, he shifted into gear.

With a glance at the dog beside him, her tongue lolling out, he said, "Need to get a pair of sunglasses."

Unexpectedly, she reached forward and licked him once on the cheek.

CHAPTER 11

BY NOON, TOM AND LADY had driven through Indianapolis, and they were headed west to Illinois when dark clouds rolled over them. Although they made up for the time lost earlier in the morning by averaging speeds well over a hundred, Tom was forced to put the top back up and show some restraint with the accelerator when the later afternoon turned into a gloomy drive though steady rain.

Although still brooding over Heather, Tom couldn't help but periodically smile at his new friend in the passenger seat. Her presence made the solemn, gray trek somewhat bearable.

Day was reaching into evening as they crossed the Mississippi River into Iowa. Not long after they passed through someplace named Davenport, which he'd never heard of and never expected to see again, the fuel gauge was edging close to *E*.

"What do you think, Lady?" he asked. "Stop in a small city or somewhere a little farther out in the country?"

Lady sat up and looked around before dropping her head back onto her forepaws.

Tom nodded. "Yeah, I agree. We'll wait a bit."

They drove an extra thirty miles or so for good measure before leaving I-80, which they'd picked up after crossing the river. Tom stopped at the end of the off-ramp out of old habit rather than real need and surveyed the area. A large sign to his right, emblazoned with the Kiwanis seal, welcomed them to quaint little Neston, home to an actual Main Street and one lonely gas station.

He turned the car into the Stop-n-Go and pulled up to one of four pumps, which looked to be working still. With luck, the control system inside the convenience store would as well.

Tom stepped away from the Mustang, and Lady slid out behind him. She made a quick check of the area then trotted toward the building through a soft, steady rain. He followed close behind, glad to have an extra set of eyes and ears—keen ones, at that.

The door to the store was unlocked, which was good. He pulled it open, and Lady slipped in before him. She did a quick check of the store, looked back, and chuffed once.

"I guess I have a bodyguard now too." He smiled.

He found everything in the place in working order and first set the appropriate pump to fill. Tom then grabbed several bags of assorted snacks, including more jerky, potato and corn chips, a few candy bars, some Twinkies, and a bunch of pretzels.

None of it would likely taste that great, but odds were good that it contained enough preservatives to last for years before turning. It also probably didn't include any actual nutrition either, but at least it wasn't canned. He also grabbed several bottles of water and a few dusty two-liters of Coke.

Tom carried his hoard of junk food out to the car and filled it up. After looking up into the overcast sky, he gave Lady a frown. "With this rain, it's going to be dark early today. I guess we need to find someplace to lock in."

The town was remarkably flat, much different from the hills he was used to back in Cincinnati. That was different, but it gave him an excellent view up and down Main Street as he stood waiting for the car to fill up.

Neston was home to a number of modest little businesses, including a diner, a barber shop with a ladies' salon next door, a post office, a laundry called the Soap 'N Suds, and a local branch of Farmers National Bank. The town hall and city offices sat directly across the street from the gas station, either of which could have made for a decent place for the night, in a pinch. But they were too big inside for Tom's liking—too much to keep an eye on all night.

A mile or so farther down the road, though, set apart from the rest of the stores, was a little bar with a broken sign. The word "Hole" was still readable near the bottom, but the upper section had been knocked out of the frame altogether.

"Let's call it the Watering Hole. What do you think?"

Lady glanced that way, shook the rain out of her coat with a rattling of tags, and sat down next to him, as if muttering, "Whatever."

He patted her a few times as the pump clicked off. After he replaced the handle, a sly grin crossed his face.

"You know what, girl?" he said. "I could go for a

drink. And I bet that little place has more than one way in and out too. Doesn't look like it has too many windows either. Probably checks off all of Ana's boxes."

She gave him a single short bark and hopped back into the car.

He dropped into the driver's seat, still grinning. Definitely time for a stiff drink. Maybe two.

The bar was a little more than a mile away from the station. He drove the Mustang roughly half that distance and parked beside the Soap 'N Suds. Without a garage to hide the car in, the least he could do was not leave it right outside like a big neon sign screaming, "Look for me inside!"

Tom shoved his new collection of CDs and buffet of junk food into the pair of plastic bags he'd grabbed from the food mart. With that and his hundred-pound flashlight, he and Lady set off down the road at a jog. As before, she stopped from time to time to sniff the air and look around. Confident, Tom huffed forward in the disappearing daylight.

After crossing the Watering Hole's gravel parking lot, Tom peered through the smoked glass window in the center of the bar's wooden door but couldn't see anything in the darkness beyond. He gave the handle a slight tug, and the door swung toward him easily. Beyond that was another solid wooden door, this one without a window.

Lady entered first and checked around quickly. He followed her to the inner door, letting the outer one fall closed. He pulled the next one open a few inches, barely enough for her to slip inside. She chuffed an okay, and Tom followed behind her.

The one-room Watering Hole was like most other dive bars Tom had experienced in his life. A dull wooden bar ran the length of the right side and was dotted with fixed, round-topped bar stools covered in ragged vinyl that had once been nail-polish red. Behind the bar stood a dusty cash register and a mirrored wall of liquor bottles likewise covered in grime. The smell of stale beer and decades of cigarette smoke still somehow hung heavily throughout. He wouldn't have said it was a pleasant odor, but it was familiar. Tom smiled.

At the end of the bar, facing him from the back wall, was a door labeled Employees. To the left of that door was a hallway with a sign reading Restrooms. On the left side of the room, opposite the bar, an old jukebox stood next to an even older-looking cigarette machine. The space between was filled with tables and chairs. Directly to his left, lined up along the front wall, was a coin-operated pool table, a lane to throw darts, and a pinball machine.

The inner door swung shut behind him, casting the room in almost total darkness.

"Dammit." He tensed with a gut punch of panic.

Lady didn't growl or bark, though, so he forced himself to relax.

Tom clicked the flashlight on and swept the room. A set of three light switches hung on the wall next to the employees-only door. He flipped them up one at a time, holding his breath. The first switch turned on the main lights over the bar area.

"Ha!" he exclaimed before immediately flicking it off again.

The second switch powered on a softer set of lights

above the bar back, hidden within the frame. They didn't add much light beyond the bar area, so he figured he could live with that.

The third switch appeared to do nothing until he poked his head through the nearby door and found a brightly lit stockroom.

Inside, he found little of interest: an emergency exit, a few shelves of liquor bottles and mixers, and a swinging door leading into another room with stacks and stacks of beer cases and silver kegs. It had likely been a cold room a few years before, but the refrigeration equipment must have given up at some point.

The emergency door in the back of the room, though, was just what he'd been looking for. It was the kind that couldn't be opened from the outside. That gave them a quick way out, if needed, without having to worry about anyone—or anything—else coming in that way.

Tom went back into the bar area and flipped the stockroom switch off. The lights over the bar weren't much, but they were enough to keep him from hunting around for more.

Four dark neon beer logos hung above the bar. He didn't dare turn them all on, but two made for a decent compromise and added a familiar comfort to the place.

Lady padded back over to the front door and chuffed once, softly.

"What's wrong?" Tom asked.

The dog woofed again and pawed the inner door, which swung slightly on its hinges.

"Yeah, yeah, I was getting to that."

The inner one had no lock, but the outer set had two

deadbolts and a slide bolt, all of which he latched. They were safely locked in for the night.

Back inside, he stood near the pool table and the only window to check the overall light level. Satisfied that they weren't announcing themselves to the world outside, he looked at Lady and found her sitting patiently next to the bar, looking up at the bags from the gas station.

"Hungry?"

She barked once in reply.

He grabbed a small bag of potato chips and some beef jerky. Offering them to the dog, he asked, "What'll it be? Tired of the jerky yet?"

She sniffed at the jerky bag. Tom ripped it open and dropped it for her. It was empty in seconds. Lady looked back at him hopefully.

"I don't have much more of that. How about we wait a little while and share the next one. You're thirsty, I bet."

She wagged in agreement. He slipped behind the bar for some water and maybe that drink of his own.

Finding a small refrigerator right away, he reached in and pulled out a surprisingly cold bottle of Bud. Somehow, the little appliance hadn't given up yet, unlike the equipment in the cold room. Still, cold or not, the beer inside was over three years old, so it had to be headed downhill.

He levered it against an opener affixed to the bar and took a pull from the bottle. It was a long way from the best beer he'd ever had, having picked up a strange, sour flavor. He'd had worse, though—much worse, actually. He took another long drink before setting it down.

Turning around, he considered the bottles on the

wall before selecting the Maker's Mark, its red wax top conspicuous even covered in dust. "It's time to toast being alive, girl."

He pulled the top off, filled a shot glass, and raised it to his canine companion. "Here's to us. Apparently, both of us are either too stubborn or too stupid to realize the world doesn't want us around anymore." Throwing his head back, he emptied the glass. The bourbon slid down his throat just as he remembered it: a hint of vanilla, a pleasant and familiar burn, and a slight cough. The rest of his beer followed suit.

Lady whined softly as he reached into the minifridge for another Bud.

"Oh, I'm sorry, girl, I forgot your water. Here I am, drinking alone."

A search of the shelves under the bar revealed a stack of small bowls likely intended for complimentary peanuts for barflies. More interesting, though, a baseball bat with the words "Speak Softly" inscribed on the barrel leaned in the corner. Even better still, Tom found an old Smith & Wesson revolver just below the cash register. He couldn't guess its caliber but did know the gun was big and heavy in his hand.

He spun the cylinder to check its load. Satisfied, he slipped the handgun into the waist of his pants against the small of his back.

After picking up the bat and a bowl, he reached for the cold-water handle beside the dish sink. Before turning it on, the bar's soda gun caught his eye. He pulled it from the holster mounted to the bar, pointed it at the sink, and hit the button labeled W. Water gushed out and ran down the drain. Four of the other buttons also worked, spitting out two brown and two clear liquids, respectively. After grabbing a tumbler, he took a quick taste of each: soda, diet soda, lemon-lime soda, and soda water.

Tom put down a bowl of water for Lady, partially filled a tall glass with bourbon, and topped it off with caramel-colored soda. "A couple of ice cubes would be nice," he mumbled, "but I guess beggars can't be choosers."

Taking his glass, he walked toward the front door, sipping as he went. He passed through the swinging interior door, the jingle of Lady's tags right behind him. With little else to do, he relaxed while watching the rain fall steadily outside the smoky windows. If he was lucky, maybe he'd catch the monsters coming out into the night.

CHAPTER 12

THROUGH THE SMOKED GLASS SET into the outer door, Tom watched the bar's parking lot and the road beyond, wondering if any of those Feral things would shamble out of hiding spots in the rainy night since the sun had fully abandoned them. Was the world really that different after dark than the empty, desolate place he'd spent the day?

He waited for a gang of the monsters to appear from nowhere and aimlessly bob and limp around the little town. None did. Ten minutes passed, and nothing moved outside but the wind and rain.

Tom finished his drink, savoring the burn of the bourbon in the back of his throat. After returning to the bar and pouring another, he mumbled, "Maybe she's just paranoid."

Lady, lying curled up on the floor, looked at him out of the corner of her eye but didn't move otherwise.

He rambled on, undeterred. "She made me think one of those soulless things would be ready to pop out from around every corner like a jack-in-the-box. But I was in that school for weeks and saw nothing. Just that one—

that was it. Maybe we can relax a bit and save ourselves the ulcer."

The next drink was a little stronger than it probably should have been. After all, he'd eaten nothing but a few pieces of dried beef since the day before. And his tolerance couldn't have been what it used to be, which explained the not-unpleasant buzz at his temples. Each drink was going down easier than the one before it too. He needed something in his stomach before he ended up the kind of drunk he'd regret.

He devoured a bag of barbecue potato chips, a bag of nacho-cheese tortilla chips, half a package of jerky—the other half of which was nearly inhaled by Lady—and a pair of Twinkies before sighing contentedly.

Following the quick supper, Tom pulled a set of darts from the shabby, pock-marked cork dartboard. He launched one dull missile after another at it but put more darts into the wall than near the center circle.

Grumbling about being out of practice, he switched to the pool table, content to simply knock the balls into the pockets. After missing seven out of eight shots, he appraised his stick with one eye closed. "Thing's crooked as a dog's leg," he muttered.

Lady raised her head briefly at the mention but went right back to sleep.

Dropping the stick on the table, he poured another drink and shuffled to the jukebox. "Now, this has some potential," he said.

The machine was dark and silent. Tom lurched around the old boxy Wurlitzer, grasping blindly behind it for a power switch. Finding it at last, he was rewarded with a bright snap of lights and a few chimes as it came alive.

Once it was on and running, he browsed through every last song available, trying to find something he recognized. After feeding it singles from the cash register and picking a dozen or so choices at random, he nodded to himself, smiling. "That ought to get us through the night, Lady. Or at least until I pass out."

Tom frowned at his already empty glass and hiccupped. "Then again, maybe I should take it a little easier."

He set the empty tumbler on the bar and instead popped the cap off another bottle of Bud. Tom grabbed it, the bat, and what was left from the roll of quarters he'd opened to play pool and turned his attention toward the pinball machine in the corner.

He'd never actually been much of a fan of pinball. He was a member of the Nintendo generation and, before that, had played video games like *Centipede* and *Pac-Man* at the mall arcade. Back in those days, he had the right pattern for each level memorized and could make that little yellow guy gobble up dots all day long.

Pinball machines, on the other hand, brought his dad to mind. "Pinball," the old man would claim, "was organic. It takes real skill. There's no pattern that can beat it. You shoot the ball, and physics takes over. And every game is different."

Feeding quarter after quarter into that old machine, he lost all track of time. "You might have had a point, Dad," he allowed. As an old AC/DC song, "You Shook Me All Night Long," played on the jukebox, Tom lost himself in the game. His eyes slashed over the table, focused on the silver ball rolling up and down the machine's slanted playing surface. His feet tapped out the beat of the music as he sang along. For a few brief moments, Tom forgot where he was, forgot the surreal world surrounding him.

The song reached its climax, and Lady, who had been lying on the floor a few feet away, jumped to her feet. Little more than a flicker of motion in the corner of his eye, it caught his attention. He turned to find the fur on the back of her neck standing up. Her teeth bared, she took a step toward the front door.

The door seemed to swing slightly toward them but then settled back into position as if kissed by a puff of air.

Tom reached for the baseball bat, and his hand tightened around the wooden handle. Lady lowered her head and took a cautious step toward the door.

The door flew open with a bang, and a pale human-like form stepped into the room and shrieked. Part scream and part growl, it was at once reminiscent of pain, hunger, and strangely, delight. A shiver raced down Tom's back, and the hair on his neck stood up.

The Feral in the doorway was short and partially hunched over, and it seemed even less like a person than the one from the school. Sharp, jagged teeth gleamed in the darkness for half a second before it charged across the room toward him.

The thing moved faster than he'd expected. In the blink of an eye, it would be on top of him. Hands shaking, Tom gripped the bat with white knuckles. His arms twitched to swing, driven by panic. But he had to wait for the right moment.

Lady leapt at the Feral. She hit it squarely in the chest, stunning it and breaking its stride. Jaws wide, she snapped at its gray mottled neck, ripping a chunk of flesh away. It shrieked again, grabbed her, and tossed her across the room like a stuffed animal. She crashed into a chair with a painful yelp.

With its own eggplant-colored blood pouring from the gash where she'd bitten it, the plaguer turned back to Tom, and he swung with whatever strength his body still had. The barrel of the bat found purchase at its temple, but instead of a sickening crunch, it made only a dull thud and glanced off. The monster staggered sideways from the blow but quickly regained its footing. A cold emptiness filled Tom's stomach.

Righting itself, it glared at him with dead, black eyes and growled a challenge.

The bloody baseball bat slipped from his hand and clattered to the floor. He stepped back, away from the monstrously gleaming teeth.

As he stumbled against the pinball machine, its plunger stabbed him in the lower back. The machine clicked and chimed behind him as the Feral took a step forward. Tom was cornered.

Something else, something cold and hard, pressed against his back—the revolver.

Tom grabbed the weapon by its grip and pulled, but the cylinder got caught on his belt. The Feral snarled, raised claws dripping with its own blood, and came forward. He was barely a step from the awful thing's reach when the gun finally came free of his pants. Swinging it up, he cringed, knowing the thing would be on him before he could get the weapon pointed at it.

Expecting claws to dig into his skin, Tom screamed. Instead, the Feral lurched sideways again and hit the ground. Lady had taken another run at it but this time only rammed it rather than trying to hit and bite at the same time. She fell to the ground on top of it and rolled away.

Tom pointed the revolver and pulled the trigger.

The recoil of the first shot nearly ripped it from his shaking hands. Worse, the bullet dug into the floor just to the side of his target. The Feral screeched and covered its face, though, in pain at the bright flicker of muzzle flash. It must have been looking right at the gun when he fired.

One more chance.

Tom tightened his grip and steadied himself. Aiming as carefully as he dared in that one heartbeat, he fired a second shot. This time, he found his mark. He recovered and fired again. He squeezed the trigger over and over until he realized at last that the gun was clicking harmlessly and he was screaming at the top of his lungs.

The cylinder was empty, and Tom's arms burned from the effort of containing the recoil, but the Feral lay motionless on the ground in front of him.

He dropped the revolver with a clunk, stepped over the lifeless form, and walked to the bar. His hands shaking enough to make it a struggle, he pulled the top off the Maker's bottle and took a long drink, reveling in the burn of the whiskey as it made its way to his stomach. He coughed twice, leaned over, and threw up.

When nothing was left in his gut, he spat, wiped

his face with the back of his hand, and stood. He took another drink of bourbon and rinsed his mouth with it before spitting that onto the floor as well. Then he raised the bottle to his lips a third time but set it back down instead.

Lady sat up and licked one of her forepaws. He whistled her over to him, and she limped across the room on three legs.

"Are you hurt, girl?"

She woofed twice softly. Seemed as though she would be all right.

"You're a good girl, Lady. You saved my ass there. That's what we're going to have to do, though… stick… with…" He trailed off, recognizing a familiar wheeze from across the room. Tom's eyes became the size of saucers, and his mouth fell open. The Feral drew itself up onto its knees and turned toward him. Throwing its head back, it screeched, fangs out, as the other one had outside the school.

Leveling a look of rage in his direction, it growled again, a low, furious roll filled with hate.

Lady, her hackles up, barked back at the monster in a frenzy, but with her injured foreleg, didn't charge again. The bat and gun lay on the ground over by the pinball machine, and the Feral, nearly back to its feet, was blocking the way.

They were defenseless, and in a few seconds, that thing was going to come at them again. And now, it wasn't just a monster. It was pissed.

CHAPTER 13

THE PLAGUER STAGGERED TOWARD THEM, its movements labored, slower than before. The four or five shots that found their marks had had some effect, if not the desired one.

Lady continued to bark as the pair backed away. Tom looked around, frantically searching for something to subdue the monster.

With nothing else promising, he grasped the back of a chair. Having seen the best a gun could do, though, he didn't have a ton of hope that smashing an aging bar chair over the thing's head would accomplish much.

He took another step backward, his left hand brushing the top of a vinyl bar stool. The storeroom door should have been behind him. They could make a run through the stockroom and out the emergency exit.

Tom looked over his shoulder at the door, hesitation clouding his face. The night was pitch black out there, and morning was still a long time away. Worse, because he'd been so clever and parked half a mile away, they would have to sprint there to the car while praying other Feral—which, inconveniently, wouldn't be riddled with bullets—weren't milling around nearby.

Without warning, Lady began barking again, with both more volume and tempo. She stopped retreating from the Feral even as Tom made a half turn to run for the back door.

The front door crashed open.

"I told you—" Ana froze in the doorway, her look of anger quickly replaced by one of horror.

The plaguer spun to face her and released a guttural howl.

Tom cringed and covered his ears. He should have been out the back minutes ago, running as fast as he could. Thinking he could stand up to anything capable of making such a chilling, animal cry had been bald stupidity.

The Feral lumbered toward Ana, teeth and claws ready to tear her apart. To Tom's surprise, she stood her ground. "Run!" she screamed.

Flush with terror, he ran several steps toward the stockroom door but stopped when his eyes caught the flashlight sitting on the bar. Tom grabbed it and spun toward the Feral.

"Hey, ugly, look at me!" he bellowed, stomping forward.

The monster turned back to him, mouth open, saliva oozing from jagged teeth. Tom clicked on the high-powered flashlight, throwing a spectacular beam of light directly into the monster's face. It screamed, squeezed its eyes shut, and covered them with a forearm.

Ana raced forward and grabbed its head, a slender hand on either side of its face. With a quick motion, it spun around unnaturally. The sickening crack of vertebrae filled the air, even over the blaring music. The now-limp Feral collapsed in a heap.

Lady continued to bark at Ana, head down and fur standing up.

"If you want the mutt to live," she hissed, pointing at the dog, "calm it down before it attracts something else. And turn off that damned music."

Tom knelt beside Lady, patted her gently, and scratched her neck. "It's all right, girl, we're okay. The Feral's dead. This is Ana. She's a friend of mine."

The dog stopped barking, but a low growl continued to rumble in her chest. She held her head slightly down forward, refusing to take her eyes off Ana.

"I need to come in, Tom. We don't have time for this."

Stroking the fur on Lady's back, he whispered reassuringly. Still, the dog would not be soothed.

"Ana," Tom said, "come over here, slowly, and offer your hand. Show her she can trust you."

"Tom, we do not have time—"

"I know!" he spat. "I know we don't have time. But she's going to try to tear you apart otherwise."

Ana sighed hard but took a slow step forward with her hand extended. Lady, in response, opened her mouth in a sneer, offering her canines. She covered them up again quickly, though, as Tom continued soothing her. The rumbling growl in her chest held steady.

Ana reached the pair and dropped to one knee, offering her hand. The uncertain shepherd sniffed at it, showed her teeth one last time, then nosed the woman's hand onto her head.

Ana scratched between her pointed ears carefully, and the low growl finally stopped.

Tom exhaled. "I can't believe she did that. She took to me right away."

"Dogs and I do not usually get along," Ana replied. Without a moment's pause, she stood up. "We need to get out of here. Right now. Is there a stockroom?"

"Yes," Tom answered.

"Is it well lit?"

Tom raised an eyebrow. "I guess with all the lights on, it's pretty bright. Why?"

"That Feral isn't dead. He'll be dragging himself up again before too long. But if you surround them with light, they seem to think it's daytime and basically stay put indefinitely. Are there any windows in there?"

"No, I don't think so." Tom flipped the appropriate switch on the panel by the stockroom door and pushed the door open to give Ana a good view.

Ana clucked her tongue. "Well, it isn't perfect, but hopefully, it will do the job."

She stormed over to the jukebox—which clicked to the next of Tom's picks—and yanked the plug from the wall. "Honestly, Tom, what were you thinking?" she scolded. "I told you to be quiet, inconspicuous. Yet here you are with more lights than a carnival and making more noise than a frat party. On top of all that, you're at least half drunk. I'm astonished that you avoided getting mauled and eaten long enough for me to get here." Stomping back to the Feral on the floor, she rolled it over and grabbed it under the shoulders. "Come here and take its legs," she barked.

Following her instructions, they lifted the plaguer off the floor and headed for the stockroom. Its head flopped back and to the side unnaturally, gruesomely.

"Its neck is completely broken," he said, horrified. "How does something in that condition get back up at any point?"

"As we speak, it's healing itself. It may never hold its head upright again, but it will walk again… soon."

Tom looked the head lolling back limply with a mixture of disbelief and terror.

Taking a deep breath, he said, "Look, Ana, I'm—"

"I don't want to hear it, whatever your excuses are," she said. "We aren't playing a game here, Tom. You can't assume that because it's just a little light or a little music, it won't be enough to attract Feral or worse. You can't take those kinds of risks with your life. Not when I'm risking mine as well.

"When I tell you no visible light, that means none. And if you're making noise that can be heard ten feet away, you're making too much. Do you think Lady there could hear that jukebox from the street? I'm sure she could have, and a Feral's sense of hearing is at least as sensitive as hers."

Lady, trailing behind them as they navigated cases of beer with their heavy load, chuffed once in agreement.

Tom hung his head. "You're… yeah, okay. I'm sorry. I thought everything was good enough."

"'Good enough' will get us killed."

"From here on out," she continued, "you do exactly what I tell you the way I tell you! Not just close. To the letter. It won't be fun, and it won't be easy. You will be able to relax when we get to Seattle. But if you do something as stupid as this again, I might just go ahead and kill you myself."

Lady's ears perked up, and she cocked her head at Ana, as if unsure whether the threat was real and required a disapproving growl. She let it slide.

Tom looked up at Ana across the Feral's lifeless body, his mouth working silently. With nothing else to say in his defense, he simply stammered, "Yeah, I was being stupid. I'm sorry."

Ana nodded. "Let's get this done and get out of here. Set him on that table over there."

The pair shuffled over to a worktable on the left side of the room. With a gesture from Ana, they dropped the heavy burden with a thud. He half expected the Feral to groan or stir, but it remained lifeless.

"We need to get moving. I didn't see the car outside. Where is it?"

Pulling the keys from his pocket, Tom replied, "There's a new Mustang parked up the street, beside the laundry place. That's the car I brought here."

She eyed the keychain dubiously before taking it from his hand. "A Mustang," she said disapprovingly. When he opened his mouth to explain, she raised a hand to forestall him. "It doesn't matter. Let's just get out of here. I'll go get the car. I'll pull up to the front door. Be ready to sprint out and jump in."

They returned to the main bar area. "Do you want Lady to go with you? She seems to be a pretty good guard."

"No, she should stay with you. Grab your stuff and be ready."

Tom nodded and turned to his pile of CDs and junk food on the bar.

Ana stopped in the doorway and turned. "Tom, despite being an idiot, you did well with that Feral on your own." With that, she disappeared into the dark, rainy night.

CHAPTER 14

TOM STOOD BESIDE THE BAR with his convenience-store bags in hand, foot tapping.

"How long do you think she'll be gone?" he asked Lady, sitting at attention beside him. The Soap 'N Suds couldn't be more than half a mile away. She'd surely be back in less than ten minutes.

He looked over his shoulder again, through the stockroom door they'd wedged open. With every glance, Tom expected to find the Feral shambling toward him. But the thing lay where they'd dumped it, motionless. Nevertheless, he couldn't take his eyes off it. He stared, waiting for some sign that it was ready to stand up again: a movement, a groan, a twitch of the hand.

"She better hurry up, or I'm going to lose it."

Needing a distraction, he surveyed the wreck of a bar room. The revolver and the baseball bat lay on the floor near the pinball machine. The bat probably wasn't worth dragging along, but he was damn sure going to bring the gun. Maybe it hadn't done the job quite well enough this time, but that was likely the fault of his poor aim as much as anything else. Two or three slugs in the head would almost certainly kill a Feral. Ana had said you just had to do some damage to the nervous system.

"I'd bet a couple of decent shots through the skull would do exactly that," he said, gripping the heavy weapon.

He checked the cylinder and nodded, finding it empty. Ducking behind the bar, he gave the shelves a second look. With a mumbled "Here we go," he drew out a box that looked just right for bullets but frowned at its lack of weight. Tom shook it, hoping for at least a few rattles inside. Nothing. Empty.

He slid the gun back into the waistband of his pants anyway. He'd never been much of a gun proponent before, but the heft of it against him was comforting. They'd just have to stop someplace and pick up more rounds.

That done, he tapped his fingers on the bar, trying to will Ana back with the car. He forced himself to look forward at the front door, not back into the stockroom. Before long, though, he was staring at the Feral on the table again. Mental pictures of it sitting up and baring its teeth flashed through his head again and again.

"I hate to leave it," he muttered. Sooner or later, the power was going to fail. When that happened, the room would go dark, and that Feral would be back to wandering the world in search of helpless living things. Or worse, he and Ana might somehow come across it again down the road.

The image of a world full of people being terrorized by those things made him shiver. Heather's death was still a gaping wound, but at least she wasn't here, surrounded by this craziness. She'd gone on to somewhere better, someplace without a child's nightmares walking around freely.

The whole situation was so surreal, his past life seemed at odds with the grimness around him. He almost thought his memories to be pleasant fictions, make-believe meant to cope with the constant fear of living like this. Or better, maybe this was just a nightmare, one he would eventually start awake from, then he would roll over and wrap his arms around Heather as the bad dream faded away.

But none of that was true. He didn't need to be pinched. Just a few minutes before, he'd hit that Feral with a baseball bat hard enough that his hands stung at the impact. The muscles in his arms still ached from the recoil of firing that big Smith & Wesson.

No, he'd woken up to a grisly, twisted version of the world he used to know.

He thanked whatever gods he could think of that he hadn't been awake for the time between, when everything changed. The newspapers Ana had left for him made no mention of horrifying monsters with cruel fanged teeth and dead-looking eyes. Where had the Feral come from? When did they become a regular nightly occurrence? Was it after the disease finished its grim work and most everyone was already dead, or were the Feral a kind of side effect of Charon somehow?

Tom shuddered, imagining wives tucking their sick, feverish husbands into bed at night, only to wake up and find monsters beside them.

More likely, though, the Feral had come after the populations had been decimated, when there were no journalists left to sensationalize them. After all, modern journalism was nothing if not attracted to gruesome details of dark bedtime stories.

Then again, maybe Ana censored all those articles, keeping any mention of the plaguers away from him. He wouldn't put it past her, since she already had a record for holding information pretty close to her chest.

He trusted her, though, by necessity. And he had to keep trusting her. He owed her a huge debt as it was because she'd gotten him away from Alexander and brought him out of his coma and back to life. More than that, even, he needed her. He would be completely alone without her.

"Don't get me wrong," he said, smirking at Lady, "I appreciate your company, but you're terrible at conversation."

Still, what if Ana was slowly turning into one of those things? She'd said that anyone surviving the plague had been "changed." What did that mean? She seemed normal enough—perhaps a bit too thin and a little aloof, but that seemed to go along with the conditions of living these days.

Then again, the image of Ana breaking that Feral's neck with her bare hands, effortlessly, played over and over in his head. That wasn't something a "normal" person could do.

It was time to hear the whole story, and he wasn't going anywhere until he got it, no matter how many real people she'd saved.

Real people. Others like *him*. If only the other two she'd gotten out before him had managed to hang on. It would be nice not to be the only one stumbling around without any real idea of what was going on. Maybe there were others. Did Alexander have a collection of coma patients hidden away somewhere, free of Charon and its changes? God help them if they managed to wake up somehow, alone, confused, and at the mercy of some madman or worse, those damn Feral.

His cheeks colored with the blossom of anger. Waking up had been hard enough, and he'd had Ana to help him through it. He couldn't imagine coming out of a coma in a strange, dark place and being confronted by something like the monster on that table. He didn't have the words to describe that horror.

The fear and anxiety he'd bottled up and carried around for the past two months finally spilled out. Warmth surged through him.

He didn't think about picking up the bat or walking into the stockroom. But standing over the Feral on the table, he reveled in the sudden sense of power the anger gave him. His arms tingled, and his mouth puckered in a grimace.

The pounding of his heartbeat thrummed in his ears like tribal drums.

He raised the bat over his head, focusing all that rage and hatred on the Feral. The power of it, an inferno welling up from deep in his chest, poured through him, rushing into his arms and spreading to the hands gripping the handle of that Louisville Slugger. The bat fell with a wet crunch across the bridge of the plaguer's nose. Cold blood splattered everywhere as the Feral's face collapsed beneath the force of the blow, covering him and his clothes, as well as the ceiling and walls nearby.

Screaming, he bludgeoned it over and over until nothing remained but shards of cracked skull and bloody ooze.

The surge of hot strength subsided, and he staggered back a step, face blank. Absently, he wiped the back of one shaking hand across his cheek, leaving a crimson smear.

"I can't get rid of all of you," he whispered, "but you'll never walk around outside again. And I'm not hiding anymore either."

After those few seconds of violence, he felt like a new man, reborn.

Lady barked sharply from the doorway, shocking him out of his daze. A car horn blared outside.

Still clutching the bloody bat, he marched through the bar and calmly out into the rain, Lady at his heels.

CHAPTER 15

Tom opened the Mustang's passenger door, and Lady jumped into the backseat out of the rain. Standing beside the car, he raised his face to the sky and let the falling water rinse away the Feral's blood.

"Oh my God, Tom, you're covered in blood! What happened? Are you all right?" Ana's voice held a slight tremor, betraying either shock, mild fear, or both. Her eyes fell on the blood-slick bat still held tightly in his right hand. "Oh," she gasped.

He leaned into the car, ducking just under the roof. "I'm fine. I decided I wasn't okay with just leaving that thing until the lights went out. So I took care of it."

Momentarily speechless, Ana paused several long seconds before responding. "I see. You sure you're okay?"

"I'm fine—much better," he said. Then, "How many others like me are there?"

"Get in the car. We must get out of here. Now is not—"

He cut her off before she could deflect. "How many others, Ana?"

"What do you mean?"

"I know there were two before, and both died. How

many other coma patients does Alexander still have? How many are still being used for some kind of research or worse? How many?"

"How do you know about the others?" She frowned, looking up at him from the driver's seat. "Never mind. We need to go, Tom. We can talk about this while we drive. Get in. It's not safe here." It was not a suggestion.

"Answer the question."

A flash of disbelief crossed the pale, sharp features of Ana's face. She narrowed her eyes and picked around the thumbnail of her right hand. "Two that I am certain of. There were five of you originally. The first two, well, I suppose you know what happened after I snuck them out. You were third. He still has two more. Why?"

"I'm going back for them."

"Tom, that's ridiculous," she blurted.

"I'm going back for them," he repeated, allowing no room for argument. "You don't have to come. You've done more than enough already. Besides pulling me out of there, you've saved my life twice from those damned Feral. I can't ask you to help with this. I know it's foolish and likely to get me killed. Just tell me where they are, and I'll find a way to get them myself."

"Tom, you can't expect to walk in and grab them. You'll never make it out alive."

"Probably. But I can't leave them there, helpless, for whenever Alexander decides he's through with them. Or for one of those Feral to wander by. I can't just turn my back on them, head west, and hope for the best.

"You got me out and two others before that. So there's obviously a way. Just tell me where to find them. I'll find someplace here in town to hole up until morning, and then I'll head back to Cincinnati."

She turned away from him and looked out through the car's windshield, toward the expressway overpass, a mile down the road. Struggling with some internal debate, she continued digging at the skin around her thumbnails. He'd never seen her like this, without her typical decisiveness and sense of control.

He smiled, glad to have regained a little control over himself, even if it was at her expense.

Seconds passed—fifteen, twenty, twenty-five—while she stared out into the rain. Every moment he stood beside the car in the darkness, he felt more vulnerable. His clothes were soaked through, and the adrenaline of bashing that Feral had run its course, leaving him cold and tired. The dry, empty seat he was looming over looked very inviting. But he clung to his resolve.

He couldn't let her think he was weak. Regardless of what he'd said, he desperately needed Ana's help. Together, they might have a slight chance of succeeding. Without her, he had none.

Finally, she placed her hands in her lap and forced them to be still. She nodded to herself and said, nearly whispering, "Fine. We'll go back."

He exhaled, visibly relieved.

She looked back at him, and her authority returned. "But we're going right now, tonight. We have to get there before morning, and we're only taking one shot at it. If he's moved them or we come across any kind of snag, I'm calling it off. No discussion. I'm not spending the next week hunting around Cincinnati blindly, hoping not to accidentally stumble upon one of Alexander's thugs or plaguers. Are we agreed?"

From the back seat, Lady twisted her head sideways at him.

"Let's go." He slipped the bat behind the passenger seat, took out the revolver, and set it on the dash as he slid into the car beside her. He hesitated before pulling the door shut. "Wait, I left my CDs inside."

She gave him a flat look. "Buckle up. You're not going back in there. We'll get more later."

He shrugged and closed the door. Ana stomped on the accelerator. The Mustang took off in a spray of gravel, fishtailed onto Main Street, and roared toward the expressway.

Pressed against his seat by the sudden burst of speed, Tom gave her an alarmed look. "Slow down! Do you always have to drive like a maniac?"

"We don't have much time," she replied, calm as ever. "There's just enough night left for us to get back, hide the car, and make it to the hospital before dawn."

"Besides," she added, "wasn't a car like this made to go as fast as you can push her?"

The corners of her mouth rose in a sly grin reflected in her dark eyes. It was the same genuine smile he'd gotten when he drove away from the warehouse that morning. It softened her sharp features and brightened her whole face.

"Ana, I need to know what's going on. You haven't told me everything."

Her face darkened. The grin evaporated.

"What do you mean?" she asked, focusing on the road. "You know as much about Alexander and everything going on as I do. I don't know what more you'd want me to tell you."

"Tell me about you, Ana."

She snapped her head around to face him, meeting Tom's eyes. "What do you want to know?" she replied cautiously.

"You said everyone who survived Charon was different… not human any longer. I assumed you meant the Feral. But you meant people like you too, didn't you?"

She hesitated. "Yes. I was wondering when you would get to that."

"And?"

"You're right. I'm not like you, not anymore. For some of us, the disease mutated into something different. It didn't kill us but changed us instead. Not cognitively, of course. We're still much the same people, intellectually, as we were before. But there are significant physical changes. I can't eat most vegetables or grains any longer and can only digest some forms of meat. Cooking it seems to render it useless to us. I'd been a vegetarian for years, so you can imagine the difficulty in having to learn to live on raw meat. Of course, that's the least of my problems now— finding edible meat is getting harder and harder. I also have an intense sensitivity to light. If I'm hurt, though, I heal faster than normal because my cells regenerate unnaturally quickly. It's as if I'm taking the kinds of steroids that made athletes invincible."

He gave her a quizzical look. "Is that it? That doesn't sound too bad. I mean, it's pretty awful, really, but if the alternative was dying, at least you can cope with this."

"And I can no longer have children," she added quietly.

For a few seconds, he was dumbfounded. Having children in this mess was the last thing he'd want to consider. But circumstances alone rarely kept someone from wanting to have a baby. If she'd planned on being a mother someday, but Charon had taken that chance away... He didn't know what to say.

Finally, he found his tongue. "Ana, I'm... so sorry. I know that doesn't mean much."

She stared ahead, blinking, concentrating on the dark road ahead of them.

An uncomfortable silence settled between them. After a few miles, she said, "Thank you. I appreciate that. It... means more to me than you could know." After another brief pause, she went on, "At any rate, we don't reproduce. At all."

"Is that why...?"

"Yes," she replied, seeming to predict the question. "That's why you're so important. If there is ever going to be any hope of rebuilding the population, it starts with you."

He turned toward the dark countryside drifting by outside. He'd never seen a night so black.

"Okay, but now I really don't understand why we left in such a hurry. If you need regular, unaltered people for that, why didn't you try to get the other patients out?"

"Partially because I wasn't sure if what I was doing would work. I didn't know if I could manage to keep you alive at all, let alone bring you out of the coma. Remember, I failed twice before you, and I could not risk accidentally killing all of you at once.

"After succeeding with you, though, we decided that just getting you away from Alexander and to Seattle alive was good enough for a first step. I'm not the only one Colin has out looking for… unaltered… survivors. Hopefully, one of the others will come back with the kind of luck I've had."

Tom rubbed his eyes with his knuckles. "You mean that Colin decided you should take me west?"

"Yes," she replied.

"So you're defying his orders by taking me back to Cincinnati?"

"Sort of, yes."

Again, he didn't know what to say. "Thank you. I hope he isn't too upset with you."

She smirked. "I'm not too concerned. The odds are in favor of us never leaving Cincinnati again. Colin can't be too mad at me if I'm dead."

He chuckled at her uncharacteristically sarcastic remark, likely the result of weathering a long, emotionally trying day. In other words, he was one dumb pun from being slap happy, and it actually felt good.

The state was infectious. Ana was soon cackling along beside him, and Tom ended up laughing so hard that he had tears in his eyes.

As they both regained their composure, he turned to her and said, "So you're not going to slowly transition into a Feral?"

"No, don't be silly," she answered, still rumbling with light laughter.

"Thank God. I was afraid I was going to have to shoot you too, before long."

Then they were both laughing again, fitfully, as they sped through the night toward Cincinnati.

CHAPTER 16

TOM WOKE UP WITH SOMETHING cold and wet pressing against his ear. He opened his eyes to find a dog's shiny dark nose inches from his face. Lady gave his left ear a flick with her tongue from the back seat. He had reclined the passenger seat at some point in the night, hoping to get some sleep.

"Good morning to you too," he mumbled. His mouth was dry, and his breath couldn't have been much better than the dog's.

When he sat upright and returned his seat to its usual position, a sharp pain flared in his lower back. A good stretch would be in order when they stopped. Sleeping in a car wasn't as easy as it used to be in college.

Rubbing the stiffness out of his neck, he realized the rain had stopped. Morning hadn't quite come yet, but a hint of daylight, just the suggestion of it, really, was visible on the horizon. The countryside surrounding them when he'd fallen asleep had been replaced by looming city buildings. The darkness, though, was the same.

The city was so dark, in fact, that even with dawn approaching, something felt out of place.

"Doesn't look right," he mumbled, more to himself than Ana.

"It's the light," she replied. "Well, the lack of it."

"What?" he asked. "Oh."

He'd never driven through a dark city. The place should have had streetlamps glowing here and there as well as plenty of smaller residential lights, even in the wee hours of the morning. All that was missing. Furthermore, they were driving without headlights.

"Are you crazy?"

"We must not be seen."

He sighed. "What time is it?"

"Almost dawn," she replied.

"Where are we? About there?"

She nodded. "Yes. I think we got lucky and timed this about right. Arriving in the dark will help avoid notice, and once the sun comes up, we should be able to move around on foot without fear of running into Feral."

"So that's why you're driving without the lights on? I can't see but a few feet past the hood of the car. Aren't you worried about running into something?"

She gave him half a smile. "I see well enough in the dark to avoid obstacles. Besides, there isn't anything out there I'd hesitate to run over."

"There is that, I guess." Just out the window to her left, the sky brightened to a pale indigo, but it wasn't where he expected. "We're driving south?"

"Yes," she answered. "If we were going to run into anyone looking for us, they would expect us to be coming from the west. I drove well north of the city before leaving the expressway and have been driving through town on side streets."

Tom nodded and fell silent next to her, staring out his own window.

The city of Cincinnati had been founded on the banks of the Ohio River and grew upward out of the river valley into the hills above. As a result, many of the city's streets were sloped to match the natural geography of the area, so he wasn't surprised that they were traveling sharply downhill.

His stomach rumbled as they passed a dusty corner market with broken windows. Smiling, he said, "Hey, could you stop the next time we pass a bakery? I'd love a donut and some coffee."

That earned him a sideways glance. "Too late," she replied dryly. "We're here."

The Mustang slowed as she applied the brake, groaning against the momentum. Ana whipped the car to the left, onto a cross street that banked back uphill. She pulled over to the curb and killed the engine.

Glancing at the rearview mirror, she said, "The hospital is just across the street and a block down."

Tom peered into his own side-view mirror, and Lady poked her nose up over the back seat to get a look out the rear window.

He'd been expecting a scene from an old war film. In a movie, whenever the small band of heroes worked their way behind enemy lines in, the place would be crawling with lookouts and guard dogs.

Sure, that was pretty far-fetched, but he still expected to see at least a guard or two. But not a thing moved in the increasing morning light other than the occasional thicket of overgrown landscaping, pushed around by a slight breeze. He couldn't quite see the hospital itself, though. The view was blocked by a building beside and behind them.

"I can't see it. Can you?"

"No."

"What do you expect?"

"I'm not certain," she replied. "I used to know when they'd make visits, but I haven't done any surveillance recently. In the past, evening was the more active time around here, not morning. Regardless, it would be best to assume that someone is in there. So don't make any more noise than is necessary once we step out of the car."

Tom nodded. "I got it."

Lady shook her head vigorously from the backseat, causing a jingle of tags that startled them both. They looked at each other then back at the dog.

"I should take off…" Tom started.

At the same time, Ana said, "She doesn't need…"

They both stopped midsentence.

Tom smiled and started again, "I'll take her collar off."

Lady chuffed in agreement.

Moments later, the collar sat on the dashboard, forgotten, as the three of them looked across the street. When a pale-yellow ribbon of daylight reached over the horizon in front of them, Ana finally said, "Okay, it's time. Follow me."

They opened their doors and got out. Lady hopped onto the sidewalk behind Tom and sniffed the air. Satisfied, she looked back at him. He nodded, grabbed his

Louisville Slugger—it *was* his now, no two ways about that—and closed the door. His fingers itched to pick up the revolver too, but without any ammo, it was little more than a paperweight.

Ana met him on the sidewalk. Darting to the building beside them, she pressed her back against it and gave Tom a curt wave. He followed with Lady at his heels.

They slid carefully, backs along the wall, away from the car and in the direction of the downhill street they'd just turned off. When they reached the corner, she glanced around.

"Nothing moving," she whispered, barely audible. "I'm going to cross the street and approach the entrance. Stay here until I wave you over. If you see anything or"—she looked at Lady—"smell anything, get back in the car and go. Don't wait for me."

Tom gave her a thumbs-up, and she turned her back toward the entrance. After one more look toward the street, Ana dashed across.

The hospital building was a hulking stone structure designed with neo-Greek flair. Still in good condition, it stood out conspicuously from the crumbling buildings on the surrounding blocks.

A dozen white fluted columns stood in front of it, six to each side of the main entrance. Ana ducked between the two at the farthest right corner of the building, disappearing from Tom's view into the darkness beyond. He hoped to catch sight of her in the aisle between the pillars and the wall beyond but couldn't make out anything in the shadows.

Ana's pale face appeared briefly as she made her way

between columns. But she disappeared again just as quickly, swallowed by the surrounding darkness.

With agonizing slowness, he tracked her progress to the front entrance, one fleeting glimpse between pillars at a time.

Finally, she emerged near the bank of doors at the center of the building. She still wasn't completely visible, but he could see well enough to recognize her. She looked down the aisle to the left of the entrance for several seconds, making sure nothing was hiding. Then she faced Tom across the street and put her hand up, palm out.

Turning back to the door, she took the handle of the center one and opened it just enough to slip her head inside. A few nerve-wracking seconds later, she reappeared. Wedging her foot against the door to keep it from closing, she turned back and gave Tom a brief wave. Assuming that was the all-clear signal, Tom sprinted over, Lady at his feet.

He reached the entrance, panting from the run.

"Take a minute to catch your breath," she whispered.

As Tom waited for his breathing to return to normal, Lady padded up to the door and pressed her nose into the opening made with Ana's foot. She sniffed inside several times, withdrew, sneezed once and shook her head forcefully.

"Something wrong in there?" Tom asked.

Lady sat down on the concrete and looked around casually.

"I guess she's not concerned," he said.

Ana nodded in reply. "Yes. All right, quietly."

She opened the door wide enough for each of them

to slip inside one at a time. Lady entered first, as usual, followed by Tom and finally Ana. She held the door as it drifted closed behind them, preventing it from banging against the frame.

Once inside, Tom gasped and cursed too loudly then covered his mouth and nose with his hands. The smell hit him like a body blow from a heavyweight boxer, completely taking his breath away. The acid in his stomach roiled at the foulness.

Lady's initial reaction after sniffing inside made perfect sense now. He swallowed hard against the urge to retch violently.

Good thing he'd eaten nothing since before the Feral attack at the Watering Hole.

He glared at Ana over his hands. "You could have warned me," he hissed.

"I am so sorry," she whispered back. "Yes, I should have. Hospitals are filled with the smell of death and rot, still, even three years later. Most of the bodies of the plague victims are just bones now, but places like this are packed with them, and the air doesn't move. I've gotten used to it and rarely think of it anymore. Some places, though, especially large public buildings pressed into service as massive makeshift clinics at the height of the epidemic, we can't even go into without being overwhelmed."

Dropping his hands and forming fists, he closed his eyes and held his breath for a few seconds. After exhaling slowly, he drew in another breath, through his mouth as much as possible.

Tom could taste the stench in the air and felt it blanketing his skin. He hoped the sensation owed more to the stuffiness of a building that likely hadn't had working climate control or air circulation in years than because he was actually "feeling" a smell.

"Let's get this over with before I puke," he said.

Ana nodded and made her way through the main lobby, past a waiting area, the gift shop, the visitor's information desk, and a handful of dead potted trees. Her pace was aggressive and steady, but she took each step carefully, moving in silence.

Tom followed a step behind, trying to mimic her gait with little success. He did manage not to slap his boots against the tile floor, though, which was as much as he realistically hoped for, considering they were walking past hundreds of the dead.

Lady stole behind them, stopping every fifty feet to sniff around. How she could be using such a sensitive nose here was beyond understanding. And even if a Feral was lumbering after them, catching its scent in air so saturated by the smell of decay would have to be almost impossible.

If they got out of here, she deserved some beef jerky just for trying.

They made their way through the hospital, Tom's shoulders slumping, along with his resolve to find survivors. The temperature inside was easily over ninety degrees, and the odor clung to him.

It didn't help that their progress was excruciating. Every hundred feet or so, they'd stop to give Ana a chance to listen intently and Lady a few seconds to sniff the stagnant air.

Neither seemed to register any alarm, though, which came as a small surprise. He heard a variety of unsettling noises in the hallways: a shuffling sound from someplace behind then, a soft ping off in the distance, and even an occasional scratching in the walls.

Despite that, as they made their way down long corridors, past countless corners, and up a flight of industrial stairs, he didn't see so much as an eyebrow twitch of concern from his companions. And since they didn't seem worried, he forced himself to pretend he wasn't either.

At last, they reached a pair of swinging gray double doors with an engraved plate that read Intensive Care.

"This is it," Ana whispered.

Tom nodded in understanding, and she pushed the door open slowly. A piercing squeal tore through the quiet of the building as it turned on its hinges, and they both grimaced. Lady slipped past them into the unit, and they followed her in. Ana strode ahead with purpose, past patient rooms on each side of a long hallway that came to a sharp left-hand turn.

Tom caught up with her two doors after the corner, standing outside one of the rooms, frozen.

Looking inside, he said, "What'd you—" He stopped with a gasp.

The room was in shambles. Equipment was thrown everywhere. Most of it was broken open, spilling wires and circuit boards onto the floor. An expensive-looking bed with a host of levers, switches, and visible wiring rested on its side against the far wall. By far, though, the worst thing was the crumpled grayish heap lying in a hospital gown in the center of the room.

The heap was a body, beaten, battered and contorted—a woman, as a matter of fact, although Tom couldn't have guessed her age. Her skin was leathery and dry, like the Egyptian mummies he'd read about when he was younger.

"How long... um... how long do you think she's been like this?" he asked.

Ana paused. "I don't know. This wasn't done recently."

He stepped into the room, Lady at his heels.

Her arms and legs were arranged at odd angles, like a rag doll thrown away by a toddler. The gown didn't completely cover the remains, and several gashes from what looked like claw marks stood out in furious red contrast to her ashen skin. Worse, though, was her throat. It had been ripped apart, as if a pack of wild dogs had been at it.

He bent at the waist and convulsed, his stomach churning again.

Barely able to keep from throwing up, Tom dashed from the room to keep what little he might still have in his stomach. He crossed the hallway to the nurses' station and spread his arms wide on the counter for support.

Ana came up next to him and placed a hand on his.

"What was her name?" he asked when he could speak without being sick.

"Tom, don't."

"Tell me her name," he insisted.

She sighed. "Melanie."

"Which room was the other one in?"

Ana looked over her right shoulder. "Two doors down."

Tom turned to investigate that room, but Lady trotted to the doorway and stopped. After a brief glance inside, she faced them and woofed twice, mournfully.

He buried his face in his hands, struggling to compose himself. Ana approached the second doorway anyway. Reaching it, she gasped.

"Tell me," he said.

"No, Tom, it's… worse. That first one was bad, but this one looks like there were twice as many."

Twice as many—the concept was unfathomable. One of those nightmarish monsters was enough.

"How many, do you think?"

"That room, maybe two. Three at the most. This one… It's horrible."

She walked back to him, still leaning over the counter. "There's nothing we could have done. It doesn't matter if we'd come a week or a month ago."

"What happened? Did Feral just happen to wander in here? Why wouldn't Alexander have some kind of protection for them if they were important like you said I am?"

She shook her head and answered without looking up. "I don't know. It doesn't make any sense."

He thought again of the gray crumpled heap, seeing in his mind only that devastated throat. "We should go," he murmured, turning back the way they'd come.

The trio started back in the direction of the gray double doors. Halfway up the hall, before reaching the corner, Lady stopped and growled, taking an aggressive posture.

Tom froze. He scanned both ends of the hall, head swiveling back and forth, expecting to find a plaguer advancing on them. Seeing nothing, he knelt to soothe her, afraid the noise might draw unwanted attention.

Before his hand reached her, she began barking wildly, flinging saliva with every snap of her jaws. The sound was familiar: a combination of aggressive threat, warning, and outright alarm.

"Tom!" Ana shouted. At the end of the hallway, two Feral rounded the corner, snarling.

CHAPTER 17

TOM WAS FROZEN ON ONE knee, his arms and legs so heavy that they could have been made of concrete. Beside him, Ana took in a sharp breath. The pair of Feral stood at the corner, baring jagged teeth and snarling like rabid dogs. Strangely, though, they didn't move any closer.

"Back the other way!" Ana barked, a hint of panic ruffling her typical calm.

Another set of gray double doors stood at the other end of the hall. If they could reach them and lock them from the other side, they might have a chance.

Still, Tom squeezed the bat in his right hand and considered charging forward. Scowling, he began to shake, rage replacing his initial terror. Surely, those two were responsible for the brutality in those rooms.

They needed to pay for that.

"Tom," Ana whispered, kneeling next to him, "Not now. We have to get out of here. Wasting your life won't bring them back."

He shot her a look of disgust. "They did this. We need to make sure they never do it again."

"I don't know what's gotten into you." She cursed,

grabbing the back of his shirt collar, "but you need to calm down."

Something in her eyes calmed him, and the heat of his anger faded.

A more rational sense of dread replaced the lust for blood seeping out of him. He stood and backed toward the other end of the hall. Ana moved with him as Lady stood her ground in the middle of the hallway, still growling. The Feral, inexplicably, held their position.

Reaching the doors, Tom felt along the surface of the door behind him, never taking his eyes from the threat fifty yards away. He whistled to Lady. "Come. Let's go, girl." Still not turning, he pushed against the door. It didn't budge. "Door won't open," he said. "Tell me if they move."

Spinning around, Tom examined the door, hoping to find a bolt lock or some other way to release it—nothing, not even a handle.

A loud clack came from the other side, along with the unmistakable sound of a bolt sliding.

"Did you do something?" he asked.

"No," Ana said, turning.

The door swung away from them, opening to reveal a group of scruffy-looking men, grinning like madmen.

"Run!" Ana screamed.

Tom dashed away, toward the waiting Feral, and raised his bat. "Run where? I'd rather take my chances with…."

Before he could finish, a firm, cold hand gripped him by the neck, lifted him an inch or so off the ground, and pressed him against the nearest wall like he was nothing more than a small dog on a leash. Had he resisted even the tiniest bit, his neck would have broken easily.

Back pressed to a wall, face-to-face with his captor, he tried to bring the bat up again. Before it got to his waist, though, the man squeezed Tom's wrist. His hand was like an iron clasp, and the bat clattered to the floor harmlessly.

"My, aren't you a feisty piece of meat." He chuckled in a low, gruff voice.

Across the hallway, Ana had been subdued as well. Three men were holding her, though, one on each side and one squeezing her by the neck like him.

Lady started toward them, growling her displeasure.

The only one not busy restraining them took a few steps towards the dog, cracked his knuckles, and gave her a wicked grin. "Come here, puppy."

Tom hadn't known the shepherd for long, but he knew she wouldn't give up until she was dead. And something horrible in the man's eyes said that was exactly his intention. Lady might have gone on living in that music store for who knows how long if Tom hadn't stumbled into the back room. He wasn't going to let her die on his account—not if he could help it.

"Lady, no!" he croaked. "Run!"

She hurtled toward the man, barking and growling, giving no sign she'd heard Tom's command. The hand tightened on his throat, keeping him from repeating it.

"Let's let the doggy play with Reg," the man holding him croaked in his ear.

Lady came within the man's reach, snapped at his outstretched hands, and feinted to his left. He lurched to grab her just as she changed direction and slipped around behind him. A second later, she was out through the doors the men had entered.

With a quick turn, the man took a few steps to follow, but the one holding Ana's neck said, "Let it go, Reg. For once, we have something more important than a dog."

Reg turned back with a pleading look. "Let me get it, Lars, I know I can track it."

"No," Lars replied, "come here and hold this one. I want to get a look at her pet."

Reg grumbled as he replaced the leader, his hand around Ana's neck.

Although all the men in the group were thin, Reg was the shortest and skinniest overall. A mess of black, greasy, straw-like hair framed an angular face with a pair of dark, sunken eyes, a narrow nose, and disproportionately large, cracked lips. The most fitting description Tom could think of was weaselly. Back before the world had fallen apart, this guy would have been the one all the clerks in a store would watch for shoplifting.

Lars, though, was the opposite. He was tall, a head and a half taller than Reg, and while not exactly thickly built, bore himself with the gravity and confidence of a well-muscled man. He'd probably been familiar with the inside of the gym for most of his life. His face was longer and more evenly built than Reg's, surrounded with shaggy chestnut-colored hair sprinkled with gray. His eyes were a bright, clear sea blue that stood out in sharp contrast to the lack of color everywhere else.

Those eyes fell on Tom, the calculating gaze of a hunter—worse, a hungry hunter with its prey in sight, waiting for the moment to strike.

"How do you stand it?" Lars said to Ana, emphasizing the word "do" with a plain, Midwestern accent. "I'd forgotten how strong the temptation is, how hard it is to control yourself when it's right there, waiting for you to take it."

He leaned in closer, close enough that Tom could smell an odd, metallic scent on the man and feel breath on his cheek. The tall man inhaled deeply, closed his eyes, and fell silent, almost reverent.

"Get away from me!" Tom tried to scream, but the steel hand around his throat allowed only a grunt to escape.

Luckily, that was enough to shake Lars out of his trance. His eyes sprang open, startled, and he lunged backward, away from Tom.

Turning back to Ana, he said, "I really don't know how you do it. Refresh my memory. How long have you been together?"

Ana stared back, a cold fire in her eyes. She said nothing.

"Tell me, or I'll have him ripped from neck to navel."

"You're bluffing," she spat.

Giving her an amused smile, Lars picked up the baseball bat. As he ran his fingers over the words inscribed along the head, he asked, "What's your name?"

"Ana."

"Finally, the spy that has eluded us for six months has a name." Gesturing toward the rooms behind them, he went on, "As you've seen, Ana, Alexander has lost interest in his little science project. He does, though, want to know why Colin cares so much about this leftover. I won't lie. I'm sure he'd rather I didn't kill him, but he left it to my discretion. And I assume you know my reputation, already?"

Ana inclined her head a few inches.

"Good. Now, once again: How long has it been?"

"Just over two months," she sighed.

"Incredible. Two months you've been living like this, alone out here, and yet you've managed not to…"

"I am no animal!" Ana shouted, struggling against the hands holding her.

Lars chuckled. "She's not an animal, fellas," he said.

The others joined in the laughter.

He smiled at Tom, his eyes once again the hunter's, watchful and waiting. After a long, appraising look, he turned back to Ana. "You're in luck. For the moment, I'll pretend I'm not one either. What's your little pet's name?"

Tom tried to voice his indignation and again failed to produce more than a weak croaking sound.

"Tom is a man," she replied, "just as you were, once. Show him some respect."

"You'll forgive me if I don't fall over myself respecting a piece of meat that likely won't survive the night."

Tom's eyes flicked to the pair of Feral still standing at the end of the hallway. His stomach lurched at the thought.

Facing him, Lars said, "Tom, is it?"

He replied the only way he could, giving a slight nod.

"Okay, Tom, this is Will." Lars pointed at the Asian man holding Ana's right arm and shoulder. "His real name is something like Wei Lan Po, but we all just call him Will. Will controls those two ugly bastards at the end of the hallway, and he does whatever I tell him. Isn't that right, Will?"

"That's right, boss."

"Just in case Tom doesn't believe us, why don't you bring them a little closer?"

Will whistled through his teeth, and the Feral rumbled down the hall toward the group.

"That's far enough."

The other man clucked his tongue, and the monsters stopped, frozen in place.

Tom's eyes bulged. They were *trained*? With those vicious teeth and claws, how could anyone train something so dangerous and unpredictable? Who were these people, and what else were they capable of?

"That make the right impression, Tom?"

He nodded again.

Lars gestured to the gruff-looking man holding Tom against the wall. "Good. Then I'm going to have my buddy here let go of you because I don't want to have to carry you all the way back. If you try anything stupid, get to thinking maybe you can make a run for it, or even flinch the wrong way, Will's going to have his two dogs on you before you can wet yourself. You understand?"

Again, a nod.

"Let him down, Cade."

Cade's grip went slack, and Tom slid down the wall and to his knees, rubbing at the soreness on his neck, surely marked by a furious red handprint. He drew a deep, ragged breath, painfully aware of how little air he'd gotten while being held.

Lars shook his head. "Get him up. We need to go."

Bending over him, Cade took Tom by the underarms and hoisted him back to his feet. Once upright, he swayed woozily.

"The subway, chief?" Cade asked in that gravelly voice.

Lars sighed in resigned irritation. "Of course the subway, idiot." Then, to Will, "Keep the same distance between us as we move."

The smaller man nodded.

"Good," Lars said, turning to Ana. "Now, Reg is going to let you go too, and these two will keep a hand on you for good measure. I want some insurance, though, that you're not going to try anything dumb. If I even catch a whiff that you're up to something, Will's gonna let his pets loose to play, and that means Tom will look like a gutted steer before you get your head turned around. Got me?"

She pressed her lips together into a fine line, and her eyes narrowed. Having little choice, though, she agreed. "Fine. Let's get this over with."

Lars chuckled again. "A woman after my own heart. Let's go, boys. Reg, you're first."

CHAPTER 18

T HE SKINNY MAN SLUNK THROUGH the open doors where the group had entered, followed by Ana, with an escort to either side; Tom, with Cade steadying him; Lars, still carrying Tom's baseball bat; and eventually the pair of Feral.

The motley procession made their way through the stuffy hospital corridors at a brisk pace. Tom nearly had to jog to keep up. He stumbled once or twice, but Cade kept him upright.

Moving so quickly and showing little regard for keeping quiet proved that Lars wasn't concerned about coming across anything dangerous. If he didn't care about running into Feral, either his men knew where to expect them, or all the ones in the area had somehow already been… trained. It was like hiking through a forest, surrounded by someone's pack of pet wolves.

At least Tom's predicament helped him forget about the repugnant odor throughout the hospital. By the time the odor reasserted itself, forcing him to wrinkle his nose, they'd made their way down several long hallways and at least three flights of stairs. The excursion ended at a large, navy-blue steel door with no markings or handles.

Without hesitating, Reg picked up a pry bar resting against the wall nearby, worked it into the gap between the door and frame, and popped the door ajar with little effort. A blast of cool air blew against Tom's face as the door swung wide. It was stale and slightly wet, but compared to the stench of the hospital, it was one of the sweetest things he'd ever smelled.

Beyond the door frame, though, was nothing but inky blackness.

"He won't be able to see in there," Ana said.

Lars frowned. "Useless meat. Fine. Cade, hold on to him tight. If he starts to fall, keep him upright. I'll take his other arm."

The leader glared at Ana. "Remember what I said. It may be dark in there, but I'll know if you're up to something."

"What is this?" Tom asked, voice still cracking.

"A subway tunnel," Ana replied.

"When was there a subway in Cincinnati?"

"Never, but there are tunnels. The city started work on a subway in the 1920s, but it was never finished. Much of the tunnel work was done, though, and that's what you're looking at."

"Enough with the history lesson," Lars growled. "Watch out in there. There aren't tracks or anything, but there's plenty of rubble and uneven footing." With that, he pulled Tom and Cade through the doorway and into the darkness beyond.

Ana's escorts brought her through next, and the two groups moved away from the light of the doorway. The Feral followed, then Reg came through and closed the door. As he sealed the door, they were plunged into complete darkness.

Terrified at the thought of moving through the tunnel blind, Tom felt the muscles in his arms, legs, and neck go rigid.

"It's okay," Ana said from somewhere to his right and behind him. "There's nothing in front of us. Just keep walking."

"So touching," Lars mocked. "Just keep putting one foot in front of the other, Meat, like you've been doing all your life. It's a short trip, and I don't want to attract any uncontrolled plaguers."

As Tom trudged through the darkness with little or no control, the journey certainly didn't seem short. It couldn't have been more than a ten-minute hike in the tunnel, but to Tom it seemed an hour, at least—an hour in which each moment brought an unexpected noise from off in the distance or a jagged pull on his arms, an hour during which the tension tied his shoulder blades into a knotted lump and holding his head up in the dark strained his already sore neck.

Eventually, the group veered slightly to the right, leading to the opposite side of the abandoned subway.

A dozen footsteps or so later, Lars gave Tom a sharp tug on the arm. "Stop here. Cade, get the door."

The man on his right stepped away, and Tom heard him approach what he thought would be the tunnel's sidewall. Some indistinct shuffling followed, then Cade picked something up off the ground.

Metal rang against metal, piercing the silence of the unfinished shaft. *Clang. Clang. Clang.*

A few heartbeats later, a muffled answer came in return. *Clang. Clang.*

Rocks on the ground were knocked around as someone moved closer to where Tom waited with Lars. The scrape of metal being drawn against metal came next, followed by a movement of something heavier. Then a yellow rectangle appeared in the wall right in front of him as a sealed door opened from the other side. Soft light spilled out of the corridor beyond into the tunnel where they stood.

To Tom's eyes, it was like the midday sun.

He held his hands up in front of his face, reveling in the small details of his fingers and palms. He smiled, thrilled to have all his senses again.

Lars nudged him toward the doorway.

Tom frowned. His hands were trembling, and he crossed them over his chest to hide it. A cold weight grew in his belly. Ana had avoided these very people for a long time, and he'd led them both right to them.

"What are you going to do with us?" he asked.

"We probably won't kill you right away," Lars said, sneering, "but if you'd rather, we could leave you alone out here in the tunnel."

His men chuckled. Still gripping Tom's arm, Lars pushed him again, less gently, and he stumbled up and across the threshold.

Beyond the doorway, they came to the door-keeper, an older-looking man with a plumber's wrench. He was just as pale and gaunt as the rest of them but stood with a slight stoop and moved like a movie zombie. Strange to see a man of his age given a task like guarding a door. How few survivors could there be if that was necessary?

Lars dipped his head as they passed and offered the man a perfunctory "Old-timer." The elder man waved them on.

The others made their way through, and the old man sealed the door just after the Feral. Tom, Ana, and their respective escorts kept moving down the corridor, keeping their distance from the monsters.

This new area was an underground tunnel but different from the subway. The floor and walls were all white-washed stone masonry, coming together in an arched ceiling barely a head above them. The short height gave it a cramped feeling but not enough to be claustrophobic. The air was slightly damp and smelled both a little sweet and sharply pungent, like mud after a heavy spring thunderstorm.

A series of hooked lights, the kind mechanics would use beneath the hood of a car, had been hung at regular intervals. Mirrors were positioned both opposite the lights and between them. Extension cords ran along the bottom of the wall on the right side of the tunnel, stretching as far as he could see. Tom was grateful for the light although it was much dimmer than it had seemed when that door first opened into the darkness of the subway.

"Are you operating this part of the grid somehow or using generators?" Ana asked.

"Generators," Lars replied. "Plenty of gas and kerosene around these days."

Bricks in the walls were cracked and had fallen out in spots, and dirt, debris, and refuse had gathered in piles here and there. Altogether, the tunnel seemed like a dungeon in the depths of some ancient medieval fortress. The place seemed old—very old.

"What is this?" Tom said.

"I don't know, but it's clever," Ana replied, eyes darting around, taking in as much as she could.

Lars smirked. "This is a lagering cellar, part of the city's old brewing tradition. They've been here since the 1800s, I'm told. Between these tunnels and the subway system they never completed, you'd be surprised how quickly we can move around the city without ever going topside."

The huge cellar, deep below ground, was a marvel. Strange that he could live in a city all his life and know so little about it. Somehow, in one day, he'd learned about an abandoned subway system as well as subterranean spaces that had been around for over a century.

What other surprises would the end of the modern world reveal?

Lars barked a command for them to move, and they made their way forward. They walked straight for a few hundred feet then turned left through a stone archway. They passed several other seemingly closed archways, as well as a few steel doors set into the stonework. He halted them in front of one of those doors.

Releasing Tom, he grabbed a tarnished key from a hook on the wall and slid it into the lock on the door with a practiced motion. After a quick twist, the door creaked open several inches.

Lars poked his head through the doorway, withdrew, and pushed the door open for the rest of them. Taking Tom by the arm again, he shoved him inside.

The space beyond the door was the same arched stonework, but it had been made into a separate room instead of a corridor. It was maybe half as wide and about thirty feet deep. Eight or ten feet from the back wall, a steel cage with a hinged door ran the width of the room, creating a separate area. Tom didn't know what brewers would have used it for back when beer was stored here, but he knew exactly how Lars intended to use it.

"Move it. Into the cell. And don't do anything you'll regret. It'd be a shame to come all this way for nothing."

Ana nodded her head.

Thoughts of escape raced through Tom's mind, but not having much of a real chance to get away, he shuffled through the cell doors.

For good measure, Cade gave him a little shove on the back. Tom stumbled but righted himself without falling, a minor victory.

Will and the other man holding Ana escorted her all the way to the far wall of the cell, where they turned her around. Three metal clamps he hadn't seen before hung from the stonework. Their purpose was immediately clear: a larger one high on the stone wall for her neck and two smaller ones for her arms. They were going to bind her to the wall.

Tom took a step forward, intending to somehow prevent that.

Lars put a firm hand on his shoulder. "Easy there, Meat. Use your head. What do you really think you're going to do?" Looking at the Feral near the room's door, he added, "I can kill you without even taking a breath, or if you'd like, you could still get torn to pieces."

Tom's shoulders slumped.

Three clicks echoed through the chamber as Ana was locked into the restraints. She dangled above the ground, held up by the bands around her arms.

Tom gave her a look of reassurance. To his surprise, he didn't find shock or panic on her face but a hard determination.

Lars chuckled. "Don't worry. She won't be up there long, I'm sure."

Tom began to say something encouraging just as Ana's eyes widened in surprise. "Tom!" she screamed.

And everything went black.

CHAPTER 19

HOW HAD THINGS GONE SO wrong, so quickly?

A few hours before, they'd been on their way west and at least relatively safe. Admittedly, not everything had gone as well as planned. Tom stopping at that bar in Iowa had been a disaster, and they were lucky to have left in one piece. Still, they'd been out of Alexander's reach. Another few hours west from there, they would have reached Colin's territory. They wouldn't have had to worry about even accidental encounters with Feral.

Somehow, though, Tom had gotten this ridiculous idea to come back to Cincinnati for survivors, and worse, she'd been fool enough to agree to return with him.

Before this, he'd been easy to Influence. He'd done exactly as she wanted when she wanted, with little pushing. The man she found in that bar, though, was different. Not only did he not respond to her subtle Influence, suddenly she found herself following him.

Colin would be furious.

Ana took a deep breath, cleared her head, and focused. The hard steel bands holding her neck and arms in place cut into her skin painfully. Under normal circumstances, she likely could have bent them or applied enough pressure on the clasp to snap it open. But being pressed against the wall completely deprived her of the necessary leverage.

Even if she could somehow power through her bindings, the two Feral from the hospital were standing guard just beyond the steel bars of the cell. While getting free and managing to subdue both of them wasn't out of the question, by the time she managed it, stronger, smarter reinforcements would be on hand.

She was trapped until someone decided to do something with her.

Ana glanced at the heap on the floor a few feet away. Tom had fallen like a sack of rocks when Lars hit him on the back of the head, and he hadn't moved since. She hoped the blow hadn't caused any serious damage. Even a moderate concussion would probably ruin Colin's plans. Her Master was going to be angry enough as it was.

She closed her eyes, took several slow, measured breaths, and allowed calm to sweep through her. She'd practiced this type of meditation regularly a lifetime ago, before Charon came along and changed everything. She needed to relax and think. Eventually, an opportunity to retake control of her situation would appear. She just had to be ready to act when that moment came.

Time slipped away as she concentrated on her breathing and considered her alternatives. When she finally heard the bolt on the room's outer door slide back, she had no idea how much time had passed. Could it have cycled back to nighttime already?

Lars entered the room, leaving the door ajar. He ignored the plaguers completely and marched between them to the cell door. After producing the key, he unlocked the gate and entered. Without breaking stride, he stepped over Tom and set himself in front of Ana.

His eyes were nearly on a level with hers due to his height. "I'm going to release you, and you, me, and one of my ugly friends back there are going to Alexander's office for a chat. I imagine I don't need to tell you what the Feral we're leaving down here is going to do if something goes wrong."

Ana exhaled forcefully. "They're yours?"

Lars nodded his head slightly. "Not directly, but they belong to Family."

Considering the implications, that left her with little alternative. "Smart."

"You've avoided us long enough. We're not taking chances."

"Fine. I give you my word—nothing clever." She sighed.

Nodding again as though he'd expected exactly that, Lars pressed her chest against the wall with one hand and, with the other, released first her neck restraint and then her armbands. He pulled her forward, off the wall, and set her feet on the ground hard.

"Follow me," he said, turning for the door.

As he walked away, she considered attacking, taking her chances with the Feral and any others that might come running. She might have been able to take Lars if she surprised him, but with Tom unconscious, she'd have to carry him out. In these dark, winding tunnels, they'd be doomed.

Instead, she followed Lars out of the cell, pausing briefly to check Tom for a pulse. Upon finding that his heart was still beating, she left the cell and closed the steel door behind herself. Her captors might have seemed unconcerned about leaving that Feral down here with him, but she wasn't so confident. The monsters were, after all, monsters. And if Tom woke up, the last thing he needed to do was wander out of the cell. In Alexander's lair, the inside of that cage was probably the safest place for him.

Lars led her between the two Feral to the outer doorway. The guards growled quietly and showed their pointed fangs as she walked between them, trying to pay them no mind. One of them broke away and followed her, another escort.

She entered the tunnel beyond the door and took one last look at Tom over her shoulder. She wasn't one for wishes, but she quietly made one to get out of the situation somehow.

Their journey through the cellar was quick. Ana had been expecting a mazelike series of twists and turns, but the opposite was the case. They walked down one arched stone hallway, turned right, and crossed a huge room that was empty but for a handful of old broken wooden kegs.

At the far end of what had been a vast storage room for beer long ago, they came to another door, unlocked and leading to a smaller room beyond. Lars nodded for her to proceed, and Ana mounted the single step between rooms. Once they were both through, he led her to a set of stairs in the back left-hand corner of the room.

The steps rose directly in front of them, made a ninety-degree turn to the right, and continued to ascend, where they ended in an open archway. Through the arch, the space beyond was more finished than the storage areas below. The walls were covered in stucco rather than simple stone, but large chips of the plastering had broken off over the years, revealing reddish bricks behind it. The same style of mechanic's lamps used in the cellaring areas hung from old wall sconces that had apparently given up working some time before. Between the sconces, pictures of heavily bearded brewers with very German-sounding names, who'd probably worked there a century before, hung in dusty frames.

The room was large and open, with old wooden floors that creaked as they crossed. One or two large doors stood along all the walls, each with shiny bolts that had been recently cleaned and tended to. The area was otherwise empty, save for another narrow wooden staircase inset on the far back wall.

They crossed the room and climbed. Four or five steps up, the creaking stairs turned at a small landing leading to the next floor. The second floor was darker than a moonless night, but Ana peered in anyway, hoping to pick out details that might prove useful. They passed so quickly on their way up, though, that her usually sensitive eyes failed to adjust to the lack of light.

They emerged on the third floor in the center of a short, softly lit hallway with a closed door on either side and another roughly six feet ahead. Lars went straight to that one and rapped two short knocks on the stained wooden door.

"Come," someone called in a deep voice from beyond it.

Lars opened the door and ushered Ana through. The

Feral stopped just beyond the top of the steps, taking up a guard position.

Alexander's office was long and narrow, with the same wooden floors and plastered brick. Unlike the lower levels, though, this room was lit by a handful of gleaming oil lanterns that didn't generate half the candlepower of the electric lights used elsewhere.

A crackling fire on the far side of the room made shadows that danced on the floorboards nearby. Two sets of heavy drawn curtains hung floor to ceiling on the wall to Ana's left. In the gloom, their color was impossible to tell. They were simply a dark shade of *something*.

In the center of the room, an older-looking man with a gray beard sat behind a massive polished-oak desk stacked with books and papers. He stood and motioned them to a pair of mismatched chairs facing him.

"Ana, is it? Have a seat. Lars, if you have other work…"

He was not an imposing figure, surprisingly. Alexander was broad shouldered and barrel-chested, certainly, but of average height at best. Delicate facial features and slender hands seemed at odds with his otherwise rugged profile. He was not at all what she'd expected. From all the stories she had heard, she'd imagined him a giant.

Still, his voice was deep and commanding, and his eyes were ice cold. She could see how the force of his presence alone had earned him power.

Lars cleared his throat. "Truth be told, my lord, I'd rather stay, if you don't mind. I'm not needed for anything too badly right now."

Alexander pressed his lips together and gave his lieutenant a hard glare. "As you will. Both of you have a seat." The words were clipped. For some reason, what Lars had said irritated him.

"I'd prefer to stand," Ana replied. Then she added, "As your prisoner." She clenched her fists, steeling herself under the weight of his presence. It pressed on her, threatening to completely wash away her own will. Getting through this without giving away Colin's secrets was going to require every ounce of her self-control.

"Stubborn children," Alexander sighed before taking his seat again. "I don't know what you know about me," he continued, "but based on how long you've been sneaking around in my region, I'd bet you've heard a few things."

Ana matched his gaze. "I know you have a reputation for being direct… and brutal when necessary."

"Hard times require hard measures, I'm afraid. And you're right, I'd rather not mince words. I'll be straight with you, then. You're lucky to be alive. I had every right to end your pitifully young life the moment you were captured. You've killed… what? Two or three of my people?"

"Hardly people. But yes, I have defended myself as needed."

The older man chuckled. "Yes, well, you're lucky they were Feral. You ask me, those beasts are just extra mouths to feed. If you'd killed one of my Family, though, we wouldn't be having such a pleasant chat. Smoke?"

Ana shook her head as Alexander reached for a crumpled pack of Winstons.

"I'm lucky I can still find packs here and there." In a quick, practiced motion, he drew a slightly flattened cigarette from the pack, tore the filter off, and lit it with a chrome cigarette lighter. Making a half turn in his chair, he flicked the filter into the fireplace behind himself and exhaled a cloud of acrid smoke.

"I'll make you this offer only once. Tell me what your Master is planning for the human, and I'll let you live. After, of course, you swear to obey me."

She hesitated. Men like this were not used to being denied. "Lord Colin is my Maker. I can no more openly defy him and offer you my loyalty than I could walk out of this building untouched."

"Don't give me that, child," he snapped. "We can work around your bond, and you know it. Tell me what I want to know."

Ana looked away. "He told me to bring him home. That's all I know."

"You're a terrible liar, girl. And your human is going to pay for it. We tried what my people thought best to harvest, and that turned out to be a waste of time. If you won't give me a practical use for him, I promise he won't live through the night."

"My lord…" Lars began.

Alexander shot another glare at the younger man and pointed with the two fingers holding his smoldering Winston. "That'll do. If I want comments from you, boy, I'll ask."

The tension between them didn't seem new.

Turning back to her, he took a long drag from the cigarette, exhaled, and tossed the butt into the fire. "Last chance."

Ana hung her head. "I can't help you."

"What a pity, for both of you. Lars, bind her upstairs. We'll give her some time to think about it and test her resolve. If not, well, nature will take its course."

"Yes, my lord." Taking Ana by the arm, Lars turned for the door.

"And, son?"

"Yes, my lord?" Lars replied, looking back over his shoulder.

"When you've finished with her, bring him up. Nothing happens to him until we meet."

"Yes, my lord."

Alexander returned to the books on his desk as Lars stalked out of the office, towing Ana firmly behind him. In the hallway, the Feral standing guard turned around to face them and grunted.

"Piss off," Lars spat.

The hunched creature retreated down the stairway without any reaction to the rough treatment.

When it was gone, Lars shoved Ana back onto the staircase. "Climb."

She took each step methodically, the wood creaking below her feet.

Think. There was so little time.

Lars grumbled behind her. "Quit wasting my time. If you're going to stall, I'll pick you up and carry you."

Reluctantly, Ana increased her speed, and they climbed to the top of the staircase, two floors above Alexander's office. The pair emerged in the center of a room below a vaulted ceiling with an ornamental cupola.

The floor of the room was rough. In spots, narrow planks of the painted hardwood were missing, giving access to the subfloor below. In other spots, whole spans of boards were warped.

Unlike the simple plastered brick walls below, the entire room was surrounded with windows offering a nighttime view of the neighborhood outside. Many were cracked or had holes large enough to fit a brick though. A chill wind whistled through the room.

He led her, still by the arm, to a vertical support beam near the eastern-facing windows. A pair each of hand and leg manacles dangled at the end of short chains, affixed to the post by iron spikes.

She was out of time.

As he clamped the shackles to her wrists over her head, Ana took her only shot.

"You don't agree with him about Tom?"

"Alexander is my lord. I don't have to agree with him about anything."

The bindings snapped shut around her ankles. Outside the window, the city was dark and quiet. How long until sunrise?

She looked into his eyes, crystal blue like water on a Caribbean beach. "You're not his Descended, are you?"

"No. My Family is gone."

"I am very sorry. I'm told it's hard to lose them when you are young."

Lars grunted and turned to the dark skyline.

She pressed on. "He is going to kill you all, eventually. He can't feed you and doesn't know what to do with so many. He's in over his head."

Turning back to her, Lars's face hardened. "I know he can't feed us. I know he's completely wasting our biggest opportunity. He's old and too conservative for... times like this. But what can I do?"

"Help me. Help us. There would be a place for you. Colin has a plan. I believe we'll find a way to make more food."

Lars shook his head with a sigh. "Everyone thinks betrayal is easier for someone else."

He turned and headed back to the staircase. Over his shoulder, he added, "Good luck."

Ana knocked the back of her head against the post behind her. Lars agreed with her, and she'd planted a seed, but it had precious little time to grow. She hoped it would be enough.

Closing her eyes, she concentrated on her breathing, with nothing left to do but try to relax. And wait.

CHAPTER 20

TOM *FIDDLED WITH THE PACKAGE of artificial sweetener. She was late, but she would surely come. The scene at the hotel had been a nightmare. He should have found a better way, should have confronted her at home. By surprising her instead, catching her like that, he'd startled and shamed her all at once. They'd barely spoken since.*

He just wanted to talk like civilized adults. Yes, the scars from how she'd hurt him were still fresh, but he still loved her anyway. They could fix it. Somehow.

He slurped the rest of his espresso and looked at his watch again. Heather should have been there already.

A tap on his shoulder. "Sir?"

Tom looked up into the face of a young barista with a mass of blond hair literally spilling from her butterfly barrette.

"Yes?" he replied.

"Are you Tom?"

Dread filled him. "Yes."

"Um. Okay. Some lady just called and said to tell you she wouldn't be here."

"Oh, Christ," he sighed, burying his forehead in his hand. The headache was starting already.

"Yeah. I'm sorry. And she said you should wake up and realize she doesn't want to talk. I'm so sorry. If you ask me, she sounded like kind of a wench."

Wake up, she said. Not a minute before, he'd been thinking about how badly he'd screwed up, and that's the message she gives him? Wake up?

"I mean it! Wake up!"

Tom blinked his eyes open, the coffee-shop girl's voice still echoing in his head. The dream dissolved, leaving him unsettled. Instead of fading, though, the sense of dread grew stronger as his senses returned and he remembered his situation.

In this case, the nightmare was better than waking.

He wasn't quite standing, propped against a wall. Lars stood in front of him with a forearm across his chest. Tom's vision cleared, bringing a five-paneled wooden door into focus.

Tom didn't recognize the hallway around them. Its warm wood construction, though, was much different from the stonework of the cellar he'd seen last.

The stained door was ninety degrees to his left. To his right, a few feet away along the same wall his back was against, stood another just like it. Opposite that one was yet another. At the end of the hall was an opening to a set of stairs, wrapped in framing that matched the doors. The stain seemed fresh, not faded.

Tom's whole head was on fire. His eyes burned even in the dim light of the hallway. He reached up and explored a sore lump on the back of his head with his fingers.

"If I let go, can you stand on your own?" Lars asked.

"I think so," Tom croaked. He nodded in case he hadn't been heard, and the slight motion brought stars to his eyes. Groaning, he took his head in his hands.

The other man chuckled. "It'll get worse before it gets better," he said, knocking on the door.

"Come."

Lars opened the door and shoved Tom over the threshold. He stumbled into the room and righted himself, coming to face an older but not quite elderly man smoking at a large wooden desk.

"Sit down," the man commanded.

Tom obeyed without hesitation. The way his head felt, he wouldn't have been standing long anyway.

Lars sat down in the mismatched chair beside him.

"Son, why does he look like he's nursing a hangover?" the man asked.

Lars grinned slightly. "I knocked him out after we got him downstairs. I didn't want the two of them scheming." He paused then added, "I might've been a little overenthusiastic."

The man grunted and exhaled smoke.

"Any word from the group you sent north?" Lars asked.

"Nothing useful. It's still early."

"We really should consider moving everything—"

"Not now. We'll discuss it later."

An awkward silence fell between them. Tom straightened in his chair, swallowed, and met the older man's eyes. "Where is Ana?"

"Well, well, he's full of himself, isn't he?" the man asked Lars, chuckling. Turning to Tom, he said, "You're here to answer my questions. You will speak when I speak to you."

Tom's cheeks burned at the rebuke. Why did he feel like he was in grade school?

"Do you know who I am?" the man said.

"No." He resisted the urge to shake his head.

"My name is Alexander. And you've caused me a whole mess of trouble."

"I've heard of you," Tom replied, straining to keep from looking at his feet. "From what I've been told, I kind of expected you to kill me on sight."

Alexander tapped surprisingly delicate fingers on the top of his desk. The rhythmic motion was mesmerizing. "I considered it. But I've got a couple of other possible uses for you that we couldn't try before, when you were so fragile and asleep."

"Then again," he went on, "Ana's Master seems to have something particular in mind for you. Maybe I should wait until they get here."

"They're coming? Here?" Lars interjected. "You know for sure?"

Alexander gave him a flat look. "Yes, of course they are. Did you not hear her say she's Descended? Colin knows we have her and probably that we have him." He nodded in Tom's direction.

Tom's eyelids felt heavier than they should.

"But my lord, we're not in the best position now. With most of our strongest away, trying to—"

"I understand our position better than you do, boy. Nevertheless, I expect they'll be here within the hour. Don't worry—they won't be coming to fight. They'll want to negotiate for custody of our captives." Glancing at Tom, he added, "It's a shame we'll have to disappoint them."

Tom heard the words they were saying, but they didn't seem to be making sense.

"My lord?"

"Just smell him sitting there. I'm not giving away our last chance at a real meal."

"Don't you think we should at least—"

"No, Lars," Alexander warned sharply. "I have a starving Family and no food. I myself haven't fed decently in weeks, and here we're given the gift of a live man, one that we could use for some time if we ration him carefully."

They might as well have been talking in a foreign language.

"But—"

"Enough!" Alexander growled, smacking his palm across the heavy desk.

The fog cleared away, taking some of the pain along. Tom snapped back to attention. What were they talking about? Food? Hunger? Weren't they talking about him?

A slow, creeping horror filled him. "Are you talking about… eating… me?"

A cold smile spread across Alexander's face. "No, we're going to chain you to that wall in the basement and bleed you to death slowly. Your blood will keep my Family healthy for weeks."

Tom stood up, knocking over the chair behind him. "What the hell is wrong with you?" he screamed. "You drink blood?"

The smile on the man's wrinkled face was replaced

by a shadow of confusion. "Of course we… Oh, my," he said, eyes going wide. "She didn't tell you."

Hands shaking, Tom's reply was barely a squeak. "Tell me what?" Before Alexander could answer, Tom stole a glance over his shoulder at the door behind him. Could he make it to the stairs outside? How long before they led to an exit?

He had no chance to find out. Lars was standing behind him suddenly, a steel grip on each of his biceps. He was going nowhere.

"It never occurred to me that she wouldn't tell you," Alexander said, almost chuckling. "My, my, it would seem your Ana has some explaining to do. Pity you'll never see her again."

"Tell me what? What do you mean? What are you going to do to her?"

"Do with her? She'll die, just as you will. Take comfort in that. She lied to you, Tom. She's not like you. No one is like you. My kind has been living among you for thousands of years, in the shadows, seen only when we wish to be. Preying on you at our whim. Feeding on your blood. I, myself, am over a hundred and fifty years old."

Tom's jaw dropped. "My God. You can't be serious. You want me to believe you're… what? Vampires? That's… that's ridiculous." His voice trembled.

Alexander sneered. "Charon killed all of you, leaving us with nothing to feed on. We're starving… slowly. And I'm going to use you to keep my Family alive for as long as possible."

Tom stood before the desk, mouth agape, as a wave of revelation crashed over him. It was preposterous.

But.

What if it wasn't? What if it *were* true? If so, many things would suddenly make sense. Most of his nagging questions would have answers. All of Ana's strange behavior would make perfect sense.

This had to be some kind of nightmare, a bad dream full of children's monsters that would disappear when he woke up. Vampires just weren't real.

Deep down, though, he knew Alexander wasn't lying. He could feel the truth of it. He tried to stammer something, but all words escaped him. Then, his heart hammering in his chest, he managed to squeak, "Where... where... is Ana?"

"You've got some nerve. I'll give you that," Alexander said, chuckling again. "I can smell your fear—not just the simple stuff but waves of terror rolling off you. And yet, you're asking for her? Fine, you earned one. She's chained to a post upstairs on our observation deck, waiting to greet the morning sun. It'll rise soon, I think. A shame too. She had backbone, for as young as she is. She could have been useful. But an example's got to be made, or others will think we go easy on spies here.

"Colin's people will no doubt be a little disappointed, but we'll work things out. Lars, take him to storage and chain him up. I'll have someone come down and begin harvesting."

"Yes, my lord."

"Good. Now, get him away from me before I give in to the temptation to keep him for myself. I'd forgotten how intoxicating the beating of a live human heart can be."

As Alexander again reached for his cigarettes, Lars turned him away from the desk and toward the door. He stopped them in the doorway. "What if they do want to start a fight, my lord? Colin isn't going to be happy about this, and we don't have much backup."

Flicking his filter into the fireplace, Alexander exhaled another lungful of smoke. "It won't come to that, son. But if it does, and they have the upper hand like you think, then we'll take our prisoner and make for the tunnels. They don't know this city like we do, above or below ground."

Lars grunted and ushered Tom out of the office and back to the staircase. They started down, only to stop in the darkness on the second floor. Farther below, a soft glow hinted at a possible exit.

"Stop it," Lars whispered into his ear from behind. "You're not going anywhere I don't want you to. I'm going to let go of your arms. If you make a move to get away, I'll tear you apart."

Confused, Tom nodded, assuming the other man could see it in the dark.

The pressure of Lars's grip disappeared. "If I let you go, what will you do?"

Tom spun around, brows furrowed. "What do you mean 'let me go'?"

"Exactly what I said," Lars growled. "Answer the question."

Tom didn't know what to say. It had to be some kind of trick. But if it wasn't…

He needed to get the hell out of this place, to turn, run, and never look back. But he didn't know where to.

Where would he go? How would he get away from Cincinnati? Could he find his car—or any working car, for that matter—and avoid Feral long enough to find someplace safe?

More importantly, could he just leave Ana here to die? Alexander had claimed she'd been lying to him for months, but she also saved his life at least twice, perhaps more, depending on how you looked at it.

Either way, he didn't know if he could live with himself if he did nothing, knowing he had an opportunity to save her.

Like it or not, furious or not, he owed her. More than that, he needed her.

"I can't run away and just let her die," he whispered. "If you let me go, I've got to try to save her."

"You're not as dumb as you look, Meat," Lars replied. "Take a step to your right. You'll be off the staircase and on the second floor. Then call that mutt of yours… quietly. She's about ten feet away. I can smell her."

After stepping onto the second floor, Tom clicked his tongue in the darkness. "Lady, come."

A few seconds later, a warm, familiar coat of fur brushed against his right leg. He reached down and thumped her on the chest. She planted a wet swipe of her wide tongue across his cheek in response.

"I ought to give you a piece of my mind for not leaving like I said," he mumbled through the titanic lump in his throat. Choking back happy tears, he added, "You're a good girl."

"Not to interrupt the reunion, but we gotta move. Quickly. Here, you'll need this." Taking Tom's hand, Lars pressed a cold metal object to his palm. "That's the key to the manacles. You need to go up three floors, all the way to the top. Move quietly, especially past the floor above us. If Alexander senses you passing by, you won't make it ten feet.

"If you do make it up there, set her free and stay put. Things are going to get ugly down here, and I won't have you killed on accident."

Tom nodded. "Thank you," he whispered.

"Don't bother. I'm not doing it for you. I'm doing it for me because the old man's a fool. And there's no guarantee things will be any better for you in Colin's hands. Now, go, and remember what I said."

With Lady alongside, Tom tiptoed up the steps, praying they didn't creak under their weight. He wanted to run, to charge upstairs with abandon, especially after sneaking past the dreaded third floor safely. But somehow, he kept his pace in check.

The steps ended flush with the top floor. He peeked up over them, his eyes barely above floor level. Four support posts ran from the floor to the ceiling, two on each side of the room. A nighttime view of dark skyscrapers rising above the river in the distance filled the windows to the west. In the east, the dark neighborhood and river gave way to rolling hillsides in the distance.

Ana hung, hands over her head, from the one of the beams facing east, waiting to meet the morning sun. At that distance, she looked unconscious. Tom sprang up the remaining steps and rushed toward her, frantic. She couldn't be dead.

Lady woofed, and Ana's head snapped up. Her eyes grew wide at seeing them over her shoulder.

"My God!" she exclaimed. "How did you get up here? What's going on? Is everything—"

"Hold on. I'll explain. Let me get you down." Tom lifted the key but then stopped with a look of uncertainty.

"Tom?" Concern darkened her usually unreadable face.

He stepped back. "He told me. Everything. Alexander did."

Her brows came together, and her lips pressed into a thin line. "What do you mean?"

"He told me... what you really are." He curled his fists into balls. "Why did you lie to me?"

"Tom, I... I just..."

"Why did you lie to me?" he bellowed, cheeks flushing with anger. "*Why?*"

He raised a hand to slap her, to channel all his pain and indignation, to finally get some measure of retribution for everything that had gone wrong since that hotel-room hallway over a decade before.

His hand hung in the air over her.

And it fell as he turned away.

"How would I have told you, Tom?" she asked, nearly a whisper. "Two months ago, it was difficult enough to explain how every person that ever cared for you, that you ever cared for, was gone—disappeared in what was, for you, the blink of an eye. If that wasn't bad enough, how could I have squeezed in the fact that the only sentient beings left in the world were horror-movie monsters that looked at you as a source of food?

"Ever since we left the school, I've struggled to find a way to tell you. It's been eating away at me. But you trusted me, and I *needed* you to trust me. Telling you would've destroyed that trust. So I didn't, hoping that somehow things would sort themselves out when we reached Seattle."

Tom glanced over his shoulder. "Why haven't you fed on me? Isn't that what you people do?"

She sighed. "I've never tasted the blood of a living human. I've lived on all manner of animal blood, and for a time, I had an impressive stockpile of transfusion units. It was the only thing I was sad to leave back in that school. But no, at no time was I ever even tempted to feed on you. I don't have the right. I promised myself that I'd let myself die before killing someone."

"What does Colin want me for?"

"Colin…" She faltered. "Colin believes you can be cloned."

Tom blinked as her full meaning sank in. The thought gave him a sickening chill.

He rubbed the bridge of his nose with his thumb and index finger, trying to block the pain in his head.

"If I help you, will he leave me be? Give me a safe place?"

"I can't say for certain, but yes, I believe so. When he gave me this task, I told him I wouldn't harm any survivors or let them be harmed. He praised me for that."

"Promise me. Swear to me that you will never lie to me again."

Ana exhaled. "Tom, I swear to you on my life, such as it is, and the desperate hope that I might someday find

I've retained my soul, that I will never knowingly lie to you again."

Tom stood, considering, tapping the key against the palm of his left hand. To Lady, he said, "What do you think?"

The dog woofed, tail wagging.

Tom smirked at Ana. "And I thought she didn't like you."

A minute later she was rubbing her wrists, free of the post. "How did you get up here, anyway?"

"Alexander was planning to start, well, draining me daily," Tom said, as if discussing whether it might rain the next day. "Lars apparently thought that was a pretty stupid idea and let us go. I think he intends to help Colin."

If Ana was surprised, she didn't show it. Instead, her face went blank, and she drifted toward the steps.

Tom took her arm. "He told me that after I released you, we should stay put. That things might get 'ugly' below."

"Ugly?" she murmured, eyes distant. Then surprise flashed across her features. "Oh my God, they're here already. This could be a disaster. We have to get downstairs! We have to find Ash!"

With those words still hanging between them, Ana raced for the stairs, nearly a blur.

CHAPTER 21

Tom's mouth hung open as Ana disappeared down the steps. "Didn't expect that to happen," he mumbled.

He took a few steps, intending to follow her out of pure habit, but stopped short, uncertain. Ana just ran off toward whatever was going on below, but Lars had been pretty insistent that they should wait up here until everything settled down.

Lady woofed questioningly.

"I'm thinking, I'm thinking," he mumbled.

She dropped onto her haunches between him and the stairs, waiting.

"One thing's for sure," he said to her. "If I'm going down there, I'm not going unarmed."

Tom glanced around the dark room, searching for something to use as protection. He cursed himself for both not bringing the revolver and not making Ana stop somewhere for more ammo. That was the weapon he wanted. But it was sitting useless in the car.

Luckily, a short length of discarded framing stud was leaning in the corner to his right. He picked it up, testing its weight. It was just over three feet long, a bit longer than the Louisville Slugger. The hard corners on the old 2x4 would make it hard to hold and probably handicap his swing. The bat, with its rounded handle, would have been much easier on his hands. Still, it was better than nothing, and the heft of it was reassuring.

He took a few practice swings in the empty air.

"All right," he said to the dog, "let's go."

Lady bounded to her feet and headed down the steps.

"Slow down," Tom urged, trying to keep her wagging tail in sight without plodding down the steps noisily.

She paused, waiting for him to catch up. Once together, they descended the staircase a few agonizing steps at a time. They passed the floor with Alexander's study without incident. He took them a little faster after that but kept himself from dashing down them in pairs.

At the bottom, Ana was standing in the middle of a large room, looking at an open archway in the stone wall in front of her. Lady raced ahead and stopped at her feet, staring intently in the same direction.

"Ana, what's going—" he began, but the dog interrupted him with a series of barks.

A figure emerged from the dark archway. It resembled a Feral in a way, with the same set of pointed teeth dominated by a pair of slightly curved fangs. Its mouth and chin were covered in what had to be blood.

Plaguers usually stooped, moved sluggishly, and were covered with rags that barely clung to them. This was something else. It stood upright, moved with a casual fluidity, and was dressed well in a dark hooded sweatshirt and jeans that looked new save for several inky stains across the chest.

The sweatshirt's hood was drawn forward, obscuring the upper half of the thing's face.

"Ash," Ana breathed, "thank God."

Lady, unsure how to react, reduced her barking to a low, steady growl.

The thing, Ash, whatever it was, glanced briefly at Ana and then beyond her, right at Tom. It snarled—the angry sound of a cornered animal—and darted forward.

"No!" Ana screamed. "Ash!"

Lady ran forward to meet the advancing creature, snarling. It slowed as they met, showing fangs that dripped crimson. The dog lunged, teeth sinking into Ash's leg.

A look of shock and then a wince replaced the wicked grin on its face. A reddish stain spread through its pants where Lady's teeth had found flesh. It raised a hand to smack her away, but Ana, streaking to it, struck first. With a dull thud, she planted a solid right hook across the thing's ear.

"Ash!" she screeched, inches from its face.

It staggered backward from the blow, its hood falling away in the process, revealing a face more human than Feral.

The thing—vampire—looked like a surfer without the tan. Rugged, well-defined features, weatherworn from exposure to the elements, dominated the square face. A full head of sandy blond hair fell loosely all around it, just long enough to barely reach dark, beady eyes that glared with hate.

Ash peered at Ana, truly seeing her for the first time, as if she'd been beneath notice before. He struck back with such speed that Tom barely registered the motion.

Several bones in Ana's face cracked, the sound of branches snapping in the woods. She skidded across the floor to Tom's left.

Lady released her hold on Ash's leg and lunged for his throat but was met with a blur of motion from the other direction. With a yelp, she was swatted to Tom's right.

Still ten feet away, Ash glared, ravenous hunger the only thing recognizable in the black of his eyes.

Tom squeezed the two-by-four and raised it to his shoulder.

Ash snarled and came at him again. The vampire seemed to glide forward, faster than even Ana had run earlier.

Tom had only one chance to get this right. Giving in to instincts honed by years of childhood baseball, he gripped the wood, waiting for just the right moment. His brain unconsciously registered tiny changes in Ash's movement, processing variables he could never have calculated on paper. His hands twitched. Half a second later, he uncoiled, stepping into the swing like a professional, putting all his body weight into it.

Timing it perfectly, the framing stud slammed into Ash's head with a crunch, a crushing blow that easily would have killed a normal person.

The two-by-four snapped in two, and half of it sailed across the room before clattering to the floor. The sting of vibration surged up Tom's arms, from his hands to his shoulders, as if he'd just hit a brick wall.

Ash staggered to the side a step, maybe two, and looked back at Tom, hissing. In a blink, the vampire seized him by the throat and lifted him off the ground.

Just as before, at the hospital, he felt as though a steel collar had been wrapped around his neck. But that time, he was being held in place against a wall. This time, the feeling of cold iron was slowly tightening.

He already couldn't take a breath.

He had to do something quickly. Ana lay on the floor, motionless, several feet away. In the corner of his eye, Lady was struggling to get to her feet. By the time either could help, he would be dead.

Tom flailed about wildly with his arms and legs. He punched and kicked at Ash, smacking him repeatedly with what was left of his framing stud. With his other hand, he clawed at the hand gripping his neck.

Ash ignored all that and made a quiet shushing noise. Peering at him with those dark, empty eyes, the vampire somehow snared Tom.

Unable to look away, he stopped fighting.

"I'm going to enjoy draining every last drop of your life, man. It's been so long. You should be glad of how I'm going to savor you."

A weird sense of peace washed over him. His heartbeat slowed, and his eyelids drooped. Seconds ago, he'd been full of rage, ready to claw Ash's eyes out. But now, he just wanted to relax.

Maybe that would be best. Get it over with. All the running and trying to hide was so tiring. Life was so overwhelming. No one could keep it up forever. This was just no way to live. Let Ash drain him and get it over with. It probably wouldn't even hurt. A few moments of helplessness, then it would be done. A blessed relief.

Tom went limp and closed his eyes. He welcomed the end.

Lady barked once, sharply. His head snapped up at the noise. Something in his brain snapped as well, as if waking from a dream.

Panic again flooded through him. Ash pulled him closer, close enough that Tom could smell the metallic tinge of blood on the vampire's breath.

Summoning all his strength, he lashed out with the framing stud again. Instead of swinging, though, he drove the splintered point of the broken end into Ash's chest. He prayed the oversized stake wound find its mark.

Whether it hit the heart or not, the attack seemed to work. The grip on Tom's throat disappeared.

Tom dropped to the floor, gasping like a fish out of water. He struggled to get back up to a crouch, ready to make a run for it. Exhausted, he made it only as far as his knees.

Ash staggered back several steps, eyes wide, shocked at the piece of wood protruding from his chest. Then he laughed, a full, booming laugh that filled the mostly empty room, echoing off the stucco and stonework.

"A stake through the heart?" he said with a wide grin. "Did you figure I'd blow away in a flash of dust?" Another chuckle. "So sorry to disappoint you."

Ash took a firm hold of the two-by-four and wrenched it out of his chest with agonizing slowness. It slid free, slick and covered with innards. A gush of blood followed. He dropped it to the floor and bent at the waist, gasping.

Tom finally got to his feet, ready to run, but with nowhere to go. More vampires would likely be waiting in the tunnels below, and he could barely stand, let alone fight. He'd never make his way past them. Going back up the steps, though, would likely result in getting cornered. However, if he could find a window up there or maybe reach a fire escape, he might get out of the building alive.

Lady limped to his side, and he turned to make a run for the steps. Ana remained motionless on the floor across the room. He grimaced at the thought of leaving her, but he couldn't help her.

"Tom, stop," Ash said, his voice steady—a request, not a threat. "You're not in danger. Not anymore. Not from me, at least."

One foot on the bottom step, Tom looked back. Ash stood near Ana, wiping the blood from his face and hands with his sweatshirt. "I'm sorry I lost control. It was quite… exhilarating… below. I haven't gotten worked up like that in some time. Sometimes, it's hard not to get caught up in the blood frenzy. Quick thinking with that two-by-four. Not many people like you have ever held me off like that. It was just enough to bring me back to my senses."

Ana groaned and rolled over, clutching her head. Without opening her eyes, she muttered, "Dammit, Ash, did you kill him? Or did you stop after trying to kill me?"

Ash knelt beside her. "No, but I almost did. Dude's got a few tricks. He managed to snap me out of the frenzy without any help. Are you all right? How long since you fed?"

"It's been… a while," she replied slowly, "but I'll be fine."

"We'll have to see to that. Let me help you up." Ash stood and offered his hand.

She took it and got up off the floor.

"It's good to see you, sister," Ash added as she dusted herself off.

Still standing on the bottom step, Tom waited with a puzzled expression. A few moments before, Ash was a fanged nightmare ready to squeeze the life out of him while hissing about how much fun it would be to drink his blood. Now, he and Ana were suddenly close friends.

Lady cocked her head.

"Ana, what's going on?" he asked.

She crossed the room toward him. "This is Ash. He is Colin's right hand, his first lieutenant. Colin sent him and several others to protect you until we can get you to Seattle."

"He has some pretty unusual protection techniques," Tom scoffed, looking back up the staircase.

"Dude, let me apologize," Ash said. "I totally wasn't myself when I came through the archway. I promise you it won't happen again. Believe it or not, I'm actually the lucky one here. If you hadn't stopped me and I'd managed to kill you, Colin totally would have had my head the minute he arrived."

As Tom started to say something sarcastic, Ana cut him off. "Colin is coming here?"

"Yep," Ash replied. "He's coming to Tom instead of having the two of you try another trip across country."

Ana scowled. "That's... audacious. Alexander will almost certainly feel threatened."

"He should feel threatened. The big man has decided to branch out, expand. The trip here is to kill two birds with one stone. That's why we showed up with our fangs out."

Ana covered her mouth with her hand. "Oh my God. It will be a war."

"Maybe, little sister. Maybe not. That's up to Colin. And Alexander."

CHAPTER 22

"WHAT WILL BE UP TO Alexander?" The voice came from the archway to the cellar below. Lars presented a horrifying image: blood dripped from his hands and covered his face and chest. Half staggering into the room, without his usual purposeful stride, he was either exhausted or perhaps wounded.

As he took in the scene, a spark of recognition caught in his eyes and was instantly replaced with something darker. He hissed and, with a show of fangs, flew across the room.

He hit Ash at full speed, and the pair rose into the air for a heartbeat before crashing to the ground, splintering the wooden floorboards. They landed in a tangle, Lars on top, and careered into the wall beyond. The impact sent a shower of dust flying around them, and a spiderweb of cracks appeared in the brick and mortar where Ash hit the building.

They finally came to rest, wedged in the corner where the wall and floor met, Lars holding Ash down by the neck.

"Don't even fucking twitch, or I'll snap it," he said.

Ash opened his mouth to reply, but whatever he'd planned to say was reduced to a gargle as Lars squeezed.

"If I want you to talk, I'll tell you to talk."

Almost imperceptibly, Ash nodded.

"I was going to walk you straight up to him," Lars cried. "You didn't need to storm in here and start killing Family! Why do you think they opened the door in the first place? I told them to do it." His grip tightened.

Ana took a step toward them. "Don't kill him. There's been enough killing already."

Lars glanced back at her. Reluctantly, he released his hold on Ash and looked down at him. "I had to kill my own down there, damn you, to keep them from killing you and making this whole thing worse. I'm covered in the blood of my own Family, for no good goddamn reason."

Ash coughed a couple of times and propped himself up on his elbows. With a morbid grin, he muttered in a gravelly voice, "Gave you a decent chance to feed for once, though, right?"

Lars's right hand flashed in an arcing motion, striking Ash across the face. Blood splattered the wall, and a few teeth skittered across the floor.

Ash chuckled. "Feel better, dude?" Seeing Tom's shock, he added, "Don't worry—they'll grow back."

Lars slumped back, away from the wall. From a seated position on the floor, he hung his head, taking it in both hands as his appearance of strength evaporated.

"That human better be worth all this," he whispered, barely loud enough for Tom to hear.

Tom looked at Ana uncertainly. He glanced at the stairs then again toward the archway leading below.

Ana gave him a reassuring half smile. "Everything will be fine, Tom."

Reaching down, he patted Lady a few times on the chest. The German shepherd nuzzled his hand in return.

Ash pushed himself up off the ground and sat against the wall.

"Are you all right?" Ana asked, moving toward him.

"I'm fine." He waved her back. Looking at Lars, he went on. "Is that what you'd have done in my place? Knowing that you were entering another lord's stronghold, with orders to take it? Also knowing that the lord in question already held one of your own Family? I don't know you, man, but I know that look in your eye. You're the kind that acts when times call for it. It's the reason guys like us end up in charge of things."

Lars raised his head, scowling. "No one had to die. There are few enough of us left as it is."

"True," Ash replied. "But then again, there are entirely too many," he added coldly.

Lars's fangs materialized at the implication. "If you think you'll be killing more of my—"

Ash raised his hand. "Peace, man. No more." He paused, then smiled. "Well, maybe one more. Where is Alexander?"

Lars looked at Ana. "You didn't see him after Tom let you go?"

She shook her head. "No."

"If he left his office, either you would have crossed his

path on your way down here, or I would have seen him on my way up from below. He must still be upstairs."

Turning toward Ash, he continued, "His office is on the third floor, to the right of the steps. He'll know you're here by now. I can't believe he isn't on top of us already."

Ash eyed the steps. "Is he still up there?"

"I don't know," Lars replied.

"You're not Descended?" Ash asked, voice full of surprise.

Lars shook his head.

"Weird." With that, Ash pushed away from the wall and got to his feet, dusting himself off as he made his way to the staircase. He paused at the bottom, looking up.

"If something happens, you'll know soon. Don't wait. Take him"—he nodded in Tom's direction—"and get to the others below. There were sixteen of us, and I think at least a dozen are still alive down there. Keep the man safe."

Ana suggested, "Perhaps we should leave and come back when the situation is more…"

Ash shook his head. "No, if it isn't past daybreak already, it will be soon."

"Understood."

Ash turned back to the stairs and began climbing, two at a time. In seconds, he disappeared at the turn on the landing.

Tom stood up and crossed the room, Lady beside him. He gave a wide berth to Lars, still leaning against the wall and holding his head.

"Are you all right?" she asked as he neared her.

He nodded. "What was all that about? The 'Descended' bit, I mean."

Looking at the staircase, Ana picked at the skin on her thumb. "What? Oh, not now," she answered. "I'll explain when we have more time."

That wasn't the answer Tom wanted, but it was all he would get from her at the moment. Changing the subject, he gestured toward Lars, sitting motionless on the floor. "What's he doing? Is he okay?"

"What?" she replied in a distant voice. Before he could ask again, though, her focus returned. Meeting his eyes, she said, "Oh. He's just resting. I imagine he needs to heal. We heal quicker when either feeding or in a near-meditative state."

Realizing he was an available food option, Tom took a step back from him. "Maybe we should leave him be?"

"No. We stay here until Ash returns."

"You're safe," Lars replied, raising his head. "At least for now. Yes, I'd rather feed, but I didn't go through all this just to drain you. Besides," he added with a grin, "if I decide to feed on you, don't think you'd just slip away." He chuckled to himself as the thud of boots on the staircase echoed through the room.

Tom and Lars both turned toward the steps with the same look of concern.

Ash or Alexander?

Tom took a few steps backward as Lady positioned herself between him and the stairs.

Ash rounded the turn, and Tom gasped in relief.

"He's gone," Ash said.

"What? Are you sure?" Lars asked. "Just gone?"

"Ghosted, man. No sign of him."

"He made a run for it."

"Looks that way."

"That son of a bitch," Lars muttered then stood up with a sigh. "I don't know if that technically means his authority is mine or what, but it's good enough for me. I have no interest in trying to lead here. If Colin wants to run things here, fine, as long as he takes responsibility for anyone willing to accept him. And I want promises from you and him that the human will be kept safe and not wasted on just feeding. There has to be something we can do with him that would serve all of us."

Ash nodded. "My lord will give you his official answer when he gets here. For now, I'll accept your offer on his behalf." He extended a hand.

Lars looked at the hand and crossed his arms. "The offer is to Colin, not you. You're not off the hook with me yet."

"No worries, dude. Plenty of time to settle that score. And you can swear your oath to Colin when he gets here."

"That'll be between him and me."

A dark glint shone in Ash's eye but disappeared quickly. "Either way, get your Family up here. It's time to say hi a little nicer."

CHAPTER 23

L ARS DIDN'T MAKE ANY NOTICEABLE call for his people to gather, but somehow, over the course of the next twenty minutes, a crowd trickled in through the stone archway. They were a scraggly-looking lot of over a hundred. Most wore disheveled clothing, and many were covered in bloodstains.

When everyone was on hand, Lars nodded to Ash from the arch.

"Wait on the landing behind me," Ash said as his own group approached.

Tom, Ana, and Lady climbed to the landing and stopped. Ash took a spot on the bottom step, and his people clustered around him, forming a wall that blocked him from the locals.

Lars's Family stood together opposite the guards. Exchanging glances and hushed comments amongst themselves, they eyed the strangers with suspicion and, in some cases, dark looks.

It couldn't have helped that the newcomers seemed in better condition than Alexander's people. While members of both sides were relatively thin, the locals looked... withered. Either Seattle itself made life easier for a vampire, or Colin was doing a much better job of providing for his subjects.

Lars had greeted many of his people individually as they entered, taking them aside for a few quick words as soon as they passed through the arch. Usually, after a brief exchange, they would sneak a look in Tom's or Ana's direction, followed by a hard glare at the foreign vampires below. Then they would slink away and gather together in smaller clusters.

Tom's skin crawled. The air between the two groups crackled with tension.

"I think maybe this was a mistake," he said to Ana. "We should look for a chance to get out of here. Most of Alexander's people are giving me wild-eyed looks, and they only break it off long enough to stare at Ash with hate. I feel like a rabbit in a fox hole. We should bolt before someone figures that out."

Ana shook her head. "I'm sorry, Tom, but that's impossible now. We have to stay with Ash. You need to be with me, and I've been commanded to stay here. You don't need to worry, though. He will keep you safe from Alexander's clan. Nothing will happen to you."

That wasn't reassuring. Fifteen minutes before, Ash had been goading Lars about how many of his own people he'd had to feed on.

"I thought you were on my side," Tom huffed, frowning. "Just like that, you hand me over to Ash, and without even asking my opinion? I don't know him. I don't know anything about him. But he doesn't seem like the kind of guy I want to trust."

She gave him a pleading look. "You must believe

that I meant every word about watching out for you and keeping you safe. But Colin is my Master. He controls everything I do. I follow his orders without question or hesitation. I have no choice in the matter, no will. And he wants me—and you—to stay with Ash."

Before Tom could reply, Ash climbed another step and raised his arms.

"Cousins," he began, his voice booming against the walls, "I'm Ash. I represent Colin, Master of the West. Before anything else, I want to say how very sorry we are for the... trouble... when we arrived. I was sent to talk with Alexander about my sister, who was being held here against her will. It bums me out that we were attacked when we arrived, and your lord fled before I had a chance to meet with him. I hope those of you who are Descended from him will verify that he is still alive and well, if not here."

A slight murmur ran through the crowd, and several in the larger group nodded in agreement.

Ash continued, "It seems you've been struggling here more than some of the rest of us. Personally, I'm thinking maybe Alexander got tired of trying to take care of so many of you. Whatever his deal, Lars, who you know as his Second, has offered to allow my lord, Colin, to come and try his best to do better for you all. As your current leader, Lars agreed to let any of you say an oath to the big man when he gets here, without fear of retribution. Everyone cool with that?"

Lars stood with his arms crossed, staring blankly at Ash, and said nothing. The rest of his Family stood silent as well.

"Awesome. Anyone swearing the new oath will be taken care of and allowed to live here or in the West in total peace. Anyone not swearing, though, needs to find a new home. And if you want to leave before Colin arrives, go for it."

Another murmur ran through the crowd, and a handful of vampires slipped out through the archway.

"If you want to chat with me in person, I'll be setting up in Alexander's office. My door is open. I look forward to meeting you all." He turned to go up the steps but, on seeing Tom, spun back around.

"One last thing. As you know by now, there's a human here. I'm betting it's the first one most of you have seen... or *smelled* in a while. Mind yourselves where he is concerned. He is under my protection. If anybody messes with him, barks at him, or so much as looks at him wrong, I'll remove your head from your shoulders faster than your fangs can drop into place."

Ash spread his legs and placed his hands on his hips, offering a challenge.

"Look, you're all hungry. I get it. It hasn't been easy here. Hell, it ain't easy anywhere. But we can't waste this dude's life on one simple feeding. Eventually, he'll help to feed us all. I know you have been left to scavenge for much too long, but those days will be over soon. Colin will help you. He's going to save us all!"

A muted round of applause broke through the crowd and was followed by the low, constant hum of murmured conversation.

"Keep your fantasies. To hell with 'eventually.' I'm tired of being hungry now!" cried someone from the back of the crowd. A short, stocky man strode forward with twenty or so vampires following.

"Dane, no!" Lars cried and began to push through the assembled crowd himself.

Dane and his mob reached the front of the throng then charged into Ash's wall of guards, flying through the space in a second. From his perch on the staircase landing, Tom could see white fangs and slashing claws as the groups clashed.

Lady, who had been sitting on the step just below Tom, stood and gave a low growl that matched the fur standing on the back of her neck.

Ana's cold hand gripped Tom's arm. "Stay right there," she urged breathlessly.

Emboldened by their Family struggling with Ash's guards, several others from Lars's side of the room stepped forward to join the fight. Lars, nearly a blur, raced to the front of the crowd, and one by one, he grabbed them and tossed them backward, away from the conflict.

Facing his people, he bellowed, "Stay out of it. Anyone else who wants in that fight has to go through me. There's been enough blood today!"

Dane's group had a significant numerical advantage over Ash's—not quite twice the size but probably half again as large, and Ash himself had yet to step down and enter the fray. Even with those odds, the West Coasters were well-prepared for the attack. A blurred melee followed, highlighted by the occasional scream or a spatter of blood as a claw or set of fangs found its target.

As the skirmish progressed, several members of Dane's

group were thrown back into the crowd and away from the conflict.

Just as the numbers were becoming more even, Dane opened the neck of one of the defenders. The guard's blood gushed over his chest, and he slumped to the ground, giving the insurgent leader a chance to slip past him and approach the stairs.

Ash stepped down and squared up to face him.

Dane unleashed a pair of huge open swipes in quick succession.

Ash ducked below the first one casually and blocked the second with little effort. As the shorter man recovered, Ash countered with a punch to the head, which sent Dane staggering sideways. His defenses down, Ash seized the stout man's neck with his left hand. He twisted Dane around to face the others, pulled him close, and raised a hand.

"Enough!"

The handful of Dane's men still struggling stopped fighting and retreated to the safety of the larger group.

Dane scratched at the hand gripping his neck, gasping.

"This is your bright idea?" Ash asked, nodding toward the vampires backpedaling. "They followed you?"

Dane nodded as well as he could.

Looking across the room, Ash said, "It's your choice, Lars."

Lars stepped past the guards with a scowl.

"That was the stupidest damned thing you've ever done, Dane," he said, approaching the pair. "You know better."

Dane closed his eyes and nodded again slowly.

"Did you expect to just feed on him in front of all of us and then walk away?"

Dane gave him half a shrug and a pleading look.

"Idiot," Lars said. Taking Dane's head in both hands, he twisted until a stomach-churning pop filled the room. Then he squeezed. A nauseating sequence of crunching sounds, like an egg being crushed, followed.

Dane's head slipped, limp, from Lars's hands, the contorted face drooping against his own chest. Ash let go, and the body fell to the ground between the pair with a wet thud.

"Nice, dude," Ash said.

Lars stared at Ash, his face unreadable. In his eyes, though, a storm raged. He turned, slipped through the crowd, and disappeared into the blackness beyond the archway.

Ash climbed back up on the lower step and gestured at the body on the ground. "His head will be hung up just so no one forgets. Anybody else tries anything like that, you'll meet the same end—or worse. The human's not to be touched unless Colin or I say otherwise. Thank you all for coming. That's it for now. Colin can't wait to get here and meet you all."

The crowd broke up, and the guards came back together, tightening the circle at the base of the stairs. Ash climbed to meet Ana and Tom. As he approached, Lady, who had stopped growling when Dane was subdued, began again.

Tom reached down and patted her side. "I know, girl. I know. Try to relax."

Ash ignored Tom and the dog. Looking at Ana, he said, "Take them up to that viewing deck and lock them in. I want him sealed in there. No one gets access but you. I'll put a couple of guards at the floor below."

Tom's face flushed hotly. He opened his mouth to explain, loudly if necessary, that under no circumstances would he be held like a prisoner again. Ana squeezed his arm gently, stalling him.

He looked at her and frowned. Upon turning back to give Ash a good piece of his mind, he was startled to find nothing but empty space. Ash had already returned to his men at the bottom of the steps.

CHAPTER 24

THE CROWD TOOK THEIR TIME dispersing. Several individuals left right away, but smaller groups lingered, whispering in heated discussions. Their glances at Tom were stolen now—far less deliberate than when they'd entered the room—but still, they repeatedly peeked at him from the corners of their eyes from time to time.

Being separated from all the others probably wasn't the worst thing in the world since he was at best a political problem and at worst a last meal in pretty much everyone else's eyes. He wasn't about to tell Ana he was okay with it, though. Openly conceding that point was the last thing he was going to do.

Crossing his arms, he glared. "Locked up again?"

She fidgeted with the zipper of the cropped jacket she wore, hesitant to meet his eyes. After a moment, she forced her hands to her sides. "I'm sorry. I wish it didn't have to be this way, Tom, believe me. Just, please, go upstairs. We'll talk about it up there."

"Yeah, you're sorry. I should have figured. It seems like you're sorry a lot."

"Tom, I—"

He cut her short. "Save it."

Seeing no other real choice, he started climbing. Taking his time, he made each step a slow protest against being told what to do.

Tom reached the observation deck and stepped into the room with Lady behind him. The sun had not quite risen yet, but the sky at the horizon was a pale mix of violet and light blue, a sure sign that it wouldn't take long.

Ana stopped before reaching the point where she might have been exposed to sunlight. "Is the sun up yet?"

"Not yet." His reply was gruff.

She peeked up over the last step to confirm what he'd said then climbed into the room. He turned away from her.

"Tom, I have no choice in this. I told you, Ash speaks with Colin's authority. I can't simply ignore him."

He stuffed his hands into his pockets and grunted, staring out the window at the increasingly bright horizon.

"I am going to be up here with you every night," Ana offered. "I'm not going to abandon you. We still have much work to do together, and at least you'll be safe here now."

"What do you want me to say?" he growled. "Do you want me to tell you that it's all right, that I understand? Well, it's not all right. It's…" He stopped and sighed heavily. "Look, whatever you want me to say to make you feel better, you're not going to get it. I'm glad you woke me up and saved my life, and I'll always be thankful for that. But I've been through too much—and things just keep getting worse—to pretend I'm anything but pissed."

"Tom."

FAMINE

He pointed accusingly. "'Trust me. I'll take care of you,' said the vampire that conveniently left out the *vampire* part. And did you mention that there's no one left but vampires and those monstrous pet freaks? Didn't figure I needed to know that, right?" Face flushing, he thundered on. "And now I get an invitation to stay and hang out with all your vampire friends, but only if I'm all locked up, safe and sound, probably right until dinner time."

She flinched at every accusation.

"This isn't keeping me safe. This is keeping me prisoner. Just… go. I can't even look at you right now. Go away and lock the damned door."

An awkward silence fell between them, tension hanging in the room like the still, humid air before a summer storm.

Ana stared at the warped floorboards, seeming to consider a response. She took a deep breath, and his eyes widened, awaiting her reply. Instead, she muttered something unintelligible, turned, and fled from the room.

Her head already below floor level, she reached up and grabbed a handle strap he hadn't noticed earlier. It was attached to a hinged trapdoor, which she swung up and over to cover the stairway opening. It fell flush with the floor, closing him in.

"I'll be back at dusk," she said, muffled by the wood between them.

Four metallic clicks rattled as the trap's locks were secured. He and Lady weren't going anywhere for the day.

For the next hour or so, Tom paced the observation deck, first burning away his frustration, then trying to think of some way to entertain himself. The sun rose slowly over the horizon as he made an inventory of everything in the room. He found a few pieces of mismatched lumber tossed into the corners, a bucket of completely dried-out wall plaster, and a paint-splattered drop cloth.

With nothing else to do, he eventually sat down with his back against the post where Ana had been chained. Lady padded over and lay down beside him, resting her head atop his thigh. He gently stroked her dark fur.

"At least we've got each other," he whispered.

Before long, the stress and exertion of the previous few days caught up to him, and with the sun rising into the sky, he dozed off.

Tom slept like the dead the entire day, sitting straight up against a post and facing full daylight. He woke up to Lady nudging his hand with her muzzle as sunlight faded behind them. His back ached from the awkward position, and his neck probably wouldn't be free of kinks for weeks. It was worse than sleeping in a car.

After giving the dog a pat on the side of her chest, he stood and stretched. He coaxed a few pops and cracks from his spine and sighed.

He felt a little bit less like a wooden plank, and his stomach growled. He'd eaten nothing since the bar, however long ago that had been. A day? Two? His head was spinning slightly from standing up. Getting some food was going to have to be the first order of business.

As he settled back down against the post, thinking fond thoughts of his grandmother's French toast, the locks on the trap door rattled in succession. Each clicked open, followed by a brief pause, before the platform at last rose from the floor. His pulse quickened at not knowing who was pushing it open.

Ana's face appeared from the darkness below. Tom exhaled in relief, the muscles in his arms and shoulders relaxing.

"Good evening," she said, climbing into the room. "Did you rest?"

"As well as someone can, locked in an attic all day."

She frowned. "I'll have a bed and some other accommodations brought up. Hopefully, tomorrow will be more comfortable."

He said nothing.

"You must be hungry," she pressed on, echoing his thoughts. "I brought food." She held out a bag of potato chips and a bottle of water.

Tom looked at it then back at her. "This isn't going to work. I'm not going to live long on nothing but three-year-old snack chips. Sooner or later, you're going to have to find me some real food."

"I know. I'll speak to Ash about that tonight, but this is what I have right now. Please eat it. If nothing else, you need the calories."

He raised an eyebrow and considered telling her to take the chips to Ash and shove them somewhere he'd need a mirror to find them, but the rumble in his stomach conquered any possible defiance. He took them and the water and tore into the bag.

"Lady's going to need to go for a walk," he mumbled around a mouth full of salty fried potato. For good measure, he dropped a few chips on the floor for her.

Ana cocked her head at the dog. "I hadn't thought of that. Let me take her, I'll—"

"No. She and I stay together. I don't want anyone down there looking at her like breakfast."

Ana threw her hands up. "Fine. We'll all go for a walk outside. Quickly, though. We need to get right to work tonight. Follow me."

They made their way down the stairs, earning suspicious looks along the way. When they reached the big room on the main floor, instead of heading through the arch into the cellars, Ana led them to a large door on the south wall. She slid back a heavy bolt and pulled the handle, ignoring the creaks and groans of its hinges.

They went through and entered some kind of office space from long before. An old writing desk stood against one of the walls, and a pair of worn, high-backed chairs faced it. The floor had been a nice hardwood at some point before years and dust wore away its gleam.

Ana didn't slow as she moved through the room, making a straight line for a door on the opposite wall. She produced a key from the pocket of her jacket and slid it into the keyhole above the doorknob. It stuck slightly when she tried to turn it but eventually gave way with a loud clack. A burst of cool night air rushed in from the street.

"I thought we'd have to wander through the tunnels again for half an hour before we came to daylight," Tom said, looking around. "Or, I mean, moonlight."

"No, that's not the only way," Ana replied. "There were several entrances to the building originally, but most have been blocked or sealed. Only two are accessible now,

I'm told. The fewer ways in, the better. And those two are rarely used since we don't typically take surface streets in the city. Not when we can avoid it, anyway."

"Why not?" he asked.

"Well, besides the potential for sunlight, it's the Feral. No one will say it, but running into unfamiliar Feral is unpleasant. That's good for us at the moment, though. Since so few of us use the streets around here, I thought we'd be mostly left alone this way."

The unspoken point was clear: the fewer of her kind they came across, the better. He glanced up and down the street, suddenly feeling naked, exposed. Tom shook his head at the idea that she preferred the chance of running into Feral over being among Lars's Family.

He tailed Lady mechanically as she darted from place to place, investigating unseen scents in the dark city. Ana walked beside him quietly, content to leave him alone.

They hiked for some time in silence. Block after city block disappeared behind them as they followed the erratic path of a dog chasing invisible odors. Ana sighed heavily from time to time and occasionally put her hands on her hips but said nothing.

Finally, after losing track of how far they'd gone, he stopped in the middle of the street and whistled to Lady. She immediately gave up whatever phantom she was chasing and trotted back to him.

The night air was crisp and slightly damp, the way that only autumn can be, cold enough that his hands stung. He blew warm breath into them before shoving them into the pockets of his jeans.

"I'm going to need my leather jacket," Tom said at

last. "I think I left it back with the car. We could get it now, but I'm not sure where we are."

She shook her head. "No, we need to get back. If we don't soon, Ash will send someone for us."

"If I ran?"

"I'd have to stop you. It's too dangerous out here for you alone, especially at night."

Tom exhaled slowly and looked back the way they'd come. "I'm going to die back there," he said, not quite a whisper. "One way or another… and probably sooner rather than later. You have to help me get away."

Ana held out her hands. "You don't know what you're asking, Tom. What I want doesn't matter. I have to finish the task Colin gave me."

Tom kicked a few pebbles, watching them bounce and roll a foot or so away. "Hardly worth the effort," he mumbled. He pushed a sleeve back to reveal a forearm covered in dozens of dark, circular scars in sharp contrast to his pale skin.

"I'm covered in reminders that I've been here before, Ana. I'm not going to let it happen again."

She said nothing. Tom searched Ana's dark eyes for some glint of compromise, anything to give him a modicum of hope. She stared back, unblinking. Nothing was there but darkness and cold steel.

"Fine," he sighed. "Let's get back so you can start work."

Without waiting for her to respond, he started toward his prison, Lady padding beside him.

CHAPTER 25

B Y THE TIME THE PAIR returned to the observation deck in the former brewery, someone had brought in a hospital-style bed. In addition, a massive aging cherry desk stood in the center of the room along with a tall, swiveling desk chair and a stainless-steel table. A host of carefully arranged medical instruments gleamed atop the table, waiting for use.

"Huh. Impressive," Tom said, falling into the chair and propping his feet up in relief. They ached slightly from the long walk on the pavement. His stomach grumbled loudly, too, proof that what little food he'd eaten wasn't nearly enough.

Ana looked over the medical tools carefully, clucking her tongue in irritation from time to time. "I'm sorry, what did you say?" she asked over her shoulder.

"I said it was impressive. We weren't gone that long, and someone managed to get all this heavy stuff up here in the meantime. How do you people do that?"

She gave him a blank look. "Do what?"

"How do you get others to do things without talking to them?"

"What do you mean?"

Tom swiveled in the chair and waved his hands at the additions to the room. "You showed up at twilight, said nothing to anyone on our way out, but somehow all the stuff we needed appeared while we were gone. It was the same way with Lars last night. Ash told him to get his people together, and they just started showing up. But Lars never said a thing to anyone, at least not that I saw. How does that work?"

Ana smirked. "Well, I spoke to Ash about our needs this morning after I locked you in. As for last night, with Lars, Family can usually communicate without speaking."

"How?"

"Each of us can speak via our thoughts with the one who Made us."

"No way. Like telepathy? That's crazy."

"I find it interesting that you choose to believe *that's* crazy. You're surrounded by vampires, creatures of myth that can supposedly take the form of a bat or wolf at will. Real, actual vampires. Some of us have lived for hundreds of years or more. You apparently have no problem accepting that, but when I tell you we can communicate with our thoughts, you say it's crazy?"

He frowned. "I guess I try not to think about the vampire part. I just kind of latched onto the lie you fed me about the effects of Charon. But telepathy, really?"

"I don't know how it works," she admitted. "I personally believe there have to be scientific explanations for all of the... unusual aspects of this life, but I haven't had an opportunity to research any of it. I hope that when I've finished my research with you for Colin, he'll allow me to investigate that.

"Regardless, yes, I can speak, after a fashion, directly to Colin. He can do the same with all of his Descendants. Now, please remove your clothes and have a seat on the bed. We need to get started."

Tom sat motionless, considering. Just talking about being studied for medical reasons was easy, but when push came to shove, he didn't much relish the idea of being poked, prodded, measured, or whatever else she had in mind.

Ana, who had gone back to evaluating her tools, looked at him with a raised eyebrow. "Tom, please."

Giving in, he stood up. "You win," he said. "We're due for a nice, long, honest chat about the real world, anyway."

If she noticed his special emphasis on the word "honest," she gave no indication. Pressing ahead, she picked up a rubber strap and a syringe from the table. "Fine. The bed, please?"

He pulled his shirt off and stood near the bed. "I've heard you guys say things like 'Family,' 'Child,' and 'Descended.' They seem to mean different things."

She waited near the foot of the bed for him to finish undressing. "Family is sort of a generic term for anyone belonging to a particular Master. Vampires used to be solitary creatures, but there aren't many loners, what we call renegades, out there anymore, so we've begun thinking of ourselves as families. You might hear 'Clan' also, depending on where you are. A 'Child' is a member of a given family.

"'Descended,' though, is more specific. Colin Made me, as he did Ash. We are both, then, his Descendants.

Lars, however, was apparently not turned into one of us by Alexander, so he is not Descended from his lord.

"That came as something of a surprise, actually. It's rare to be so high in the chain of command of one who didn't make him. I can only imagine what Lars had to do to prove his loyalty and be deemed worthy of such a position."

Tom, down to only a pair of boxer shorts, tried, without much success, to look relaxed. A crisp night breeze blew through the drafty room, raising goosebumps on his bare skin. He didn't care about Lars's position within Alexander's family, clan, or whatever, but maybe asking for more details would keep him preoccupied and not focused on the bitter chill.

"Why would he have to be extra loyal or more worthy just because Alexander isn't the one who turned him?"

Ana tied the strap around his bicep and tapped his arm. "Lords are typically cautious about who they have close to them. Even though we obey them, anyone could challenge them at any time. It is not like there are many real laws among us. Anyone in a position of power, then, has to know they can trust their lieutenants absolutely. Descendants are far more trustworthy because being linked to one's Maker leaves little opportunity for betrayal. Like I said, we have little free will when it comes to them."

"You're serious about that?"

"If I did something against Colin's wishes, he would know about it almost immediately, and the telepathic bond makes it twice as hard to disobey. Had Alexander had one of his own in Lars's position, Ash would have had a much more difficult time taking over here. And both of us would certainly be dead." She drove the needle into Tom's arm, and blood rushed into the attached glass cylinder.

"Um, how is it you're not going kind of crazy? Aren't you all bloodthirsty all the time? Lars and Ash both almost lost it when they got close, and that was just them standing next to me. Drawing a sample can't be easy."

The corners of Ana's mouth twitched upward slightly. "I told you—I have never had human blood. I am not an animal. I gather from others that there's something different about it, unique. Like a drug. I've intentionally stayed away from it to prevent myself from forming a dependency. Yes, that means I'm never satisfied, but it's much easier to live with myself this way."

"Not even a taste?"

"Never. Colin forced me to try hunting once before Charon made the old ways pointless, but I refused to hurt the poor woman he'd chosen for me. I feel bad enough that I've had to resort to living on the animals I can find."

"Saved by the world's first vegetarian vampire." Tom laughed. "I'm sorry, but that's funnier than hell."

Ana raised her eyebrows. "I'm glad you find my predicament so amusing."

Still smiling, he said, "I'm sorry, I just… Well, anyway, all these years, and you've never drunk from a human? How long has it been?"

"You'd be surprised." She gave a slight smile.

"Well, how old are you? A hundred years? Fifty?"

Ana shook her head. "No. I'm younger than you, actually. I was in my late twenties when Colin turned me.

That was only three years ago. It happened just before Charon became so widespread."

Tom's mouth hung open. In horror movies and books, vampires were always ancient creatures, centuries old or more. They'd lived through the most dramatic episodes in history and wandered the globe, feeding on people. Yet Ana was actually younger than him.

"I had no idea," he mumbled, not sure what else to say.

She shrugged.

"What about the Feral? Who controls them and how?"

Pen in hand, she made a few notes in a notebook as she explained. "They're pretty much what I said before: mutations resulting from Charon. But vampire mutations, not human. Vampires that fed on someone carrying it got it just like a normal person would, and for some reason, our immunity to infection didn't work. But the disease doesn't kill us. It turns us into those monsters.

"I honestly don't understand it, but after just a few hours of contact, we become like animals. We lose the ability to speak, and our appearance changes permanently. In addition, our behavior becomes more violent, and we generally lose any kind of impulse control. It's like some form of devolution."

"What about the control, then?"

"The telepathic link survives the change, so the only way to control them is through their Maker. Whoever turned them into a vampire in the first place can make them behave as desired. But there are plenty of Feral out there without a living Maker or whose Maker is a plaguer as well. Those are all uncontrolled, and they roam the world like wild dogs. Worse, they easily outnumber us."

Tom shivered, thinking about the Feral, and the skin on his arms prickled with even more goosebumps. He dropped the topic and let her work. Before long, though, the draft and the uncomfortable silence became more than he could take.

"Three years, huh?" he said at last. "And Colin was the one who did it—turned you, I mean? Just before Charon? I guess you got a little lucky there, at least."

She stopped writing and looked up from her notebook. Her usually dark, placid eyes held a swirling tempest. He cringed, expecting an angry outburst, even without knowing what he'd said to upset her. But the thunderous look disappeared as quickly as it had come.

Instead, she replied dryly, "I do not know that I would say it was *lucky*."

Before he could reply, she returned to her notes. Then she went on, "It was actually shortly after the initial outbreak, about a week before they dropped the bomb on LA."

"Really?" Tom said. "Why'd he do it, then, at that point? Doesn't seem like the right time to be adding to the Family."

"Because he's smarter than the others. He knew what was coming and saw the danger to our food chain. Making me like him was not an accident. He had a plan in mind and chose me intentionally."

"Why you?"

"Before Charon, I was a researcher with the Centers for Disease Control. When the outbreak was first reported, they sent me out to help isolate the virus. I was supposed to figure out what was happening and try to keep it under control. Colin was already thinking about things long-term, though. When he saw what the future held, he started looking for someone with a medical background. He found me, and apparently, I fit all his criteria. He dragged me to Seattle, turned me, and tried to get me to adapt to the lifestyle before everything completely fell apart." She looked up again. "Most nights, I wish he had left me in Los Angeles," she added softly. "It would have been better than this."

CHAPTER 26

Nothing seemed the right thing to say, so Tom said nothing. He wanted to console her, but words just weren't enough. Anything he could have said would have come out hollow, empty.

A difficult silence settled between the pair while Ana continued her exam. Occasionally, she gave him instructions or paused to take another of what seemed an endless series of samples. She poked and prodded at him in a hundred different ways, making for a long, largely unpleasant experience.

After what seemed like hours of sitting in his shorts and weathering Ana's scrutiny, she stepped away. She added a few more scribbles to her notebook, sighed, and caught his eye. That was the first time since they'd stopped talking that she seemed aware of him as a person rather than an object of study.

"I'm sorry, Tom, you're shivering."

The chill had been unpleasant when they began, and those goosebumps had lingered long past his thoughts of the Feral. At one point, he thought his teeth might chip from the chattering, but he'd had enough of showing his weaknesses, even to Ana. So he chose to ignore the discomfort and, after some time, managed to forget how cold the room was altogether. When she mentioned it, Tom was oblivious to the fact he was trembling.

"I'll be fine."

She clucked her tongue and shook her head. "Nonsense. I'll make sure you have a few blankets. We have to have some around here somewhere."

Someone cleared their throat conspicuously, startling them both.

Ana spun on her heel and stiffened, ready to defend them both if necessary.

Ash stood at the top of the stairs, inspecting the room casually, as if he'd just happened to drop by with no real purpose. His surfer image seemed cultivated to encourage that idea, but Tom knew better. The gruesome way Ash had appeared when they first met guaranteed he would never buy the charade.

He gave Ash a curt nod. If he was going to have to get along with him, they might as well be civil.

Ash completely ignored the gesture. In fact, he ignored Tom altogether, as if he were beneath him—an animal not particularly worthy of notice.

"Ana, a word?" Ash said.

She sighed loudly, a little too loudly, in fact. Irritation was written all over her face. Nonetheless, she set her notebook and pen on the table and walked over.

Lady had been lying quietly on the other side of the room throughout the exam. Her head was up now, though, no longer resting on her front paws. She watched Ash intently, ears forward. With a whistle, Tom called her over for some attention. Lady stood and stretched out, her front paws extended fully and rump in the air. She yawned in that distinctly canine way—producing a half yawn, half growl—before padding over. When she stood next to him, her coat tickled the leg dangling from the bed.

"That's a good girl," he said, brushing the fur along her side as she leaned her neck against his leg and rubbed slightly.

Tom turned his attention back to Ana and Ash, facing each other near the top of the step. As quiet as the pair had been, he half expected they'd disappeared below to talk about something private. Instead, they were glaring at each other. Ana's dark eyes burned. She wasn't happy.

A low rumble of warning rolled through Lady's chest and neck. Had she not been leaning against him, Tom probably wouldn't have noticed. At the same moment, an icy chill shot up his back from the base of his spine. It was a familiar, dreadful feeling.

It was the same thing that had first tipped him off to Heather's infidelity. She would say she was going out with her girlfriends or staying late for work, but something about the way she held herself spoke to him, or the way she met his eyes gave him tiny inklings of doubt, which accumulated. Eventually, those suspicions manifested in a sharp chill that blasted all the way to the base of his neck.

This was the same feeling. Something was very wrong.

Neither Ana nor Ash said a single word as he watched them, but eventually, her shoulders slumped. She looked down at the floor, beaten, disgust plain on her face.

Colin. They were having some kind of three-way conversation with Colin.

Ana held out a hand, and Ash put something small in it. Tom couldn't see what it was from so far, but it was colorless, maybe transparent, and small enough that she concealed it in her hand quickly.

His ears burned in contrast to the frigid bite of warning between his shoulder blades.

He had to get away somehow. But with Ana and Ash standing in his path, he had no way to get to the stairs.

He sprang from the table and dashed toward the window with the most cracks. If he threw himself at it just right, maybe he would go through the glass and land on the concrete ledge just beyond. It was a desperate plan with almost no chance of success, but he had few other options.

Lady snarled behind him then yelped just as suddenly, and he fought an overwhelming urge to turn back for her. He had little enough chance as it was—if he stopped or looked back, he had none.

His bare feet slapped on the uneven floorboards. He was ten steps from the window. Eight steps, six, then four—for a fleeting instant, he dared hope to make it. With just three more steps and a little luck, he'd be out of this place one way or the other.

He shouted when Ash seemed to materialize right in front of him with a wicked grin. Tom slammed into the vampire, expecting to knock him down, but instead began falling backward. Before he hit the ground, though, something latched onto his arms and legs with an iron grip that had become much too familiar.

Four of Ash's lackeys surrounded him, each holding a limb.

He squirmed and kicked, struggling to get free, but it was no use. They carried him toward the bed without effort.

As they crossed the room, Reg, the sickly-looking vampire with the greasy black hair from Lars's crew at the hospital, passed through his line of sight. He was holding onto Lady tightly, her back against his torso. One dirty hand held her muzzle shut while the other clung to her chest.

"Don't you dare hurt her!" Tom screamed. With panic swelling in his throat, he was shocked to find he had any voice at all.

Ana approached the dog cautiously, and Lady jerked against her captor, but Reg held tight. Ana put her left hand on the dog's neck and produced a syringe in her right. The needle disappeared into Lady's neck, and Ana depressed the plunger.

Lady slid limply from Reg's grasp.

"No!" Tom cried in horror.

He barely heard Ash chuckling over the thrumming of blood in his own ears. He and Reg laughed as Lady lay motionless on the floor. Tom's whole body burned with rage. "Let go of me!" he roared, thrashing against the four sets of hands carrying him.

He might as well have been struggling against steel bars.

They lifted him up and set him on the bed, forcing his arms and legs down. He continued to buck and bounce, hoping for a miracle, but his efforts were wasted. Finally, he surrendered.

Ana stepped into his line of sight. "I'm sorry, Tom. I'm so sorry."

His face grew cold as the color drained from it. "What did you do to her? Whatever they make you do to me, don't let them have her. Keep her safe. Promise me she'll be safe!"

"I'm sorry," she repeated, raising another syringe to her eye level. She flicked the needle a couple of times with a finger, and beads of clear fluid flew from it.

"What is that? What are you doing?" Desperate, Tom screamed, "Let me go!" His throat scratchy and hoarse, he watched in shocked disbelief as Ana leaned over him.

She eyed each of the four guards gripping his arms and legs in turn. "Firmly," she commanded, as calm as ever. Finally, she looked Tom in the eye, and the same storm that had so briefly appeared there before was swirling in the darkness. A shiny tear rolled down her cheek. "I'm so sorry. God forgive me." With that, she drove the needle into his arm and injected the full volume of that clear fluid.

His stomach churned in revulsion, and everything went black.

CHAPTER 27

"**W**E HAVE TO KNOW WITH *absolute certainty.*" The voice in Ana's head had been calm and clipped. She shuddered, hoping Ash didn't notice. Hearing someone thousands of miles away speaking directly into her thoughts gave her chills, as always. It was the same prickly, uncomfortable sensation she used to get while working in the morgue late at night as a student. But she couldn't let them know how much she disliked the experience. Still being so poorly adjusted to her new life was difficult enough.

"*Colin, please,*" she thought. "*He's lost whatever trust in me he might have had. I need to earn it back. But if we go through with this, it will destroy any chance I've got to do that. Give me a little time. A few more days. By the time you get here, hopefully we'll be able to do it with his consent. He's not an animal. He should be given a choice.*"

Ash smirked, but it was Colin's voice she heard: "*Your brother claims that they are all animals, that your human should be used for meat. He also thinks we've wasted enough time and energy and taken unnecessary risks. He asks if you would have risked war over a dairy cow before you were*

Made. We should act swiftly and get it over with before Alexander's Family grows a backbone."

She scowled at Ash, imagining what he'd actually thought to Colin. Unfortunately, the connection didn't work that way. *"Tom is* not *a cow or any other kind of animal. He's a human, just as we were once. Lord, please, just a—"*

"Enough." The word was quiet and authoritative, carrying traces of Colin's formerly noble British accent.

The tranquility of his voice, even when giving commands, was not unusual. Ana had never heard him speak—or think—in anything other than measured tones. He expected his Children to do his bidding without thinking, like well-trained soldiers. According to rumor, if he raised his voice to anyone, that was the last thing they heard.

"Daughter, Ash is certainly wrong: the risk is necessary. He is, however, correct about the danger. We are balanced precariously in this situation, and if I'm going to risk a war over a human, I have to know he can serve his intended purpose. If you had managed to reach home, the potential conflict might have been avoided. But you failed, and now, we must adapt to the situation at hand.

"Now, it has become a much more complicated issue of territory. That's acceptable, as the potential gains are even greater, but so are the risks. And I will not risk so much without being certain that the prize is worthwhile."

The sting of shame from Colin's rebuke burned in Ana's cheeks. Her shoulders drooped as her resolve evaporated. He'd already made up his mind, so the discussion was over.

She hated that he could make her feel this way. She'd never consented to being Made, to giving him such power over her.

Colin wasn't quite finished. *"Regardless, time is a luxury we don't have. I expect to arrive the evening after next. Some things must be set in order before we begin hearing from our new neighbors from the other regions. Before that happens, I* will *have the support of Alexander's Children and* will *know exactly what we have to bargain with. Which means I want to know as much about our human as possible upon my arrival. So, yes, you will do it, and you will do it now."*

Ash pressed the vial of tranquilizer solution into her hand.

As her skin crawled from the force, for lack of a better term, of Colin's thoughts, he added, *"Your brother says he has help below, ready to come up and take care of any potential… difficulties. Just do what you need to do quickly, and everything will be fine."*

A rustling noise from behind grabbed her attention, and she turned to see Tom make a mad dash to the window. She gasped—he was planning to throw himself out the window.

Whether that had been his true intention or not, thirty seconds later, it was all but over. Lady was lying on the floor unconscious, her tongue lolling out, and Tom sprawled on his back on the bed, breathing regularly. She had the vague urge to vomit but knew that was a psychological reaction. Her kind simply didn't throw up.

A full day later, she was leaning against the broad desk in the pale light of early evening, watching Tom sleep. He should have been waking up at any moment. That was what she hoped, at least. Lady had moved slightly since Ana left them the night before, which was welcome news.

When the commotion finally settled, Reg had been standing over the dog with a ravenous look, and she had feared he'd already done the dog some harm. After a sharp word from her, though, he slunk down the steps, looking sullen and even more weasel-like than usual.

That one... He gave her the willies, especially the way he looked at Tom and Lady. He was certain to do something treacherous eventually. Not for the first time, she allowed it was a shame that she wasn't the kind of person who just... took care of that kind of problem.

Ana nibbled absently on the nail on the middle finger of her right hand. Frowning, she forced herself to stop. The habit—the weakness—embarrassed her, and she struggled to suppress it. When preoccupied or stressed, though, all self-discipline slipped away, and the quirks of her former life appeared, including nail biting, scratching at her cuticles, and picking at the skin on her thumbs.

At the moment, she would have liked to do all three at once.

The nail regenerated quickly. She smiled, glad that hiding that particular habit was so easy. If only getting rid of it were as simple... But for her kind, breaking old habits was harder than teaching the proverbial old dog new tricks.

Tom stirred, and a leaden weight hit her stomach. How could she tell him?

He groaned and shifted slightly on the bed. At least she'd dosed the tranquilizer about right to coincide with nightfall.

His eyelids fluttered, struggling to stay open. After a few cycles of opening and closing, they finally held, and his coffee-brown eyes focused. Tom lifted a hand and rubbed his forehead. "Unnnhhh... What happened?"

"Carefully, slowly," she said from the side of the bed. "Do you want me to help you sit up?"

He nodded. Ana took one scarred arm, lifted him into a seated position, and turned his body so his legs flipped over the side.

"What do you remember?"

"I remember..." he began. Tom cocked his head and narrowed his eyes. He snatched his arm away. "I remember."

"Tom, let me—"

"Go fuck yourself."

Again that familiar, loathsome, stinging warmed her cheeks. But nothing would be gained by antagonizing him while trying to defend herself further, especially since what she'd done couldn't be defended. But he had to trust her again, somehow.

She avoided his face, not wanting to wilt beneath the harsh glare she knew he'd be giving her.

"What did you do to Lady?" he asked.

"Nothing," she replied, sneaking a look up. "I wouldn't go along with them unless they let me tranquilize her. I didn't want her to get hurt, but we knew she wouldn't let us..."

"Let you do what?"

She hesitated then blurted out, "Tom, Colin wanted you tested. He made me inject you with something so he would be sure his plans would work."

His face flushed as he idly scratched at the spot where she'd given him the injection. "What plans? What did you inject me with?"

"It's… Tom, I…" Her hands came together, fingers chipping at a thumbnail. With a frown, she forced them into the pockets of her new white lab coat. Finally, looking him in the eye, she said, "Charon." It was nearly a whisper.

He blanched and looked as though he might throw up. "Tell me that's a sick joke."

Again, she hung her head, unable to look at him.

"What the hell were you thinking?" he shouted. "You gave me the goddamn plague on purpose?"

Instinctively, an apology almost bubbled out of her, but she caught it at the tip of her tongue and swallowed it. No amount of "I'm sorry" could ever make up for what they'd done.

"Jesus, Ana," he said, somewhat cooler. "Why?" Then, "How long do I have?"

"I'm so sorry, Tom. Colin forced me. He said he needed to know if you were immune or just lucky."

The excuse hung in the air between then, ringing hollow even in her own ears.

"I'm supposed to feel better about it because he forced you?" Tom spat. "How long until he forces you cut me open just to see if my heart is still beating? God dammit! I should have just left you hanging up there." He nodded across the room at the post where she'd been shackled before Ash arrived.

Deep down, a part of her agreed. Finally losing all self-control, she resumed nibbling on her fingernail.

"So how long? A day? Two? I'll tell you right now—you're getting me out of here. I don't care if I have to take a chainsaw to every pair of fangs in the building and then set the place on fire. I am not going to die of the plague locked up like a prisoner, surrounded by… monsters. You owe me that much, at least."

"Tom, I-I… can't. I wish I could, but it's impossible. And before you say anything else, let me tell you everything. You were given a direct dose of Charon large enough that the incubation period would have been minimal. You were exposed over twelve hours ago, which is plenty of time for the virus to get started. At this point, you should have symptoms that include congestion, fatigue, general achiness, and perhaps even a fever."

He looked back at her, face blank.

"Tell me how you feel."

Tom put a hand to his head and frowned. "Fine. My arm itches a little, and I think I strained my shoulder trying to get away. But I don't think I have any of that other stuff."

Relief flooded through her. A tiny smile barely revealed a fraction of what she felt. Could he actually be immune? Was it possible?

"Looking at you, I would have guessed you weren't feeling any symptoms. You appear well. There's a chance we may have gotten lucky. But I need to check a few things to be sure."

Tom's eyes narrowed, and she wasn't surprised. She'd expected hesitation about going through another round of tests.

"Tom, I know you have little faith in me at the moment. I won't ask for any more. But I need to do a basic examination and take another round of samples. Then, in a few hours, we will know for certain. If you would rather, however, I can just leave you alone, but that means you will have to wait twenty-four to forty-eight hours to be sure."

He straightened on the bed, apparently trying to find a more authoritative position, even still in his boxers. Making his face hard, he said, "You're wrong. I have *no* faith in you at the moment. But fine. Do it quickly and get out."

Nodding, Ana picked up her stethoscope from the table. She had a lot to accomplish and precious little time to work. She set the earpieces in her ears and rubbed the diaphragm side of the chest piece out of habit. Her hands, though, had long since stopped being warm enough to take the chill away. She placed it gingerly on his chest.

"Breathe deeply."

She listened to his breathing from several places and checked his heart rate. "Your respiration is good. No evidence of congestion at all, and your pulse is strong. Blood pressure next."

She wrapped a blood-pressure cuff around his arm. "Doing a basic exam reminds me a lot of when this all began. I examined hundreds of people in a very brief time in LA, when Charon first struck. Every single time, I prayed to find someone who didn't have it. I pleaded with God to let me hear just one person breathe normally or to find a heartbeat that was not starting to lag. How much joy it would have given me then, back before—"

Tom grunted. Apparently, he didn't feel like talking.

That was just fine. More than anything, she needed him to listen. If he heard enough, everything might still work out.

"I don't often have much chance to do this kind of thing anymore," she went on. "I enjoyed our first months together back at the high school, even though I was constantly worried about being found. Checking in on you regularly and nursing you back to strength—it reminded me why I got into medicine in the first place. Brought back memories of when I worked with the CDC in Atlanta."

The cuff swelled. Ana stopped talking to listen to the blood pump through him. Her more acute hearing made this much easier than back in those days, but even so, she couldn't quite do it without the stethoscope.

Releasing the valve on the pump ball, she listened again while the air flowed from the device. Finally, she let it deflate fully and pulled apart the Velcro holding the cuff on his arm. "Your blood pressure is normal."

"Well, thank God," he said, rolling his eyes. "I'd hate to have to cut back on my salt."

Pretending not to hear, she picked up a syringe and a pair of vials for a blood sample.

"I miss Atlanta," she said, prepping his arm for the withdrawal. "Not just the work, but I liked living there so much better than Seattle. It was usually warm, at least, if not hot, and I used to be the kind of person that was always cold. I would wear a sweater sometimes even when it was ninety degrees. It was much more my kind of place."

The needle pierced the skin of his arm and sank into a blood vessel. Knowing she'd hit her mark, she attached one of the glass vials and watched the crimson fluid pump into it. When the first was full, she swapped it for a second one, which also filled quickly. Drawing blood was a lot easier since she was able to sense exactly where it flowed beneath the skin.

"I detested Seattle. In fact, I think if anything ever happened to Colin and I found myself a renegade, I'd move back to Atlanta. I hear that the Master of the South, a very old one of us named Emily, is supposed to be pretty reasonable, as far as that goes.

"That's just gossip, of course, but it makes a certain amount of sense to me. At her age, she would be one of the most powerful of us, which also means, I suppose, she would rarely be threatened. So it's easy to believe that she might be somewhat more open-minded, especially when it comes to trying to protect and provide for her Family. I imagine she'd be willing to at least hear my thoughts about researching our kind and finding ways to feed us.

"Not that it matters at the moment, of course. I'm happy to serve Colin as he commands. But it would be nice to go back to Atlanta if I had the opportunity."

Tom, who had been transfixed by something across the room, turned to Ana. His face still impassive, he asked in an icy tone, "How much longer will this take?"

"I'm finished for now." Ana sighed. "Get dressed if you'd like."

"About time. Go, then."

"As you wish." Tom said nothing else while getting dressed, so she collected the things needed for the rest of her work, including her notebook and the samples she'd taken. At the staircase, Lady, finally having woken up as well, got to her feet and wobbled over to him near the bed.

It was a good sign that the dog hadn't charged her immediately.

Maybe the hope she clung to would not turn out to be misplaced after all.

After watching Tom pat Lady gently for a few moments, she finally said, "I'll be back tomorrow evening with the test results and to prepare for Colin's arrival. Let us know if you need anything or begin to feel symptoms. And, Tom, I… truly… am sorry." With that, she climbed down the steps, pulling the trapdoor behind her.

She had done what she could—the rest depended on Tom.

CHAPTER 28

TOM RUBBED LADY ON THE scruff of her neck. "I'm sorry, girl. Are you okay?"

She painted a sloppy tongue swipe on his cheek.

"I'm not sure how we're going to get out of this mess, but we'd better figure something out fast. Things are going to get a lot worse if we're still here when Colin shows up."

Lady backed out of his reach and shook out her whole body, head to tail. She chuffed twice.

"What's the problem?"

She staggered to the trapdoor, nearly falling over once. Tom couldn't help but be a little amused. Lady looked like she'd had a few too many drinks. Then again, he hadn't yet tried walking across the room himself.

She stopped beside the trapdoor and tapped it a few times with a paw. She chuffed twice again.

"What? Need to go for a walk or something? I guess we have been up here a while."

The dog woofed a couple more times, more firmly, and tapped on the door again. She was trying to make a point, one he was missing.

Tom stood, waiting a few seconds to make sure his legs weren't going to give way. Thankfully, they held beneath him—a little wobbly, to be sure, but workable. Still, he'd need something to eat before he felt like himself again.

He hobbled over to the trapdoor. Nothing looked out of place. He shrugged and knelt beside the dog.

"I'm not seeing it."

Lady cocked her head. She tapped at the trapdoor again.

Tom's face brightened in a flash of understanding. The trapdoor had four locks, one on each corner, and he'd heard none of them clasped shut when Ana left.

Giving the dog a wide smile, he said, "She left the damned locks undone, didn't she?"

Lady woofed again, tail wagging enthusiastically.

"That's a very good girl. I'm getting you a whole steak when we get out of here. Even if I have to learn how to butcher the thing myself." Rubbing her on the head and scratching her chest, he added, "Now, we just have to hope no one notices before morning."

The next few hours of the night trickled past like the lazy drip of a leaking faucet. Tom paced in front of the window, slow and steady, waiting for the first hint of morning to appear on the horizon. With each passing second, he dreaded every sound, expecting to hear the locks slide into place beneath them. Beads of sweat gathered at his forehead, even with the cool night breeze blowing through cracks in the windows. Each creak of the century-old building taunted him.

He should have slept. He desperately needed to sleep, really, especially as the next day was going to be either very long or very short. But a combination of impatience and anxiety made it impossible. Drifting off in the middle of an earthquake would have been easier.

After he spent an eternity staring toward the east, the sky began to brighten. The locks never rattled together. No one came to seal them in. They just needed a little more patience and a whole lot of luck.

If waiting through the night had been a trial, resisting the urge to dart through the trap at first light was outright torture. At last, when the sun stood all the way above the horizon, Tom tiptoed over to the trapdoor with Lady beside him. His fingers slipped easily under the edge of the door, and he whispered a prayer to anyone or anything that might still be listening.

Nothing was left but to lift and hope.

The fear that he was totally wrong about the locks swirled in the back of his mind, tangling with the almost impossible hope that they might have a chance to get out. The mix of the two things made him want to throw up.

He lifted slowly, carefully, dreading the moment when the door caught on the locks and held tight. But it didn't. It rose a few inches from the floor, unimpeded, and relief washed over him.

Tom's lips moved with a comment for Lady, but his nerves had a firm grip on his voice, and the words got trapped in his throat. His voice finally squeaked on the third attempt as he said, "I'll lift just enough for you to fit through. Go do your thing."

Lady put her nose to the small opening and sniffed. Then she pushed up against the bottom of the panel with her muzzle, signaling for him to lift higher. He did, and she darted into the darkness below.

Tom didn't even twitch for the brief time she was gone. Like a statue, he held the panel ajar, breath trapped in his lungs, focused on the space below. He strained to catch any sound that might rise from the stairway.

Finally, Lady's paws tapped on the steps softly, announcing her return. After coming back into view, she stopped and sat down, waiting for him.

The coast was apparently clear enough to proceed.

He raised the door a few more inches but stopped with it halfway open. Lady cocked her head at him, as if wondering what was taking him so long.

He waved a finger and whispered, "Don't move. Just a second," and lowered the panel back to the floor.

Tom stepped carefully over to the corner of the room where the cast-off building supplies had been left to rot. He grabbed one of the few remaining framing studs and turned back. Carrying the thing was probably pointless. It certainly hadn't been much help the last time around. But they might come across anything—from a pair of Feral to Colin himself—on the way to the outside door. Having something—anything—that could be used as a weapon seemed the wisest choice.

Tom set the two-by-four on the floor and lifted again, glad to find Lady fixed to the same spot. He smiled and slipped through the trapdoor. Reaching back, he grabbed the piece of wood and stole down the steps, letting the door settle flush with the ceiling above him. Holding his breath, he let go, praying it didn't make a racket.

It didn't.

Without light from the windows above, the steps were incredibly dark. Tom stood in place, giving his eyes time to adjust. Losing his balance and rolling to the bottom would be disastrous. He would literally make enough noise to wake the dead.

At least, he assumed that was how it worked. He'd never thought to ask Ana what her kind actually did during the day. They didn't go outside, clearly, and they'd talked warily enough of the sun that the traditional vampire sunlight myths had to be true. But did they have to sleep all day? Or was their rest optional?

He'd seen Ana at daybreak before, and Lars's group walked them through the subway tunnels just after dawn, so they didn't just drop off at first light like a narcoleptic. He would have given his eye teeth to know whether they rested lightly or rather in some kind of heavy trance. Since their senses seemed a lot more like Lady's than his own—making detecting clumsy humans fumbling around in the dark easier—he hoped it was the latter, for both their sakes.

Either way, he had no time to fret about it.

"Go. Slowly," he whispered, feeling the words in his throat more than hearing them come from his mouth.

The dog, little more than brownish patches of fur, took a few steps forward. He tiptoed behind her, concentrating on each footstep.

He cursed himself for not thinking to take his boots off before they began, but he wasn't about to pause now, not when they were possibly minutes away from the sunlit world outside.

Only one floor down, Tom felt beads of sweat rolling down his face, yet he had to remind himself over and over to keep moving. The temptation to stop and strain, listening for any hint of alarm, was almost too much. But Lady, with her more acute senses, was ahead of him. He had to trust her to let him know if something was wrong.

Foot over foot, step by step, the pair descended toward the main room in silence. Finally, after what seemed an eternity of creeping downstairs, shoulders tight with tension and sweat rolling down his back, Tom set his foot down on the floor at the bottom.

Aside from Lady, no other beings were in sight, living or dead. He sighed deeply, but after just a moment's pause, he pressed on. They weren't out of the woods yet.

CHAPTER 29

WITH THE MOTION OF HIS own hand, which Tom could hardly see in the dark, he waved Lady to the large door on the south wall, the same one they'd used before for their walk. Their first time out, the thing had creaked like it had been rusted shut for a decade. A noise that grating would shatter the silence of the building and could be an alarm signaling his escape to everyone. That could be the end of his chance.

He would've paid every dollar he'd ever earned for a small can of oil or lubricant. Without it, he had little choice but to grit his teeth, move quickly, and pray.

Touching the cold metal bolt gave him a shiver. It was now or never. With a deep breath and a silent prayer, he pushed the bolt to the side, hands trembling. It slid easily along its track, clearing the door with minimal noise.

One step closer.

Lady padded in a circuit around the room, stopping every few feet. He knew her ears would be twitching forward even if he couldn't see them. After walking a full circuit, instead of returning to him, she took up a position by the archway leading to the lagering cellars below. She must have assumed, like he did, that trouble would probably come from that direction if it came.

Tom gripped the handle and counted to ten. Once he took the next step and the silence was shattered by the groans and creaks of the old door, he'd have to think and move quickly. He was totally assuming—or was it hoping?—that the door through the office, the one leading outside, wasn't locked. The other day, they'd had a key. But they hadn't locked it on the way back in, to the best of his memory, so it should still be open.

Reaching ten, he gave the door handle a light tug. It nearly flew toward him, opening several inches without any noticeable sound and hardly any resistance. The corners of his mouth twitched in a small smile. Someone must have oiled the thing.

So far, everything was easier than expected.

Tom gave the door one more measured pull, conscious of moving it forward as smoothly as possible. To his horror, a squeak of rusty metal hinges filled the room.

Tom swore under his breath. Quickly, now.

He slipped through the opening and into the office beyond, ignoring the hammering in his chest. "Get out, get out, get out," he muttered. He had to focus and ignore the panic growing in his chest.

He sprinted across the room, crashing into a wooden chair in the process. It nearly brought him to the floor in a tangle, but he righted himself, threw it aside, and reached the door.

He'd risked everything, hoping that the door to daylight would be unlocked when he reached it. But he'd been wrong—it was locked securely.

A wide grin spread across his face.

The steel key Ana had used to open it protruded from the keyhole.

With a hasty word of thanks, he twisted it with as much force as he dared apply, remembering how it had gotten stuck before. It met resistance as it spun in the lock but gave way easily enough with a clack. Then, with a half turn of the doorknob and a tug, he gasped as glorious sunlight filled his vision.

Nearly overcome, Tom raised his hand to shield his eyes from the intense light.

A hard grip seized his shoulder, and his joy crystallized into sharp, cold dread.

Toms was forcibly spun around, and his view of the sunny outside world was replaced by Reg's dirty, weasel-like face.

"Think you're going somewhere?"

Tom swallowed hard and lurched backward, trying to get through the doorway and into the sun. But he couldn't move.

"Maybe not just yet," Reg said, sneering. "I thought I heard somethin' slip down past me on the steps. But I figured it was one of the others sneakin' about, one of Ash's, maybe. God knows they do enough of it. Suppose if I'da smelt or listened better, I'da knowed it was you. But my momma always said I'd miss the nose on my face if it weren't attached."

A warm, comfortable feeling washed over Tom.

The framing stud hung limply by Tom's side. Part of his brain urged him to use it—he needed only a moment's diversion to slip outside—but a larger part railed against the idea. Why bother wasting all that energy on something so pointless? Yes, he should maybe just stay here.

"Lookit my luck, bein' a bit awake," the disheveled man continued, "an' now I get to be Colin's hero when he gets here. I betcha he'll let me have a taste or two of you, as a prize. Just a few drops, o' course, not much, just enough to show everyone how it pays to be on his team. Yep, I'm almost sure he will.

"And damn, boy, do you smell good. I ain't had any real-people blood in so long. It almost hurts me to think of it. In fact, I jus' don't think I can help myself. I think I'll just take a little taste now. You gotta give yourself a treat once in a while, you know?"

The words flowed through Tom like a melody, in and out, barely registering. He frowned, drawing his eyebrows together. Was someone talking to him? Wait. He'd forgotten something, something important.

Reg opened his mouth wide, revealing a pair of dingy gray fangs. He lifted Tom's forearm to his mouth. In a bare whisper, he added, "Yeah, right on the arm where she was poking you. No one'll notice. 'Specially not with all the scars."

The vampire bit down into Tom's arm just above the wrist. Blood poured out into Reg's waiting mouth. He lapped at the pair of seeping punctures like a cat with a bowl of cream.

Tom's eyes rolled up. He drifted…

The room erupted in a frenzy of screams and fur. Tom blinked away the haze in time to see Reg's head snap back, away from him. Lady had jumped on the vampire's back, locking her powerful jaws on his neck.

Reg twisted, grabbing at the dog behind him with little success.

Shaking his head clear, Tom raised the framing stud and waited for the vampire to spin back to face him. A pair of grimy, red-stained fangs came into view, and he swung with every ounce of strength.

Focused on the German shepherd on Reg's back, the vampire's eyes grew with surprise as the lumber crunched into the front of his face. Screaming, he fumbled sideways, careening into the chair Tom had hit moments before. He, too, barely managed to avoid hitting the floor. His hands covered his mouth, now bleeding profusely. Defensively, he turned away from Tom.

Stepping up behind him, Tom slid the piece of wood across the vampire's chest for leverage. He then heaved backward, hoping they were still in front of the doorway.

Lady, having let go when the framing stud met the vampire's teeth, stood opposite them, facing Reg. She dashed forward at the same time Tom heaved, powering into Reg, hammering him square in his chest. All three of them fell through the door… into the bright daylight beyond.

Tom and Reg stumbled several steps together, away from the building and into the street. Out of Tom's control, the pair's momentum drove them backward, hard onto the pavement.

On his back, Tom hit the street first, still holding the two-by-four tightly across Reg's chest. His opponent came down on top of him, pushing all the air from his lungs in the process.

Reg wailed—a blood-curdling, high-pitched squeal—

and his whole body started thrashing. Lady barked an alarm from the sidewalk. Seeing stars and desperate to get air back in his lungs, Tom let go of the wood and heaved the weight on top of him to his right. Reg, still bucking, and now groaning, rolled clear of him.

Gasping for breath, Tom wrenched himself up, regripping the stud with blood-smeared hands. He raised the wood over his head, ready to bludgeon the vampire lying in the street as soon as he got his wind back.

Breath finally came in shallow gasps, not quite panting. With it, the acrid, bitter smell of smoke mingled with the reek of charring flesh and hair filled his nose. Tears ran down his cheeks. Nearly retching, Tom turned away and tried to blink the stinging smoke from his eyes.

Breathing and vision returned to normal. The street was quiet and still. Reg had stopped thrashing or making any noise. Tom turned back and froze, mouth hanging open. Small, blue flames engulfed the smoldering heap on the ground. Reg was motionless, quite dead, and quickly burning away.

Tom marveled at the process. The extremities turned black first and curled away like newspaper put to a match. Light, delicate ashes freed themselves from the body and floated away as the charring continued up the arms and legs. In seconds, nothing was left but the torso and head. Soon after, the chest collapsed upon itself.

Not even a minute had passed since they tumbled out of the building. In that span, Reg was reduced to little more than ash being carried away by the wind.

Tom dropped to a knee and took several deep breaths.

Lady sniffed at the black spot left in the street then walked over to press her muzzle against his chest.

He stroked her black fur in return. "No time to rest. We have to go."

The door of the building stood open still, and Tom half expected to find a beehive of activity beyond it. To his surprise, nothing moved within. No telling how long that would last, though. The fight with Reg had produced a lot more noise than he'd intended.

Turning away from the brewery, Tom looked up the street in one direction and then the other. Deep down, he'd never believed they'd succeed. Now, out in the open, he didn't know where they should go.

Lady chuffed beside him, and Tom smiled.

"Yes, I see it too."

A block away, the Mustang was parked conspicuously on the far side of the street. "Ana must have driven it over last night."

He shook his head as realization struck him like a load of bricks. Ana had planned it all, the only way she could, to keep Colin from suspecting anything. She left the trap door unlocked, left the key where he'd be sure to find it, and having shown him which exit to take, even brought the car close enough for them. She'd orchestrated all of it but quietly, passively, to avoid suspicion.

He owed her one. It was a pretty small one, considered what she'd let them do, though. She was still not high on his list of favorite people.

The pair walked to the car, and he pulled the handle experimentally. The door swung open freely, as he'd guessed. Lady hopped in and crossed over to the passenger's seat. Tom picked up his jacket from the driver's seat and pulled it on then smiled and slid into the car.

The keys were nestled in the cup holder between the two front seats. His smile grew when he pressed the Start button and the car roared to life.

She'd told him exactly where to go too.

CHAPTER 30

ANA SQUINTED THROUGH A MICROSCOPE, examining a slide mounted with a sample of Tom's blood. The piece of equipment was as basic a scope as she'd ever used, just enough to do the job, and sat on a workman's table that was almost, but not quite, the perfect height for her. A few inches taller would have been ideal, but under these conditions, she would take what she could get.

The beginner's microscope and too-short table weren't even the most inconvenient things about her working situation. The cramped lab room, which doubled as her sleeping quarters—it was the only private spot available—was deep below ground, where adequate electricity was difficult to come by. A number of pieces of lab equipment had been brought in and set up for her, but the only power she had was from extension cords going all the way back to the ground floor. Whenever she needed to use a different tool that needed power, something had to be unplugged first.

She hoped they'd move to a more modern location when Colin arrived.

The microscope's glaring white light brightened the

whole room. It was a stark contrast to the dim, fuzzy gloom put off by the pair of hanging work lights facing each other on opposite walls.

Scrutinizing the sample, Ana smiled, glad at not being bathed in shadows for once. Sunlight had been one of her favorite things in her first life, even though she'd always been fair and burned easily. In summer, she was rarely without a big hat and the heaviest sunblock she could find, but she still preferred being out in the sun with both any time she could sneak away.

Granted, the tiny microscope light wasn't as warm or welcoming as a walk in the afternoon sunlight, but it beat the ever-present shadows she lived in.

While she was scribbling something in her notebook, her ears twitched as footsteps in the hall announced someone approaching the closed door to her lab.

"Yes?" she called loudly. Hardly anyone came down unless they were looking for her. Its remoteness was part of the reason she'd chosen it, gloomy or not.

The door swung open. A young-looking vampire nodded at her, eyes shifting nervously. "Ana?"

"Yes?"

He was one of Lars's, one of the first to commit to Colin's leadership. He couldn't have been more than seventeen or eighteen when he was turned, but she could not guess how many years he'd lived, not aging, since then. "Um, Col—er—Lord Colin, has arrived. He wants you to come see him immediately."

A tremor of surprise ran through her. "Are you certain it was Lord Colin? Perhaps you are confused. Do you mean Ash? My lord will contact me directly when he arrives."

Ash sending someone for her would've been unusually pompous, even for him, but not entirely out of character. Colin, though, surely wouldn't arrive without contacting her.

Her nervous guest shifted on his feet. "No, um… it wasn't Ash. Some man I've never seen got here about an hour after nightfall. He looked… proper and told me he was Colin. I said my oath to him. Ash stood there the whole time. He told me this new guy was the big man now."

"After nightfall?" she asked, raising an eyebrow.

Ana looked at her watch. Time had completely gotten away from her again. It was a hazard of working so far from everyone else. When preoccupied, she often tended to forget the time of night and would end up working through much of her daylight rest period without noticing. Regardless, keeping Colin waiting wasn't smart.

"Take me to him," she said.

Colin's page turned and headed back up the dark hallway without another word. Ana followed in silence, hands jammed firmly into her lab coat pockets, mind spinning.

Walking at a brisk pace, they wasted little time making their way through the cellars. Back in the central room on the ground floor, her escort made for the staircase.

"Where is he? I expected we'd find him here, speaking to everyone," Ana said.

"No," the page replied over his shoulder. "He's in Alexander's office. He said he wanted to straighten a few things out before addressing everyone."

Ana frowned. A private meeting before assembling the group was unexpected. A welcome or greeting of some kind usually came before he got down to individual business. That he'd chosen to skip that spoke volumes about their circumstances.

She had little time to worry over it, though, and was standing before the doors of the former lord's office moments later. Raising her hand to knock, she heard a familiar voice say, "Come," before she struck the wood.

Little had changed in the office since her last visit. Colin sat behind the desk just as Alexander had, before a roaring fire, but without the foul-smelling cigarettes. Ash sat in one of the chairs opposite him, looking smug, as usual.

Colin was exactly as she remembered. Even seated, his unusual height was apparent. Standing, he would tower over her and Ash, as well as nearly everyone else in the building. He was thin, with long, slender fingers and a matching narrow face. With his meticulously combed white hair and finely wrinkled face, he had to have been in his advancing years when turned—or very, *very* old now. His eyes, though, a pale sky blue, were clear and confident. They were the eyes of a much younger person.

If not for them, he would have resembled someone's prim older uncle.

"It is good to see you, Lord," she said. "It has been too long."

"Indeed," he said, his tone seeming to absorb all the warmth from the room. "It seems that, left to your own devices, you're still losing track of time and not resting properly."

She flushed. "I try, but there is always so much work to do and too few hours in the night. With the exception, though, of the one time I passed out, I don't suffer for it. Still, I apologize for not being on hand for your arrival."

"Nonsense. You were not on hand because I shielded myself from you. Just before nightfall, Ash communicated to me that there was a significant problem here. I wanted to speak to him about it before making my arrival generally known."

Ana's eyebrows drew together. "What problem is that, Lord? I have not heard anything. Can I help in some way?"

"Yes, I don't doubt that you can. Before we get to that, though, tell me about the human. Do you have the results yet?"

Ana smiled. At least she had good news on that front. "Yes, my lord, my tests are complete and conclusive. Tom is immune to Charon. His system has eradicated nearly all traces of the dose I gave him, without so much as a sniffle. By now, his blood is likely completely clean of it."

"Good. Quite a shame, then," Colin said.

"My lord?"

"He is gone, Daughter. The trapdoor above was found unlocked, and the street door was wide open when Ash woke from his rest this evening. The room is empty. He and that mutt of his appear to have escaped, and one of Alexander's Family was killed in the process."

Ana gasped. "Has he been seen? Can we guess where he went? Please, set me to it. I can find him."

Colin shook his head softly. "Oh, my daughter. I have to admit I am somewhat impressed. Candidly, I am stunned with what you accomplished without tipping me off. It seems I overestimated your loyalty to the Family and underestimated your cleverness. Regardless, you know how he escaped and where he went. And you will tell me, right now, where he is headed. We've wasted too much time already."

"You know I wish to serve as best I can, Lord. For you and the Family. But I have no idea—"

"Enough!" Colin roared, standing up and slamming his hands on the desk. "Don't waste my time! Do you think I'm stupid?" Looming over her, he paused briefly to collect himself. "You seem to forget that I read your memories like a photo album. I can see you *forgetting* to take that key from the door when you returned from your walk to that car last night. And even now, remembering when you left the human alone yesterday, it's clear you neglected to set the locks. You set him free, you ungrateful little bitch, and you were careful enough about it to ensure I wouldn't stop you first."

Ana's face burned, and she threw herself out of the chair. She'd had enough. No more. Not from him. Not ever again. She glared into Colin's strangely young eyes across the desk. "I've... had it with you too... old man," she sputtered, struggling to come up with a decent insult. "To hell with you. To hell with you and *your* mutt too." She waved at Ash, still sitting in the chair beside her.

Ash raised an eyebrow and smirked, seeming to enjoy the show.

"I don't care what you do to me," she continued, "but I won't help you bring him back. With luck, he's out of your reach now. Do whatever you will. Kill me if you like.

You killed me once already—what difference does it make if you do it again? So go ahead, hang me up in front of a window, tie me down in the street, lock me in a room with half a dozen Feral, or be man enough to do it yourself. I don't care. I'm finished wasting my time.

"Of course, you'd better be sure you're done with my skills first. It's a little late for anyone else to become an MD."

Colin snarled, his face a mask of dark rage.

"Before you decide, though, I should tell you that I finally have everything I need to finish the task you set me. I can do what you wanted, and I *am* willing to do it. So maybe we can come to some… arrangement that doesn't end with my death. But I won't help you find him. I won't help you hurt him anymore."

She crossed her arms, a fire raging in her belly. She refused to look away from Colin's eyes, no matter how tremendously the force of his presence pushed her to be meek and subservient.

A minute slipped past, and neither spoke, moved, or blinked. It seemed like an hour to her, but she willed herself not to wilt.

"Why?" he asked finally. "Why would you do this to me? To your Family? I gave you a second life when the rest of the world was dying. I protected you in those chaotic months when the humans were falling like gnats and our brothers were becoming Feral by the dozens. I've kept you safe and fed when so many others were starving. After all that, why, Daughter, would you treat me this way?"

"You expect me to be grateful for *that*?" Ana fumed.

"You think I'm glad you Made me? I hate what you've done to me. I loathe it. Every night, I wake up, hoping to find out that this life is just a nightmare. The worst part of each of my days is when I realize it isn't. Before you did this to me, few things could make me as happy as a day spent in the warm sunshine, and now I'm constantly surrounded by darkness. I've huddled in shadows for three years, longing every single day to feel the sun on my skin while trying to cope with the knowledge that it would kill me in seconds.

"And that's not even the worst thing. You know quite well that I'll never have anything but contempt for you because…"

She looked away at last, inspecting the wooden surface of the desk in front of her. "Because," she whispered, "you killed my daughter when you turned me and took away any chance I might have for another."

Colin sighed and straightened. "Really, Ana. Must we go through this again? You know that I did you and your child a favor. You were barely halfway through your pregnancy when you were Made. Had I not, you and the baby both would have died of Charon long before you delivered it. I'm sure the feeling of that loss is terrible, but it wasn't my doing. It was inevitable. I simply made the decision to save the only one of you I could save." His voice was slow, patient, like a parent explaining sunrise to a child.

The condescension stung, but losing control would be disastrous. She was lucky to still be alive. Blood near boiling, she curled her hands into tight fists and replied through gritted teeth, "It was not your decision to make. It was mine. And you took it and my baby from me. And I will never forgive you for it."

"Ana, child, be reasonable. Surely you realize—"

The years of repressing everything he'd put her through were too much.

"I was pregnant!" she shrieked. "You want to know *why* I did it? I'll tell you why. You took that choice from me, so I took this choice from you. *I* decided to save Tom, to give him at least a chance at life. To make up for the life you stole from me."

Colin crossed his arms. "We settled this a long time ago, before any of this began. I thought you had decided to be sensible about it. I see I was wrong. I made a mistake, letting you spend so much time out on your own, without a chaperone. In fact, based on what I'm seeing in your memories now, I realize I've been much too lenient with you."

He recoiled suddenly and gave her a questioning look. "There are some strange things in your head, Daughter. We're going to have to talk about what you've been up to. Unfortunately, I don't have time for that discussion now."

He turned to Ash. "Who knows that the human escaped?"

"No one outside the room. More know about Reg's death, but only the three of us know about Tom."

"Good. Keep it that way. Make sure no one finds out."

"Yes, my lord."

"Is there a cell here, fit to hold one of us?" Colin asked.

"Yes, in the cellars below."

"Good. I see why Alexander chose this place. Take her down there. I'll decide what to do with her later."

"Yes, my lord," Ash said again.

"Once that is done, you are to leave immediately. Find the human and bring him back… alive. I don't care what you have to do, what steps you need to take, but we *must* get him back."

Ash gave Ana a smug look from the corner of his eye. "I will not fail you or the Family, my lord."

In short order, Ana was flanked by a pair of Ash's men and being taken toward the subterranean cellars. Ash swaggered a few steps behind.

"Why don't you give us a little resistance, princess? Something to justify a lesson. After that display in there, I think someone should teach you about respect."

"I have little doubt you would enjoy that," she replied. "I'm sorry to disappoint you, but I've accomplished what I'd wanted. Whatever happens now is out of my hands. I will accept Colin's decision willingly. And I pray that Tom eludes you."

"Don't you worry, princess," Ash said with a wicked grin. "I'll find him. And when I do, I'll make sure he regrets having gone running. Colin said to bring him back alive. Well, he'll be alive, but I can't promise he'll be happy about it. If I can't beat some manners into you, I'll have to take it up with him."

Ana's lips compressed. "You had better hope Colin orders my death, Ash. Because I swear I am going to make killing you a priority."

Ash erupted in laughter. Hours later, as she was hanging from the steel restraints in the same familiar cell, it still rang in her ears.

CHAPTER 31

THE MUSTANG SPED SOUTH ON the expressway, as fast as Tom dared push it. His daring didn't exceed eighty miles per hour, though. He wanted to go faster, but his eyelids were already drooping, as if holding up sandbags. Having been awake most of the night and a good part of the day was taking its toll, and the last thing he needed was to fall asleep at the wheel.

The car pinged, startling him from a drowsy trance brought on by the rhythm of mile after mile of uninterrupted highway. The low-fuel light glowed on the dashboard.

They'd stopped for gas already once, just outside Lexington, Kentucky, and were now only about fifty miles away from their destination. A fill-up could probably wait, but stopping seemed like a good idea. With several hours yet before sundown, he could find something to eat and a safe place to spend the night then figure out what to do next.

What to do next was his biggest problem.

Getting away from Alexander's region, which seemed to have become Colin's, was a good first step. But the United States was a big place, and even if some places might be relatively safe—largely deserted areas, maybe—he didn't know where to start looking.

Ana might have slipped him another idea, but he couldn't be certain. He wasn't exactly thinking objectively about her at the moment.

After their walk, he'd had little hope that she could or would assist him in any way. If that wasn't bad enough, she then injected him with the plague. Afterward, he could barely stand to be in the same room with her.

Several hundred miles, though, added perspective. He could see a number of very subtle things she might have done to help them get out.

That subtlety was the key. With her connection to Colin limiting her ability to help outright, if she'd wanted him to know something, it had to be hinted at. Nothing could be spoken outright.

With that in mind, going back over everything she'd said to him at the brewery led him to believe that Ana had come right out and told him what to do: go to Atlanta and find Emily—make her listen, and maybe she'll help.

Tom had to admit the idea was bold. It was also either brilliant or absolutely insane.

Searching for a different vampire lord seemed like suicide, but he wasn't going to be able to avoid Colin forever. For that matter, he didn't know how long he could realistically expect to stay alive on his own. Sooner or later, he'd stumble across a Feral, or another vampire would find him, and that, at best, would lead to more running and more trouble.

No, he needed a longer-term solution. If this Lord—or Lady—of the South, Emily, could help him somehow, perhaps in exchange for helping them feed, he'd do whatever he had to do.

Then again, he might have completely misinterpreted Ana. Maybe she had just been rambling on about Atlanta because she was feeling talkative. Maybe she was nervous because of Colin's visit. That possibility was hard to swallow, though. In the time they'd been together, she'd never been what he considered chatty. She almost had to have been trying to give him some kind of clue.

Being this close to the city, though, called for a more specific plan than "drive to Atlanta." How exactly was he supposed to set up a meeting with Emily without ending up dead first? He couldn't just call and ask for an appointment.

His first plan was to drive all over the city and spray-paint, "Man Seeks Emily," with a meeting time and place. But if that even worked, weeks could pass before someone noticed. And with Colin undoubtedly following close behind, that would be as big a sign to his people as hers. No, Tom needed to see Emily sooner. He had to find some other way.

He pulled off the highway at the next exit hosting a decent-sized commercial strip. He didn't know the name of the place, but it had everything he was looking for, including fast-food restaurants, gas stations, and several strip malls.

Even better, about a quarter mile down the road, a Walmart sign loomed high in the air. With luck, the sporting-goods department would still be in decent condition. Since he had the revolver back, he wasn't about to be caught without ammunition again.

A fresh set of clothes would be a welcome change too.

First things first, though. He pulled into a gas station with a convenience store. Tom followed Lady and her sensitive nose inside, just as they had back in that little town in Iowa.

The store was empty and, thankfully, still had power. Smiling, Tom exited with his arms stretched around a massive haul of quick-mart junk food. Nearly every single bag or can he'd found inside that might contain something edible fell into the trunk in an avalanche of wrinkled plastic and bright labels.

He popped the top off a bottle of Coke and ate a bag of nacho chips while standing beside the car, staring down the road at the Walmart.

"What do you think, girl?" he said, tossing Lady a chip. "What are the odds we'll find the place empty?"

She wagged her tail in reply, either for the chip or the question. It really made no difference. They needed the ammo.

After making the short drive down the road, Tom opened the door to the Mustang and stepped out with his gun and bat, Lady following after.

He secured the gun in his pants then ran his fingers over the barrel of the baseball bat, caressing where the words "Speak Softly" were cut into wood.

"I might have to get a pocketknife and carve 'Courage' on the other side," he said. "Don't you think it'd be more fitting, girl?"

The dog, which had trotted several feet closer to the store's main entrance, glanced back over her shoulder. Apparently not interested in the bat's inscription, she turned back and put her nose to the ground.

"Be that way," he said.

They stalked up to the door with caution, although with the sun shining, he didn't think it too likely that anything would burst out at them.

The main doors were clear glass, the automatic type that would slide apart. They didn't budge when he stepped on the pressure-sensitive pad, though. Either they were off or had no power.

He pressed his face to the glass. The building inside was dark, the kind of hazy gray that made the world seem filtered through gauze. Lights at intervals along the walls and support columns shone, though, making circles inside where the shadows were pushed back. Most likely, they were the emergency lights.

"That means some kind of electricity, right?" Tom mumbled.

He set the bat down and tried to wedge his fingers between the two panes. They moved apart but just barely. After a quarter or maybe half an inch, the doors stopped moving with a dull *thunk*, caught on a post or a catch of some kind, probably the lock.

Giving up, Tom moved to his right and tried the second set of sliding doors, with the same result.

"Well, looks like it's the hard way," he said to Lady.

He pressed his face to the door again and looked sideways, searching for a lock on the frame inside. After finding it near the top of the door, he picked up the Louisville Slugger and stepped back.

"Let's hope nothing's awake in there," he said and

lashed a swing at the glass. He struck the door exactly where he'd aimed, just next to the lock mechanism. But instead of punching through or even making a tiny crack, the bat thudded back toward him. Shockwaves reverberated through Tom's hands, up his arms, and into his shoulders.

He staggered back a step.

"If at first you don't succeed…"

Tom tapped the head of the bat on the target spot. With a deep breath, he pulled back and uncoiled once more. The bat bounced again, but this time, it came with the sound of nuts cracking. Several fine fissures appeared at the point of impact.

One more deep breath and another full swing brought the bat partially through the glass. It didn't erupt into the thousand sharp little pieces he'd hoped for, but he'd nonetheless opened a hole large enough to get his hand through to touch the lock. That was good enough.

Careful to avoid cutting himself on the glass, he spun the bolt inside until it clicked. With some effort, the doors slid apart after that. They resisted working against their motors, though, making the task a bit harder than he'd expected.

Regardless, he opened a gap wide enough for him and Lady to creep into the quiet, apparently empty space.

A long row of check-out lanes ran nearly the entire length of the dark building, from the far wall on Tom's right to just where he was standing. In front of them was the open center aisle, full of half-stocked displays. In the far back-right corner of the store, a sign hung from the ceiling over the sporting-goods department.

So much for a quick grab. They'd have to tiptoe through the whole store.

Lady put her nose in the air and sniffed several times. Her ears twitched, but she seemed to sense nothing out of place. The dog looked back at Tom, waiting for instructions.

Kneeling, he patted her. With the other hand, he pointed the bat at the far corner of the store and said in a whisper, "Back there first, but use the aisleways." He hoped she was smart enough to get the point and stay in the more open spaces. Stumbling upon a Feral in the middle of a jungle of clothing racks because they'd cut through the juniors' department was not on today's agenda.

The dog padded down the main aisle a few paces ahead of Tom.

Taking care to avoid loud footfalls, the pair stole toward the back of the store, wary of errant noises, flashes of motion, or any hint of activity beside their movement. Halfway there, Tom forced himself to relax slightly. Everything seemed quiet.

But that didn't last. Upon reaching the end of the midway at the back of the store, they turned to the right, toward the sporting goods. About fifty feet later, maybe a third of the way along the back aisle, Lady came to a dead stop and looked back toward the front of the store.

A metallic clang shattered the silence, echoing off the painted cinder-block walls.

A cold shiver raced up Tom's back, and he froze in place, listening. He didn't even breathe until he remembered it was necessary.

Lady took a few steps toward the source of the noise and sniffed the air. She growled, a familiar, barely audible rumble.

Tom had to choose: race for the ammunition, hoping to find it before something found him, or do nothing, wait, and hope for the best?

Tom lifted the bat over his shoulder and tightened his grip on the handle. It was an easy decision. He wasn't turning his back on whatever was out there.

Lady growled again, louder and lower. Then she erupted in a flurry of barks.

A Feral shambled out of the housewares, turned toward them, and hissed. It showed them curved fangs and jagged teeth and screeched a horrifying, high-pitched squeal. Tom cringed at the ear-splitting sound. It was like fingernails on a chalkboard.

The monster charged toward them at a dead run, rags streaming behind it and feet slapping against the cheap off-white floor tiles.

"Fuck you," Tom mumbled.

Lady ran to meet the running monster, still barking furiously. As they came together, the plaguer slashed at the dog, but she ducked away from its razorlike claws at the last second. She nipped at the back of its calf as it spun around, chasing her. Having learned something about Feral in their previous encounters, Lady dodged to the side, managing to stay just beyond its reach while still getting in a decent bite here and there.

More importantly, she was keeping the thing preoccupied.

Tom swallowed hard and ran forward, entirely betraying his instincts, but he wasn't about to waste the diversion.

Lady stopped darting in circles around the thing and switched to a nip-and-retreat tactic. It was riskier, as each swing of the thing's claws just barely missed her. But it kept the Feral with its back to Tom. He was on top of it before it even realized he'd moved.

Setting his feet in a wide batter's stance and shouldering the bat, Tom yelled, "Hey, asshole!"

The Feral whipped around with its claws in the air, snarling, just in time to meet Tom's Louisville Slugger with the bridge of what was once a human nose. It lurched sideways from the blow. Not giving it even an instant to recover, he swung again, this time driving the bat into the Feral's left temple. With a satisfying crunch both heard and felt, the monster crumpled to the ground.

He raised the bat into the air again and rained blows down on what remained of the plaguer's head. Tom didn't stop until his arms burned from the effort.

Standing over the lifeless form, panting, he realized he knew exactly how to arrange a meeting with Emily.

CHAPTER 32

THE COLD METAL BINDINGS PRESSED hard against Ana's neck and arms. If they ever let her down, she expected to remember the feeling for weeks.

The first hour or so hadn't been too bad. She'd easily pretended that hanging from the wall was her choice and that she felt no discomfort. After six hours, though, lying to herself no longer worked.

The empty space in the cell below mocked her, and she fantasized about being down there, free to move around. But she might as well have wished to be human again. Never mind that the cell, by itself, would not hold her—Colin would undoubtedly employ every method in his power to make her regret her clever little rebellion.

Assuming she lived much longer, of course.

To her surprise, she hadn't been roughed up at all. When Ash brought her down, she'd expected two or three of his goons to be waiting, primed to give her that lesson in respect he had mentioned. After her behavior in the office, Colin would have almost certainly looked the other way as long as Ash and his boys showed a minimum of restraint.

Instead, Ash had locked her up and barely made a few

bad jokes at her expense before bolting the door from the other side. She actually would have preferred he had taken a little time to work her over. Not only would that have delayed him from tracking Tom, but that urgency proved that finding the human was foremost on Ash's mind.

All that meant that when Tom was finally caught— and unless he was both very smart and very lucky, eventually he *would* be caught—he'd get whatever Ash had wanted to give her and more.

Well, Tom was on his own. She had done what she could for him.

The bolt on the room's only door clacked as it was drawn back from the other side. Lars entered, shaking his head with a *tsk*.

Her eyes widened at seeing him, in particular, in the small cell. Next to Tom and maybe Alexander himself, Lars was the last person she'd expected to visit.

"I see you're as surprised to see me as I am to actually find you here," he said.

"Indeed," she replied dryly. "Forgive me for not greeting you more formally. But please, make yourself at home."

Lars smirked, stepped up to the inner cell door, and planted his hands on his hips. "I never would have believed this, not without seeing it with my own eyes. A couple of the boys told me you were locked up and hanging on the wall, and I told them they were going Feral. Losing this bet's going to cost me."

Ana rolled her eyes. "I have no doubt you'll make it back from them soon enough. And if you just came to gawk...?"

"As a matter of fact, I did mostly come just to see you up there for myself. But now, I think I need to know exactly what happened. How did the Ice Princess, Colin's special girl, end up in the cell?"

"I doubt you'll believe it," Ana said.

Lars scoffed. "Two weeks ago, I wouldn't have believed any of this. I definitely wouldn't have bought that I'd turn against my own lord and hand his authority over to someone else. So go ahead—try me. I'm think I'm just about ready to start believing in Santa Claus."

"I fear it has little to do with legends of fat bearded men who give toys to children," Ana said, "and everything to do with Tom. I let him go, Lars. Just before Colin arrived, I helped Tom escape."

Lars said nothing for a moment but simply stared back at her. Eventually, he ran a hand through the mess of gray-brown hair on his head and let out a long, steady whistle.

"Boy, when you decide you're going up against it, you don't mess around, do you? I have to say I'm impressed. Pretty pissed, too, but damn, woman, do you have a set of stones on you.

"How'd you get away with it before Ash stopped you?" he asked. "And why in God's name *would* you, especially knowing it'd end up with you down here? Or worse?"

"Well," she said, "I didn't exactly walk him through the front door and wish him a pleasant trip. I actually didn't think it would work. *He* did most of it. All I did was leave a few things placed strategically to make it possible, while dropping hints here and there. Anything more, and Colin would have known before Tom had a chance. As it is, Tom was just observant enough and a lot lucky. I worry, though, that he won't be lucky for long," she added.

Lars rubbed his chin. "I suppose Colin sent a goon squad after him?"

Ana nodded as much as she could under the circumstances. "Yes. Ash, at least, has been dispatched to find him and bring him back. He probably took some buddies for fun."

"He's in trouble, then, unless he keeps getting very lucky," Lars said. "I can only guess how... committed Ash will be to fetching the spoils for his master. Just like a good birding dog."

"That's what I'm afraid of," she said.

After a pause, Lars said, "Now tell me why."

Ana hesitated. "For many reasons. My relationship with my Maker is... not typical. Mostly, though, I did it because Colin forced me to inject Tom with Charon. Colin wanted to be absolutely certain before he arrived whether it was a case of immunity or just dumb luck. So he had me infect him."

Lars swore. "You're kidding me, right?"

Ana shook her head. "You see now why I chose to help him escape."

"That sonuvabitch. Not an hour ago, he got us all together and gave us a song and dance about doing better than Alexander by working out a way to somehow use your human to feed us. Trying to make us feel better about swearing to him, even with Alexander still out there somewhere. And yet he'd already tried to kill Tom once and now doesn't even have him.

"Most of Alexander's Family is taking the oath right now. Only reason I put him off about it a while is because it wasn't sitting right with me. Maybe it's time to stir up some trouble for him. I wanted to keep as many of us alive as possible, but I'm beginning to think your lord is just using us."

"I have little doubt," Ana said. Then, "I might have a more productive task for you, though, if you'd be willing to do me a favor."

He raised an eyebrow. "You're going to ask a favor of me? Seems like we've come a long way since *I* put you on that wall a couple days ago."

Ana rolled her eyes again. "Circumstances have changed quite a bit since then, I would say, regardless of how they appear." She waved her hands in the manacles for effect. "You have not taken Colin's oath, then?"

"No."

"Good," Ana said with a sigh of relief. "Then you can go after Tom."

Lars met her suggestion with a look of disbelief. "You want me to go chasing after the human that you let go?"

"Yes," she urged. "But I don't want you to bring him back. You simply have to find him before Ash does and protect him. He needs help."

"You know where he is?"

"I suspect I do. I don't know for sure, but I hinted at a place. If he was smart enough to follow my trail out, I expect he was smart enough to follow my suggestion."

"Why should I?" Lars asked.

"Because you know how important he is. And because if Ash finds him first, there is no guarantee that I'll have a chance to finish my work. I can do it, Lars. I'm sure of it. But if Ash gets his hands on Tom, it'll be months before he'll be in any condition to help us."

"What makes you think you'll live through the day? Colin sees everything you're telling me. I'm guessing he won't be too happy you let his little secret out and then told me to go get in Ash's way."

"True, but Turning me was not an accident, Lars," Ana said. "It was a calculated decision. He has no one else to do what I can. As long as there is a chance Tom can be used to produce blood to feed us, he'll keep me alive. He can't risk killing me yet."

"And you think he'll let me just walk out of here?"

"To be honest, yes, I think he will. Ash is an effective tool for Colin, but he's equally vicious and can be difficult. Colin must be at least a little concerned about what Ash will do to Tom. I also think he'd enjoy testing whether you're Ash's equal. He likes pitting his Children against each other.

"Then again, I could be misjudging him. He might not let you out. But surely you have methods of leaving here that we are not aware of?"

Lars chuckled. "You're smarter than even I've given you credit for, princess. Fine, I'll do your little chore—not just because you're right and he'll need some help, but because I'd like another shot at Ash."

Ana's body sagged against her bindings in relief. "Thank you. I can't tell you how much that eases my mind."

"You realize that's another one you're going to owe me

at the end of this, right?" Lars smirked. "Well, if you make it to the end, that is. And I always collect on my debts."

"I fully expect to live long enough to see those debts paid, Lars," Ana said, trying to look more certain than she felt.

"The more pressing question," Lars said, "is where am I going?"

Ana hesitated. Colin was almost certainly paying close attention to their conversation. However, having no Descended of her own, she wasn't sure how much detail their connection brought. He could, at the very least, reference the images in her memory, as well as see what she was seeing. But was that the extent of it, or could Colin hear what she heard too?

She used to fear that he might be able to read her thoughts completely, but at this point, she knew that wasn't the case. Early on, she experimented by intentionally conjuring treacherous thoughts that should have sent him into a rage yet got no reaction. Thus, he likely could only "hear" the thoughts she sent him when communicating.

He could still at least see and possibly hear what she was saying, though, and that was enough to be a problem at the moment.

"Once I tell you," Ana said, "don't say anything else to me. Just go. The less you say after, the better."

Lars nodded. Either he took her meaning, or he was content to go along anyway.

"Good. I sent him to find Emily in Atlanta. To ask for her help."

Lars raised his eyebrows in surprise then cocked his

head as if wondering at her sanity. Apparently, he hadn't been expecting that answer.

Shocked or not, he kept his promise. The look disappeared almost as quickly as it had come, replaced by stony resolution. Giving Ana a half nod, he turned and was gone from the room before she could say anything else. He left her alone, again, with nothing but worry.

CHAPTER 33

I F SHE WAS GOING TO *walk past, she'd do it soon. She hadn't yesterday or the day before. In fact, he hadn't seen her once in the weeks he'd been staking out here. Every day at lunch time, though, he still wasted an hour on an uncomfortable park bench beside the riverside path, hoping to catch Heather.*

She used to go for walks on Riverfront Drive almost daily, right past the trees and benches and that unusual statue of that man reading. At least, she'd told him she did. Tom hadn't ever been here before the hotel.

The benches were hard and given to making his back ache, making him squirm frequently. Worse, he had a painfully sore throat, and his head throbbed from last night's excesses at the bar.

He shook a couple of aspirin out of the tiny bottle he carried and washed them down with a gulp of lukewarm, overpriced coffee. In ten more minutes, he'd give up for today. Looking out over the Ohio River, he lost himself in thought as brown-tinged ripples slid by.

His watch chimed once to signal the half hour—time to go. He glanced up and down the cobblestone sidewalk behind the bench one last time.

And there she was.

Heather looked lost in thought herself, meandering toward him, taking step after slow step. It showed a stark contrast to the purpose-driven wife he remembered, who had little patience for wasting time.

He should look away. She shouldn't find him staring at her. Still, he couldn't take his eyes off her. He was afraid she'd disappear if he blinked, like a riverside mirage. She was still radiant, even looking somewhat lost. His heart ached with how much he missed her.

At last, barely fifteen feet away, she noticed him. Mouth open and eyes wide, she came to a dead stop. The surprise on her face made her look like she'd been slapped.

"Tom," she said.

"Hi," he said back.

"How... how have you been?"

"Okay, I guess," he replied. "I miss you."

"Yeah," his wife said. "Wow. This is..."

"Yeah."

His hands came up involuntarily, driven by the urge to do something, anything: grab her, hug her, or simply take her hand. But he couldn't. The weight hanging between them was too much. It separated them as surely as an actual wall. How did someone fix that?

Uncertainty gnawed away at him. "Sit with me," he pleaded. "Just a few minutes. I want to talk."

"Tom, I—"

"Please, Heather, we owe it to each other. Five minutes."

She sighed but came around the bench and sat down. She sat as far from him as possible on the far end of the bench, but that was a start.

"Heather," he said, "I want you to know that I screwed up and I'm sorry. I never should have done… what I did. There were better, more constructive ways I could have… Anyway, I'm sorry."

She stared across the muddy river and said nothing.

"Either way, the thing is that I still love you. I don't know how to live without you. I'm a mess. Please come home. Whatever happened, however we got broken, there's got to be a way to fix it. There must be some way to get back to the way we were before."

Lowering her head, she whispered, "You can't go back, Tom. You can't undo what's been done."

"Fine. I get that. I understand. And I don't care. Didn't you hear me? I still love you, whatever happened. I miss you, and I want you back. I forgive you and want to get on with our life."

"Forgive me?" she exploded, shooting him daggers. "What fucking nerve."

The look on his face gave the question he didn't ask.

"This, Tom, is why we can't just fix it and go on. You still don't get it. You've never gotten it. You don't even know what the problem is, let alone how to fix it. No, we're done, Tom, truly and completely. You can't just say 'I forgive you' and hope that sticks us back together like duct tape. It won't hold us. Not now. Especially not now."

"Heather."

He reached out for her hand. She snatched it away.

"You might be willing to forgive me, but I can't forgive you."

"Forgive me?" he repeated. "I'm not the one who—"

Heather stood up. "Tom, I know exactly what I did and

exactly why I did it. And as much as I know it hurt you, and I'm sorry for that, I had to do it.

"I did it for me because I was lost and alone. You weren't there for me when I needed you. The worst days of my life, when I just wanted you to hold me, caress my hand, rub my back, and wipe away my tears, you couldn't do it. You obsessed about how we could get over it, make it better, fix it so the pain would go away—a hundred useless things that were all about you, not us. What I really wanted was someone to help me carry the grief. Instead, you abandoned me. For that, I'll never be able to forgive you."

She sighed again. "The worst part is that the stunned look on your face tells me you still don't get it. And that, ignoring everything else, is why we can't be fixed."

A hard silence fell between them as Tom fumbled for something to say.

She pressed through it first. "I came down here today because I just had a lunch meeting with my attorney. I want a divorce. She's filing the papers today."

An urgent *woof* in his ear startled Tom awake. The flimsy camping cot he'd taken from a shelf and set up in the corner of the sporting-goods department bounced as he jumped slightly at the sound. Recognizing Lady beside him, he relaxed.

Sitting up, Tom rubbed his eyes and waited for his body and brain to adjust to being awake.

"The sun's gone down?" he asked the dog.

Lady sat beside the cot and chuffed.

"All right, then—showtime," Tom said.

He stood and stretched. So much depended on him

being alert and ready over the next few hours that he longed for a cup of coffee or two. Come to think of it, everything to make a pot was probably in the store some-where—except time. He couldn't spare the time to deal with that now. Evening had fallen, and he could get an unfriendly visitor at any minute. Wandering the store in search of a can of Folgers was out of the question.

He ran down a mental checklist of his preparations. Everything should be ready.

A few bottles of water were lined up beside the cot. Tom picked one up, twisted off the cap, and took a long drink. The remaining half went into a nearby water dish for Lady. She lapped it up with enthusiasm.

Tom then opened a box of fruit-and-nut bars and removed an individually wrapped pack. It smelled lightly of honey, raisins, and brown sugar. More important was what he didn't smell: decay or any other kind of funk that'd make him think twice before eating.

He tore the wrapper open and split the bar in half, sharing it with Lady. She gobbled hers down quickly, not seeming concerned about whether it was spoiled. Tom ate his half more casually, but it still disappeared in three bites. He repeated the process with two more bars then opened another bottle of water, using half of it to wash down the dry breakfast. As before, he poured the remainder into the dog's bowl, where it disappeared just as quickly.

He favored Lady with a grim smile. They'd probably just had the most nutritious meal either had eaten in a week.

"What I wouldn't give for a warm thermos of Ana's canned soup," he mused.

Lady cocked her head and wagged her tail, anxiously waiting for another trail bar.

"No more for now, girl. Maybe later. We've got work to do."

Tom picked up the Smith & Wesson, at last heavy with bullets again. He tucked it into his pants, as usual. Gun in place, he grabbed his newest acquisition, a pump-action shotgun, and hoisted it over his left shoulder. Finally, he gripped his Louisville Slugger with his free right hand. It was probably not really necessary anymore, but he still trusted that weapon the most and wasn't about to leave it behind. The shotgun had to prove itself before he gave up the bat.

"Let's go," he said.

At the main entrance, Tom leaned the bat against a wall and pressed his face to the glass of the outside door. The world was a shade of soft blue with a few pale creases of orange and yellow yet streaking the horizon. The sun was down, but night had not completely fallen yet. The sky was dark enough for his purposes, though.

Seeing no sign of any movement in the parking lot or beyond, Tom clicked the switch above the main doors. They glided apart.

Lady trotted out onto the sidewalk, making sure no surprises awaited them. She wagged her tail and looked back over her shoulder—all clear.

Tom had set up a portable stereo system just outside the door, hours before grabbing the nap. He popped the hinged CD compartment open and pulled a disc case from his back pocket. He didn't recognize the band at all, but the back cover featured a group of rough-looking guys with tattoos and a lot of hair. The goal was to play something loud, and that seemed as good a choice as any.

He slapped the disc into the player, closed the lid, and pressed Play then Repeat. After a quick period of speaker hiss, the small device belted out exactly what he wanted: something like the power metal he'd listened to years ago. The first track featured an aggressive combination of drums and electric guitar leading into a stream of vocals that sounded like half shouting, half vomiting.

That should get some attention.

Back inside, he switched the doors off again, leaving them open. Lady followed, taking a seat just beyond the pressure mat.

"Stay," Tom said, scratching her on the head. "And when you get a nibble, Lady, don't you mess around. Just come to me."

She licked his hand once in response and turned back toward the world outside.

Tom grabbed the bat and retreated inside. Reaching the back of the store, he took position between a pair of shelving units half full of footwear, running perpendicular to the main aisle.

The wait was relatively brief. He barely had time for that tense sort of boredom to set in before Tom heard a sharp, urgent bark from Lady. With a deep breath, he slung the shotgun over his shoulder, drew the revolver, and backed up to the far end of the row of shoes. Two more aggressive barks rang through the store, followed by an ear-splitting screech.

Tom wiped sweat from his forehead. He'd gotten the attention he wanted. A Feral had taken the bait. Now to reel it in. The trick, of course, was to not get killed in the process.

Another bark followed, this time closer, somewhere off to his right. Then he heard the familiar *slap slap slap* of bare feet on the tiles. The catch of the day was close.

From his vantage point at the end of the row of shoes, Lady suddenly appeared from his right and disappeared to his left just as quickly. Then one of the biggest plaguers he'd seen yet lumbered after her, grunting.

He hoped it was too preoccupied with the chase to catch his scent.

When it didn't turn back toward him, he slid up the row as quickly and quietly as possible and spun to his left, springing into the main aisle. The moment his boots cleared the merchandise shelf, the Feral skidded to a stop and spun around.

Only 20 feet away, the hulking thing growled at Tom.

He raised the revolver in both hands and leveled it at the monster coming toward him. Exhaling, he pulled the trigger. The shot sailed wide of its mark.

Slipping into a mental void to clear his head like when he'd shot cans with his BB gun as a kid, he took aim again and fired a second time. The shot hit right where he wanted, blasting the monster's right shoulder.

The Feral stopped and screamed in a familiar display of fangs. Tom, still focusing on the empty, quiet place in his head, ignored the show of aggression and fired again, this time at the other shoulder. Blood splattered the foot-wear shelf.

Enraged, the monster dashed forward, screeching as it ran, claws raised and teeth out.

No more games. He had to hope that was enough of a show.

Squeezing the trigger repeatedly, Tom emptied what was left in the revolver's cylinder into the Feral's head. The thing pulled up abruptly and collapsed backward.

Wasting no time, he dropped the pistol and whipped the shotgun off his shoulder.

"Stay back," he commanded Lady.

He'd intentionally chosen shells with a narrow spray to limit the potential for either of them to get hit accidentally. Still, no point in taking unnecessary risks. She ducked behind a row of ladies' sandals.

Advancing a few paces, Tom placed the gun's muzzle a few inches above the plaguer's head. He fired, pumped, and fired again, reducing it to reddish pulp.

With plastic shot casings bouncing hollowly against the floor, Tom inspected his handiwork. What used to be the Feral's head was now a modern-art piece.

Satisfied, he shouldered the weapon, leaned against a display of tennis shoes, and took a few deep breaths. His hands shook, and his heart pounded from the adrenaline surging through him.

"Are you all right, girl? Come on back out."

Lady padded out from the footwear department into the walkway. Instead of dashing to him with her tail wagging, she froze and began barking again.

Tom attempted to spin around, but a pair of cold hands held him fast by the head and shoulders. He couldn't move without breaking his own neck.

"You smell delicious." A woman breathed against his ear. "This must be my lucky day."

CHAPTER 34

TOM SWALLOWED HARD. EVERYTHING HINGED on the next few moments.

Lady stopped barking but continued to growl at whoever was holding him.

"Sit, girl," he said, making his voice as steady as possible, given the circumstances.

She barked again for good measure but did as she was told.

"That was nice of you," said the woman, still close. "Saved me the trouble of killing her first. Maybe when I'm finished with you, I'll let her go. No reason I should be the only lucky one today."

She spoke in barely a whisper, with her mouth pressed close to his ear. Whoever she was, she had a prominent Southern drawl, the kind that provided a certain level of genteel charm. He'd always thought that particular accent enticing, and in another time or place, he might have been attracted.

Tom cleared his throat. "Listen, lady, let's just all calm down and chat for a minute. Let me go so we can have a nice, civilized conversation."

"You've got a heckuva a set of balls for a man alone in

a discount store with no friends but a dog," she said. "It'll almost be a shame to drain you."

She tightened her grip on his head and shoulder then inhaled deeply, murmuring to herself. Tom sensed anticipation mixed with some measure of contentment, like just before someone would dig into a heaping plate of food at Thanksgiving.

She hissed, and Tom could guess what would come next.

"No, no, wait!" he yelled, struggling to pull away. "I need to speak with Emily. Don't kill me. I have something Emily can use!"

The woman hissed again, louder and angry. Still, fangs didn't rip into him anywhere.

She shoved him away. He tripped over the plaguer's feet and went sprawling to the floor, tangling with his shotgun. Thankfully, he managed to avoid most of the puddle that remained of the Feral's head.

"So much for being civilized," he muttered.

Tom rolled over and got his feet. Lady darted between him and the vampire.

As he got a good look at her at last, the sarcastic remark he'd meant to make vanished. For a moment, he was dumbfounded. Her eyes were a deep green, the color of clover in spring, her lips were full and just red enough to sharply contrast the paleness of her face, and a mass of auburn hair fell around her shoulders in perfectly untamed waves. His breath caught in his throat.

The only thing spoiling the image was the dark look of irritation on her face.

Her eyes flashed dangerously. "You've got one minute

to tell me why Emily should give a damn about you. After that, I don't care how big your balls are—I won't be interrupted again."

He'd never had much luck talking to pretty girls, and suddenly his life depended on it. He almost wanted to laugh.

"Uh… okay…" Tom stammered. "Um, what's your name?"

She crossed her arms beneath the curves of her chest and sighed. "Lindsey. Get on with it."

"Lindsey. Okay, Lindsey, I'm Tom. I was being held first by Alexander and then Colin, up north in Cincinnati. There's some kind of power struggle going on up there, and I'm in the middle of it. I managed to escape, but I'm sure someone will be coming after me, so I need protection. Because sooner or later, someone like you is going to accidentally… uh, do what you do. But you can't let that happen because I'm apparently immune. To Charon. That disease."

Tom finished in a breathless rush. Lindsey raised an eyebrow. "As persuasive speeches go, you might want to practice that one in the mirror a few more times. I'm not quite sold."

"Look—" Tom began.

She waved it off. "So you're immune, huh? Right. Sure you are. And I'm going to start working on my tan tomorrow. No, I'll tell you what you are. You're a good meal wasting my time. On top of that, you just killed one of my pet Feral. He used to be my favorite Descended. So, hon, I think I'll just go ahead and do, you know, what we do."

Lindsey took a step toward them. Growling, Lady lowered her head and offered her own curved, ivory canines. The woman grinned, a warm smile that sparkled in her eyes and erased the irritation from her face. "I'm going to enjoy—" she began.

Her head snapped up and her eyes glazed into a vacant stare as she trailed off, leaving the half-finished statement hanging between them. The bright smile she'd worn briefly was replaced with a stiff blankness, like a store mannequin's.

She had to be talking to someone… by thought. Still hard to get used to the idea.

The look disappeared as quickly as it had come. She cocked her head and glared.

"Maybe I won't drain you just yet," she said after a moment's thought. "If you're so sure you want a chance to talk to Emily, I'll let you have it." The words sounded confident, but her tone betrayed a subtle hint of question, as if she was mildly confused.

Tom breathed a sigh of relief. "Lady, sit. Everything's fine."

"I don't know that I'd say that, exactly," Lindsey countered. "You're still my claim, and I'm not about to let you get away from me. You won't be out of my sight anytime in the near future."

"Sure, fine, you'll kill me tomorrow, and all that," he said, dismissing the comment. "So now what?"

"We have a little ways to go to meet her. But I'm not carrying you, so I reckon we'll have to wait for someone to bring us a car. Unless you've got one?"

Slinging the shotgun over his shoulder, Tom nodded.

"As a matter of fact, I do. And I didn't want to leave it here anyway."

"Fine. But I'm driving."

He took a few steps forward and picked up his revolver, coming within arm's length of Lindsey. He hoped she could smell him from that distance—the possibility that he might be teasing her made him smile.

"Hold on a second," Tom said. "I need to take care of something."

Lindsey crossed her arms again and tapped a foot. "Be quick. The longer you keep Emily waiting, hon, the shorter your conversation with her is likely to be."

Slipping a small green-and-gray camouflage backpack from his back, Tom knelt. He unzipped one of the pack's many pockets and withdrew a box of bullets. Then, with a flick of his wrist, he flipped open the gun's empty cylinder.

"I have to admit," he said, "I'm surprised you're letting me reload my guns."

Lindsey snickered. "Why? They might save me trouble, depending on what we run into."

"You mean uncontrolled Feral?" he asked. Surely the horde of mindless zombie vampires out there was the only thing worth worrying about.

She frowned and gave him an appraising look. "Yes, them. Uncontrolled ones can be a pain."

Tom's smile widened at having set her off balance. She hadn't expected him to know much about her kind, apparently.

"Besides," she continued, "What are you going to do with that little thing that would hassle me? You know what I am."

Tom laughed. "Of course. You're a horror-movie monster, which is now apparently an everyday thing for me."

She cocked her head the same way Lady would when trying to figure him out. "You're an odd guy. And I'm no movie monster, hon. I'm the real thing."

With another chuckle, Tom slapped the revolver's cylinder closed and slid both the gun and the box of bullets back into his pack. He stood up, shrugged it back on, and picked up his shotgun and bat.

"Odd is one way to put it. I'm leaning toward borderline insane, myself. All that aside, I'm ready to go if you are."

She turned and headed toward the store's main entrance without waiting for him to catch up. "Come on," she said over her shoulder. "Let's get this over with."

At the front of the store, Lindsey strode right through the still-open automatic door. Tom, however, paused, waiting for Lady's usual approval.

Already in the parking lot, Lindsey said something toward the spot she expected him to be. She stopped short, realizing no one was following her. "What are you waiting for?" she called back to him.

Having gotten the all-clear from Lady, Tom joined her. "It's probably not something you worry about too much," he said, "but some of us have to check that there aren't any boogeymen around before we go rushing outside at night."

"I reckon I can understand that," she allowed. "I'd have warned you, though. You're no good to me tore up. That'll be my job when the time comes."

"Wow, you know how to really make a guy feel special," he replied dryly.

Lindsey said nothing. Instead, she gave him a flat look, held out a hand, and said, "Keys."

He nodded toward the Mustang. "That's my car. The keys are in it. I figured I was better off not carrying them around."

Lindsey checked out the car and clucked her tongue. "First guy I've seen in two years, and you're making up for something just like every boy I went to high school with. Let me tell you, you won't impress anyone with a big muscle car nowadays."

After opening the passenger door, Tom let Lady climb into the back before settling in and arranging his weapons on the floorboard. "You women just can't help but give me grief about my choice of car, can you?"

Lindsey raised an eyebrow. "Women? Who else have you been talking to?"

"I'm afraid you'll have to wait until I meet Emily to hear about my adventures. I don't want to have to go through it twice." He wasn't ready to give his story away to her just yet, either. Better to leave her curious.

He also had a weird sense that he was sort of playing hard to get.

"Come to think of it," he added, "How do I know you aren't taking me out to the middle of nowhere to drain me, away from prying eyes that might make you share?"

She chuckled. "Look, hon—"

"I have a name."

"My meals don't usually get names."

"This one does, and it's Tom."

"Fine. Look, Tommy, if I was ready to have you, it wouldn't matter if we were in the Walmart, the middle of the street, or halfway through supper in my daddy's old farmhouse. I said I'd take you to see her, and that's what I'm going to do. When the time comes, you can bet I won't play with you. I'm not a cat-and-mouse kind of gal."

He wasn't about to bet on any of that. His plan had worked out so far, though. Nothing for it but to go along and hope for the best.

They were back on the expressway almost immediately, headed south toward the city.

"How far?" He hadn't planned on carrying a conversation, but his nerves kept him at it.

"A short ways," she said. "The place we're staying now is on the north side of town."

"Staying now? She moves around?"

Lindsey nodded. "Emily keeps her feet moving. I reckon she gets bored pretty quick. I've heard her say how much better she liked things before. Days are too much like each other now."

"How old is she, really?" he asked. "I've heard she's one of the oldest."

The question earned him another appraising glance. "Can't say for sure. She's old, one of the oldest I know of. But I wouldn't be asking her if I were you. Actually, there's a prime tip for you, hon, if you want to keep your skin intact. Don't be rude when you meet her. Whatever it is you're hoping for, bad manners will likely just get you dead. And it would disappoint me a lot if I lost my prize on account of his basic lack of a civilized nature."

"Great. So she's old and prickly," he said with a sigh. His plan seemed less like a great idea with every mile.

The woman smiled, green eyes sparkling. "Now, she's not all bad. And it ain't a sure thing she'll kill you. Heck, if you're lucky, maybe she'll even invite you for dinner."

She didn't mention whether he'd be a guest or the main course.

CHAPTER 35

AFTER CREEPING ALONG THE DARK alleyway, Birdy set down one of the two cages he carried and knocked on the door in front of him. He whistled to himself, waiting for Hap, the guy who ran the place, or Ben, the younger one who helped him, to come to the door.

He shifted from foot to foot and looked longingly at the open street at the mouth of the alley. The tight space made him nervous. Hap, though, wouldn't let him use the same door as his customers.

"The guys that come here would tear you up and make you do for free what you're making a profit on now," the grizzled, white-haired vampire with the jagged scar on his cheek would say every time Birdy stopped by with something to sell. "You need me for our little arrangement to work, and it won't work if my patrons find out where I get my goods."

The arrangement actually suited Birdy just fine as it was. Sure, he could've made more on the live animals he trapped if he sold them to customers directly, but he didn't care to deal with the kind of vampires that sought out an establishment like Hap's. They were the aggressive, type-A sort that had made his first life miserable decades before. After he'd been turned, he finally felt like he had power over something, and he'd made every single one of his victims know it before they died.

But now, with the people gone, things were back to the way they were before, and he hated it, mostly because Hap's customers and others like them saw him as too weak to be one of them. Still, they seemed to prefer the blood of hot, still-living victims than the cold blood of Lady Emily's rations, and that preference was making him rich.

For every live animal he delivered, Hap would sell it for a minimum of two ration tokens, more for a larger animal. They would then split the rations between them. Birdy hadn't felt any real thirst in months, and he hadn't used or traded even half the tokens he'd made.

The door cracked an inch. Ben, Hap's assistant, peered out. "Good to see you, Birdy. You got a delivery for us?" he whispered.

The whispering meant customers were in the front of the place, so they would need to do their business quickly and quietly. Birdy nodded in reply but said nothing. At Hap's suggestion, he didn't talk when others were around so that no one might recognize his voice.

Birdy didn't have much to say anyway.

Ben opened the door and let him in. They walked through a tiny office and into a cramped kitchen area. The unlit space was tight with large appliances and work counters. It seemed impossible that a restaurant crew had once operated in such a confined space. He set his shrouded cages on the floor and looked at Ben expectedly.

Ben lifted the dark shrouds from each cage, one at a time. The first one held four birds, a large black crow, a cardinal, and two songbirds of one sort or another. The other cage was split into separate sections holding various rodents and woodland creatures, including a fat rabbit Birdy was hoping would bring him maybe half a dozen tokens in profit.

Ben held out ten fingers. Birdy put up ten and then flashed his right hand alone, suggesting another five, fifteen altogether for the lot. Ben frowned, showed him just a pair of fingers, then made a slashing gesture—twelve rations, final offer.

Rubbing his narrow, hairless chin, the hunter pretended to consider, but he'd already made up his mind. Twelve was fine. After making him wait a few extra moments, he nodded to the assistant, who smiled and slipped through a dark, heavy curtain into the front of the establishment.

Left alone, Birdy took a position by the canvas curtain and listened.

"I don't know if I'll have anything to offer you guys tonight," Hap said, slightly muffled. "But if you ain't got any pressing business, it'd be worth your time to wait a bit."

A chorus of laughter responded, three different laughs. "It ain't like we have to get back to the office or home to the wife and kids, Hap. I can hang around a while. Got any whiskey?"

"You're in luck, Dell," Hap replied, "I got a bottle each of bourbon, scotch, and rye. I picked up the rye one just for you. What's your pleasure?"

The voice belonging to Dell laughed again. "You

know me too well, old man. I'll take the rye, and the boys here... Well, what'll it be, boys?"

"Scotch," one said, sounding pleased.

"Got any gin?" another mumbled. After a pause, then, "All right, well, scotch I guess."

"I'll see to gettin' some gin for next time, Willis. Ben, get their drinks, I'll see to that other thing."

Birdy licked his lips at the thought of a few slugs of whiskey. He'd always appreciated the heat at the end of a cheap shot and the comforting numb sensation that followed soon after. In his opinion, the effects of alcohol were much more pleasant as a vampire. He'd never gotten more than a decent buzz this way, just a nice, warm, happy feeling. And hangovers didn't exist anymore, no matter how much he drank.

Maybe when Ben came back with his tokens, Birdy would barter one for a bottle of whatever Hap wanted to rid himself of.

An old-fashioned bell hanging above the front door in the other room chimed, sounding flat through the canvas. Footsteps announced more customers, though the heavy curtain kept Birdy from smelling them in the other room. The separation worked more to his advantage, he figured, since it kept them from smelling him too.

"Evening, fellas," Hap said. "I'm Hap, and this is my place. What can we do for you?"

"Hap, dude, nice to meet you," someone replied. The voice carried an accent Birdy hadn't heard in several years. He couldn't place it for sure, though—maybe someplace up north or out west.

The guy went on, "This the sort of place dudes like us

could score something warm to drink for the right price? Maybe catch the gossip?"

"Yup," the owner replied. "Talk is always free, and a warm meal can usually be had for a few rations. I have to admit, though, you don't look or sound like you're from around here." Even Birdy, who was usually slow to such things, caught the implication: foreign rations from foreign lords weren't any good to Hap.

"Don't worry, buddy," the person said, "we'll make sure you're paid right. What's on the menu?"

"Nothin' just now, but I 'spect a delivery soon. These other fellas get first pick, but if you're willing to wait, I'm sure you'll be glad you did."

"Sweet."

A pair of unfamiliar voices chuckled in agreement. The tone of their laughter made the hair on Birdy's skin stand up.

"While we're waiting," the foreigner continued, "heard anything about a human running around here?"

Birdy's ears twitched. A human? A *real* human? Around here? Sure, rumors about them popped up every so often, but he hadn't heard a trustworthy account of someone finding an actual person for at least a couple of years.

"Odd you should ask," Hap replied. "Dell, here, was just sayin' that somebody found one a little ways out of town, of all places."

"I could hardly believe it, myself," Dell said. "But I do odd jobs for Lady Emily sometimes, so I'm around the Chalet. I heard her tell someone exactly that. One of her Descended seems to have found a real person, with a mutt even! And if that don't beat all, the man said he wanted to talk to Emily. They were s'posed to be headed into town, last I heard."

The stranger whistled. "Dude. I don't know that I would have bought that if you weren't there. That's massive news. I bet the Lady's place is buzzing."

"Nah," Dell said. "I heard her say she wanted t' keep it pretty quiet until she got the guy. But he should be there by now, so I figure it's okay to tell a few people. Seems like you had some idea about it already, anyway. But still, just let's keep it between us."

The stranger coughed. "I did hear a little something floating around. But don't worry—I'm pretty sure everyone in this room is going to keep quiet. Now, about that warm meal…"

Birdy frowned at the man's voice. Something was out of place.

"I told you, buddy, I don't got anythin' right this minute. Maybe you oughta come back in a few hours." Birdy nodded to himself in the darkness. Hap didn't seem to like something about the new guy either.

"I never was very patient," the man said. "Maybe we'll just see what we can get now."

A thud sounded through the canvas, followed by several cracking sounds in quick succession. Then came a wet popping noise.

Two people screamed. Ben, for sure, was one, and the other sounded like Dell's gin guy, maybe Willis? It didn't matter—Birdy had heard enough. Time to go.

Underlining his decision, a heavy grunt in the other room was followed by a loud crash. Someone muttered something Birdy couldn't understand but then broke off, gurgling thickly.

Birdy dashed toward the back door and fell over his own cage of birds with a curse, having forgotten them in his haste. He tumbled to the floor, and the cage was knocked sideways in a ringing crash of metal. A symphony of angry squawks filled the kitchen.

He barely registered the noise before he was off the floor and racing for the door. Halfway there, though, something heavy pressed against him from behind, changing his course slightly.

He tried to reach for the knob on the alleyway door but was forced to put his hands out to soften the impact of being driven into the doorframe.

He hit it hard, face turned to the side, cheek smashing against it with a splintering crack. A cold hand reached around his neck, and a heavy weight held him in place. He struggled to push back away from the door but couldn't move.

"Easy, dude," the newcomer whispered. "You're the hunter, right? You bring… Hap, was it? You bring Hap the animals?"

"Yes," he croaked, "Birdy."

"Well, little birdie, I'm Ash. And today might be your lucky day, dude. Then again, it might be a pretty bad day. It depends on whether you're going to be a friendly guy or not. What do you think?"

"Friendly," he muttered, nodding repeatedly. "I'll be friendly."

"Good. Let me show you something." Ash pulled him away from the door, spun them both around, and marched Birdy through the canvas-covered opening, down a short hallway, and into the front room.

The handful of other times Birdy had seen the room, it had been the picture of order. Hap kept a clean, well-organized place. Now, it looked like a bomb had gone off. Tables and chairs were overturned, and five bodies littered the room. Ben sat against the wall on the far side, his head limp against his chest. Hap was doubled over the bar, face to one side, staring off into the distance. Two more were slumped forward in their chairs, and a third sprawled out on a broken tabletop that had fallen to the floor. Ash's companions each stood over one of the bodies in the chairs, lapping up the blood pumping from their necks.

"See, we break their necks first," Ash said as if explaining something as common as how to tie a knot. "Then we cut the spinal cord from behind so we don't lose too much blood. That usually gives us enough time to feed before they heal and get some fight back in them."

"But… the law…" Birdy stammered.

Ash squeezed the back of his neck hard. "Now, you're not gonna be all judgmental, are you? Because I haven't made up my mind about you yet. You seem like a cool dude. I like handy dudes. What I don't like is letting the useless ones skate by, wasting good blood that could be going to the rest of us. Not a one of these pathetic lumps was good for anything, so they might as well feed those of us trying to make the world better."

Ash's face loomed beside Birdy, close enough to give him a good look at his eyes, which blazed, alive and unyielding. The guy's whole face beamed with a kind of furious zeal. Birdy had never seen anything like it. He was staring at the face of insanity—a very dangerous insanity.

Birdy stammered, hoping to say something that wouldn't get him killed, but Ash saved him the effort. "Someday, not too long off, there's only going to be one Master, Birdy," he whispered, "and that day, I'm going to keep the cool, handy people around. The rest, the useless, judgmental ones, are going to end up like Dell and Hap here. I don't think you want to be like them, do you?"

Birdy shook his head, still in Ash's grip.

"Good. That's being smart, dude. Now, you split on out the back. And take your animals with you this time too. I think we're set for food here for a while. But I'll be looking for you again, dude, to do some work for me or my guys. So you be waiting to hear from me. Got me?"

Birdy nodded again.

"Yeah, that's good. You go on now," Ash said again, letting go.

Not waiting to be told a second time, he flashed through the hallway and into the kitchen. Slowing just enough to grab his cages and open the alley door, Birdy fled into the night, trying not to think about the abomination taking place in the front room.

CHAPTER 36

THE MUSTANG FLEW DOWN THE country road, much faster than if Tom had been driving. He had thought Ana was aggressive behind the wheel when they fled from the high school, but Lindsey could have passed for a professional stunt driver. With her taking razor-sharp turns at such high speeds, luck more than anything else was keeping down the fruit-and-nut bars he'd eaten. Lady had it even worse, though. Without a seat belt, she slid or rolled across the back seat every time the car pitched around a turn.

The drive so far had included two different interstates, several state routes, and a countless series of twists and hard turns on back roads. Tom was completely turned around. They could be headed back to Cincinnati, for all he could tell. If something went wrong and he ended up running for his life again, getting away would prove to be quite a challenge.

Just as he was starting to think they really were maybe heading north, Lindsey whipped the car to the left into a partially hidden driveway. The path snaked left and right several times before ending in a circular turnaround before a huge, colonial-style mansion. Lights blazed from all the windows, and shadows flickered and moved behind the curtains.

"This is the place?" Tom asked.

Lindsey gave him a flat look. "No, I just like driving past this one. I'm thinking of buying it as a summer home."

Tom chuckled. He told himself he was just reacting to her sarcasm, but the bass drum in his chest and the quiver in his hands suggested he might be nervous to the point of hysteria.

"What did you call it again?"

"The Chalet."

"It's, uh, it's impressive," Tom said, eyeing the mansion. "It's nice to see a place with some light and life in it."

Lindsey nodded. "Emily has workers manning the local power plant in shifts, so there's electricity throughout most of the area. Mostly, though, it's so all the lights can be turned on every night. She says she's not going to live for eternity in the dark.

"Oh," she went on, "and this one mansion isn't 'the Chalet.' Emily calls whatever roof she's staying under at the moment 'the Chalet.' I don't know why, for sure, but she's done it as long as I've known her."

After stepping out of the car, they made their way up a cobblestone-lined walk ending in a long covered porch spanning the front of the house. A set of massive double doors with elaborate stained-glass sidelights loomed ahead.

"You look a bit out of place loaded for battle, Tommy. Are you sure you want to carry those around? The baseball bat, especially, makes a nice, friendly statement."

Tom gave her a narrow glance. "I think I'll hold on to them if you don't mind."

"Suit yourself, but it's not like they'd do you any good. And if you're bound to keep them, don't go waving them around when you meet Emily. She might get offended."

"I'll try to remember that," Tom replied dryly. He thought—but wasn't sure—he caught a twinkle of amusement on her face.

The door on the right opened silently as they stepped up onto the porch. Someone had been watching their approach.

A man filled the space in the doorway. He was barely more than five feet tall, with brown hair and eyes. He was, quite possibly, the most average-looking person Tom had ever seen. His only distinguishing feature was a slightly irritated, disapproving look, as if Lindsey was a housecat carrying a dead mouse home in its mouth.

"What can I do for you, Miss Lindsey?" he said, lacking any inflection.

"Let us in, Nelson. She's expecting me, and you know it."

The average-looking man, Nelson, sniffed. "As we've discussed before, I would appreciate being greeted with a little more respect. I am, after all, Emily's personal assistant and head of household at the Chalet."

Lindsey chuckled. "Look, Nelson, you might want all manner of sunshine blown up your ass, and Emily might have enough patience for your nonsense, but nothing changes the fact that you're basically the butler and sometimes the doorman around here. Now, since we're expected, why don't y'all get out of our way and announce us. I need to discuss my claim over this human here."

The short man stiffened, clearly stung. "I see," he muttered. "I am afraid that Lady Emily is occupied with another matter of some urgency at the moment. But if you will follow me, I'm to provide your *claim* with a secure room where he can wait until she is available for you both."

He stepped aside, allowing them in. Lady padded ahead but came up short when the man cleared his throat hard.

"You know how she feels about those things," he said.

Tom looked Lindsey squarely in the face. "She's family and goes where I go. I'm not leaving her out here alone, especially now that we've made it this far. Your… relatives… will be eyeing her like the Christmas goose."

"Oh, lord ha' mercy…" Lindsey sighed. To Nelson, she said, "Fine. The dog's with us. It's on me."

Turning back to Tom, she added, "That mutt doesn't leave your heels. If there are any problems, believe me, you'll both pay for it. I swear I'm beginning to think you're more trouble than you're worth."

Following the tense—although thankfully brief—exchange at the door, Nelson led them from the enormous, richly appointed foyer through the house.

They climbed a curved, sweeping staircase easily twelve feet wide. It separated at the top into two paths leading in opposite directions, each to one of the mansion's wings.

Proceeding to the right, Nelson broke the silence. "I

would imagine the east wing will offer you more comfort or at least more security."

"Why?" Tom asked.

Nelson sighed with feigned exasperation. "Because no one likes sleeping on the side of the house where the sun comes up. Those of us lucky enough to have earned a room to ourselves above ground prefer the west wing."

Looking at Lindsey, Tom asked, "Am I not safe here? Do I need to be concerned?"

She stopped in the middle of the long hallway. "Tommy, if I were you, there wouldn't be a place on this Earth I'd feel safe. If you ask me, how you managed to get this far with your blood still in your skin means you're either blessed or cursed, one or the other."

"Great, so I need to sleep sitting up with a loaded shotgun across my knees?"

"Well, it ain't all that bad, especially after Emily's decided what to do with you. If you felt brave, you probably could walk around. Emily doesn't keep any Feral in the house, so you don't gotta fret there. But you're gonna smell mighty tasty to anyone getting a good whiff of you, hon, and not all of us have my self-control. Keeping you away from the bulk of the others will keep temptation to a minimum."

Nelson coughed from a doorway at the end of the hall. "If you would be kind enough to join me."

They caught up quickly, stopping in front of a white three-panel door. Nelson produced a key from his pocket and unlocked the door, revealing a large bedroom beyond. The décor was the kind of old-fashioned Tom didn't think still existed, including several Queen Anne chairs with actual doilies and a canopied bed with a lace duvet. It reminded him of when he stayed at his grandmother's house overnight as a kid.

"Give him the key," Lindsey said.

"As you are fond of pointing out, Lindsey," Nelson said, "I am head of the household here. As such, I expect you to be content with the way—"

"Give him the key," she repeated. The steel in her voice gave Tom a shiver.

A rosy flush, unlike anything Tom had seen before on a vampire, bloomed on Nelson's face. He scowled but nevertheless held out the room key to Tom.

"I expect that back before you leave the Chalet. Or, well, I guess I'll just take it back when we're finished with you." Nelson turned away without waiting for a reply and disappeared back toward the stairway.

"Never you mind about him," Lindsey said, watching his silhouette grow small. "He's been a self-important little cuss since I first laid eyes on him. He likes to bluster, but he won't bother you. Besides, you're mine." She gave him a wolfish grin.

"Lock the door," she continued, "and try and relax. Maybe get some rest. I'll fetch you when Emily's ready to see us."

Tom nodded and shut the door as Lindsey walked away. He locked them in as she'd suggested then watched Lady busily sniff everything in the room. When she finished, she padded back over to him by the door and looked up.

"Well, what should we do?" he asked. "Take her advice and stay here or go looking around?"

Lady didn't even pause. She lay down immediately, stretching out on the floor against the heavy door, head on her forepaws and eyes closed. Tom chuckled to himself, earning a disapproving peek out of one eye.

"You're right. You're right," he said around a yawn, aware of his own bone-deep exhaustion. The short nap at the store on that uncomfortable cot hadn't even put a dent in it. Tom leaned his shotgun and bat against the nightstand and shrugged out of his backpack, setting it carefully on the floor. He climbed onto the bed fully clothed without pulling the blankets down, too tired to care about rumpling the lace cover.

Tom's eyelids drooped heavily. After what seemed a particularly long blink, he was startled by a low woof from Lady. He was surprised to find her no longer lying in front of the door but just below him on the floor beside the bed. According to the old-fashioned clock on the nightstand, he'd been asleep for nearly four hours without moving a muscle.

As he rolled over, his intention of slipping back to sleep was thwarted by a firm knock at the door.

"Rise and shine, Tommy," Lindsey called.

"Yeah, just a second," he replied, swinging his feet over the side of the bed.

After a brief pause to stretch and rub his eyes, Tom shuffled to the door. "Are you alone?"

"Yes," she replied.

He fished the key out of his pants pocket, unlocked the door, and opened it just enough to look out into the hall. Lindsey met him with an open smile, holding a navy blazer on a hanger.

She was even more stunning than before. Her auburn hair had been pulled atop her head in a way that accentuated its reddish streaks. She'd changed clothes, too, into a light-blue dress that brought out the emerald in her eyes. Her smooth ivory skin was a perfect contrast to the tones of her outfit and makeup. She was the first one of her kind Tom had seen for whom their inherent paleness wasn't a detractor.

"Morning, sunshine. Here." She pushed the door open with her empty hand and pressed the clothing to his chest.

Tom took it with a look of confusion. "What's this?"

"A suit," she said. "Put it on. You've been invited to dinner. Oh, and no guns."

"Dinner? With who?"

"Lady Emily, you dolt. She's having a formal dinner for once since you're around. I hope you remember your table manners. You know a salad fork from a dinner fork, right?"

Tom rolled his eyes. "You're kidding me."

Lindsey's grin grew wider. "Oh no, not at all. Get your tie straight. You've got ten minutes until drinks are served."

She turned away from the door, the sound of her chuckles following behind.

CHAPTER 37

THE PAIR ENTERED THE CHALET'S formal dining room ten minutes later, followed closely by Lady. Tom felt like a new man. The suit he'd been given fit better than he would have believed, considering someone must have sized him up by eye. The clean white shirt with it had been freshly pressed and starched, and the accompanying tan slacks had a sharp military crease. A navy-and-green paisley tie completed the ensemble.

Heather would have called him a car salesman for the outfit and would have turned her nose up at the tie in particular. She'd always been picky about those and notoriously hated paisley. For his part, he didn't much care what ties looked like—they were nooses to be avoided whenever possible. But he needed Emily's help. If she wanted him to wear a tie—or a tiara, for that matter—he'd do it. He'd dressed himself with care, trying somehow to will the idea of her helping him into the outfit.

Tying the necktie, though, nearly bested him since he hadn't tried in over a decade. Muscle memory got him through it in the end, and he ended up pleased with the result. Lindsey fussed over it with a few sharp tugs, complaining that it wasn't quite straight. But it looked about the same to him after she "fixed" it.

Nelson greeted them in the dining room with a curt bow. His eyes lingered over Tom's new clothing as he straightened, registering a look of surprise that disappeared quickly. "Emily will be with you in a moment. Would you care for a drink before dinner?" He asked politely enough, but the chill in his voice made it clear he didn't much care either way.

"Why, yes, Nelson," Lindsey answered, "Tom and I would love a drink. Could you fetch something for us?"

He sniffed with derision but turned on his heel and crossed to the bar on the far side of the room.

"Do you even drink?" Tom asked.

Lindsey chuckled. "Nelson and I have been picking at each other for decades. He's not high on me because I don't need to beg him for Emily's favor. I'm not high on him because he's a pompous little shit who wants his ass kissed for being the butler."

She said it quietly but still loud enough—likely on purpose—for Nelson's sensitive hearing. He looked up from pouring bourbon into a tall glass pitcher and glared back at her. Tom expected a scathing reply, but he simply gave her a hateful look and went back to making drinks.

"Jesus, do *any* of you get along?"

"Only as needed," said someone behind them in a smooth voice, "which these days is making for strange bedfellows."

Tom spun to find a casually dressed woman in the doorway behind them. She had chin-length toffee-toned hair with gold highlights, sharp gray eyes barely touched with crows' feet, and a broad, warm smile. Attractive but not breathtaking, she seemed a handsome, sturdy-looking woman in her middle years.

Hard to believe she was centuries old or more.

"Tom," Lindsey said, "This is Emily, Lady of the South."

"We don't need any of that nonsense, Lindsey, and you know how I feel about it," the woman said, waving a hand. "It's my distinct pleasure to meet you, Tom. I hope you feel welcome here."

Emily extended a hand. Tom shook it tentatively.

"Oh, now, I won't nibble you—probably," she said, laughing. "Thank you ever so kindly for indulging me with dinner. I used to love dinner parties and balls and masquerades before that. Afraid there's not much of those sorts of things anymore, of course. Has me feeling a little socially deprived, as you can imagine."

In her songlike Southern drawl, it came out "dee-prihved." Tom, entranced, nodded mutely in agreement. Well, *of course* finding decent social engagements would be difficult after the end of the world.

Lady chuffed softly beside him. He frowned down at her, blinking away that gauzy feeling in his head. How did they do that to him? "I'm sorry… I seem to have gotten lost there for a second."

His host gave Lindsey a deliberate look but then patted him on the arm. "Oh, that's quite all right, child. With what you've been through, I'm surprised you're still standing upright. Nelson, how about that drink? I find myself a bit dry at the moment."

Nelson materialized at Tom's right with a tray holding three tall glasses filled with mint leaves and a pale, caramel-colored liquid.

"I hope you like mint juleps, Tom," Emily said. "I simply fell in love with them when I moved here. I'll stray occasionally, of course, and have been known to enjoy a sip of champagne every now and again, but nothing seems to satisfy me like a julep. And Nelson has become quite the hand at mixing them just so."

Lindsey took a glass from the offered tray, then Tom followed suit. Emily raised her glass in a toast. "To new friends and opportunities."

"Here, here," Lindsey cheered before upending her glass and emptying half of it.

Emily herself took a more moderate drink but still more than Tom's measured sip. The prospect of tying one on was tempting, but he'd learned that lesson in Iowa.

Eyeing him over the lip of her cup, Emily said, "Speaking of satisfaction… My, Lindsey, you were right. He is a pretty young thing, isn't he? My eyes haven't seen so tempting a morsel in years."

"Ma'am, I, um, well, that's very flattering," Tom stammered.

Emily reached out and brushed his shoulder then squeezed his arm above the elbow. "Oh, now, don't be shy. A man as well-formed as you should be bold. I do think you could do with some thickening up, but I've still half a mind to take you to bed right now. Lord knows it has been long enough since there's been a man around to give this old girl an indecent few thoughts."

Tom's whole face burned. Surely, she was kidding.

Lindsey gave him a Cheshire-cat grin. Worse, she offered no clue whether or not Emily was joking.

He tugged at his collar.

Emily rescued him, laughing lightly. "Listen to me going on, forward like a common street girl. Forgive me if I've put you off, but I've been around too long not to jump at chances when I have them. And believe me, chances are few and far between these days."

"Come," she continued, "let's sit down and eat. Nelson, the soup, please?" Emily started toward the long, rectangular dining table that dominated the room but stopped midway and turned back to them.

"Oh, and I should mention that I don't make a habit of letting dogs in the house, let alone the dining room. I've long had a policy that I'm the bitch here at the Chalet, and one bitch is quite enough."

Tom, gathering his wits, blurted, "She stays with me." His cheeks burned again as soon as the words left his mouth.

Emily's face became impassive, and she arched an eyebrow. "I'm not accustomed to being barked at in my own home."

Lowering his head, Tom said, "I'm sorry, ma'am. We've been—"

She waved his apology away. "Of course. But perhaps you might think first next time?" As Tom nodded stiffly, she continued, "As you're a guest in my home and you seem to have an attachment to your... dog, I'm inclined to make an exception this time as a courtesy. So long as you and she both return that courtesy, I'm sure we'll all get along just fine. She does seem well-mannered for an animal. I have Descended that could take lessons."

"Thank you, ma'am."

As she sat, her eyes twinkled. "You'll be in even bigger trouble if you continue to call me 'ma'am.'"

They settled into their seats, with Emily at the head of the linen-covered table and Lindsey and Tom each at one hand, opposite each other. The moment they were seated and settled, Nelson appeared with a bottle of wine and a tray of wide soup bowls.

The soup was a thick, slightly spicy pumpkin puree that was warm and hearty. That and a quickly emptied glass of wine went a long way to helping Tom relax. Spooning up the last drops from his bowl, he wondered where the pumpkin had come from since he couldn't imagine them farming. But he let the question go unasked.

When he finished, Tom was surprised to find both ladies had nearly emptied their own bowls, working their spoons diligently at their own last few drops. He'd expected they would daintily take dabs of soup every now and then, out of politeness. They didn't need to eat, after all.

Clearing his throat, he said, "That was great. I haven't had much in the way of decent food in quite some time. I have to admit, though, I'm surprised to see you eating so… heartily."

Emily, with a chuckle, put her spoon in her empty bowl and wiped the corners of her mouth with a napkin. "Oh, son, you really don't know the first thing about us, do you? True, we don't need to eat, but living on Feedings alone can get damn dull, I don't mind saying. Especially without much in the way of hunting these days. I find that a good meal now and then, of real food, mind you, breaks up the day-to-day. And wine… Oh my, I simply couldn't do without it."

She paused for a few seconds and turned her head quizzically. "Are we the first ones you've seen eat real food?"

"Yes," Tom replied, nearly dumbfounded. "Truth be told, I haven't seen anyone eat much… of anything."

Emily's rolled her eyes. "I declare, that girl who's been helping you along… What was her name?"

"Ana," Lindsey offered.

"That's right, Ana. Seems she's doing a fairly poor job. You wouldn't make it three days on your own out here."

The dismissal grated. "For the record," Tom replied, "it's been almost two days, and I'm not dead yet."

Emily smiled. "I did say 'three,' didn't I, son?"

Tom sighed. "Well, Ana played it all closer to the vest than I would have liked. Might have been nice to know what was going on earlier. But that's beside the point now. I said goodbye to her when I left Cincinnati, not exactly on the best terms." A thought struck him. "How and what do you know about Ana, anyway?"

Lindsey smirked after cleaning the last of her own soup off a spoon. "Oh, we know plenty about you and her by now, Tommy. I didn't when I picked you up at that store, but there are certainly rumors about you two in the air if you know where to listen. You're nearly celebrities."

Tom took another sip of his wine, which Nelson had refilled without a word. "Great. I'm vampire gossip."

In an attempt to comfort him, Emily patted his hand

again, which made him want to recoil from the chill of it. "Better to be gossip than the alternative, dear."

"I wouldn't worry much yet, Tommy," Lindsey said. "Most of what we hear is vague. It boils down to the talk of a human out there, somewhere. So far, that's it."

"I see. And about Ana?"

"The gossip's not much different than about you," Emily said, with emphasis on the word "gossip." "But we've always got a few ears to the ground. We heard that Colin has had Ana looking for humans since the plague, and he Made her specifically for her medical background. We also hear she was pregnant at the time, which came as quite a shock. Becoming one of us kills the baby, so turning a pregnant woman used to be quite taboo. Since then, she's been—"

"What?"

Emily gave him a blank look. "You didn't know? She didn't tell you?"

"Uh… no," he stammered. "She doesn't talk about herself much. Like I said: close to the vest."

"Well, now you know why," Emily said. "Poor thing's in just a mess. Likely one of the youngest of us, if not *the* youngest, and the world is all out of sorts. She'd have been better off left to die. And I hear she has a rocky relationship with her kin. But even with all that, she's supposed to have a big role in some scheme of Colin's."

Tom said nothing as Nelson collected their empty bowls and replaced them with plates of some kind of roasted bird and potatoes. He poked at the fowl with his fork, glad for the distraction.

"So you kids had a falling out?" Lindsey asked, cutting into her bird.

"Ana told me in the beginning—" Tom began.

"When you woke up from the coma?" Lindsey interjected.

Tom looked at her, an eyebrow raised. They did seem to have learned a lot about them both in a short time.

"Yes, after I woke up, when I was still weak. She told me she was going to help me get better and take care of me. Later on, when I understood… what had happened… she promised to look after me. Keep me safe."

He paused, not wanting to go on. Both women watched him in silence, hanging on the pause.

"After all that, all the promises, all we'd been through, she betrayed me. A bunch of Colin's goons held me down, and she injected me with that... Charon."

Lindsey and Emily shared a guarded look he couldn't decipher.

His hostess sat back in her seat. "Now, that's just a pity. You're no use to me with the disease. I have to admit, though, you look pretty healthy to have the plague."

"Didn't Lindsey tell you? Apparently, I'm immune."

"Oh, she told me you told her that. But you'll forgive me if I'm a tad skeptical."

"I don't have any proof, if that's what you want. But it's been three days since I got injected. I should be dead by now, right?"

Emily upended her wine glass and poured more for everyone. "I'll have to consider that when I set my mind to what to do with you. Some proof, though, would be helpful."

"Well," Tom said, "I don't want to see her, but Ana can give you that. Or don't you have your own doctor or something?"

"Not one that knows medicine past the Civil War." Emily laughed. "I might find an old sawbones or a fellow to apply a few leeches to bleed the evil spirits from you. Then again, I wouldn't recommend bleeding openly around here."

"Great," he mumbled.

"Look at it this way, son. I can't let a body feed off you until I know for sure. So that might help you stay alive. Then again, I don't know how long I want you hanging around, teasing the Family, either. Especially if one taste might turn them Feral. I've had my fill of those *things*." She spat the word like a curse.

Tom shook his head. "So you might have helped me, but since you can't be sure I'm not sick, I'm on my own?"

"Oh, not so fast," Emily said, smiling. "We'll see. As I said, I've yet to decide what I want to do with you. It will certainly help your case, though, if you're breathing still when I do. It doesn't hurt, either, that you're kind of cute." Her face became much more serious as she leaned toward him. "And you might want to cut that poor little girl some slack, son. She's in a bit of a spot."

"We're all in a hard spot, ma'am. I trusted her with my life, and she nearly killed me."

Lindsey gave him a questioning look from across the table. "Do you know why?"

He tossed his napkin on the table. "She said Colin ordered it. But that's no excuse, if you ask me."

As Lindsey shook her head in disbelief, Emily erupted

in laughter. "Oh, son, you have no idea, do you? If her Maker told her to do something, she had no more control over herself than you had in that coma. I might tell Lindsey here to get up from the table, spin your head around like a weather vane, and then go stand outside until the sun came up. She'd do it, too. She'd hate it, especially with that little shine in her eye telling me she's taken to you. And she'd scream like a baby when the sun hit her and she burned away. But she wouldn't be able to help herself."

Tom glanced at Lindsey, who looked away, embarrassed either by Emily's comment about her liking him or by her powerlessness against her Maker's wishes—likely a little of both.

Tom asked Emily, "Then how'd Ana help me get away?"

Emily sat back in her chair again, raising both eyebrows in surprise. "You're pulling my leg, son."

"No, ma'am. She left locks undone, keys where I could find them, even slipped me the suggestion to come here to find you. There's no doubt in my mind she did it all on purpose."

Picking up her glass, Emily again took a long drink. "An introduction to this young lady may be in order. Sounds like she's got a good touch of vinegar to her." Lowering her voice, she added, "Not so sure about Colin, though. Maybe he isn't all he's been made out to be."

Falling silent, she idly tapped a well-manicured finger on her crystal goblet, lost in thought.

CHAPTER 38

"Uh, ma'am?" Tom said, breaking the silence.

Emily turned to him and set her glass on the table. "Forgive me. Now then, I have certainly enjoyed our dinner, but the sun will be up soon, and I still have a few pressing matters to attend to before I turn in for the day. Let's get down to the real business, then. What do you want from me that's worth all this trouble?"

Tom drained his own glass, stalling. After clearing his throat, he said, "Ana pointed me in your direction but didn't really tell me why. She said that with your experience and position, you were maybe the only one that might listen to her ideas for fixing the problems... your kind has."

Their biggest problem was their food supply, of course, a fact he stumbled past quickly.

"So I guess she thought, by the same token, maybe you'd consider helping me stay alive. Alexander wants to use me for food, Colin as a guinea pig, and I can only run for so long. I desperately need security or someplace to hide—a place where I won't fear for my neck every time the sun goes down."

Emily gave him a sympathetic look. "I do hate to burst your bubble, but I doubt you're going to find a safe place anywhere. I'm sure I don't need to tell you, but every one of our kind who sees you is going to look at you like a prize pig. And if they get a good whiff of the blood running through you, many of them are likely to lose control. That's going to be a hard burden to bear anywhere, in any situation.

"Why would I give you protection anyway? Why should I protect you when that means keeping you away from my own children, just following their natural instincts?"

"Surely," Tom stammered, "there has to be some way I can help you that doesn't include my dying. Ana said she thought she had something figured out."

"But, son, she's not here. Even if she were, she's Colin's daughter. She can't just pack up, move to Atlanta, and start working for me. Not without his approval. And as I've said, I have no one like her. Whatever else Colin may be, it was clever of him to Turn her before the disease spread too far. Horrible, too, given her circumstances at the time, of course, but regardless, I haven't got a scientist in the Family, ready to pick up where she left off."

Emily took another sip of wine, letting her words sink in. With a nod to Lindsey, she continued, "Setting all that aside, my daughter has first claim on you. Even if I choose to take the decision away from her and offer you protection, by my own rules, I would have to compensate her. I don't know that I have anything of such value at the moment."

Meeting Lindsey's gaze, Tom said. "So… what? She

gets to decide what to do with me? Because I'm pretty sure she made up her mind about that back in the store."

Lindsey smiled back at him, her ruby lips spreading in a grin that lit her face. "Don't be so sure, Tommy. You barely know me."

"Regardless," Emily said, "I haven't decided. I'll admit the urge to keep you around as my own plaything for a bit is tempting. But that's just me being selfish."

"Plaything?" Tom asked, eyes wide. Then, with a long, controlled sigh, he added, "Fine, whatever, if that's what it takes to keep my skin intact."

Emily chuckled, face sparkling with mischief. "I'll think about it. Tell you the truth, though, you haven't made much of an argument."

"What do you mean?" Tom asked.

"You want protection, but you haven't convinced me that giving it to you is worth the mountain of hassle it'll cause. And if I can't do something useful with you, you'll just be hanging around the Chalet, confined to your room, Lindsey's, or mine, to keep the fighting to a minimum. That's not a life good for anyone here. For you, it's prison."

Tom frowned over the silver spoon on the table in front of him. "I see," he mumbled.

Emily stood up. "Look, son, the only thing I am sure of now is that daylight's rising, and I have work to do before Rest. Let's talk again tomorrow, and I'll let you know. You think about it. Come up with something helpful for both of us."

"I'll show him back to his room," Lindsey offered.

His hostess nodded. "It was my pleasure to meet you, Tom. I'm very glad you could join me for dinner."

Before Tom could even say good night, she nodded at Nelson, and the two of them disappeared through the back door, where the food had been brought in. He and Lindsey made their way to his room in silence, their dinner conversation a heavy disappointment.

Upon reaching his door, Tom unlocked it and said, "Good night... or is it good morning for you?"

She smiled at the question, the first truly warm smile she'd given him. "Wishing me a pleasant Rest would be the polite thing."

"Well, then, have a pleasant Rest, Lindsey," he said.

She cocked her head at him. "Thank you. That's nice of you to say, especially considering I'll probably feed on you tomorrow."

The warmth of her smile belied the threat. For some reason he couldn't put a finger on, he trusted her. He returned the smile. "I'll believe that when I see it."

Lindsey smirked but didn't contradict him. After a moment, she said, "We'll see. In daylight, I reckon it's safe to wander around in the Chalet, but be careful. Be in your room before sundown, and don't go belowground. Get some sleep too."

He nodded at the warning, which was sounding commonplace. "I'll see you tonight, then." As she nodded, he closed the door and locked it.

Lady was already lying on the floor by the bed.

Tom dropped the blazer, pulled off the tie, and fell onto the bed, hoping to get some sleep. But it eluded him, unsurprisingly, since he'd only been awake for a few hours. After tossing and turning for some time, he gave up and sat up.

Soft light was coming in through the room's sheer-covered windows.

"What do you think, girl, want to watch the sunrise?"

Lady opened her eyes and gave him a recriminating look.

"Tough," he told her. "Porches like the one here are made for sunrises and sunsets. Come on."

He slipped on his black leather bomber jacket, and they headed out into the hallway and made their way through the quiet house. The lights had been put out, but the promise of daylight was enough to brighten the Chalet. The silence that had fallen over the building was eerie compared to how busy it had been earlier, but Tom didn't mind. At least for once, he wasn't worried about finding a nightmare around every dark corner.

The front door was open, which struck him as odd, considering the security at the brewery back in Cincinnati. Did they always leave it open, or was that an accommodation for him?

Tom and Lady stepped out onto the long porch and walked along the east wing of the house. Reaching the corner of the decking, Tom leaned against the railing and admired the soft shades of pink peeking between the trees surrounding the mansion.

The morning air was sharp and cool, and Tom was soon blowing warm breath into his hands. When he stuffed them into the pockets of his jacket, his left hand brushed against something flat and smooth.

Heather's note.

Tom drew it from the pocket and traced over his name, neatly lettered on the front of the envelope. How long had passed since he picked it up in their apartment? A week? Six days? Five? All the time ran together in his head, one unbroken sequence of days and nights that belonged to someone else.

After some quick calculation, he concluded that five days had passed since his first encounter with that Feral in the empty high school—five days since this nightmare began.

Eyes closed, he slid his fingers across the face of the envelope, feeling the rough texture of the paper, the sharp edge where the flap tucked into itself. He followed the creases where his name had been signed with a fountain pen and imagined Heather's fingers feeling the exact same thing when she held the note years before.

Tom hesitated as he had back in the apartment. Did he want to read about it all over again? Didn't he have enough to deal with already? Surely, this could wait for better circumstances.

But he was out of time and knew it. He wasn't ready to read the note and probably would never be ready, but he might not have another chance. When Emily and her clan woke up in a few hours, she would decide what to do with him, and the odds weren't in his favor.

The flap opened easily, as it had days ago. Tom pulled the vellum note out of the heavy envelope and unfolded it. The paper was covered with Heather's distinctive handwriting, full of broad loops and carefully formed letters, each written with exactly the same slant on the line.

For some reason, that brought the smell of her to mind.

Taking a deep breath, he steadied himself.

My Dearest Tom,

I think this is going to be the last letter. I've got it, that Charon flu that's killing everyone. I'm so weak I can barely hold the pen, but I couldn't go without telling you goodbye.

It's a little strange, knowing that I'll be the first of us to go. I've been waiting for a phone call from the hospital every night for the past ten years or to get that sympathetic look from the desk nurse when I showed up for my afternoon visit. But you've never given up, not in all this time, and for some reason, it makes me believe that somehow, you'll make it through this.

I haven't been allowed to see you for a week, but I called today, and the new girl at the desk—one I guess I'll never get to know—told me you were still doing well and showed no symptoms of being sick.

I always thought I'd be more afraid if I knew the end was coming, but I'm actually kind of peaceful over it. I'll be with our little Matthew soon, and the idea fills me with so much joy I can't describe it. I can't wait to hold him again, feel his warmth, smooth the little tuft of fine silk hair on the top of his head, and tell him that it's okay now because Mommy's come to be with him forever.

I will never stop being sorry for how I hurt you, and I hope someday, somehow, you can find a way to forgive me.

Forever yours,

Heather

He wiped a few warm tears from his cheek and tenderly put the letter back in the envelope.

After hopping over the porch railing, Tom grabbed the box of letters from the Mustang, parked just a few feet away in the turnaround.

Returning to the porch, he sat down in one of the dozen or so old-fashioned rocking chairs spaced evenly along the front of the house. He placed the box in the chair beside him.

Tom returned the first envelope to the box, pulled out the last one, removed the note, and unfolded it.

My Dearest Tom,

I was stunned when that policeman came to the door two weeks ago. At first, I was afraid you'd let your temper get the better of you for once and done something stupid. When he told me you'd been in an accident, I was afraid I'd lost you forever. But he said you were at the hospital, barely alive. I've hardly left your side since.

I can't believe I had to almost lose you before realizing how much I need you. I don't know whether to hate or thank the drunk that plowed into you at that intersection. Without him, I might have gone through with that stupid divorce. Because of him, though, you might never come back to me.

The doctors tell me you're in a coma that could last anywhere from a week to the rest of your life. Either way, when you wake up, I'll be there waiting for you. I hope you won't still hate me for everything.

When we lost Matthew, I could barely get by, day to day. No one should ever have to make funeral arrangements from labor and delivery. When we buried that tiny coffin, I believed that most of what you loved about me was buried too. I was broken, reckless, stupid, and didn't give a damn. I didn't think I could live our life anymore, didn't think I could live with you.

Someday, I hope you'll find a way to forgive me for being so stupid. I'm so sorry for all the ways I hurt you only because I was so broken myself. You deserved better than what I gave you. You're the kindest man I ever met, Thomas Woodford, and the only man I ever truly loved.

You tried to help me move on, to move forward together with our life, to see that no single thing, no matter how difficult or disappointing, is worth giving up over. You tried so hard for me, and in return I broke your heart.

I am so very, very sorry.

You need to understand that I filed for divorce because no matter what lies I told you or myself, the truth is that I couldn't take the way you looked at me after that day, with the hurt so clear in your eyes. I didn't think you could ever love me again. After everything I'd done to you, I couldn't go on hurting you.

I suppose that's all the least of our worries now. I've cried myself to sleep every night lately, thinking about how I almost lost you and how I'll need a miracle to get you back.

But I believe in miracles, and I know that someday soon, you'll come back to me. I promise you I will be here waiting when that day comes.

Always yours,

Heather

Tom folded the letter along its aging crease, put it back in the box, and wiped his face again. With reverence, he took the next-to-last envelope from the box and removed the vellum note inside.

After reading that one, he moved on to the next then the next and the next, one a month, every month, for ten years. They were full of love and hope, news of the world and his family, and more importantly, healing.

He spent the morning reading letters from the wife he'd loved and lost, who apparently came back to him only when it was too late for both of them. When he finished, after reading that last note a second time, the sun was high in the sky above the trees to the east.

It shone warmly on his face, glinting off the streams of tears rolling down his cheeks.

Tom put his face in his hands and wept without reservation, sobbing softly with Lady at his feet—not for the world that was gone or the one he was trapped in, but for the wife he hadn't been there for a decade earlier, when she needed him. And he wept for the love that brought her back to him anyway.

He knew exactly what he wanted from Emily now, and it wasn't protection.

CHAPTER 39

AFTER THE TEARS STOPPED AND Tom's cheeks dried, he rocked lazily while the sun slid across a blue sky filled with soft white clouds, enjoying the simple pleasure of late morning on a front porch. For the first time since the day he confronted Heather in that hotel-room doorway, he was at peace—at peace with himself, if not quite perfectly at peace with his world.

That was something, at least, a good start.

He nodded off at some point midmorning and woke slowly, rubbing a kink from the back of his neck. The sun hadn't yet reached its peak, and sore neck notwithstanding, he considered staying put and taking a longer nap in his chair. But while he was relatively safe at the moment, that probably wouldn't be the case as the sun started to fall. On the off chance he didn't wake up before then, he decided he should get back behind the locked door of his room.

With Lady at his heels and the box of Heather's notes under his arm, he went back inside the Chalet. Rather than going straight to the room, though, he briefly explored the ground floor.

The mansion was as beautiful as it was massive. Every

room was decorated with what seemed to him impeccable taste, even if maybe more traditional than he'd have gone for. Few expenses had been spared when it came to the furniture, lighting fixtures, floor coverings, and even accessories.

He and Lady started in the library, with walls lined two stories high with books. Next came the dining room, which led to the kitchen through the door Emily had used after dinner. After that, they entered some form of sitting room or parlor, which itself led to a large office with a massive dark wooden desk and half a dozen wing-back chairs. Then they wandered through a game room complete with a pool table and a collection of dark, silent video and pinball game cabinets.

Finally, they made their way across another sitting room, this one full of leather couches and chairs and decorated with oil-based paintings depicting an English foxhunt. Exiting the far door from that room led them back to the foyer with its grand, sweeping staircase and breathtaking crystal chandelier.

The second floor was less interesting. The western wing had a number of accessible rooms but even more that were locked. Behind the unlocked doors were rooms like the one he had been assigned. They varied in size and décor, of course, and some were even multiple-room suites, but all seemed to function as bedrooms.

Having done enough wandering around to become comfortable with the basic layout of those two floors of the Chalet, Tom followed Lady back to their own room in the eastern wing. Once past his door and locked in, he took off his jacket and boots and crawled into bed.

Lady flopped on the floor beside him without ceremony. Exhaustion and lack of sleep caught up with them both quickly.

Tom slept like the dead.

He woke to muted gray light filtering in through the sheers covering the windows. The sun had already set, and the world outside was catching up quickly.

Grunting with the aches and pains earned over the past few days, he reached toward the ceiling, trying to work all the kinks out. Lady followed his lead, stretching out with her forequarters down and her hind in the air as she yawned. Afterward, she shook vigorously.

Not wasting time, he stood up and dressed. He put his old jeans on but chose to wear the white button-up shirt that came with the suit. Having a clean shirt, something he'd taken for granted for years, was a luxury now. He was keeping this one.

With his jacket on, boots tied, pack in place, and weapons ready, Tom left his room in search of Lindsey and Emily, sure that they'd be finished with Rest. He locked the door behind himself and headed for the office he'd seen earlier that morning. It seemed the most reasonable place to start.

At the top of the stairs, he decided that waiting in his room for Lindsey to get him might have been the wiser course. He passed no one in the hallway, but several of Emily's Family were making their way along the opposite wing. Others passed through the open foyer below.

Each of them gave him a deep, appraising look as they went about their business.

A few even stopped dead in their tracks and stared at

him with half-blank, almost wild eyes. Tom stood at the top of the steps, frozen, uncertain. If they weren't struggling with the urge to feed already, getting closer meant filling their noses with the scent of his blood. But he couldn't stand there all night.

Tom took a tentative step forward, down the sweeping staircase. One of the vampires below, a hulking beast with a handlebar mustache, gave him a wicked smile. Fangs appeared from nowhere as malice darkened his face.

Tom retreated to the top step, but he was too late. The man with the mustache stalked toward him. Lady leapt down two steps, growling ferociously.

Tom dropped his bat and raised the shotgun to his shoulder.

As the man reached the bottom step, Lindsey flashed through the foyer. In the blink of an eye, she was behind him, one hand clutching the back of his neck and the other his left arm. She whispered something in his ear, and the dangerous look on his face became one of surprise and fear. His fangs disappeared.

Lindsey spun Handlebar Mustache away from the steps, released him, and pointed toward the door. He gave her a pleading look that she ignored. With one last angry glare at Tom, he turned and left the Chalet.

Tom picked up his bat, caught up with Lady, and walked downstairs. Reaching Lindsey, he said, "I guess I owe you one."

"I seem to recall telling you to get to your room before nightfall," she said, disapproval plain on her face. "You should have stayed there until I came to get you."

"Sorry," he said, keeping his voice firm. "I woke up

feeling better than I have in days. I'm ready to fight the whole world. I wanted to see Emily as soon as possible."

She rolled her eyes but smiled. "I see. Trying to cut a deal with her before I caught wind of it? You're not going to weasel away from me." She laughed and winked at him. "Come on. She's in her office."

Emily looked up from writing something at her desk when the pair stopped in her doorway and Lindsey rapped twice on the frame.

"Good evening," Lindsey said. "I hope we aren't interrupting?"

Emily smiled in return, but it was brief and plastic, not like the ones she'd given Tom the night before. Though the night was young, she looked weary already. "Good evening. Nothing that can't wait. Come in." She waved them forward.

They crossed the room to her desk and took seats in a pair of leather-covered chairs opposite it.

"What can I do for you?" Emily asked.

"Forget about protection. I know how to help you, but I need your help first."

Emily gave him a quizzical look. "Explain that for me, son."

"We have to go get Ana."

"Tom, that dog don't hunt. We've already talked about it. She's Colin's, and that's that."

"Look, if the only way I can help you is with her, then I'm going to do whatever it takes to get her back. So I'm going to go back for her one way or the other. But I'll have a lot better chance if I'm not alone."

"That's a pretty tall order, son," Emily replied, capping

a fountain pen and setting it on the desk. "Last night, you were looking for any old port in the storm, so long as I told you it was safe. But now you're fixin' to head back into the hornet's nest… alone? What changed your mind?"

He raised a hand and extended a pair of fingers. "Two things. First, I've got no other choice. I'm not prepared to curl into a ball and die."

"Second, I've been given a second chance. A second chance at life and a second chance to make up for lots of old mistakes. And I'm going to make the most of those chances, risk or no risk. This is how the world is now. This is my life. If I go back up there and I'm killed trying to find her, that's one thing. But at least I'll know I tried. If I won't even try, I might as well be dead."

Lady's tail thumped against the hardwood floor where she lay between the chairs.

Tom looked from Emily to Lindsey to gauge their reactions. Emily put a finger to her lips and tapped a few times. Lindsey's eyes were fixed on Emily, with that now-familiar faraway look. They were communicating.

"And what about Colin and Ash?" Emily asked. "They won't just let you walk in there and take her away. She'll probably end up killing you herself. I don't care how feisty she is—she can't fight her Maker."

"I'll kill them both if I have to, starting with Colin," Tom said, glaring in challenge. He hoisted the bat on his shoulder to underscore the threat.

Emily chuckled. "You know, I believe you think you could. I've half a mind to turn you loose and see what happens."

"Let me help him," Lindsey said, leaning forward. "Colin's got no right to do half of what he's done. Infecting Tom with Charon was just plain dumb. And we can't let some West Coast asshole swing through and take over Alexander's region. He needs to be taught a lesson and either burned or sent back west."

"Do not forget your place, child," Emily snapped. "Your britches aren't big enough to question lords, girl. I'll tell you what to think about what Colin's done."

Beside him, Lindsey hung her head. "I'm sorry, my lady. I spoke too quick. I just—"

Emily waved her apology away. "Nonsense. Just remember that there is a time and a place, Daughter. For what it's worth, I don't entirely disagree with you."

"But?" Lindsey asked.

"But no, I can't send you to get one of Colin's Family, especially when it could lead to stirring up—or outright fighting—another lord. I won't risk a full war with him and the entire region north of us over this. It's not worth it."

Tom sighed. "I'll go alone, then."

"You not going anywhere, son," Emily said, leaving no room for argument. "You're not running off to get yourself killed. You were lucky as hell to get away the first time, even with help. You go back there alone, you aren't coming back."

"So what am I supposed to do," he asked, burning with a mix of disappointment and irritation, "wait around until one of your Family decides to have a go at me?"

"Yes, I do expect you to wait until—oh, Nelson, come in."

Tom and Lindsey both turned to find Nelson hovering in the doorway.

"My lady, a guest has arrived for you," the steward announced. "Would you like to see him? He claims it is urgent."

Emily's brow furrowed. "Yes, fine, show him in."

Nelson stepped aside, and a rugged-looked man strode purposefully into the office, shoving a scraggly, disheveled vampire in front of him.

"Good evening, Emily," Lars said. "It's been much too long."

CHAPTER 40

TOM SPRANG FROM HIS CHAIR and turned to face Lars, his back to Emily's desk. "What's he doing here?" he nearly shouted.

"Believe it or not, I'm here looking for you, Meat," Lars replied.

Squeezing the grip on his shotgun, Tom narrowed his eyes. "If you came to fetch me for Colin—"

Lars laughed and waved a hand, dismissing the warning. "You've got yourself all worked up, don't you? I'm sad to disappoint you. That's not why I came."

Confused, Tom frowned. "Then why?"

"Ana asked me to find you before Ash did. He's the one Colin sent looking for you."

"I was afraid of that," Tom said.

Lars nodded. "You have no idea how pissed he was. But he's kept it quiet. Only a handful know, and it's mostly all his people."

"And Ana?"

"She's alive. Or, at least, she was when I left. And lucky to be, if you ask me."

"Does Colin know that she…?"

"That she helped you? Yep. When I left, she was hanging in that cell where I first put you. Seems Colin isn't sure what to do with her. Apparently, she's pretty valuable to him, so he hasn't done anything yet. Of course, she's only valuable to him if he has you too." After a brief pause, Lars added, "I'd bet his indecision won't last too long, though."

Tom turned to Emily. "You have to let me go now. The longer I stay here, the angrier Colin's going to get. Sooner or later, he's going to kill her."

Emily gave him a sympathetic look. "Son, I'm sorry, but I can't let you charge back up there, guns blazing, especially if you already stoked Colin's fire. She's a big girl, and I'm sure she knew what she was getting into. Don't think she'd appreciate you stumbling back into Colin's hands after everything it's cost her to get you away. And, look now, Ash is hunting you too. I've never met him, but the stories I've heard tell that he's not only a fine tracker but plenty nasty to boot."

Tom dropped back into his chair and set the gun across his lap as Lady whimpered softly from the floor beside him. "Emily, please, if you would just—"

Lars cut him short. "Lady, I've got some other news for you."

With a hand still holding his disheveled companion's arm, Lars led him to a couch along the wall to Lindsey's left, beneath several pictures of sailboats. The man wore a dirty green trucker's cap and a hole-riddled plaid flannel shirt. His jeans had long ago faded to near colorlessness, so pale that barely a hint of soft blue was left. His hair was dark brown, curly, and shaggy beneath the cap and looked in need of a good washing.

Lars gave the man a shove, and he dropped onto the couch without resisting. He slipped the cap off his head and focused on his feet.

"What exactly have you to tell me, that you've brought me one of my own?" Emily replied. To the man, she said, "Birdy, isn't it?"

He nodded. "My... Lady," he stammered.

"Tell her, Birdy," Lars said, his voice carrying a low undertone of threat.

"He told me... he said..." Birdy stopped and looked up at Lars pleadingly. "I don't think he wanted me to tell anyone... He's not right... dangerous." Each word dribbled out slowly, one at a time.

Lars gestured toward Emily. "See her? She's trying to be very patient with you right now, Birdy, because she's a better leader than me. But she's your Master, and if she loses her patience, she can skin and gut you like those squirrels you sell. Now spit it out."

Cowering, Birdy lowered his eyes and nodded several times. Finally, he whispered, "He killed them. All of them. He and his boys."

A grave look washed over Emily. "Who did, Birdy? Where?"

The words came at last, in a rush, one on top of another. "At Hap's. They knocked them down and cut their necks and fed on them. Hap and Ben and three others I didn't know."

Emily's face grew dark, a tempest brewing. "Who, Birdy?"

Wringing the old faded hat in his hands, Birdy met her eyes. "Some crazy man. Called himself Ash. He said there'd only be one Master someday and that I should help him make it that way."

Silence fell over the office, every breath held. Emily sat back in her chair without breaking eye contact. Her fingers tapped a calm, repeating pattern against the top of her desk, and her face became unreadable stone.

Just when Lindsey cleared her throat softly and was about to speak, Emily finally asked, "What else did he say about this one-Master business?"

"I… I don't know. Nuthin'. He just said that. And that the good ones would feed on the… judgey ones."

"That's all?"

"He came into Hap's sayin' he wanted a warm meal. But then he asked questions."

"What questions, Birdy?"

He squirmed beneath her stare as if he'd rather be anywhere else in the world. "Wantin' to know if anyone been talking about a human."

"What did they say?"

"One of the ones that wasn't Hap or Ben—Dell, I think—said he'd heard o' one." Looking away from her, Birdy turned toward Tom, his eyes widening as if just realizing they were in the same room. "It was you," he said. "They was talking about you." A wildness came over his face. "Brother, but you do smell good," he whispered.

"Birdy," Emily commanded sharply, drawing his attention back. "Was there more? Did he ask other questions?"

Looking back at his feet, he shook his head, his shaggy curls dancing like a curtain in front of his face. "No, ma'am."

"Thank you, then. That'll do for now. You two stay here, now, at the Chalet until all this blows over."

Birdy slumped visibly, as if a weight had been lifted away. "Thank you, ma'am," he said.

"Don't be silly," Emily replied. "Would you like Nelson to assign you a room, or will you be all right on your own?"

Standing up, he replaced the dirty cap on his head. "No, ma'am, I can see to myself. Thank you much for the kindness."

"You're Family, child. What's mine is yours. Now, run along and don't bother yourself with this unpleasantness anymore."

He gave Tom one last hesitant look but then turned away with a start, like someone trying to keep from nodding off in a chair. He disappeared from the office.

"He was always a nervous one, Lady," Lindsey said as soon as he was gone. "He could be a problem here." She didn't look at Tom but didn't need to.

Emily nodded. "Don't worry. I already have someone keeping an eye on him." To Lars, still standing beside the couch, she said, "You know I don't stand on being formal, Lars. Have a seat. Bearer of bad news or not, you are a sight for mighty sore eyes. And yes, you're right, it has been much too long."

Rather than dropping onto the soft cushions of the couch, Lars leaned against one of its arms with an air of casual readiness that fit him perfectly. "I do regret not having made a trip south since... well, the disease. Things north of here have kept me busy. Quite busy in the last week, especially," he added, offering a wry smile.

The rattle of ice announced Nelson in the doorway behind them. "You could use a drink, my Lady?" he said.

"Why, yes, Nelson, thank you," she replied. "I believe everyone else will have one also. I know most of us have just woken, but you know what they say about desperate times."

Nelson set down a tray of glasses, ice, and bourbon and went about making them each a drink.

Lindsey leaned toward Emily. "Sounds like Colin and Ash are up to something. What are you going to do?"

After taking the glass offered by her assistant, she drained it in one gulp and held it out for a refill. Nelson poured from the decanter still in his one hand as the others took drinks from the tray offered in his other.

Again, Emily took a deep pull, this time emptying only half her glass. "I've protected myself and my Family for a thousand years, and in all that time, with all the bloody feuds and fights, I do believe I've never heard anything quite as disturbing as what Ash did right beneath my nose, to my own people."

Another quick gulp.

Standing, she set her glass on the desk. "Nelson, call the Captain and have him fire the Dragon. We're going to see about this."

Lindsey smiled and drank her own bourbon in one swallow.

"The Dragon?" Tom asked, uncertainty plain on his face.

"It's about time I paid a call to the new lord in the north. I'm not sure I want a war, but nobody comes into my backyard and kills my Family without being called to account. I'll have Ash's head, one way or the other, and Colin's too if his answers don't suit me. And we'll see about this 'one Master' nonsense. Get whatever you need. We're leaving within the hour."

CHAPTER 41

ORTY MINUTES LATER, LINDSEY COLLECTED Tom and Lady from his room and led them back to the Mustang. She had changed clothes since the meeting in Emily's office and was covered in black, head to toe. He nearly remarked at her Cold War–spy wardrobe but thought better of it after seeing the set of her jaw and her determined look.

"Where is everyone?" Tom asked, settling into the car. As he fastened his seat belt, Lady gave him an envious look from the small seat behind him.

"They'll meet us there," Lindsey replied. "We're taking the car because I have to drive you. The others will walk or run."

"All the way to Cincinnati?" His mouth hung open. "How long will that take?"

"No, no—someplace much closer," Lindsey said with a smirk, spinning the Mustang through the turnaround with a squeal of rubber. "Have we got a surprise for you."

After a thankfully short but heart-stopping drive that included Lindsey's typical abuse of the accelerator and neglect of the brakes, they pulled into an industrial park dominated by an enormous warehouse. The inky black of night surrounding them hid the building's details, leaving it a dark, shapeless form that loomed over them.

"We're going in there?" Tom asked as he stepped out of the car, more than a little uneasy.

Lady sniffed around, sharing his anxiety.

Lindsey walked to the front of the Mustang, parked facing the building. "Trust me, it'll be fine."

"Right. If I end up dead because of something in there, I'm going to haunt you for the rest of your life. And since you're mostly immortal, I'd take that threat pretty seriously if I were you." He gave her his best grin, hoping to lighten the sense of dread the place was giving him.

She laughed. "I'll keep that in mind. Follow me, Tommy."

Lindsey disappeared though an open doorway next to a pair of huge barn-style doors.

"I guess we've followed her this far…" Tom said to Lady.

The dog cocked her head as if not sure she approved, but she went in anyway.

He followed but stopped almost immediately. Lady's tail, which he almost couldn't find, was a few yards ahead of him, but the rest of her was hidden in the darkness ahead. "Lindsey?" he called in a whisper.

"Keep walking," she replied, somewhere ahead of him. "There's nothing in your way."

Hands forward, the way he played Marco Polo in the pool as a kid—except holding on to a baseball bat—he took one hesitant step forward at a time. Nothing solid was within arm's reach to either side of him, and the way sound carried gave the impression of open space. A soft bump on his leg let him know Lady was walking beside him.

"What is this place?"

"Some kind of warehouse or industrial plant, I guess. I'm not sure. Doesn't matter anyhow." She was close, ahead just a few feet or so.

Finally, his right hand, fingers stretched forward awkwardly while trying to hold the bat, reached a flat, solid surface. A half second later, the other brushed against something softer, like fabric, over something more firm.

"Whoa, there, Tommy. Hands to yourself," Lindsey said from his left.

"Oh, God. Sorry." He could almost hear her grinning at his embarrassment.

"Are you ready?"

"Uh, sure. For what?"

"This." A splinter of pale light appeared just in front of him, finally making her visible. It widened, and he realized she was opening a door. In the growing moonlight, he was again struck by her smile and the twinkle of her eyes. Even dressed in all black and done up conservatively, she was striking. He didn't actually have a stupid crush on a vampire, did he?

She looked like a kid at Christmas. Tom started to point out that she was almost bouncing, but the heavy, acrid smell of smoke filled his nose. He coughed instead.

"Is something burning?"

"You betcha!" she said, holding the door wide open. "Look."

He stepped into the doorway. "Well, I'll be damned."

The door opened to an outdoor loading dock half

covered by a tin roof. Where it ended, a raised concrete pad continued, and beside it, a huge locomotive belched black smoke into the pale night sky. A handful of shadows skittered around beneath the hulking steel monster, busily attending to it.

"The Dragon," Lindsey whispered over his shoulder. Her voice was almost reverent.

"Is that an... old steam train?"

"Bet your ass. Emily uses it to go longer distances than she wants to go by foot. She hates cars."

They crossed the warehouse space and came out from beneath the roof onto the open platform. Closer now, the locomotive's details stood out clearly. Painted reptilian wings stretched along the side of the engine's boiler and back along its tender, and an enormous dragon-head carving was mounted at its nose, pointing forward over the cattle catcher.

Emily's workers stopped to glare briefly at Tom and Lindsey as they neared the train, but they went back to work without a second look.

Three coaches were attached behind the engine, two of which were brightly lit from within.

"That first one," Lindsey explained, "has a few large cabins in it. Emily uses one of them for her office on board, another for her Rest. The others are for anyone. Usually, there's a card game or something going on. The second car has individual berths. You'll be in one of those. The last car is for Resting on trips that are longer than one night. Its windows have been replaced with covers so no sunlight comes in."

"Wow" was the best Tom could muster. "That's awesome. Who drives it?"

She led him to the second coach and climbed up the steps. "They call him the Captain. I've met him, but only once—a man salty enough to curdle milk by lookin' at it. Supposed to have been an officer in the Civil War and an engineer most of his natural life afterward. This was his idea. Emily loves it."

Lady scrambled up after her, and Tom followed. "The Chalet, the Dragon, the Captain? "Emily certainly seems to have some flair, doesn't she?"

The coach's central corridor was lit by the flickering light of candle lanterns at regular intervals. Pairs of doors faced each other across the aisle every few feet, undoubtedly passenger compartments.

Lindsey stopped at the door numbered 17 in brass numerals. She opened it and shrugged. "Maybe, but she's over a thousand years old. At her age, I reckon it's okay to be a little off. Adds color. Especially when the world's as screwed up as this one."

Gesturing into the cabin, she added, "This is you, Tommy. I'm going to check with Emily. Stay here until I get back."

The passenger car seemed newer than the engine itself and was not without comforts. The seats, two heavily cushioned benches opposite each other, were well padded and upholstered with velvet. A set of built-in lights didn't seem to work, but a lantern had been hung by the door.

Tom took off his shotgun and pack and leaned both the gun and his bat against the wall. He dropped onto the rear-facing bench and stretched his legs onto the one opposite. Lady jumped up onto the seat beside him and put her head on his lap.

He stroked her fur, trying not to think about what they were doing.

The train shuddered into motion moments later, almost exactly an hour after Emily had made the decision to go. He appreciated how well her operation seemed to run, compared to what he'd seen with Alexander and Colin.

He liked Emily more than he wanted to admit. Maybe that wasn't so bad, though. He did need friends in the worst way. But how to tell if he could trust her?

Roughly half an hour into the trip, Lindsey came back to the cabin. She slipped inside and took the seat facing Tom.

"We should be there in eight or nine hours, just enough time to get to them before sunup. You might be staying on the train, though. Emily hasn't decided yet."

Tom frowned but nodded. "Oh. Okay."

They rode in silence for some time, each absorbed in what they were doing, content to try to relax in the sway of the coach while the Dragon clacked along its track. The dark countryside slid by outside, mostly a blur.

"Lars and Emily seemed pretty familiar."

Lindsey raised an eyebrow. "What do you mean?"

"He strolled right into her office like they were old friends and then warned her of trouble theoretically caused by his own new lord. That kind of thing doesn't seem super-common with you people."

"They're kind of old road buddies. Emily has known Lars for a long time. She and his Maker used to be… companions, I guess you would say."

"Companions? I thought you were all mostly kind of loners back in the day."

"Mostly, we ain't much for being social with our own, yeah. But it can get pretty lonesome from time to time. And then, think, Emily's over a thousand years old. That's a long time to be without any company. Sometimes, you might try to live with the humans, hiding in plain sight. Or other times, a couple of us, maybe even a small group, would live and hunt together for a while."

"So Emily used to hang out with the guy who Made Lars?"

"The woman who Made Lars, but yes," Lindsey replied, leaning her head against the seat back and closing her eyes.

"I don't get it. He's got this old relationship with Emily, but he's been living in Cincinnati with Alexander? What is he, a spy or something?"

She chuckled. "No. Emily has lots of spies, but Lars isn't one of them. He just happened to be in the North when Charon hit, so he stayed there. He's helped her out from time to time because he seems to have a soft spot for her."

"Spies?"

Leaning forward, she said, "Yeah. In the past three years, we've gone from chaos to a little bit of order, but the six lords don't always get along. So they all have their people, sources in the other regions, digging for info. How'd you figure we found out so much about you and Ana so fast?"

Tom turned back out the window. "I did wonder about that."

"I'm surprised," Lindsey added, "Colin didn't do something like this sooner. I'm sure he's been looking for a way to get off the West Coast."

"Why?"

"The place is too damned sunny. If you were me, would you want to live there?"

"Huh. I thought everybody loved California."

"LA's a crater now too."

"Oh, right. So Emily's going to go throw him out?"

She shrugged. "She hasn't told me—"

A knock cut her short. Lindsey stood and slid the door open a few inches. Nelson's face appeared in the gap, and he said something too quiet to hear over the sound of the train. She nodded, and the steward disappeared.

"Emily wants us. Let's go."

Tom sprang up and gathered his things. In the corridor, they bounced against the walls as they made their way forward. At the front of the car, Tom hesitated before gingerly stepping across the coupling into the next one.

He purposely ignored the amused look Lindsey gave him.

Emily's coach was similar but with a more dimly lit aisle. Instead of many evenly spaced pairs of doors, this one had only four, clustered together near the corridor's halfway point. One pair stood facing the two others, suggesting four separate rooms.

Lindsey walked to the farther door on the left and entered without knocking. Tom stayed right behind her, Lady at his feet, not sure what to expect.

Emily's office was well appointed but not to the same level as her rooms in the Chalet. A compact cherrywood rolltop desk stood in the far corner of the room, closed. A pair of couches faced each other in the center, one opposite the door and the other with its back to it.

Emily sat facing them. Lars, his back to the door, shot them an uninterested glance over his shoulder.

"Welcome aboard the Dragon, Tom," Emily said. "A few more hours, and we'll be there."

"Thank you," Tom replied. Not wanting to mince words, he pressed, "I need you to let me get Ana out of there."

"That's why I called you in here." From a rose-covered teacup, she sipped a thick, dark liquid that he didn't want to think much about. "I will tell you right now, son, I don't much like the idea of sending you or somebody else in there to break that girl out. I'm not much for putting my nose in another's business. In fact, I'd skin the hide off anybody that got in the way of me dealing with one of my own. But Colin's on thin ice with me for this business with Ash, and the fact of the matter is I can't let him make the decision on what to do with you. Plus, we both know that I need your friend."

"So…?" He tried not to seem too hopeful.

"So, you got one chance, son. If you can get her out, and she's willing to leave Colin, do it. Lindsey will help you. Don't get killed, and don't get my little girl killed either. I expect to keep Colin and his people busy with our visit so you can slip in and out quick. He'll be hamstrung unless he wants to attack me personally. And he'd regret that."

Before Tom could say anything, Lars added, "You got your chance, Meat. Sure you're up to it?"

"You do your part, I'll do mine," Tom answered, ignoring the flutter in his gut.

Lindsey crossed her arms. "Good. So what's the plan?"

Emily patted the seat beside her. "Tom, you come on over here and sit down, and Lindsey, you take a seat too."

With Lady at his feet, Tom settled in beside her as the four of them worked out the details.

CHAPTER 42

THE DRAGON STEAMED ACROSS THE Ohio River an hour or so before dawn, already slowing in preparation for its arrival in Cincinnati. It came to rest in a massive industrial train depot on the west side of the city. Stepping off the coach onto gravel, Tom admired the dark silhouette of the city he'd lived in most of his life, from a completely new perspective.

Rocks scattered beneath Lindsey as she stepped down behind him.

"Such a beautiful skyline," he murmured. "I didn't appreciate it at all years ago, and now I keep seeing it in an entirely new light."

"We all have regrets, Tommy, things we'd like to change," Lindsey said. "Nothing to do but remember them, keep them in mind as you go. And this time, make better ones."

He nodded and reached down to pat Lady.

"Ready?" she asked.

"Just a second," Tom replied. After shrugging out of his pack, he unzipped it and pulled out his revolver. He made sure it was fully loaded, pushed it into the usual place against his back, and replaced the backpack. Then he slung the shotgun, heavy with shells, over his shoulder. Gripping the bat, he nodded to Lindsey in the dark.

"Okay, let's go."

The clang of footsteps on metal rang behind them, and they turned to see Emily descend from the train. Lars followed.

"We were just going, Lady," Lindsey said.

Emily nodded. "You be careful, Daughter. I'd hate to lose you. We'll do what we can to help. Good hunting, now."

Farewells exchanged, Lindsey, Tom, and Lady made their way across the rail yard, east toward the city.

They crossed several sets of train tracks before reaching a tall gate in a chain-link fence separating the depot from a street leading into the city. The gate was secured with a heavy chain, which Lindsey pulled apart like a child's paper chain of snowflakes. It fell to the ground in a musical cascade of links. "I'm sorry, Tommy, were you planning to get the door for me?" She winked.

An oversized white pickup emblazoned with company logos sat abandoned on the far side of the gate. Lindsey was at the driver's door before Tom could blink.

"I was hoping I could drive this time," he said. "I do know the city better."

"You gotta be faster than that." She laughed. "Now, be a sweetheart and slip over there and try to find the keys." Lindsey nodded at the passenger door.

With a sigh, Tom walked around the truck and opened the other door. But the search for keys proved fruitless.

"No luck."

"Me either." She frowned.

"Maybe we'll get lucky with the next one?"

"I don't think so," Lindsey said, grinning. "Ever hot-wired a car?"

"Are you kidding? Who actually knows how to hot-wire something?"

"Watch and learn." She chuckled.

A few minutes and several choice curses later, the truck's engine sputtered to life.

Tom shook his head in disbelief. "Where did you learn that? Wait, don't tell me. You spent the seventies working as a night mechanic or something?"

She climbed up into the driver's seat. "You manage to live through today, and maybe I'll tell you."

An ear-splitting screech interrupted them—Feral, a pair of them. They shambled toward them from the shadows of an alley a block away. The first was tall and lanky, to the point of being almost skeletal. Scars crisscrossed its face, shoulders, and chest, and a tattered sport coat hung from it like a drape. A fringe of matted brown hair fell around its neck. It screeched again, raising a pair of filthy claws.

Beside it, a shorter version bared its fangs and hissed. Stouter than the first, it was by no means heavyset but seemed to have been wider to start with. Stark white hair fell over a prodigious forehead in a messy tangle.

Lady jumped ahead to meet them, barking furiously.

"Time we show 'em you've got a set. You want Fat Man or Skinny Boy?" Lindsey asked.

"The fat one maybe? Slower?" Tom replied.

She shook her head. "No, he'll be the leader. He probably gave Skinny his scars. I'll take him. They'll make for you right away, as soon as they catch a whiff of you, I mean. When they do, I'll swing behind and grab Tubby. Ready?"

Heart pounding, Tom swallowed. This whole excursion was his idea. He'd asked for the trip, even claimed—half seriously—he'd kill both Ash and Colin somehow if he had to. He couldn't back down from a couple of Feral, regardless of how cold the pit of his stomach had become.

He nodded and stepped away from the door of the truck, shouldering his shotgun. "Who's hungry?" he shouted in the dark.

They both squealed, not unlike pigs called to slop, and dashed toward him. Lindsey stepped away from her side of the pickup and walked to her left, trying to flank them as they moved toward Tom.

Abruptly, they pulled up and turned her way.

Seeing their sudden change, she stopped too, confusion on her face.

"What the hell are you doing? He's the tasty one." She pointed at Tom.

Both ignored the gesture and held their places. Lady continued to bark between the pair and Tom, but they ignored her too.

After a few seconds, they growled and sprinted toward Lindsey. Tom and the dog both took off right after them.

The skinny Feral arrived first. Lindsey easily parried his outstretched claw and hit it with an open palm to the chin. The thing's head snapped backward, and momentum carried it to the street.

Fat Man took a swing at her head as she recovered. Ducking slightly, Lindsey raised her shoulder to catch the brunt of the attack and staggered a few steps to the side with the hit.

Her blood sprayed over the asphalt from a set of deep gashes.

Lady reached the stocky monster a few steps ahead of Tom and bit down hard on the back of its calf. It swatted at her, but she sidestepped, and the claw passed by harmlessly. The Feral lost its balance and lurched forward.

Tom, close enough now to point the muzzle of his shotgun a few inches from the back of the thing's skull, squeezed the trigger. Fat Man's head exploded in a red mist, and the body collapsed, twitching.

The skinny one, in the meantime, grabbed Lindsey's leg as she stumbled past it. With a yank, it pulled her down and scrambled to get on top of her, leading with its fangs.

"Oh, hell no!" she cried and hit it square in the nose with an open palm. Blood gushed down the plaguer's chest, and it fell back to the ground.

Lindsey scrambled up, straddling her attacker's chest. Taking a firm grip of each side of the Feral's head, she twisted, grimacing. Popping sounds announced that Skinny's neck was broken.

"Give me the gun," she said, standing up. "No wait, the bat."

Tom grabbed his bat from the truck and watched, unaffected, as Lindsey repeated what he'd done that rainy night some days before in Iowa.

He'd been someone else before that moment, someone who might have cringed at the sight of such brutality. He wasn't *that* Tom anymore.

When she finished, Lindsey wiped the Louisville Slugger off using Skinny's oversized sport coat and handed it back. "I reckon he's not getting back up. I have to admit that's pretty satisfying," she said, matter-of-factly.

"What was that about? Why'd they go after you?"

"I don't know. Something changed when they saw me. They must have been under control." She wiped blood off her face.

"Great. So they know we're coming?"

"Maybe. Probably."

"Does that change that the plan?"

"No," Lindsey replied without hesitation. "If things go right, Emily should arrive before we do and distract them. We'll still just sneak in."

"Yeah, okay," Tom said, replacing the shell he'd used in the shotgun.

"Good. Now, let's get out of here before another flock of them show up."

The truck's engine was still sputtered along, to Tom's surprise, belching an occasional puff of dark exhaust. They climbed inside the cabin, letting Lady take the space between them on the bench seat. Lindsey dropped the transmission into gear with a thunk and gave it gas slowly. The pickup rumbled forward along the unlit street.

A few blocks later, she stopped being gentle with the aging motor and resumed driving like she was trying to outrace the devil himself. They whizzed past run-down industrial plants that spoke of the manufacturing history in this part of the city.

Eventually, that area gave way to a more residential district, although more than a few homes seemed on the brink of falling down. They crossed under an expressway, drove up a hill, and slowly came back down into the core of the city, just northwest of downtown's skyscrapers.

Continuing east, they passed several blocks where buildings here and there appeared to have been recently rehabbed, restored to their original nineteenth-century Italianate condition.

Lindsey pulled the truck to the side of the road. "This is about where Lars said to stop. We'll go the rest of the way on foot."

They'd parked in front of a bar's large clouded front window.

He glanced inside with a touch of longing. "I could sure go for a drink."

"Maybe later, if we're all alive," Lindsey said. "Come on. We need to find this place and get indoors." She nodded at the western horizon, where a soft blue glowed above the buildings.

"Oh, yeah, sorry. Let's go."

They crept up a few more blocks as slowly as they dared with the sun coming up, watchful for any hint of more Feral or other vampires. Fortunately, nothing else moved around them.

Lindsey stopped in front of a tall brick building with a board covering its front entrance. "This is the place Lars told us about."

"Are you sure we can trust him?" Tom whispered. "What if we walk into a huge trap?"

"Emily trusts him," she replied, scrutinizing the panel. "That's enough for me. Besides, if he's led us into a trap, she'll know about it the instant it's sprung on us. He'd be dead before he even noticed the pissed-off look on her face."

Digging her thin fingers into the crevice between the brick doorway and the barricade, Lindsey gave it a tug, and the wooden sheet swung forward easily, just like a door. Darkness lay beyond.

"Very clever," Tom breathed.

Lady sniffed at the opening. Satisfied, she padded through. Tom went next, and Lindsey stepped in last, letting the panel close behind them.

Determined not to fumble around in the dark, Tom slipped off his pack and took out a flashlight. He snapped it on, causing Lindsey to groan and cover her eyes.

"You could give a girl some warning when you're going to do that next time, Tommy," she hissed.

"Sorry."

They stood in place as her eyes adjusted to the light. The room was shrouded in a dusty gloom the flashlight barely defied. How sensitive must her vision be for that little light to have such a blinding effect?

Tom swept the light over the room, but it wasn't much to look at. The space was largely empty and covered in a thick layer of dust. A trail of footprints led across the room to a dark opening on the far wall. Lady followed the tracks and stopped at the passageway. She looked back, expectantly.

"Let's just go," Lindsey muttered, still blinking in the dim light. "I'll be fine in a minute."

They crossed the room side-by-side. Reaching Lady, they found the opening wasn't a hallway but a ramp descending into darkness. More footprints stood out on the dusty walk.

"Just like Lars described," Lindsey said. "Follow me. Quietly."

CHAPTER 43

T HE RAMP LED TO A level landing, where it turned to the left. Another short ramp brought them to a musty-smelling tunnel hundreds of feet long, farther than the flashlight's weak beam of light could brighten.

The tunnel was just wide enough that they weren't squeezing their shoulders along the sides, and it was built the same as the one below the brewery. This didn't have the tall ceilings of the lagering cellars, though, and Tom had to duck slightly below the stonework, which came together in an arch not quite six feet above the floor. The walls curved toward the ground also, coming together in a thin rivulet of water running over dirt.

Neither spoke. Lindsey led the way as the odd group stole through the long hallway, Tom's own breath and pounding heartbeat the only sounds in his ears.

The long, dank tunnel opened into a vast, empty room, thick with stagnant air. The footprints, deep indentations in dirt here rather than oblong shapes in a thin layer of dust, made a path to and from a hole at the base of the wall to Tom's right. It was just large enough for an average-sized person to pass through in a crouch.

"Through that, we'll be inside Colin's lair," Lindsey

whispered. "That should open into a room along the same hallway as Ana's cell. Through that room, up the hallway, and we're there. In and out quick, and we come back this way."

Tom nodded.

"Ready?"

"As I'll ever be."

Lady stood waiting at the opening, head down. Lindsey peered through it, listening for signs of activity in the far room. Satisfied, she waved the dog ahead.

Lady darted through the opening. A few seconds later, her muzzle reappeared, as if she wondered whether they were coming. Lindsey and Tom both squatted down and shimmied after her.

The room on the far side was just as he remembered: walls and floor lined with heavy stone bricks outlining a dark, musty room. And just as in the tunnels, pieces of crumbling brick and mortar had fallen away from the walls and collected in piles.

Unlike the other room, though, this one was a single space. It wasn't separated by a wall of steel bars and made into a prison cell. It also lacked the dim, mechanic-hook lights. It did, however, have the same heavy door opposite where they'd entered, leading to the outer hallway.

Tom killed the flashlight and returned it to his backpack. After swinging the shotgun off his shoulder, he thumbed the safety off and made sure a shell was chambered. "Let's go get her."

Lindsey stood at the door and listened again. She then tested the doorknob, which turned easily. It wasn't locked. After holding up a hand with all five fingers spread wide, she counted down in the silence by folding her fingers into her palm. Finally, she crimped her thumb, leaving only a fist in the air. Then she opened the door and strode through.

Lady came next and immediately released a barrage of low growls. Tom rushed through on her heels, dropping his bat to the floor with a clatter. His finger twitched against the shotgun's cold trigger.

Three men stood facing them a few feet away, clustered around the next door, fangs exposed. Lindsey hissed and bared her own but put a hand on Tom's shotgun, keeping it pointed down.

The youngest looking of the three turned to the tallest one, standing between the other two. "Do we have to capture them, Neil, or can we have them for ourselves?" His face shone with something reminiscent of lust, making his preference clear.

Lindsey smiled darkly. "Come on over here, puppy, and try either one. I dare you."

His wild, hungry look was replaced by a flash of uncertainty. He hissed back at her.

Finally, the third one, the one closest to Ana's cell, said, "Neither. I don't see nothing. And you don't either."

Tom recognized the thickly built frame from when he'd been brought in with Lars's group. Cade was his name, he thought.

"What's that mean?" Neil asked.

"It means we get the hell outta here, Neil. That human's been nothing but trouble, and I think I heard of *her* before. If she's who I think, she'll rip you up like a paper bag. And that other lord, who's older than dirt if I'm a day, is upstairs with her whole clan. I get the creeps just looking at that one."

"But," Neil blurted, "Colin said to stop them."

Cade shrugged his wide shoulders. "Don't care. You know what's going on up there. I'm not getting into it. Lars would say the same. Especially with Alexander still out there someplace. He's my real Maker, the only lord I care about. You do what you want."

"What about you, Dillon?" Neil asked the third one.

Dillon glared at Lindsey. "I'm not…" he began just as his eyes went blank. A few seconds later, he blinked and turned to Cade. "Did you get that?"

Cade nodded smugly and smiled. "He's here. Let's knock some heads."

"This isn't our problem," Dillon said to young Neil. "Alexander wants us." With that, Dillon and Cade turned away and were gone, leaving Neil looking confused and frustrated.

"Come on, puppy," Lindsey taunted. "You want me to pet you on the back?"

He hissed again but didn't move. Finally, he muttered, "You're lucky. Next time, you won't be." He vanished into the darkness after the others.

Lady padded up the hallway toward the cell door as Tom took a breath. "What was that about?"

"I don't know, but he's right, we got lucky. The three of them at once would have been rough, even if the little pup was a total pushover. Either way, that worked out better than I'd hoped. With luck, more of Alexander's family is thinking the same thing."

Tom picked up his bat from the floor.

With a sigh, Lindsey said, "Look, you can't carry both that and the shotgun. You need both hands. You've been struggling with it since we left."

"I know," Tom replied, "but I don't want to leave it. If I run out of shells, I might need it."

She rolled her eyes. "Tommy, you've been a damned pain in my neck since the moment I found you. Give it to me."

He handed her the Louisville Slugger, and she shook her head in disbelief. "The world's most perfect killer, and I'm carrying a billy club around. Come on."

Reaching the door to Ana's cell, Lady put her nose to the ground and growled softly.

"I smell it too," Lindsey whispered. When Tom cocked an eyebrow, she mouthed the word "Feral."

As before, Lindsey raised a hand, fingers out, and counted down. When she made a fist, she twisted the knob and shouldered the wooden door inward. Lady rushed in, teeth bared. Lindsey followed, the bat high over her head.

As Tom crossed the threshold, a bare-chested Feral with white tufts of hair dropped on the floor in front of him with a thud. The Louisville Slugger in Lindsey's hands dripped crimson.

"Do you want me to…" Tom began, but the words died on his lips as she mashed the plaguer's head like a baked potato.

But it wasn't her brutality that stole his voice.

Lady, standing at the wall of steel bars, whimpered softly.

Tom knelt beside the dog and rubbed her chest. "Fuck."

On the far side of the bars, the restraints fixed to the wall hung open, empty. Ana was gone.

CHAPTER 44

LINDSEY CAME OVER TO STAND beside him. "Dammit. Colin must be protecting his bargaining chip."

"Now what?" Tom asked, determination in his voice.

"Hold on a sec," Lindsey replied. Her green eyes went empty.

Tom picked up the bloody bat and wiped it clean on the Feral's ragged pants. He examined the end of it, afraid the force she'd used might have split the wood, but it seemed as solid as ever.

Lindsey took it back. "Emily wants us to get out. She's not happy, but there's nothing else we can do. We don't know where the girl is, and Emily doesn't want us lost down here."

Tom scuffed his boots on the dusty floor, considering. At last, he said, "No."

"Look, Tommy, I—" she started.

"No, Lindsey," he said, meeting her surprised glare. "I'm not walking away from her. You don't want to come, fine. I understand you have to do what Emily commands. But I'm not leaving here without Ana. I'll have Lady track her, and I've got plenty of shells. I'll be fine."

He turned to the door and whistled. Lady woofed softly, padding after him. As he reached for the door handle, Lindsey suddenly stood in front of him.

She took his arms and looked him deeply in the eye, unblinking. "Tommy. Tom, you will *not* do this. You're coming with me. We're leaving—going back the way we came."

Lady growled a warning.

Tom looked down at the dog then back at Lindsey. "I said no. You can kill me, you can come with me, or you can leave me be. But I'm not going back. I don't want to fight about it, but I won't be pushed. I'll say it again. I'm not leaving here without her. So please step aside."

Lindsey raised an eyebrow. "How in the…?"

Tom cocked his head but said nothing and held his ground, waiting for her to move.

Lindsey glowered.

Just as he began to wonder how he would physically move her from the doorway, she gave a half smirk that cleared the tension. Shaking her head with a look that was equal parts confused and amused, she stepped out of his way.

"Thank you. Tell Emily I'll do my best to make my way back to the Chalet."

She chuckled. "No way, Tommy boy. You're not going off without me. Emily can take it out of my hide later."

Tom cocked his head, giving her a confused look. "I thought you couldn't just up and defy your Maker?"

Her mouth compressed tightly. "Normally, yeah. But Emily's… busy right now. Something bad's about to happen up there. She's pretty focused, so that makes it easier to misbehave. Now, let's get moving before I change my mind."

Cracking the door to the hallway, Tom poked his head out. Nothing was moving in either direction.

After they stepped out of the room, he squatted, face-to-face with Lady. "Find her."

The dog looked over her shoulder, the same direction the trio of guards had run off. She woofed once and licked Tom on the cheek. Springing up, she darted away.

"If she finds her, I'm somehow getting you both a steak," Lindsey said, incredulous.

Tom chuckled. "I already promised her one myself. Come on."

They jogged through the hall after the German shepherd. Although Lindsey could have easily outpaced Tom and kept up with the dog, she hung back with him instead. Lady, ten yards ahead, stopped at a corner in the hallway, barked once, and disappeared to the right.

At the corner, they came to a large open space littered with broken wooden barrels. Lady stood expectantly at a door on the far side of the room, sniffing at the gap above the floor.

"Good work, girl," Tom said as he reached her, nearly panting.

He stroked the dark fur along her back as Lindsey set her ear to the door. She frowned. Then with a barely audible gasp, her eyes flared open, and she took on that far-off look. Whatever that meant, it couldn't be good.

"What it is? What's wrong?" He pushed down the urge to shake her, knowing it wouldn't help. Instead, Tom sighed with impatience.

Finally, she blinked and exhaled. "Oh shit."

"What?" he nearly yelled.

"They're fighting upstairs. It's a bloody mess. And Alexander's back."

"We can't help that. We have to find Ana."

"You don't understand. This door leads right to the main room up there. I can hear the fighting through…" She broke off midsentence and went stock-still again.

"Dammit!" Tom threw his hands up.

Lindsey turned back to him, her face a grim mask. "Emily saw Ana. Ash is here too. He has her bound in chains, and he's dragging her up the staircase in the middle of all the fighting."

"Did Emily stop him?"

"No, for God's sake, it's chaos up there. She's just trying to keep her Family alive. She couldn't get near him."

"Fine," Tom said, exasperated. "Then let's go." He put his hand on the doorknob.

Lindsey covered his with her own, stopping him.

"Tom," she said, still close to his ear, "it's a nightmare up there, and there's no way to her but through it. Are you sure?"

He met her eyes, trying to make his face as implacable as a rock, trying to ignore the quiver in his gut. "We're wasting time. He's taking her to the observation deck—I know it."

"Okay."

After one quick breath, Tom opened the door. Beyond it was a small room with a stone staircase that twisted up and to the right. At the top was the open archway leading to the main room on the ground floor.

He could see flickers of shadows dance past it, brief glimpses of fanged vampires. Grunts, groans, cracking sounds, splattering noises, and the occasional scream all filtered down from above.

"That's it," Lindsey said beside him. "Through that arch, we'll be in the thick of it, and it's gonna be an angry beehive. Hit the top step at a dead run and don't stop for anything, even your momma. If anything or anyone comes close to you, shoot it and keep going. I don't care what you see, hear, or feel. Get to the staircase at the far side and up. Got me?"

Tom couldn't tear his eyes away from the archway. He nodded. Even if he'd had something more to say, he couldn't find the words.

"Good. Go."

He said a silent prayer and started for the stairs, whistling for Lady. She moved with him, staying at his feet.

Lindsey blew past, taking the steps in long strides, seeming to bound up them in one fluid motion. She stood on the landing where the stairs turned, waiting for him before he even hit the bottom step.

He took them a pair at a time, though, and caught up quickly. Just as quickly, though, she leapt forward and was at the next-to-last step before the arch.

As he dashed up behind her, the din of battle filled his ears. With each step, he could see more and more of the space beyond the entrance. There had to be hundreds of people—vampires—exchanging blows, almost all of them covered in splotches of red.

He'd never seen anything like it in his life.

Somewhere deep inside him, a voice screamed to stop,

wait, turn and run. Charging wildly through a blood feud between three groups of vampires—especially hungry ones—was illogical at best. This was some kind of suicide he was contemplating.

Slowing down, though, pausing even for a second, would kill the adrenaline-fueled courage that was the only thing keeping him moving in the face of everything in front of him. And he had no time to wait, no time to think. Whatever kind of life Ana had, it depended on him getting up there and stopping Ash.

He shoved the fear away, burying it as he reached for the empty place in his mind. He squeezed his shotgun until his knuckles turned white, and he hit the top of the steps running. Lady ran beside him, matching his pace and not bothering to growl or bark.

And then they were beyond the archway, in the nightmare.

Tom didn't manage to move two paces ahead before having to duck to his left. A tall blond woman to his right with the longest fangs he'd seen yet swiped a claw across the face of a shocked male of medium build, giving him several deep gashes to the cheek. The male fell backward, right into Tom's path.

Lindsey surged ahead from behind him and hit both vampires, one immediately after the other. With a loud slap, she smacked the male to change his direction, clearing him out of their way. She gave the blonde an elbow to the face that landed with a sickening crunch.

Racing along an invisible path from the archway to the staircase, they crossed groups of fighting vampires every few feet and had to duck, hit, or dodge their way past.

Sometimes the combatants would take notice of them, and sometimes they wouldn't. Sometimes they avoided interfering completely, and other times, the only way forward meant knocking someone out of the way.

Lady darted and hopped through gaps in the crowd, largely ignored.

A sticky shower of blood surrounded them, filling the air. With each foot closer to the stairs, errant droplets splattered them, warm and thick.

Halfway there, a dazed male stumbled, alone, directly into Tom's path. Tom weaved to the right to go around, but a ravenous, hateful glare flashed in the vampire's eyes. He knew exactly what was coming toward him. He opened his mouth, hissing, and jumped forward to feed.

Lady sprang first, clamping her jaws shut on the attacker's wrist, and he was forced to step sideways to shake her off.

Following Lady's attack, Tom swung the shotgun around, intending to drive it into his attacker's chest, but was a hair too slow.

Still, the muzzle of the gun batted the vampire's outstretched arms away, keeping them from grabbing Tom's neck. Lindsey rushed past, not much more than a blur, and grabbed the vampire herself.

Squeezing him by the throat, she looked around, searching for something to do with him. She needed time to bind him, time to subdue him and somehow keep him from coming back after them—time they didn't have.

Not thinking, Tom put the gun to his head and, without hesitation, sprayed two-thirds of it across the room in a cloud of red.

The body dropped to the floor in a tangled heap.

And they were running toward the steps again.

Each step closer brought another leering face, pair of slashing claws, splash of blood, or victim into their path. And every new threat, every obstacle, was met and removed in a fraction of a second, action and reaction flowing together in a complex dance that Tom would never have believed possible.

His jaw clenched tightly, and his every muscle tensed. Sweat and blood streamed down his face as he focused on each new thing in his way.

Lars, blood dripping from his fangs and down his chin, pushed a man with a ratty brown ponytail to the ground. Then, what seemed like half a heartbeat later, he was twisting the arms of a broad woman behind her back while driving her headfirst into a stone wall.

Emily flashed into and out of his view as well, through a break in the crowd of fighters, fending off at least three attackers at one. She, too, was covered in blood, her hair flying wildly about her face as she moved. It was the first time she'd been anything but meticulously well-kept.

Briefly, Tom even caught sight of Alexander, his grizzled features shining red.

Finally, with one last push to finish the frantic sprint, Tom mounted the staircase and raced upward, panting. His chest and legs burned from the effort. Somehow, though, they'd managed to cross the chaos behind them. Lady scrambled a few steps past and stopped but continued to look upward, impatient to continue.

Lindsey hit the steps a few seconds after Tom but was forced to turn around and literally kick one of Colin's thugs back into the waiting arms of a group of her own Family. She joined Tom just as he caught his breath.

"Let's not ever do that again," Tom muttered, taking in the scene. "It's a miracle we got through that in one piece."

"That was the easy part, Tommy," Lindsey replied, cold as ice, using a sleeve to wipe the blood off his face and then her own.

He nodded. "Let's do what we came here for."

Lady disappeared around the corner of the rising stairs. Tom stormed up after her, stomping on each step. Looking over his shoulder without breaking stride, he said, "Should I slow down, try to sneak up to them?"

"No," Lindsey said, just behind him. "Every second counts. Besides, if he's paying attention at all, he already knows we're coming."

They charged on as fast as they could, running single file up the narrow steps.

When they reached the top, the trap door to the observation deck was already thrown back, and pale light drifted over the last few steps. Lady jumped through the opening without hesitation, and Tom followed barely a second later.

Shouldering his shotgun, he froze, feet planted wide for balance. Grinning at him wickedly, Ash was busy securing Ana to the same post again, facing the windows.

"Be right with you, dude. Just finishing up here."

CHAPTER 45

"**T**HEY'RE HERE, AND THE SUN'S not up yet!" Tom yelled down to Lindsey.

Almost before the last word left his mouth, she was standing beside him, frowning at the predawn light streaming in through the windows.

"We have to be quick," she urged.

Ana, facing away from them and dangling from the post with her hands manacled above her, turned toward them over her shoulder.

"Tom? What are you...? Get out of here now! Run!"

"You get her down," Tom said to Lindsey, more calmness in his voice than he felt.

"Tom, no…" she began.

He ignored her, already jogging toward Ash. Lady was barely a step ahead of him, growling deeply, hackles raised.

He and the dog veered to the right of the post. Lindsey sprinted away from them, to her left, intending to approach Ana from the other side.

Ash didn't take the bait. Leaving the post, he was on Lindsey in a flash, catching her by the throat midstride. "Aw, that's cute, taking orders from a human. A perfect example of why we need to be feeding on the weak of our own kind. The herd needs thinning."

Tom fired the shotgun, the blast deafening in the mostly enclosed space. Shotgun spray tore through Ash's arm, and he dropped Lindsey.

She clutched her side, where several small, shiny wet spots blossomed against her black jacket. She'd been hit too, even with the narrow-spread shells. Regardless, Lindsey jumped up and darted away from Ash. He turned to follow, but another boom echoed through the room.

The second blast tore through Ash's shoulder, and he looked back at Tom with eyes full of rage. Fangs and claws out, he charged.

Tom pumped the gun again, but the vampire tore it from his grip before he could squeeze the trigger. Ash flipped the weapon across the room with his uninjured right hand in a single, fluid motion.

Cringing, Tom leaned forward and to his left, away from Ash, expecting a strike from the vampire's free hand. The dodge worked as the vicious blow caught him on the right shoulder rather than the head. Still, the crackle and pop of breaking bones rang in his ears.

Screaming in pain, Tom crumpled, trying to break the fall with his one good arm.

He landed hard on a pile of cold metal chains, the shiny steel links cutting into his forehead and the side of his face. Rolling over his broken right shoulder, he groaned in agony. Expecting Ash to be leaning over him, ready for the kill, Tom raised his good hand defensively. Instead, a black-and-tan streak of fur sailed over him and hit Ash squarely in the midsection. Lady latched onto the ripped, bloodied flesh of the vampire's damaged left arm, still growling.

Ash screamed in a mix of anger, surprise, and pain, and grabbed the dog by the neck with his other hand. He yanked hard to pull her away, but her powerful jaws clung to his forearm.

He pulled again and succeeded, but she came away with a gooey chunk of his flesh in the process. Ash screamed again. Furious, he flung Lady away. She crashed into the desk on the far side of the room with a yelp and slid, limp, to the floor.

Finally regaining his feet, Tom pulled the revolver from his waistband and squeezed the trigger several times. The first two shots went wide, but the next two slammed into Ash's chest, on his already damaged left side. He stumbled backward a step but then used the momentum from the impact to spin around and dash forward. He swatted the gun from Tom's hand, and a fifth shot splintered the floor several feet away.

In the same motion, Ash snapped Tom's head to the left, exposing the right side of his neck. Tom struggled, but his right arm was useless, and he couldn't reach his attacker with the left. He was overcome with exhaustion anyway, much too tired to fight anymore.

Ash leaned towards him, fangs dripping.

So tired. Definitely better to just get it over with.

Then the triumphant look on Ash's face melted away, and his eyes went wide in surprise. Tom's baseball bat slid across the front of Ash's neck, and Lindsey's face appeared over his shoulder.

Ash flew backward, away from Tom.

"Tommy, snap out of it. Get the shotgun!" Lindsey shouted.

Tom blinked against the haze in his vision and rubbed his temples. As he shook his head clear, the room snapped back into focus.

The shotgun lay on the floor behind him. Rushing to it, he picked it up with his left hand. As he stood, something dark flashed in the corner of his eye.

Ana, free of her bindings, stood by her worktable, fumbling frantically with her tools.

"Ana, help us stop him!" Tom shouted.

Either not hearing him or ignoring him, she just kept working with whatever she had in her hands.

A spike of cold fear shot through him again, eclipsing the pain in his shoulder. Had he been wrong? Would she not help them, or worse, refuse to come with them? Had all this been for nothing?

"Tom!"

The urgent call brought his attention back to Ash and Lindsey, still struggling near the post. Ash had somehow gained control over her, holding her right arm—the one with the bat—with one hand and her neck with the other.

However, Tom had done enough damage that Ash couldn't simply break her neck in one motion—yet. He'd be healed enough to do it soon, though.

Tom set his feet and raised the shotgun to his left shoulder, one-handed.

Ash, who was facing away, spun around and threw Lindsey into him. The gun fired as they collided, and buckshot sprayed the ceiling, wasted.

They hit the ground again, Lindsey landing on Tom's

chest and knocking the wind out of him. She rolled away and got back to her feet as he coughed, struggling to get up with stars in his vision.

Ash stalked toward them, swinging his left arm over his shoulder, testing it. He grabbed Lindsey, who was still stumbling, twisted her around, and pulled her to him. One arm encircled her chest, the other her throat.

She squirmed, helpless.

"I'm so sick of you. Both of you. All of you. You're pathetic and weak."

Ash glanced to his right, to the windows facing east. Slivers of sunlight crept across the floor.

"I'm taking you downstairs, dude, and sucking every last drop of sweet, terrified blood from you. And I'm not going to Influence so you feel all warm and cozy about it either. You're going to scream when I tear your throat out and lap up your blood like a cat with a bowl of cream. And your girls are going to stay up here and get a little sunburn."

Getting up, Tom staggered backward, to keep from Ash's reach. He stumbled over the chains that had cut his face before, nearly upended him again. He spotted his revolver to his right and snatched it just as a chilling scream filled the room and a streak of black streamed through his peripheral vision.

Ana stood next Ash. Her long hair hung all around her face, not completely hiding a wild, hateful expression. Lindsey staggered away from them.

Ash's mouth dropped open. A syringe protruded from his neck, plunger depressed. Whatever had been in it was coursing through him.

He lurched sideways. "What... what was in that?"

Ana spat in his face. "Enough tranquilizers to stop a herd of elephants," she said, voice slicing through the dusty air, "plus twice the Charon you made me give Tom. I want to see if *you're* immune."

Ash reached wildly for the syringe, struggling to grasp it, but couldn't. His coordination was already failing him.

"Tommy, help me," Lindsey said beside him, whispering. She held a length of the chain in her hands.

Tom nodded, not quite able to process what he was seeing.

She darted forward and snapped a manacle to Ash's arm.

He offered no resistance but gave each of them in turn a blank look. "This... It can't be..." he sputtered, tongue heavy in his mouth. His eyes rolled back into his head, and he crashed to the floor, shaking the whole room.

Lindsey offered Tom the end of the long chain. "I don't know about you, but I don't want to see what he's like Feral. Wrap this around that post."

He did as she asked, stepping through the warm sunlight near the pole. He walked around it then away again in the opposite direction. The chain clanked against the post with each step he took closer to the staircase, where Ana and Lindsey had retreated.

Lindsey took the chain from him, a glimmer in her eye. "I'll see you in hell," she said, giving the chain a hard tug.

Ash's unconscious form slid along the ground toward the post, which acted as a pivot. A few feet at a time, he edged closer to daylight. Lindsey grunted with the effort.

His arm reached a sunlit patch on the ground first and burst into bright blue flames almost instantly. With one last determined grunt, Lindsey yanked Ash's head and torso into the deadly patch on the floor.

He moaned slightly as the fire spread, consuming the body. In less than a minute, nothing but charred cinders and a shower of lightly floating ashes remained.

Weary beyond words, Tom nearly collapsed. But he had one more thing to do.

He shuffled across the room, ignoring the quiet discussion Ana and Lindsey were having as they made their way down the steps.

Lady lay motionless beside the desk, exactly where she'd landed.

Dropping to his knees with little grace, he stroked her coarse black fur. Something was stuck in Tom's throat—he could barely breathe.

"Are you okay, girl?" he croaked. "Wake up, girl, you're going to be all right."

No response. The lump in Tom's throat threatened to choke him. A hot tear slid down his cheek.

"Come on, girl."

He scratched the fur on her neck, digging through it to reach her skin below. After several breathless moments, he finally found what he was looking for. A pulse, the faintest hint of one, beat rhythmically against his fingertips.

"Thank God," he sobbed, more warm tears following. "Thank you, God."

He slipped his left hand under her head but couldn't

pick her up with his worthless right arm. "I need…" he croaked, still struggling to speak. "I need help."

Ana ran up the steps, eyeing the windows. Nodding to herself, she jogged over to Tom and knelt beside him.

"She's alive," he whispered, "but my shoulder's a mess. I can't lift her. Will you?"

Ana nodded, saying nothing. She scooped the dog up gently and ran back to the steps without waiting for Tom.

Slowly, he pushed himself up off the floor and made his way to the staircase. Both women were already below. They waited for him there, safe from the sun's deadly rays. Tom paused at the top step and glanced at the black, powdery remains of Ash.

He smiled. His shoulder was broken, he was bleeding, and the whole thing had nearly been a catastrophe.

It had gone about as well as he'd dared to hope.

Fumbling down the stairs, he met Ana and Lindsey in the darkness on the fourth floor, sitting near the steps. Both looked tired, which was saying something for them.

He plopped down on a step, grunting at the sharp ache in his right shoulder.

"Well, now what? I'm not going back down through that," he said, referring to the fighting below.

Lindsey beamed. "We can go on down whenever you're ready, hon. It's all over. For now, at least."

CHAPTER 46

AT THE BOTTOM, THREE CLUSTERS of vampires watched them enter the room. Tom felt like a rabbit entering a wolf's den.

Lars stood with one large group near the archway leading below. He spoke quietly to those around him, the remains of Alexander's Family. Alexander himself was nowhere to be found.

Colin's contingent was the larger of the two other groups, huddling together, surrounded by the family Emily had brought with her. Colin was sporting several deep gashes on his face as well as quite a few rips and blood-tinged patches on his now-dingy white dress shirt. Blood still seeped slowly from his left eye. Standing at the front of his own Family, head up, jaw jutting forward, he was defiant still, although clearly having lost face in the exchange.

Emily sat, looking perfectly serene, in a desk chair fetched from the office next door. Her face had been wiped clean of any bloody evidence, and she'd put on a sweater to cover her own injuries or blood splatters. Even her hair had been carefully tended to. She looked as if she might have been having tea the last time Tom saw her rather than slicing someone's throat open with her bare hands.

Every eye was on Tom as he stepped off the bottom stair. One of Colin's group in particular, a woman with dishwater-blond hair, stared at him, unblinking. The moment his boot touched the floor, she bared her fangs and rushed at him, hissing.

She managed only two strides before a pair of Emily's guards intercepted her, wrestled her to the ground, and twisted her head until a series of cracks echoed through the nearly silent room.

Emily shook her head and made a tsking sound. "I was hoping y'all would listen when I said no one coming down those steps was to be challenged, let alone hurt," she said in her genteel Southern lilt. "As I said, one of them is a regular ol' man. But that doesn't make a bit of difference. Tom did me a big favor upstairs, helped me take care of a problem I had. He is part of my Family, now, under my protection. I will not see him harmed." Looking at Tom, she added, "If you feel even the slightest bit uncomfortable, son, I want to hear it right away."

He nodded. "Thank you." Patting Lady in Ana's arms, he said, "My girl here, too, of course?"

She watched him for a moment, a polite smile on her face, without saying anything. Then she nodded. "Of course." Grinning more widely, she turned to Colin. "Now, then, Lord Colin, if you could help me in seeing to the safety of Tom and his pet during our stay, I would be greatly in your debt."

Tom wasn't sure, but her eyes seem to sparkle with mirth as she gave Colin strict instructions regarding a dog.

Colin's fists curled, and his jaw clenched, but he nodded. "I would be... happy... to look after the well-being of this... man... and his... animal." His body language suggested that nothing could be further from the truth.

Emily politely thanked him nonetheless. Then she asked Lars, "Have you made your decision?"

He stepped toward her, a little away from his people. "Yes, Lady Emily. I'm grateful for the offer to come to Atlanta, but whatever Alexander's faults, he's my lord still. If it's the same to you, we'd like to go find him and help him throw Colin out of the region. Unless you've reconsidered?"

Emily shook her head. "No, son, I'm sorry. I did hope that Alexander would reassert his authority here, but he ran off again before the fight was over. As Colin was in charge when we got here, I won't replace him for you. If Alexander wants to be lord, he'll need to settle that himself. It's not my place to mediate for them. At least, not for now."

Nodding, Lars replied, "As expected. I'll take those loyal to Alexander, then, and we'll be on our way."

He turned, but Emily called to him again. "Son? You did well with your Family during that little... disagreement. You put their well-being before anything else, which is something to be proud of. If you ask me, the right man might already be leading those people there."

Lars colored slightly, and he looked down. "That's kind of you to say, and I thank you, but I'm no Master."

She gave him a nod, and he waved his Family through the arch.

As they filed out, Tom shuffled over to him. "Lars."

The husky vampire turned, one eyebrow raised.

"At first, I thought you were a real sonuvabitch. But you proved you people do have some honor. I thank you for that. For everything."

Lars smirked. "You did good, Meat. You did real good. Better than I figured, at least. You watch yourself now. We've done a lot to keep you alive this far. I'd hate to waste all that effort."

Tom returned the grin and offered his left hand. "I'll see you around."

"Yes, you will," Lars replied, shaking it. Glancing at Ana over Tom's shoulder, he added, "And don't forget you owe me. Twice now. I'll be around to collect before too long."

Ana gave him that rare, genuine smile, the one that sparkled in her dark eyes. "I remember."

Lars was gone almost before they could blink.

"Now then," Emily said, "Lord Colin, we need to come to an arrangement."

"I, um, do appreciate you choosing to remain neutral," he replied, choosing the words carefully.

"Nonsense. What goes on up here is none of my business. In fact, if your man hadn't gone rogue in my neck of the woods, I'm sure I wouldn't have even needed to come."

Colin looked down, shamed by the subtle rebuke.

"While I'm here, though, I was wondering if you might do me a favor. I have this human to care for, who appears to have been injured, and I haven't got anyone with medical experience on hand. Perhaps you could lend me somebody with the necessary background?"

The muscles in Colin's temple tightened and released as he clenched his jaw, grinding his teeth. He hadn't missed Emily's underlying threat: *"Give me Ana if you want to be left alone."*

He grunted and nodded. That was the most his pride would allow.

"Very good," Emily said, pleased. "You'll release her to me?"

Colin nodded again, adding a huff.

Emily's face darkened. "I believe I'll need to hear you say it."

He glowered at her. "I release Ana to you. And believe me, I won't forget this… favor."

Ana stood looking over his shoulder, still holding Lady and trying not to look too happy. She failed miserably, though, and grinned as he'd never seen before.

"Thank you," Emily replied. "Now, unless there is another matter, perhaps we should all get some Rest?"

The factions separated, each going its own way. Most of Colin's people climbed the staircase to the darkened floors above, and Emily led her people into the tunnels below.

Tom spent the day in Ana's small underground lab space, watching Lady breathe on an exam table while Ana and Lindsey both found someplace to Rest. Eventually, he nodded off, sitting awkwardly in a chair, leaning forward with his head cradled on his left arm.

Hours later, Tom woke up to something warm and wet painting his cheek in long strokes. Every muscle in his body ached, and his shoulder burned, but the dog's terrible breath on his face melted that all away.

Lady stood over him, licking his face hard, apparently all right. He let her go on a bit longer than he should have. He just couldn't bear to make her stop.

Finally, he sat up and gently pushed her away, rubbing the thick fur under her neck. "You gave me quite a scare yesterday."

She jumped down from the table and paced around the room a few times before stopping beside his chair. The message was clear: *Look at me. I'm fine.*

He patted her on the back.

A swift knock came at the door, and it creaked open.

Ana popped her head in and gave them both a quick smile before entering. "I am quite glad to see her up and moving. I was going to start worrying about head trauma otherwise."

Lady sat down on the floor next to Tom, panting contentedly.

"She really is a very good dog." Ana looked right at Lady. "Yeah, I said it. Thank you."

"She is," Tom agreed. "I'm lucky she found me. So what's the plan?"

"Time to go. I just came to gather…" she paused, frowning to herself, "some things to take with us. Apparently, Emily has a train?"

He sensed a secret in that pause, but he wasn't going to ask. She could have her secrets. She would tell him what he needed to know.

Smiling, he said, "Yes, it's like a huge, century-old steam engine. It's one of the coolest things I've ever seen."

"Interesting. I look forward to seeing that." Wasting no more time, Ana went to work, collecting odds and ends from her lab. Mostly, she gathered notebooks, clip-boards, and that sort of thing, but after making a stack she was satisfied with, she grabbed a small cooler and opened a dorm-room-sized freezer in the corner. She set a few things from it inside the cooler and then added some chunks of foggy dry ice.

"That should do until we reach Atlanta. Quite a shame to leave all this equipment, but I suppose Emily can replace it for me. I hope she has a working freezer."

Tom chuckled. "I'm sure she'll have no problem out-fitting you."

Ana gave him a serious look and handed him the cooler. "I'll take all the paperwork. Can you please carry this and promise not to let it out of your sight? Don't allow anyone else to even hold it. I can't begin to tell you how valuable it is."

He took it from her and held it as if it might explode. "Uh, I'm sure whatever's in here, we can get more of it."

She took a breath to add something, but when Lindsey appeared in the doorway, she said, "Just keep it safe," her eyes glowing with intensity.

"Evenin'." Lindsey grinned, holding Tom's shotgun in one hand and his bat in the other. "I thought you might want these before we left."

Ana gave her a dark look for interrupting but said nothing. Those two were going to be like living with jealous cats.

"Thank you," Tom replied. "I'd feel lost without the bat."

"It was useful," she admitted. "Let's just hope you don't need it again anytime soon. Are you ready?"

They both nodded.

"One thing I don't understand," Tom said, looking at Ana. "Why did Colin just let you go?"

"In order to gain and maintain control in this region, Colin needs time to gather more Family and those loyal to him here, especially if Alexander is going to resist," Ana said.

"Right," Lindsey interjected, "so the last thing he needs is trouble from Emily. Truth be told, she had him over a barrel already, between the Ash business and losing the fight. But instead of making him pay for all that, she made him a deal. He could work on his takeover as long as he handed over the daughter he was trying to kill anyway."

"Thanks to Emily, I am finally free of him. I owe her—and both of you—quite a debt."

Smiling, Tom said, "I think we're even now."

"And you can thank Emily on the Dragon," Lindsey added before disappearing through the door.

Tom filed out behind her, followed by Ana, who didn't even pause to look back.

The walk through the dark lagering cellars and subsequent trip to the rail depot went without incident, a procession of mismatched hot-wired cars winding their way through the dark hill-and-valley streets of Cincinnati.

When they arrived at the Dragon, it was pointing south, somehow having been turned around for the trip home. Thick clouds of smoke drifted lazily from its exhaust stack.

Moments later, they were chugging toward Atlanta. Tom chose the same compartment as before. Ana and

Lindsey sat with him briefly but were called away to speak with Emily. For some time, Tom stroked Lady's fur as she dozed, and he stared out the window at the passing countryside.

After an hour or so, he stood up and stretched as best he could in the small cabin. "Let's get some air."

She dropped down off the bench and padded to the door. After opening it, Tom peeked into the hall. Finding no one, they staggered down the passageway like drunks, bobbing in response to the motion of the car.

After passing through the doors at the front of the car, Tom stopped in the open space between coaches and took a few breaths of air. It had a chill to it, appropriate for late October. He was going to miss this autumn weather when they got to Atlanta.

The train was steaming through a heavily wooded area, and although the colors of the leaves were muted in the soft moonlight, he sensed the brilliant, fiery combination of reds, golds, and yellows out there.

Heather would have loved standing here with him. Fall had meant so much to her.

"I will not waste everyone's time studying why he usually does not respond to Influence, Lindsey," Ana said, stabbing the air with her finger as the door from Emily's coach opened behind him. "And if you do not stop making a point to tell me he is your 'claim,' we are going to have a problem."

"Aw, that's cute, kiddo," Lindsey replied, "but maybe you could use a lesson in—"

Tom forced himself not to laugh out loud. Yep, jealous cats. Rather than let the bickering spiral into something more serious, he turned to the pair as they crossed the threshold to the second car. "Ladies."

They gave him a startled look and exchanged an uneasy glance, concerned at what he'd heard.

"We were just coming to talk to you," Lindsey said, clearly off-balance. "Go over some guidelines."

"I decided to get a little air. It's a beautiful night out," he replied. "I'll be back in the cabin in a few minutes. I'd like to enjoy this for a little longer."

Ana put a hand on Lindsey's arm. "Could you give us a minute?"

Lindsey cocked an eyebrow, and one side of her mouth turned up in a bit of a suggestive grin. "Okay, sure. Don't be too long."

After she left them, Tom and Ana stood together, watching the trees stream by, neither wanting to break up the rhythmic rocking of the train.

Finally, Ana whispered, "Thank you."

"I had to. You would have done it for me."

"I assumed you were done with me, that you'd be happy never to see me again," she said. "After what happened with Ash."

"I only escaped because you found a way to help me," he answered.

"Still, you shouldn't have done it. You could have—no, probably should have—been killed. You don't know the risk you took."

"No, not entirely," he said, almost a whisper, staring at the trees melting past them. "I still don't understand what you think you're going to do with me. But I had to try to help you. To make it up to Heather. A lifetime ago, I ignored her when she needed me, turned away from her when I thought she'd betrayed me. And by the time I realized how dumb I'd been, it was too late."

He turned to Ana, forcing back a new lump in his throat.

"The life I have now is a second chance, one that you gave me. I wasn't going to make the same stupid mistake again."

"Tom, I don't know—" Ana began.

He put a hand over hers. "Ana, don't. It doesn't matter. Just… I did it because, well, you're family."

She looked down, black hair falling around her face, sniffled, and wiped her eyes. Clearing her throat, she took a deep breath and smiled back at him. "Thank you," she said, squeezing his hand.

Returning to steadier ground, she added, "Now, come inside. I want to look at your shoulder. You need a sling for sure."

Tom smiled crookedly at her. "All right. Just give me a minute, and I'll be in."

Ana left him gazing out over the quickly changing landscape, content to feel the cold night air rippling through his hair.

For the moment, he was at peace, knowing for the first time that he would wake up safe tomorrow.

Tomorrow was all he wanted.

ACKNOWLEDGEMENTS

I started working on the first draft of *Famine* a little over 10 years ago, without any expectation that it might eventually become even a full length novel I'd finish, let alone publish. It took 18 months from scrawling out that first uncertain chapter to finally tapping out "The End" on its first draft. Ironically enough, that initial experimental chapter didn't even end up being the opening to this final version of the novel. How *Famine* got from there to here still boggles my mind, especially as it took the work, love, and support of so many different people. Without them and their constant encouragement, Tom and Ana would live only in the dark hidden corners of my imagination, or, at best, somewhere in a locked trunk.

I'm not sure I'll ever be able to say "Thank You" enough for all the help I got along the way, and to be honest, I'm mildly terrified writing this that I won't sufficiently remember everyone who made it possible. But as Tom figured out, eventually you have to stop being afraid and start doing the work or you might as well just never wake up.

Of course, first and foremost I have to thank my amazing wife, Amy, and all four of my wonderful, unique kids. When I told Amy in late January of 2010 that I was going to make that year the year I proved whether I could really become the writer I'd always believed was living in my bones, she told me to go for it. She's never batted an eye at even my craziest of schemes, regardless of whether I've decided to blog 120,000 words in a 12-month period or resolved to wear a different pair of socks every day for a full calendar year. And, yes, that was actually a thing I did in 2018—there's a picture of every pair on my blog.

Gracias, Querida, I could never have done this without you. Te amo mas que….

Even with all the love, support, and copious editing assistance from my wife, it still pretty much takes a village, and I never would have been able to get *Famine* out of my head and onto paper without my colleague, Becky Schwarz. As I finished groups of three chapters over the 18 months of initial drafting, she'd read them, mark them up with notes that would do any professional editor proud, and tell me to hurry up with the next group. She pushed me when I needed it and was invaluable during the frustrating lulls when I wasn't sure if *Famine* was ever going to be finished. Tom and Ana couldn't have gotten to the end, alive or otherwise, if not for her, and I don't entirely know that I would have either. Thank you, Becky. Penny war friends for life, yo.

Now, just finishing a manuscript that's nearly 100,000 words long, or of any length, really, is a feat not to be sneered at by anyone. But finishing a draft doesn't make an infant novel ready for publishing. Revisions beget revisions and even after you've gone through it a half a dozen or a dozen times, you can always find ways to tweak it. But eventually you have to hit save one last time, hold your breath, say a prayer, and let other people have at your story.

My beta readers are the best support people an author could have, and they never disappoint when it comes to giving me feedback—both good and bad—about my work. *Famine* was the first time I had gone through the process, and every comment I got back fueled my drive to make the story the best it could be, so I could maybe share it with the rest of the world. Without the time and keen insight of Stephanie S., Stephanie M., Tasha, Tom and Carla, Lisa, Justin and others, this story would never have become what it is today. I don't have the words for how much their help has meant.

Most of those people feel like family to me now, but of course I have an actual family that's just as responsible for getting this novel to you. My parents and my brothers and sister have been hounding me to get *Famine* out into the world for a long time now, and I wouldn't have made it this far without knowing they were right behind me, cheering this story on every step of the way. And, yes, Kara, the sequel, *Fury*, will be out soon, so you can finally find out what happens next.

I know this isn't everyone I should be thanking, and I have no doubt that as soon as the final version of the manuscript goes to the printer, I'm going to think of half a dozen other people I need to include. There are also literally hundreds of other writers I've chatted with online that I should mention, especially the XLGA and the entire #writingcommunity on Twitter. But they tell me the acknowledgements should probably not be as many words as the story itself, so just know that I appreciate all of your love and support, and can only hope to be there for many of you as you've been there for me.

Bringing the story of *Famine* into the world was one thing. Making it into an honest-to-goodness book, though, was an entirely different adventure. As my fledgling Ferrousox Press is a largely one-man operation (well, one and a half if you include the editorial stuff I make my poor wife do), I could not have done this without some serious professional outside help. I can't say enough good things about *Famine's* editor, L. Kelly Reed from Red Adept Editing, and Glendon Haddix and the team from Streetlight Graphics took a handful of my half-formed thoughts and turned them into a cover that I could stare at for hours. I owe them all a ton.

I'd be remiss if I didn't give a tip of the proverbial cap to the City of Cincinnati itself. The basis for *Famine* wasn't really a single thing, and there was no one moment of epiphany when it appeared in my consciousness fully formed. In early 2010, though, with several pieces of the plan swirling about, I realized I wanted something to make my post-apocalyptic vampire novel different. It needed a great setting, and I wasn't going to settle for some nameless wasteland. As luck would have it, the city of Cincinnati was beginning to bear the fruits of both an urban renewal project and a craft beer brewing renaissance. Being a lifelong resident of the greater Cincinnati area (as well as a lover of beer), I was immediately caught up by both. In case you're wondering, yes, both the subway tunnels and underground lagering cellars referenced in *Famine* are real, actual things. I took some liberties with their relative locations, admittedly, and I tried to describe the lagering tunnels in as much detail as I remember. And, yes, you can get a tour of them yourself. Come to Cincinnati and check out Queen City Underground Tours. You won't be disappointed.

Finally, I want to thank you, kind reader. For all the many different options for entertainment available today, I'm ecstatic that you chose to tag along with Ana on Tom's rescue mission and hung on for the ride that followed. I hope you found that ride everything you wanted it to be, and if you're looking for more from Tom, Ana, and Lady, there's more to their story, and it's on the way.

ABOUT THE AUTHOR

JR Andrews is the pen name for real life human Jason A. Rust. Born in Indianapolis, he has lived all but the first six months of life in Northern Kentucky, just across the Ohio River from Cincinnati, Ohio. JR has a wonderful and very tolerant wife, four very individual kids, two very lazy dogs, and a very active imagination. An avid reader and lifelong lover of Fantasy and Science Fiction, as JR Andrews he writes stories set in a world where the proverbial *&#% has already hit the fan or is just about to do so.

Famine is JR's first published novel. Its sequel, *Fury*, is planned for release in mid-2020.

You can find him on Twitter: @AuthorJRAndrews
Facebook: AuthorJRAndrews
Instagram: AuthorJRAndrews

Made in United States
Orlando, FL
07 December 2022

25724182R00248